EVENING NEWS

EVENING NEWS

--- A Novel ---

Marly Swick

LITTLE, BROWN AND COMPANY

Boston New York London

First Edition

The characters and events in this book are fictitious. Any similarity
to real persons, living or dead, is coincidental and not intended
by the author.

LIBRARY OF CONGRESS CATALOGING-IN-PUBLICATION DATA

Swick, Marly.
Evening News : a novel / by Marly Swick. — 1st ed.
p. cm.
ISBN 0-316-82533-6 (hardcover)
I. Title.
PS3569.W467E9   1999
813'.54 — dc21   98-12840

10 9 8 7 6 5 4 3 2 1

MV-NY

Printed in the United States of America

ONE

HIS SISTER, TRINA, IS SITTING IN HER PLASTIC *wading pool, bright blue with purple whales stamped on it. She looks like a butterball turkey, splashing around in her diapers and pink rubber pants, banging her plastic shovel, trying to get his mom's attention. His mom, as usual, is reading a book, furiously underlining with a yellow Magic Marker. After she graduates from college, she wants to go on to law school. She wants to go right away, but his stepdad — Teddy calls him Dan to distinguish him from his real dad — wants her to wait until Trina starts kindergarten, which won't be for three more years. Trina can walk, sort of, and babble enough to get what she wants — juice, chicken noodle soup, pick me up, put me down, that sort of thing. His mother sits with her lawn chair facing the pool to make sure Trina doesn't drown. Every so often she gets up and slathers more suntan lotion on the baby's pudgy skin or picks up the bright plastic toys that Trina keeps throwing out of the pool onto the weedy grass. She is a good-natured baby; everyone says so. Always smiling and clapping her hands like an appreciative audience at any dumb thing you do — funny faces, tickling, peekaboo. For some reason, she thinks he is especially hilarious. Even during her rare temper tantrums, he can always get her to forget she's angry and start to laugh.*

It is the end of April. Back in Nebraska, where his dad still lives, there is two feet of snow on the ground, his dad told him on the phone the day before. His dad always tells him how lucky he is to live in year-round sunshine. But Teddy misses the snow, even though he barely remembers it. He was only four when they moved away, he and his mom.

It is a Sunday afternoon. He is standing in the Beemers' master bedroom, looking out the window at his own backyard while Eric stands on a hassock and rummages through the top drawer of his father's bureau. Eric's mother is down in the rec room, riding her Ex-cercycle and listening to loud rock music. Eric's father is a pilot for United, and his mother worries about his being around all those pretty stewardesses all the time. Teddy overheard Mrs. Beemer telling his mother this and vowing to lose five pounds by their tenth anniversary, which they are going to spend on some beach in Mexico. Eric pulls a pair of balled white gym socks from the back of the drawer and extracts a small key. "Voilà!" he says, like a magician pulling a rabbit out of a hat.

Teddy watches nervously out the open window, the ruffled curtains fluttering in the breeze, as Eric walks over and unlocks the nightstand drawer next to his mother's side of the bed. Teddy's own mother has her back to them, busy underlining something in her book. The Beemers' dog, Ninja, is busy digging a hole by the chain-link fence, panting, as if trying to make a mad dash for the water in the wading pool. Eric's father got the dog at the pound a few weeks ago after the house across the street was burglarized while the couple was at home asleep. He was worried because he was away from home a lot of nights. In addition to the dog, who hasn't really turned out to be such a hot watchdog, Mr. Beemer bought his wife a handgun. Even though she said she didn't want one.

"It's a .38 caliber," Eric announces as he slides the gun from the back of the drawer, where his mother hid it in a Kleenex box. The gun is silver and black, smaller even than a squirt gun. Eric whirls around, squatting and squinting, taking aim at various targets the way cops do on TV: the china figurine on the vanity table, his parents'

wedding photograph on the wall, the dog digging in the yard. Teddy keeps glancing anxiously in his mother's direction. He knows she'd kill him if she saw him anywhere near a gun. He sees his sister toss her juice box onto the lawn. She points and grunts, but his mother doesn't pay any attention to her. Trina stands up and takes a wobbly step toward the side of the pool, toward her Juicy Juice box lying on the dead grass.

"Here." Eric hands him the gun just as the loud music from downstairs stops. They both freeze guiltily for an instant, and then it starts up again, a different tape.

Teddy's real dad in Nebraska is a hunter. Teddy likes to hear the stories about when his dad was a kid, like him, and would go hunting every fall with his father and older brothers. One of whom is dead (a car accident) and the other, Teddy's uncle Brice, doesn't like to hunt anymore. His dad keeps saying he will take Teddy hunting someday, but his mother says over her dead body. Teddy takes aim at a row of scraggly trees at the back of their yard, pretending there is a big buck rustling in the leaves. He holds his breath; everything seems perfectly still. It is as if he can hear the deer's heart beating. Then suddenly the phone on the nightstand explodes, loud and shrill, startling him, and at the same time Eric grabs for the gun, panicked that his mother will come upstairs.

His sister splashes onto her butt in the water. At first Teddy thinks she has just lost her balance as usual. Then his mother screams. The dog starts barking. "Holy shit!" Eric whispers, touching a ragged hole in the window screen. Teddy's mom is standing in the pool, lifting his sister out of the shallow water. She looks around frantically, spots them standing frozen at the open window, and shouts to call 911. Her book is floating in the water. Eric runs downstairs to the rec room. The gun is lying on the thick beige carpet. Teddy picks it up and places it back inside the Kleenex box and slides the nightstand drawer shut, but he can't find the key. He hears Eric's mother on the telephone in the kitchen, giving the address, spelling out the name of their street, B-U-E-N-A V-I-S-T-A, as if the person on the other end is deaf or retarded.

Later, when he thinks about it, he can't remember what he was thinking. It was as if he were watching himself on television. He tosses Mr. Beemer's white gym socks under the bed. The china shepherdess on the vanity table has somehow fallen onto the floor. He picks it up and checks to make sure it isn't broken. Miraculously, the shepherdess's staff and little lamb are still intact. Relieved, he sets the figurine back on the mirrored tabletop, catching a glimpse of his reflection. From this weird angle he is all nostrils and teeth. Like a monster. He looks out the window. His mother is kneeling in the water, with her back toward him. He can't see Trina. He races downstairs and out the back door, across the yard. As soon as she sees him, his mother starts shouting, "What happened? Did you see what happened, Teddy?"

He shakes his head.

His mother is sitting in the wading pool, cradling his little sister, saying her name over and over. The water is turning pink, like Easter egg dye. Eric's mother runs out onto the back porch and hollers that the paramedics are on their way. His sister's eyes are open, the eyelids trembling. He squats in the soggy grass next to the pool and starts making all the funny faces in his repertoire, sticking out his tongue and rolling his eyes into his head and stretching his lips, trying to make her laugh. Even though it is hot and bright out, he is shivering. His mother has the wadded-up beach towel pressed against Trina's chest, but you can still see the blood. The towel is white with red chili peppers. It is big enough to wrap around her two or three times. His stepdad calls Trina his "little burrito." When he hears the siren in the distance, Teddy tries even harder — wiggling his fingers in his ears, leaping and chattering like a chimpanzee, shouting "Mookie, Mookie!" the name of his sister's favorite stuffed animal. He must look like some kind of lunatic. Out of the corner of his eye, he sees Eric standing beside his mother at the edge of their lawn. Mrs. Beemer is sweating and panting in her black leotard and white sneakers. Eric, his best friend, is staring at him as if he were a total stranger, someone he has never seen before, an alien from another planet.

ON THE MOSTLY SILENT, STUNNED DRIVE HOME from the hospital, the accident was all that Dan wanted to talk about, the logistics of it. Why? How? Who? Giselle kept shaking her head and mumbling, "I don't know." Already she sensed an ominous difference between them: he wanted to know everything, and she didn't want to know anything. Hadn't they lost enough already? She kept glancing in the rearview mirror at the empty car seat, half expecting to see Trina slumped like a sack of flour, thumb stuck in her mouth, sleeping. She could not shake the feeling that they had forgotten something. You hear these stories, she thought, of big families stopping at a gas station on vacation and accidentally driving off, leaving one of the kids behind in the rest room, and no one notices for maybe ten miles. *Bobby's not here! We must have left him at the Texaco station!* And they turn the car around and speed back and there he is, sipping a Dr Pepper and eating M&M's in the office with the manager. Whenever they tell the story for years to come, it's a big joke. Everyone, including Bobby, laughs.

"What do you mean, you don't know?" Dan shook his head in frustration, as if she were a particularly dense student. "I thought you were right there."

"I was, but . . ." She shrugged and rolled down her window. Her head pounded. She felt sick to her stomach. At the hospital a police officer had shown up while she was pacing in the corridor waiting for Dan to get there. A baby-faced rookie with a cowlick and a stammer. It was hard to imagine him writing up a speeding ticket, let alone conducting an investigation. He must have seen what a state she was in. He didn't push it much after she said she hadn't seen anything, she didn't know anything, all she knew was that her daughter had a hole in her chest and no one was offering any assurance that she was going to be all right. She had seen the look the paramedics exchanged as they lifted Trina's little body onto the stretcher to carry her to the ambulance. The grim blizzard of activity when they had screamed into the emergency entrance. When the two doctors finally came out of the operating room to deliver the bad news, one of them — the sympathetic blond woman doctor — took her aside while the other one — an Omar Sharif look-alike with an Oxford accent — spoke with the cop. Out of the corner of her eye Giselle had seen him jotting down notes. Then he must have taken off. By the time Dan arrived, sweaty from tennis, pale with anxiety underneath his sporty tan, Trina was already dead and the cop was mercifully gone. The cop's tone had been less suspicious than Dan's. But then, to be fair, it wasn't his child.

Just as Teddy wasn't really Dan's child. He hadn't even asked about Teddy. *Her* son. He was only concerned about *their* daughter. And who could blame him?

On what they now referred to as their first date — a hamburger in the student union after class — Dan had told her that he never got involved with women who had children. Rather than being annoyed, she had felt crushed. For weeks she had been fantasizing about being alone with him — and now this. After she got back home to her ugly little apartment and paid the baby-sitter, she crawled into bed beside her sleeping son and cried herself to sleep.

Ever since she had enrolled in the composition course at Cal State–Northridge, Tuesday evenings had become the high point of her week, the one thing she had to look forward to. She was belatedly finishing her B.A., which had been sidetracked by her unplanned pregnancy and subsequent marriage to Teddy's father, Ed, back in Lincoln, Nebraska. Most of the other students in the class couldn't get into the literature Dan assigned; they were there to learn about punctuation so that they could get better-paying jobs. They were frustrated that Dan seemed to be more concerned with their souls than with semicolons.

Their assignments had been aimed at exploring their own personal experiences in order to see how they had arrived at their opinions and values. All semester, in his nearly illegible scrawl, Dan had praised and encouraged Giselle's writing. Having just moved across the country and being in the final stages of her divorce from Ed, she'd had a lot on her mind to write about. She hadn't known anyone in California apart from her antisocial brother, a special effects nerd at Disney, and as a single mother of a four-year-old, she didn't get out much. So after Teddy was in bed, Giselle had looked forward to writing and rewriting each week's essay. She wrote about her Catholic parents' un-Christian reaction to the news of her pregnancy, about her gay sister, the culture shock of moving from Nebraska to California, the ups and downs of motherhood. Before they ever touched each other, Dan had known more about her thoughts and feelings than her ex-husband would or could know in a million years, even though she and Ed had practically grown up together.

"I can't believe this," he said as they slowed to a halt in a sudden snarl of traffic. Up ahead an old pickup truck was stalled, smoke streaming out from under the open hood. Cars honked impatiently. At first she thought he meant the traffic, but then she looked at his face and knew he meant Trina. Unlike Ed, Dan cried easily. A movie, a book, a story on the news. Giselle had never before known a man so unembarrassed by his emotions. She thought it must be because he was half Mexican. At the hospital he had taken one look at her face and before she could even get the sentence out, he'd brushed past her into the room where Trina was and let out a howl — that was the only word for it — that seemed to go on and on.

Once, in class, Dan had choked up and tears had welled in his eyes as he read aloud the final paragraph to a short story. Some guy in the class had said he thought the ending sucked. The story was "Rock Springs" by Richard Ford; at the end this car thief, whose girlfriend has just declared her intention to leave him, is standing in the parking lot of a motel, looking for another car to steal and thinking about the sort of life he might have had if things had turned out differently. As Dan read the part about Earl staring into a station wagon with toys scattered in the backseat, his voice started to wobble. You could have heard a pin drop in the room even though the boy who had criticized the ending sat there rolling his eyes. Afterward, Dan pulled a handkerchief out of his back pocket and blew his nose and said, "It's like music. You've just got to listen." And then he'd looked over at her, his kindred soul, and smiled when she nodded.

"I know." She had to raise her voice over the chorus of indignant honking as the drivers' collective temper tantrum escalated. "I can't believe it either." She broke into a fresh spasm of sobs. He shut his eyes and lowered his forehead to the steering wheel and banged his head against the hard plastic over and over, as if trying to knock himself unconscious. She reached over and grabbed hold of his hair to stop him. The car behind them blasted its horn. The traffic was moving again.

It was the last class of the fall semester, and she had been feeling like it was a lost cause, this terrible stupid schoolgirl crush of hers, when Dan had suddenly turned to her as the students were filing out of the classroom and he was packing up his book bag. "Would you like to get a bite to eat?" he'd asked. "I'd like to talk to you about your work this term."

She had been too nervous to eat her hamburger. She just sat there nodding as he praised her work and encouraged her to take some more advanced English classes. She could feel the chemistry between them doing its thing, and then out of the blue he'd made that pronouncement about not getting involved with women who had kids. When she'd asked why, he'd shrugged boyishly and said, "Conflict of interest." And smiled. And that, she thought, was that — until he'd called her up a couple of weeks later and said he had an extra ticket to a Hollywood Bowl concert. Would she like to go?

At first she had kept Teddy out of sight as much as possible, spending more than she could afford on baby-sitters. But Dan had never brought up the issue again. And after they'd been seeing each other for a couple of months, he was the one who suggested that the three of them spend some time together. And then once Trina was born, the issue ceased to exist; she was no longer a woman with a kid. They were a family. Or so she'd thought.

When they pulled into their driveway, the neighborhood seemed unusually quiet. Hushed. She suspected that the neighbors who had witnessed all the commotion with the paramedics, the wailing ambulance, were hiding behind their miniblinds, peering out at them. Bill Beemer's red Corvette was parked in the driveway next door, and Giselle wondered whether Lois had had him contacted up in the friendly skies and summoned home or whether it was just a coincidence that he happened to come back when he did.

"I see the asshole's back," Dan muttered. "Probably on the phone with his attorney."

The two men had never hit it off, although she and Lois liked each other well enough — mostly, Giselle supposed, because their sons were practically inseparable. Bill Beemer was a real man's man, beer and football on the weekends. He had invited Dan over

to a Super Bowl party when they'd first moved in and seemed un-
nerved when Dan let it slip that he didn't know which teams were
playing.

In the past she had sometimes stuck up for Bill, trying to encourage neighborly goodwill. "You don't have to be soul mates,"
she'd tell Dan, "to eat hamburgers and drink a couple of beers."
When he was at home, Bill liked to entertain, to preside over his
state-of-the-art gas grill, and Lois was always inviting them over
for barbecues. It was awkward to beg off when they lived right
next door — the usual white lies about having a previous engage-
ment wouldn't work. "He's not that bad," Giselle would tell Dan.
"He means well." But she wouldn't defend him anymore. In fact,
she wouldn't have protested if Dan had announced his intention to
bash the guy's face in.

They walked inside the house and just stood there for a moment in the small foyer, not knowing where to go, afraid to step in
either direction, as if the house were full of land mines. She saw
Dan staring out the sliding glass door through the living room to
the backyard, the empty wading pool. She reached for his hand,
but he chose that moment to walk across the carpet and open the
sliding door. She couldn't stand to watch.

Standing alone in the empty room, she felt unreal, as if she
were standing on a stage. The director had told her what her part
was — the grieving mother — but had neglected to give her the
script. *My daughter is dead,* she thought. *Your daughter is dead,* she
told herself. *What do you do now?* This was a subject that none of
the parenting books addressed. She turned and looked at herself in
the hallway mirror, surprised to see her reflection there. The glass
was still smeared from Trina's lips. Dan would hold her in his arms
in front of the mirror, point to her reflection, and say, "Who's that
pretty little girl?" And Trina would point to herself and then kiss
herself in the mirror, laughing.

From the end of the hall she could hear the computer beeping
in Teddy's room and the low rumble of her brother's voice. She

knew that she had to go in there and tell them, but she didn't want to. She wanted to go lock herself in her room, shut her eyes, and be alone. Not move a muscle. Not even breathe. Through the window she could see Dan lugging the wading pool farther away from the house to drain the water. She could hear him struggling and cursing and crying as he struggled to drag it across the grass. She leaned forward and pressed her own lips against the smudgy imprint of Trina's mouth. When she licked her lips, she tasted apple juice. Or maybe it was just her imagination.

She wanted to go to sleep. She wanted not to be awake.

She walked down the hall to Teddy's room. He had begged to come to the hospital with them, but the paramedics said it was against procedures. Giselle had told him he could come and visit his sister in the morning, first thing. She hadn't wanted to leave him there with Lois and Eric, but there wasn't really any choice. And no time to ponder alternatives. She rode in the back of the ambulance with Trina, holding her hand and praying, trying not to think about how the accident had happened, as if Trina had been struck by lightning. From the hospital she had called her brother at his office and begged him to drive over and stay with Teddy until she got home. Her desperation must have communicated itself even to Todd, who seemed to live in a high-tech world of his own making; he'd agreed to drop whatever it was he was doing without any argument. That and the fact that his nephew was probably the only human being whom Todd seemed genuinely attached to in real life, as opposed to virtual reality.

Her brother and son were seated in front of the computer Todd had given Teddy last year, for his ninth birthday. They were playing a game on the brilliantly colored monitor. Todd seemed absorbed, pressing keys and muttering to himself, but Teddy was hunched in his chair, staring vacantly into space, literally — a poster of the planets taped over his bed. They both turned to look at her. When Todd saw her face, he shut off the computer screen. The brilliant colors dimmed to gray. They waited for her to say something. She opened her mouth, the words lined up in her mind at the ready, but nothing came out.

"She's dead," Teddy said. "I knew it."

Giselle sank down onto the edge of his bunk bed and held her arms open. He let her hug him. She patted his back to soothe him, the way she used to do when he was a colicky baby, and waited for him to dissolve into tears. But his body was stiff; he didn't seem to be there. After a couple of seconds he broke free of her embrace and ran down the hall, out the front door. The screen door banged shut behind him. She sat numbly for a moment until her brother's laserlike gaze prompted her into action. Then she ran to the door and called Teddy's name, called for him to come back. There was no answer. He was nowhere in sight. Already gone. She knew she should run after him, but she was too exhausted to move.

Dan was still in the backyard, kneeling in the crushed grass beside the wading pool, tipping it so that the remaining puddle of bloody water could drain faster. Her soggy book, *The Scarlet Letter,* was lying in a muddy puddle. She had an exam in American Lit to 1860 on Monday. A few hours ago that had been the most pressing source of anxiety in her life. Dan was poking his finger through the bullet hole in the side of the vinyl pool. A look of disbelief on his face. The bullet might as well have been a UFO. She flashed on Teddy standing there as she had climbed into the ambulance, crying and shouting, "It was Eric! It wasn't me!"

Even though it was eighty degrees out, she felt bone cold. She couldn't think what to do. The bathroom seemed like the only safe room in the house. She didn't want to see Trina's room. Not now, not yet. She needed to get out of her bloody clothes. She couldn't wait another minute, even though she heard Dan call out her name as she walked through the living room. Her brother, the coward, was hiding in Teddy's room. Even as a child, Todd had hated emotional scenes. Well, it didn't get more emotional than this. Giselle hurried into the bathroom, tore off her sundress, and blasted the water in the tub. She wished she could lock the door behind her, but Dan had removed the locks as a safety precaution, so the kids couldn't lock themselves in. As soon as Trina had learned to crawl, he had spent the better part of a Saturday kidproofing the whole house.

Giselle let herself go, moaning as she lowered herself into the scalding water. She stuffed a washcloth in her mouth and bit down hard to muffle the groans, and berated herself for studying, for ignoring Trina, when she should have been playing with her, paying attention to her. They had this new fishing game Dan had bought for Trina — the object was to hook bright plastic fish with a rod as they floated in the water. It was supposed to develop hand–eye coordination. Maybe if they'd been playing Go Fish, the bullet would have missed them both. Or maybe it would have hit Giselle instead. Anything, anyone but Trina. Giselle was a selfish mother who cared more about her own career goals, her own future, than about her child sitting there, large as life, needing her mother. She slid down and held her head under the water, not breathing, wishing she were dead. But then Teddy's face surfaced like a cork in her mind, the dread in his eyes when she'd walked into the room, the dead tone of his voice, his shallow breathing as she tried to pull him closer. And she realized that she was still being selfish; she should have gone after him no matter how tired she was. It was his loss as much as hers.

Friends of theirs had always marveled at how much attention Teddy paid to his little sister. Their sons, they complained, had no use for their baby siblings. But even when Trina first came home from the hospital, Teddy wanted to hold her, to help change her diapers, to tickle her and make silly faces. When she got old enough to sit up, he'd set her in a big spaghetti pot and tie a rope to the handle and drag her all around the house. He called it a magic carpet ride. Trina loved it. She would laugh and squeal and bang the side of the metal pot with a spoon until Giselle ordered them to stop making such a godawful racket.

Dan had been touched and delighted by Teddy's obvious affection for his little sister. Giselle had worried about the effect of a new baby on Teddy, a new baby whose real father lived in the same house, not halfway across the country. But from the moment Trina was born, they were all more of a family. Dan and Teddy had seemed to feel closer to each other. They were the men of the house; Trina and she were the "chicks." "Chicks," Dan would say, shaking his head and winking at Teddy when Giselle or Trina did something silly, and Teddy would nod and grin. She shut off the faucet and grabbed a towel. She might have lost one child, but she wasn't going to lose another. She was still a mother.

While she was drying herself, she heard Dan say something to her brother, and then he flung open the bathroom door. "Where's Teddy?" he asked. His voice echoed off the bathroom walls, loud and harsh, and the look on his face was cold and distant. She held the bath towel in front of herself, as if he were some stranger who had just barged in.

"I don't know," she said, reaching for her underwear. "I was just going to look for him."

"What do you mean, look for him?" Dan glanced down at her bloody dress lying on the tile floor and kicked it across the room. "Where the fuck is he?"

Her heart pounded. Dan rarely lost his temper. When they argued, which wasn't all that often, his voice remained low and reasonable. Almost as if they were having a classroom discussion.

"He ran outside when I told him about . . ." Her voice choked up.

"Trina," he enunciated precisely. "Catrina."

"Do you mind?" He was blocking the doorway; she brushed past him into the hallway. "I'm getting dressed."

He followed her into their bedroom. She glanced into Teddy's room, which was empty. "Where's my brother?"

"He left. Said to call if we needed him." Dan sat on the edge of the bed and watched as she pulled on her jeans. The expression on his face looked critical, as if he were staring at a picture hanging crookedly. Then he sighed and lowered his head into his hands. Giselle walked over and wrapped her arms around him, pillowing his head against her breasts. She hadn't bothered to put on a bra. He lifted up her T-shirt and pressed his face into her bare breasts and started to cry. She held him tighter. His sweat had dried now and smelled sour, the sweat of fear rather than of vigorous exercise. She wanted to lie down beside him; she wanted them to cry together. He was mumbling how he couldn't believe it, how it couldn't be true, and she was brushing her lips against his hair, whispering, "I know, I know," but part of her mind was worrying about Teddy, and as if reading her thoughts, he suddenly pushed her away and sat up straight.

"It was Teddy," he said. "He was the one who fired the gun."

"No, it wasn't. It was Eric." She tucked her T-shirt firmly into the waistband of her jeans. "He had his father's gun."

Dan just shook his head slowly. "I talked to Bill. He says Teddy was holding the gun."

"He's lying," she said. "Teddy knows better. He wouldn't play with a gun. I know he wouldn't."

"Teddy admitted it to the police."

"Admitted what?" She glared at him.

"That he was holding the gun and doesn't know what happened. The phone rang, Eric bumped his arm, he was startled or some damn thing, and the gun went off. He said he was aiming at the trees in the back."

Giselle pressed her hands over her ears. "I'm not going to listen to this shit." She grabbed her sandals from underneath the bed. "I'm going to find Teddy."

"Stupid fucking kids!" Dan pounded his fist on the night table. "How many times do you have to tell them something?" The cheap ginger jar lamp jumped with each blow, sliding closer to the edge until it flew off and shattered on the wooden floor.

"What about Bill?" she shouted. "What sort of idiot keeps a loaded gun where kids can get at it?"

Dan shook his head. "He claims it was in a locked drawer and the key was hidden. The asshole really did call his lawyer. Already. He's scared stiff I'm going to sue him." Dan gave a snort of contempt, then covered his face with his hands. "For what? What's he got that I want? His fucking Corvette?"

She buckled her sandals and stood up. "I've got to find Teddy." She hesitated in the doorway. "Are you coming with me?"

He crushed one of the larger lamp shards underneath the heel of his tennis shoes. "I don't want to see him right now. Not yet." When he saw the look on her face, he added, "I'm sorry. Just not right now."

"However it happened, it was an accident," she said. "He's nine years old, for chrissakes!"

"I know," he mumbled, not looking at her. "Bill doesn't think they're going to file any charges. He talked to the police."

"Charges?" she repeated blankly. "What kind of charges?"

"Manslaughter, I guess." He let out a deep sigh and slipped into his teacher tone of voice: "Unintentionally causing the death of another without malice."

"It was an accident!" she shouted. "They're in the fourth grade, for chrissakes. Are you crazy?"

He shrugged. "I'm not a lawyer."

She felt cold again. Somewhere she had read some statistic: 70 percent of marriages did not survive the death of a child. Or maybe it was higher. Eighty percent. Ninety percent. At that moment it might as well have been 100 percent.

"Just give me a little while," he called after her as she slammed the door.

The clouds had moved in. It looked like rain. Suppertime. She could smell the charcoal grills fired up in some of the neighbors' backyards, everyone hurrying to cook their burgers and steaks before the rain let loose. As she walked to the end of their driveway, she thought of the chicken marinating in the refrigerator, ready for Dan to barbecue, the bowl of potato salad she had made that morning. A potato-sized lump lodged itself in her throat, and she almost turned and went back inside, unable to face the normal world going about its normal business. Or the thought of running into someone. Either way. If they'd heard or hadn't heard yet. The stilted offer of sympathy — what could you ever say? — or some oblivious bit of chitchat about the weather or whatever. What would she do? Hold up her end of the small talk? Blurt out, *I can't talk to you right now. Our daughter died today and I'm looking for my son, who accidentally shot her. Ciao.* She remembered how guiltily inadequate she'd felt when her cousin Ruth's younger daughter was run over a couple of years ago, how she'd actually picked up the phone to call her and then set it down again, and how she'd labored, instead, over her stilted condolences on a sympathy card.

Fortunately, it wasn't a particularly friendly neighborhood — just a diverse assortment of people, mostly renters like themselves, who pretty much kept to themselves — except for the kids. There were a couple of boys — one black, one white, both older than Teddy — shooting baskets in the driveway of a house on the corner. Across from the run-down stucco ranch with the burned-out lawn, the curtains always drawn shut, and lots of cars coming and going at odd hours. Drug dealers, they suspected. They had warned Teddy to stay away from there, to walk on the other side of the street when he went to the playground. Just as they had warned him (repeatedly) never to talk to strangers, never to ride his bike without his helmet, never to play with matches or guns.

Giselle didn't really know where to look. His only real friend within walking distance was Eric Beemer, but she didn't think Teddy would be over there, and she didn't want to see them. Especially Bill. If he hadn't bought that fucking gun that Lois never wanted in the first place . . . He was one of those guys who always thought he knew best, who was always bragging about getting the best deal on a car or big screen TV or whatever. Lois was okay, though. Giselle knew that Lois must be feeling terrible. If she were in Lois's position, she supposed she wouldn't know what

to say or do. But she wasn't. And she didn't have any sympathy
to spare. Lois could have put her foot down, for once, about that
goddamned gun. She should have been upstairs, keeping an eye
on the boys, instead of sweating off calories on some fancy Exer-
cycle (which Bill had picked up for "next to nothing, just like
new") in some vain attempt to hang on to her asshole husband.

The playground at the end of the street was deserted except for
a father pushing his little girl on a swing while her brother was
trying to climb up the slide part of the slide instead of the ladder.
The father yelled at him to knock it off: "Use it the right way or
not at all!" The little girl was blond and blue-eyed, maybe a year
old. The boy was sulking now, throwing rocks into the sandbox.
His father looked at Giselle and heaved a sigh of exasperation.
"Kids," he said, shaking his head. He smiled, obviously happy to
see another adult, a member of the same oppressed tribe. She
couldn't bring herself to smile back, and his smile faded.

"I'm bored," the boy pouted. "I want to go."

"We just got here!" his father barked back.

She looked inside the fort, built on top of a complicated climbing device that looked like a brightly painted nuclear reactor, but
it was empty.

"You seen a nine-year-old boy, blond, red T-shirt?" she asked
him.

The man shook his head again. "We just got here," he repeated
in a more civil tone. "I guess everyone thinks it's going to rain."

Giselle nodded. "Would you tell him his mother was looking
for him if you see him?" She was amazed by how normal she
sounded. *Your daughter is dead,* she told herself. The man was
looking at her intently. She supposed her eyes must have been red
and puffy. She wished she'd thought to put on her sunglasses even
though it wasn't sunny.

The boy throwing rocks looked up at her. "What's his name?"

"Teddy," she said, and waited for a moment to see if the boy had
anything else to say, but he didn't. So she turned around and left
the playground.

It started to rain as she walked back down the block. Slow, heavy drops. She didn't know where else to look. It occurred to her for the first time that maybe he had done something really crazy. Run away. Hitchhiked. Taken a bus. Did they sell bus tickets to nine-year-olds? She should have checked the stash of money that he kept in a Stars and Stripes Band-Aid box in his dresser drawer, gifts from his father and grandparents. She had no idea how much he actually had; he never seemed to spend anything. The last she'd heard, he'd been saving up for his own video camera, but he hadn't mentioned that in a while. Or maybe he had and she just hadn't been listening. Maybe she had been too busy worrying about some exam.

Teddy was a shy and cautious kid. He wasn't the type to run away. But then he wasn't the type to mess around with a loaded gun either. He was a worrywart really — the result of living for so long with a moody single mom. When Trina was born, they got a crib monitor. Teddy had asked what it was for, and Dan explained to him about SIDS. For days after that Giselle would find him in his sister's room, hanging over the crib, checking for signs of life.

If it was true what Dan said about Teddy's being the one who shot the gun — and she didn't believe it was — she couldn't imagine what he must be feeling, what he must be thinking. Scared to death. Sick with guilt. Her parents had, despite her protests, managed to instill in him a heavy dose of Catholic guilt. Sin and damnation. After he'd spent Easter weekend with them one year, Teddy had started to cry when Ed built a fire in the fireplace, something Teddy usually loved. He clung to her, sobbing and whimpering about hell. Only three years old. Neither Dan nor Giselle believed in God, but she knew from her own childhood how hard it was to shake off those Catholic bogeymen. Just the other day, out of the blue, Teddy had asked her if taping rented videos was a sin. *Manslaughter.* The syllables kept thudding through her head. They couldn't be serious. It was absurd, unreal. They were talking about a nine-year-old boy who still liked to watch Saturday morning cartoons in his pajamas. And aside from all that, Teddy didn't do it. Eric was lying. He had always been afraid of his father, afraid to own up to even minor infractions — a broken dish, a bicycle left outside in the rain. The kid seemed to shrink inside his clothes the minute Bill walked into the room. It was sad to see.

She looked at her watch. *Teddy must be home by now,* she thought, and started jogging toward the house. She worried that Dan wouldn't handle it properly, that he'd lash out at him, say things he'd regret later, once he could think clearly again. What would this do to Teddy, a thing like this? She didn't really want to think about Teddy at all right now. She just wanted to lie still and think about her baby. She resented having to worry about him, to chase after him, when all she wanted to do was to lie somewhere quiet and dark, hidden and soundproof. All she wanted to do was lie perfectly still and contemplate the enormity of the loss. Which she still couldn't quite fathom. It was too large, like trying to imagine a million billion. She could imagine maybe a day without Trina. A week. Maybe even an entire month. But a million billion days without her was inconceivable. Her mind just went blank.

Dan's mother's Buick was parked in the driveway. Luisa was sitting in the kitchen drinking tea and crying, clutching a monogrammed handkerchief in her fist. Her mother-in-law was the only woman Giselle knew who actually used handkerchiefs — embroidered, from Mexico. Her dark, silver-streaked hair, usually twisted into an elaborate chignon, was hanging in a braid, as if she'd been ready for bed when her son called her, even though it was only seven-thirty. Ever since her husband died three years ago, Luisa rarely ventured out after dark. Trina was her only granddaughter. Dan's brother in Tucson had three boys. When she saw Giselle, she let out a strangled sort of high-pitched wail — like a bat in a cave. Giselle walked over and bent down, allowing her tiny mother-in-law — just barely over five feet tall — to embrace her awkwardly and briefly. Luisa was a painter — she had known Frida Kahlo back in Mexico City, in her youth, before she married Dan's father and moved to L.A. It was the first time Giselle could remember seeing her without her mascara and silver jewelry.

"Is Teddy here?" Giselle asked, out of breath from the short sprint. Her only exercise of late had been chasing Trina around, picking up her toys, lifting her in and out of her car seat. Before Giselle got too pregnant, she used to meet Dan at the gym on campus three days a week. They would work out on the machines for forty-five minutes and then eat lunch together at the student union. A pleasant routine that she missed.

Her husband and mother-in-law both shook their heads.

"The poor boy," Luisa moaned, but she was looking at a framed portrait of Trina on the dining room wall. Last Christmas, wearing a red velvet dress with a lace collar that Luisa had given to her. A coquettish little señorita.

Lying in the hospital bed with her dark bangs still damp from swimming, her cheeks burned pink despite Giselle's vigilance with the suntan lotion, a white sheet tucked under her chin, Trina could have been sound asleep. She had always been an arrestingly beautiful child with her dark Gypsy eyes and long lashes. Strangers on the street would exclaim over her. Giselle and Dan used to worry that someone would steal her; they never left her unattended for even a moment in a shopping cart or in her car seat. Not for a single minute.

"I couldn't find him." She noticed the open bottle of bourbon on the counter and poured herself a shot, grimacing at the taste. She rarely drank hard liquor. She saw Luisa frown and look away. Giselle knew that she did not measure up to Luisa's image of the ideal daughter-in-law. Luisa had never approved of Giselle's leaving Trina at day care while she attended classes. And now look what had happened! Even though Giselle had been home, right there, when it happened.

"Did you check next door?" he asked.

"I don't want to go over there," she said.

"I don't blame you." He held out his bourbon glass for a refill.

"I don't think he'd be there anyway." Giselle sighed and paced around the small yellow kitchen.

"Maybe we should call the police," he said. "Jesus Christ, the police, twice in one day. Any minute now I'm going to wake up on the tennis court with Harvey, and none of this will have ever happened." He took a slug of his drink. "Damn. I promised him I'd call and tell him how she was." Harvey was his best friend on the faculty. His main ally. "I just don't feel up to it."

"I know," she sighed. "Maybe I should call Ed."

"That loser," Dan snorted. "And tell him what?"

"That Teddy's lost his sister." Giselle glared at him. She almost snapped, *What's come over you?* but then realized how ridiculous she'd sound. They both usually made a point of not bad-mouthing Ed, even outside of Teddy's presence. She stared at the phone, thinking she should call but not wanting to. Somehow it would make it all seem more real, more terrible, if possible, than it already was.

The clock on the wall above the sink read 7:40. Almost Trina's bedtime. On any other night they would have just given her a bath. The water would be draining out of the tub, leaving half a dozen rubber toys beached on the bottom, which Dan had covered with safety nonslip adhesive decals in the shape of smiling fish, and Giselle would be rubbing a fluffy towel over her sweet flushed baby flesh, her sturdy little legs, her distended tummy with its "outy" belly button, her dimpled butt, the rosebud vagina. She would be half asleep on her feet but struggling valiantly to uphold her end of the conversation. She was just learning her colors. She would point to Giselle's water-spotted blouse ("Pink!"), the curtains ("Yellow!"), the sailboat capsized in the dry tub ("Blue!"), and Giselle would nod and smile, kiss the top of her damp head and murmur, "What a smart girl you are!" Then Giselle would slip on one of the dainty nighties trimmed with lace that Luisa had made for her granddaughter and carry her into her bedroom, where Dan would tuck her in and read her *Koko's Kitten,* Trina's current favorite book, which she demanded to hear every night. She knew and would complain if you omitted so much as a single word, but usually she would fall asleep before the end, hugging her stuffed monkey, Mookie.

As Giselle picked up the toys from the tub and folded the towels, she would hear Dan's voice grow softer and softer, fading to a whisper; then she'd see the light blink out and hear him tiptoe down the hall to the living room, where Teddy would be watching TV for another hour, until his bedtime. And if she wasn't distracted by some worry about her coursework or bills or what she could scrounge up for Teddy's lunchbox, she might think to herself how fortunate she was to have somehow been granted this second chance, this whole new winterless life in California.

Occasionally, by way of contrast, she would flash back to Ed getting up in the dark, scraping the ice off the windshield of his old truck while the engine feebly warmed up, and as she struggled to spoon some baby cereal into Teddy's reluctant mouth, how depressed she'd feel at another day stuck alone in the small apartment with a fussy baby while Ed was off working at a job he hated, so that they could all keep on keeping on, just like thousands of other young and careless couples who had made the same stupid mistakes. Sometimes at night she had this dream that she was at an abortion clinic — there were protesters yelling outside the window — but the nice doctor and nurses seemed not to hear them; soft, serene classical music was playing inside the clinic. They had given her an injection of something and she felt floaty, above it all, free as a bird. Then Teddy's shrill crying would wake her up and she would lumber out of bed, heavy with fatigue and guilt, to nurse him back to sleep while Ed buried his head under the pillow and resumed snoring. It wasn't that she didn't love them. She did. It was just that she hated their life.

Giselle noticed Dan staring at the wall clock. Then, abruptly, he scraped his chair back and walked down the hall to Trina's room and shut the door. She held her breath. She was afraid that any moment she would hear his voice reading the first sentences of

Koko's Kitten: "Koko's full name is Hanabi-Ko, which is Japanese for Fireworks Child. She was born on the Fourth of July. Every year I have a party for Koko with cake, sparkling apple cider, and lots of presents."

Although normally Giselle conversed comfortably enough with Dan's mother, tonight they seemed unable to think of anything to say or even to look at each other. It dawned on her that most of their conversations had been about Trina. When they heard what sounded like a hoarse sob from down the hall, Luisa stood up and refilled the teakettle, diplomatically blasting the water to preserve her son's dignity. She liked sweet herb teas that smelled of oranges and roses.

"I'm going to check the garage again," Giselle said. Luisa looked startled and confused. "For Teddy," she added. Her mother-in-law nodded vaguely, as if the name didn't quite ring a bell.

It was pitch dark in the garage. The light had burned out weeks ago, and Dan hadn't got around to changing it. That was one of the few things she missed about Ed — how handy he was, how efficient at fixing things around the house. She stumbled over to her old Honda Civic and opened the door for the overhead light. For an instant she thought she saw Teddy curled up in the backseat but in the next instant realized it was just an old blanket thrown over a pile of accumulated junk. Then she checked Dan's car, which was identical to hers, only a year older, one of the coincidences that had seemed so remarkable when they were first getting to know each other. The same shade of blue and everything. His car, however, was much neater than hers — nothing but Trina's car seat and a Fisher-Price busy box in the back. In the kitchen the phone rang. She heard Luisa say, "Just a minute, please." Then she came to the garage door and said, "It's for you."

"Teddy?" Giselle asked hopefully even though she knew that Luisa would have said so if it were.

Luisa shook her head.

"I don't want to talk to anyone."

"It's Teddy's father." Luisa frowned. "Calling from Nebraska."

Giselle could hear the faint disapproval in her voice. Dan's mother didn't believe in divorce. Usually they all tried to pretend that Teddy was immaculately conceived. Giselle hurried inside and grabbed the receiver off the counter. Her heart was hammering. She knew that Ed wouldn't be calling unless he had heard something. He always called Teddy on Saturday morning — nine o'clock on the dot. You could set your watch by it.

THE PARKING LOT OF THE MINI-MALL IS NEARLY
*deserted. Sunday evening all the stores close early. Although even
on a Saturday, there wasn't much activity. It was just another tacky
strip mall with a dry cleaner, florist, copy center, beauty parlor, deli,
shoe repair, and an all-night drugstore. But it was the only shopping
center within biking distance of his house. He'd had to cross a busy
four-lane highway, which his mother had told Teddy he was not allowed to cross — when they moved into the house on Buena Vista, she
had drawn him a map of the area in which he was allowed to ride his
bicycle — but he figured that, under the circumstances, breaking that
rule was the least of his worries.*

*To kill time, Teddy drank a couple of Cokes in the deli until it
closed. Since then he's been hanging out in the drugstore, pretending to
look at magazines. He doesn't know what he's doing, really; he just
knows he can't go home. He feels sick to his stomach every time he
even thinks about seeing his mother and Dan — or walking past his
sister's room with its bright posters and mobiles. When they moved
in, it was a thin pale blue, like skim milk. He helped his mom paint
it pink with lavender trim. Teddy got to use the roller while she
painted the windowsills with a small brush. She was studying for a
Spanish exam, listening to Spanish tapes while they painted. They*

still sometimes joke around, repeating the dumb sentences on the tapes, making up ridiculous nonsense conversations when they're waiting in line or stuck in traffic or something. ¿Que hora es? El sombrero de medico es en la mesa. *He and his mom share this goofy sense of humor that Dan doesn't really appreciate. But Teddy knows Trina would have. You could already tell by what she laughed at.*

He buys a Snickers and a Goosebumps paperback so that the store clerks won't think he is a shoplifter and sits down in one of two folding chairs by the prescriptions counter. An old man with a metal cane is sitting in the other chair, waiting for his medicine. Teddy notices the man is wearing a hearing aid and breathing heavily. He looks like he might die sitting right there in the chair before they get his prescription filled.

There is a whole series of these Goosebumps mysteries, and Teddy has already read most of them, including this one, which is one of his favorites, Trapped in Bat Wing Hall, *but he doesn't actually own a copy of it — Eric and he trade them back and forth. It is one of the cool kind — sort of like a video game — where you can choose what is going to happen next. It would say something like "If you want to open the door, turn to page 76. If you want to go back downstairs, turn to page 35." So there were actually two or three different ways the story could go. And you, the reader, were sort of, like, in control of your destiny. You could make good or bad choices. If your first choice didn't turn out so hot, you could turn back and do something else instead. When Dan first saw it, he skimmed through the book and said to Teddy's mother, "Hmmm, interesting. It's like metal fiction. Those experimental writers like . . . ," and he rattled off some foreign-sounding names that Teddy had never heard of.*

His mother nodded as if she understood what his stepfather was talking about, and Teddy said, "What's metal fiction?" And Dan said, "Meta-fiction, not metal. *The writer plays with your sense of what's reality and what's artifice." And Teddy looked at his mom, who whispered, "I'll explain later." And she did. She said that most of the time the writer wants you to forget you're reading a story and to believe it's actually happening, it's really true. But some writers like to play tricks on the reader, sort of pull the rug out from under you, so that you're always aware that it's just some story that someone is making up and the writer making it up could make it go this way or that way because none of it is really real. None of it is real life.*

The pharmacist calls out, "Mr. Salazar," and the old man sitting next to Teddy kind of trembles his way slowly to the counter to pick up his pills. The druggist, a pretty Asian lady who reminds him of Connie Chung, looks over and smiles at Teddy. "Are you waiting for a prescription?" she asks. He shakes his head and looks back down at his book. She has to repeat everything to the old man in a loud voice before he understands where to sign and why the pills cost more than they did the last time.

Teddy can't concentrate on his book. He keeps thinking. He wishes that real life were like how the book was written: If you want to pick up the gun, turn to page 13. If you want to tell Eric you have to go home, turn to page 7. And there he'd be, walking across the yard to the wading pool, complaining that he's hungry and wants a snack. And he would go inside the house and bring out three Oreos, two for himself and one for Trina.

But this is real life. There is no flipping backward, not even in his mind, at least not for long. All he can think of is how he killed his sister. But even though he is thinking about it all the time, it is also like he isn't thinking about it, because every time, over and over, it seems to strike him fresh, catch him by surprise, like a fist slamming into his stomach. He sees his sister plop down on her butt in the water, a look of pure surprise on her face, the way she always looks when she falls down. He hears his mother screaming. He feels the panic he felt when the policewoman took him into the bedroom to talk to him alone. Her partner, a bald-headed black man, took Eric into the kitchen to talk to him. Teddy knew from the movies that the police wanted to hear their stories separately so that they could compare them later, catch them in lies. Teddy was crying and shaking so hard, he could hardly talk. His officer was nice, though. She reminded him of Mrs. Honey, his third-grade teacher. She told him just to tell the truth and not be scared, because everyone knew it was an accident, and they just needed to know how the accident happened for their records. Police procedure. She made it sound as if these things happened every day. As if he'd accidentally pitched a baseball through someone's window and smashed the glass. "Just tell me what happened," she said nicely. "Take a deep breath." She handed him a Kleenex to blow his nose. "By the way, I'm Sergeant Lacey." Under other circumstances he would have been thrilled to talk to an actual police sergeant.

Teddy had wanted to lie and say that Eric was holding the gun, but he knew from movies and the OJ trial — which his mom had watched on CNN whenever she was home, saying it was better than law school — that they had a million scientists who could figure out exactly what had happened. Fingerprints and powder burns and bullet angles. He knew they'd figure it all out scientifically — plus Eric would tell them it was him anyway — and Teddy would just be in even bigger trouble if he lied.

"Did you know the gun was loaded?" the policewoman asked him.

The question caught him by surprise. It was an obvious question, but somehow he didn't remember thinking about it. He didn't remember Eric's saying anything or asking anything himself about whether or not the gun was loaded. It was hard to remember what he'd been thinking. He guessed he wasn't really thinking. He couldn't have been.

Teddy shook his head. "I didn't know there were any bullets." Which wasn't really a lie. He didn't know there were and he didn't know there weren't.

"Did Eric tell you it was unloaded?"

He shook his head again. "I don't remember. I think I just, um, you know, assumed."

She snapped off the tape recorder and patted him on the shoulder. "I think that's enough for now, Teddy."

The "for now" scared him. What about later? He wanted to ask her but he was afraid to know. He followed her silently downstairs to the kitchen. The black officer was talking to Eric's father. Teddy couldn't see Eric or his mother anywhere. The black cop was really tall, like Michael Jordan. He knelt down in front of Teddy and looked him straight in the eye. Teddy flinched, thinking maybe the officer was going to arrest him. Take him away in a squad car. Maybe even hand-cuff him. But all the officer said was "Your uncle's next door, son. You can go on home now." His voice was soft and he looked sad, as if maybe he had a boy about Teddy's age and was thinking about him.

"Are you waiting for someone?" the Asian lady pharmacist asks Teddy. He knows she is trying to figure out what he is doing sitting there all alone on a Sunday evening. It is almost dark outside.

"My mother," he lies. She isn't the police; Teddy figures he can tell her anything he feels like. "She must have forgot or she's late or some-thing." The woman still looks worried, so he adds, "Do you have a pay phone?"

The pharmacist smiles encouragingly and points to a corner on the other side of the store. "Behind the cosmetics."

Teddy walks over to the phone and turns around to see if the phar-macist is watching him. She is. So he has no choice. He picks up the receiver and drops in a quarter.

"I want to make a call," he tells the operator when her voice comes on the line. And suddenly he does. He doesn't know why he hasn't thought of it sooner. "A collect call. To Edward Bedford. Four oh two, four three five, four three three three."

"And whom should I say is calling?" she asks, sounding bored, as if she could care less.

"Teddy," he says. "His son."

WHAT THE HELL'S GOING ON OUT THERE?" ED demanded to know before she even got out a hello, before she even had the receiver all the way to her ear.

If he'd started off with an offer of sympathy, she probably would have dissolved into tears, but his brusque accusatory tone immediately put her on the defensive. She felt her spine stiffen, her jaw clench. Luisa must have sensed the fur bristling; she tiptoed into the living room with her cup of tea and turned on the television.

"You tell me," Giselle said. "I take it Teddy called you?" She poured herself another shot of bourbon. She wanted to know where her son was, but she didn't want to come right out and admit that she didn't know.

"He was crying, not making much sense. He says he killed his sister."

Giselle stopped breathing. She could hear the tone Ed's voice took on when he was scared shitless but trying to pretend as though he wasn't. She wanted to hang up, to slam down the receiver as if it were an obscene call.

"You still there?" Ed said.

"He said he killed her?" she asked, trying to keep her voice steady. "Those were his exact words?"

"I didn't have a tape recorder, but, yeah, that's what he said. Something about hunting deer. He sounded crazy. I thought maybe he was on drugs." Ed believed that everyone in California was crazy or on drugs or both. He believed the Midwest was the last bastion of sanity.

"There was an accident," she said. "Teddy didn't kill her."

"You mean she's not dead?"

"No, I mean —" Her vocal cords went dead. She took a sip of bourbon and cleared her throat.

"She's dead," he said flatly.

Giselle let out a sob. She bit down hard on her lip and tasted blood mixed with bourbon. She thought maybe she was going to faint, and sat down hard in one of the kitchen chairs.

"Oh, Jesus." He groaned. "Jesus Christ almighty."

Dan appeared in the kitchen doorway and poured himself another stiff drink. His eyes were red, but he seemed calmer. He gave her a questioning look and she mouthed, "Ed." He sighed and retreated into the living room.

"I don't know what to say," Ed said finally, as if he'd run through every possible response in his repertoire and found them all to be inappropriate.

For the first time she appreciated his inarticulateness. Even in the best of times, verbal communication was not Ed's strong point. She had never enjoyed talking to him on the telephone, not even when they were first dating and in love. Giselle would wait around the house for him to call, but then when he did, she'd have to struggle to keep the conversation afloat.

"Where's Teddy?" she asked him. She blew her nose in a paper napkin lying on the counter.

"He was calling from a pay phone at Drug Fair. He says he can't go home. He wants to come here. To Lincoln." He hesitated for a second. "Maybe it's not a bad idea."

"Over my dead body!" Giselle snapped. Suddenly all the anger that she hadn't been able to direct at any target — not at Teddy, not at the doctors, not at the cop, not at Dan — took off like a Scud missile aimed right at Ed. "I just lost one child, and now you want to take the other one. I can't believe you."

"Listen," he shouted back, "I was just thinking about Teddy. What's best for him right now. After all —"

"He needs to be here," she cut in. "We need to get through this together, as a family." At the word *family* she felt this band of pain squeezing her chest. She pictured the three of them sitting silently at the supper table, Trina's high chair sitting out in the garage.

"I don't know," she sighed. "I don't know. I just think if we send him away now, he'll think it's because we blame him. Like a punishment. That we don't love him anymore."

"Yeah," Ed conceded glumly. "Maybe." He was silent for a moment, stymied.

Suddenly it occurred to her that if Teddy really did shoot Trina — and why would he say he did if he didn't? — maybe, legally, he wasn't even allowed to leave the state. The thought took her breath away. She didn't know anything about the law in these cases. She'd read about these things happening in the newspaper — kids accidentally shooting one another — and thought, *How terrible,* but never stopped to think about the law.

"How did it happen? Where'd he get the gun?"

She had been waiting for him to ask, surprised it had taken him this long to get around to the details. The five Ws of journalism. Or was it four? In another lifetime she'd been assistant editor of their high school newspaper.

"I asked where he got the gun," Ed repeated accusatorily. As if she were the one — and not he — who had a stupid redneck NRA bumper sticker on the back of his pickup.

"I don't really want to get into it," she snapped. She figured what he was really asking was, *How could it happen? Where were you?* "I understand you've got questions and you've got a right to know — I'm not trying to be evasive — I'm just too fucking tired right now. Okay?"

"Do I have a choice?"

"I'm sorry," she amended, softening her tone. She didn't want to antagonize him. She wasn't exactly coming from a position of strength here. She could just imagine what his family and friends in Lincoln were going to say.

"I'm sorry, too," he said, so low that she could barely hear him. "About your little girl."

His mumbled apology caught her by surprise. She'd been waiting for him to say, *I told you so,* to blame her for leaving him and moving to California. For taking their son off to the killing fields — gangs, drive-by shootings, earthquakes, fires.

"I'm going to go get Teddy now," she told him. "I'll call you tomorrow morning."

"I'll be here."

"Good." She was about to hang up when he said her name, or rather the nickname she had left behind.

"Gigi?"

"What?" She picked up her car keys off the counter and jangled them, impatient to be off.

"Do you want me to come out there? I can, you know. I can be there tomorrow."

His voice sounded awkward, as if he were asking her out on a first date. Back in high school her best friend, Laura, used to say that Ed reminded her of Lennie in *Of Mice and Men.* Strong and gentle and a little slow. Laura hadn't really meant it as an insult, and somehow Giselle hadn't taken it as one. She was touched by his offer. She knew how much he hated to fly, his white-knuckled terror.

"I don't think so, Ed," she said gently. "But thanks."

"Are you sure?"

"Let's wait and see." She hung up before he could say anything or hear her crying again.

In the living room Dan and Luisa were sitting on the couch holding hands. Giselle had never seen a son and mother so affectionate with each other. At first it had worried her, made her wonder if Dan wasn't too close to his mother for comfort, but she had come to the conclusion that it was just cultural. His brother was the same way. Angela Lansbury — *Murder, She Wrote* — was on the TV. Dan had already muted the volume, as if they had just been sitting there waiting for Giselle to hang up.

"He's at Drug Fair," she said, not meeting Dan's eyes. Now that she knew he was right — it was Teddy — she couldn't bear to look at him. "I'll be back in five minutes." She hesitated for a second, not sure whether she wanted Dan to volunteer to come with her or not. But he didn't. Any other evening she might have asked, "Do you want anything?" And he might have answered, "Some Rum Raisin" or "The new *Esquire*" or "We're almost out of toothpaste." He might have added, "Be careful, honey," as she walked out to the garage. But tonight she didn't ask if he wanted anything and he didn't say anything.

During the short ride to the mini-mall, Giselle rehearsed what she was going to say to Teddy. It felt sad and strange to be worrying about what she would say to her own son, as if years had elapsed since they last saw each other, some awkward gulf of time during which he might have changed beyond recognition. At a stop sign the car across from her honked and flashed its lights. She had neglected to turn on her headlights. She sat up straighter and clutched the wheel firmly. *Just concentrate on your driving,* she told herself. *All we need now is a car accident.* She turned the radio dial to an easy-listening station and focused on breathing deeply, a relaxation technique she had taught herself during those sleepless nights after she'd left Ed and moved to California, wondering if she'd done the right thing. Sometimes she'd wake up gasping for breath. She went to a doctor and said she thought she had asthma or some kind of new allergy, but he'd said they were panic attacks. She asked for some Valium, but he was one of those young bearded New Age–type doctors. He wrote down the name of a bookstore — the Bo Tree — and recommended a couple of relaxation tapes. So Giselle would lie in bed and listen to the rustle of waves or a deep, distant gong from some Tibetan mountaintop, feeling foolish. She felt that already she was turning into the sort of flaky - California type that Midwesterners made fun of. But Teddy loved the tapes. He'd drift right off to sleep with an otherworldly smile on his lips. He even stopped grinding his teeth at night.

It was raining heavily as she turned into the empty parking lot, headed toward the brightly lit Drug Fair, and parked the car. As she sprinted to the store, sandals splashing through the puddles on the asphalt, she thought how if it had only been raining this afternoon, Trina wouldn't have been in the wading pool, and . . . so on. *You can't think of that right now,* she told herself. *You have to concentrate on Teddy.*

At the doorway Giselle almost collided with someone coming out, holding a white prescription bag. She couldn't think of his name. He and his wife had been in their Lamaze class a couple of years ago. He held up the small white bag. "Ear infection. Again," he sighed, "poor kid." Giselle mumbled something sympathetic and brushed past him.

The store was so brightly lit, it blinded Giselle for a moment. Then she walked briskly from one aisle to the next — greeting cards, cosmetics, shampoo and hair dye, toys. She walked up the toy aisle just to make certain, then went on to feminine hygiene, vitamins, cold remedies, canned foods, and summer promotional items — hibachis, folding chaise longues, and tiki torches. When she got to the last aisle, she felt panic mounting. What if he'd left the store after talking to his father and run off somewhere? She should have checked to see if his bike — a shiny black monstrosity that looked like a miniature Harley-Davidson (a Christmas present from Uncle Todd), Teddy's pride and joy — was in the bike rack out front. She was about to walk back outside and look for it when her eyes caught a flash of bright red: Teddy's Cornhuskers T-shirt (a Christmas gift from his paternal grandparents). She looked more closely, and there he was, huddled up, wedged into a narrow alcove between the cash machine and a postcard rack. He was folded up like a little lawn chair, his face pressed against his knees. She felt an urge to crawl in there with him, huddle together, but the space was too small. She thought maybe he was asleep, but when she said his name softly, just once, his head whipped up. When he saw her standing there, he cringed like a beaten dog.

And suddenly his hangdog expression triggered something inside her. Giselle wanted to yank him out of there, shake him, and shout at him, *What were you thinking? How could you have been so stupid? Don't you know what you've done?* Even though it was obvious that he did know. His eyes squeezed shut and he began to cry silently, his narrow shoulders shuddering, the vulnerable stem of his neck exposed as he blotted his tears against his blue-jeaned knees. There was a skinny little snake of a braid at the nape of his neck — a current fad among the kids in his class — that seemed to tremble like an exposed nerve ending. Trina used to delight in pulling on it until he yelped, "Ouch!" Dan had told them that in the olden days, courtiers used to wear them and they were called lovelocks. The word sounded like some sort of wrestling term.

Shaken, taken aback by her sudden brutish impulse, she reached out and tweaked the braid, as she often did, playfully. It was a routine. She would tug and he would stick out his tongue, as if the two were connected. But this time he didn't play. He just grabbed her hand and held it so hard, it hurt.

"Come on," she said, tugging him up. "Let's go home."

She noticed an obese woman in pale green hospital scrubs watching them, Giselle in particular, suspiciously. As if sizing her up as a possible child abuser. Was this a tantrum over a candy bar or something more sinister? The woman had her arms full of half-price chocolate Easter eggs. Giselle wondered if she actually worked at a hospital or just wore the loose pajamas for comfort. When the woman saw that Giselle saw she was watching them, she didn't look away as most people would have. She stood her ground. "Come on, Teddy," Giselle whispered. "People are looking at us."

At that he opened one eye and looked up, right at the formidable woman in green. Then he looked at Giselle and must have seen something that reassured him, because he stood up, wiped his nose with the back of his hand, and managed a trembly "okay."

Giselle held his hand as they walked out of the store and started across the spooky, wet parking lot, the way she used to do when he was younger. Suddenly he stopped and said, "My bike." His voice sounded timid, but his posture looked stubborn.

She wanted to leave the bike for later. She wanted to say, *It's raining. We'll get it tomorrow.* But under the circumstances, she was afraid he would interpret it as some form of punishment, of rejection, so she sighed and turned back. "Okay, go get it."

He ran back to the bike rack, the heels of his trendy sneakers flashing on and off in the dark like fireflies. Silently, he wheeled the bike, carefully avoiding puddles, to the car and tried his best to help as Giselle struggled to fit it into the Honda. Mostly he just succeeded in getting in the way, and she just managed to restrain herself from snapping at him, "Let me do it." She felt a sharp tug as she tried to straighten up. The shoulder strap of her purse had twined itself around the bike's handlebars. She swore under her breath, trying to free it, then just flung it on top of the bike and slammed the hatchback.

Teddy sat meekly in his seat as she started the engine and turned on the lights. She could see him crying again and she sat there for a second, exhausted and overwhelmed by how difficult this was going to be, how every word and gesture at this juncture seemed to call for a delicacy and restraint that seemed to require too much energy. She could barely lift her feet off the ground, let alone tiptoe through a minefield. And then, on top of all that, she berated herself for feeling this way. Shouldn't the right words and gestures just come naturally? She was his mother, after all. Where was her unconditional maternal love? Was anything in this world ever truly unconditional? Didn't everything have its breaking point? She wasn't God, after all. She remembered her cathechism: God is good. God is great. God has no beginning or end. It occurred to her that it was just as well she didn't really believe in

God. Maybe some mothers could lose a child and keep their faith, but she knew she wasn't one of them. She leaned over, patted Teddy's knee, and said, "It was an accident. No one blames you."

"Really?" Teddy's voice sounded heavy and waterlogged, as if it were bubbling up from the bottom of some deep, dark pond.

"Really." As she shifted the car into reverse, she flashed on Dan's fist pounding the night table and his voice muttering, "Stupid kids," the lamp shattering into pieces on the floor. She wondered how many other lies and half-truths she would have to tell before they were through this. Teddy mumbled something she couldn't hear. She stepped on the brake and turned to him impatiently. "What?"

"Your seat belt," he said. "You forgot to put it on."

A spark of love flamed up inside her. Giselle crushed him against her, practically strangling him in his shoulder belt, and let out a couple of choked sobs — as if she were the one being strangled — even though on the way over she had ordered herself not to cry in front of him. At least not tonight. But he seemed relieved. She felt the brittleness melt a bit as he patted her back and whimpered over and over, "I'm sorry, Mom, I'm sorry."

"I know," she said, digging in her pocket for a tissue. "I know you're sorry." She wanted to say, *Tell me it wasn't you. Tell me it was Eric.* Instead, she bit her lip, and whatever superhuman force that allows mothers to lift cars off crushed infants enabled her to keep her mouth shut.

The short ride home was silent except for the radio playing what Dan called elevator music. Teddy sat rigidly, clutching his Goosebumps paperback in his lap. She found herself driving slower and slower, as if the car were dragging its feet, as they approached Buena Vista. Luisa's big Buick was gone. She no longer drove at night, so Giselle assumed that Dan had given her a ride back to her condo, which was only a few minutes away. She doubted that he'd be gone long. Usually she handed Teddy the Genie — he got a kick out of levitating the garage door — but tonight she just punched the button herself, pulled into the crowded garage next to Dan's twin Honda Civic, and turned off the motor. He just sat there. They both seemed reluctant to go inside. Finally she said, "You have to remember that Dan's still in shock. We all are," she added, not wanting it to sound as if she were criticizing Dan. Already she could see the danger in taking sides. "He might not know what he's saying right now. You might need to give him a little time — a couple of days — to, you know, get hold of himself." When Teddy didn't say anything, she asked, "Do you know what I'm saying?"

"What about my dad? He said I could go there." Seeing the look on her face, he added, "I mean for a while."

"I told him we'd call him in the morning. First thing." She got out of the car and locked the door, then opened the hatchback to get her purse. "Can we just leave the bike till morning?"

"I don't care," he said sullenly. "Why can't I go to Nebraska?"

"You have school," she said. He just looked at her as if they both knew this was a ridiculous answer. She sighed. "We all think it's important that you stay here right now. We need to pull together as a family. There's Trina's funeral and —"

"I don't want to go to the funeral!" he interrupted. "Don't make me go. Please, pleee-aase." He sounded on the verge of hysterics. She hadn't even thought ahead to the funeral. The word coming out of her mouth shocked her. Her knees buckled. She leaned against the car to steady herself. He was tugging frantically on her purse strap, pleading with her.

"I don't know, Teddy," she sighed again. "We'll see." She shook him off, maneuvering her way past the lawn mower and a box of stuff for Goodwill to the kitchen door. "Let's try to take things a step at a time. Okay?"

Teddy just stood by the car. "I wish we'd never moved to California."

She wanted to turn around and smack him, but she forced herself to ignore the comment.

So he repeated it more loudly: "I wish we'd never moved to California!"

Jesus, is he deliberately trying to provoke me? She turned around and glared at him. "And I wish you'd had the good sense not to play with a loaded gun."

He smiled to himself as if he'd just proved a point. "I knew you blamed me. It's all my fault."

"That's not true!" she snapped, angry at herself for letting him provoke her. *He is the child. I am the adult.* Something she would probably have to repeat to herself, like a mantra, thousands of times, in the hours, days, weeks — maybe years — to come. "It's no one's fault."

"How can something be no one's fault?" he asked. He sounded genuinely interested, as if he were waiting for a real answer.

"I don't know." She sighed again, louder and longer. "Sometimes things just happen." She held the door open, waiting for him to precede her into the house, not taking any chances that he'd bolt. She thought how handy religion could be at a time like this. "It's God's will," she could hear her mother's reedy voice saying. "He works in mysterious ways." And Giselle's father would nod in pious agreement. Although he would also probably beat the shit out of the poor kid and never even see any flaw in the logic.

The feeling in the house was beyond emptiness, a vacuum, sucking them down into it. She let out a small cry. Trina's new pink tricycle was standing in the middle of the living room. Giselle was sure it hadn't been there when she left. Dan must have moved it. Teddy stared at the bike as if he'd seen a ghost. She was glad for these few minutes alone with him. She hoped she could get him into his pajamas and into bed before Dan got back. Skip the bath. In the morning the terrible reality would be waiting there for them, like an endless bad dream, but at least they might have more energy to deal with it. It was one of the great truisms: Things always look better in the morning. Trite but true, at least up to this point in her life. This time she had the feeling that the opposite could just as easily be true: Things will look even worse in the morning. And in the afternoon. And in the evening. And on the day after. And on the day after that. Maybe — who knew? — as time went on, there were some things that got harder and harder to take. Like frostbite — as the numbness wore off, the pain burned hotter.

She thought of that young couple with the baby, a big news story a while back, who got lost in a snowstorm. The wife had to stay behind in a tiny cave with the baby for two days while her husband hiked out for help. At the time Giselle had wondered what the wife had to feel as she watched him disappear into this white wilderness, and what they had said to each other before he'd actually set out. Months later Giselle saw them on *Primetime Live* or *60 Minutes*. One or both of them had lost some toes to frostbite. The baby was perfectly fine. A miraculous story of love and endurance. Survival. She had thought, watching them talking and holding hands, how very possible yet disappointing it would be if, some years down the road, they ended up getting a divorce. They were, after all, still so young — even though they seemed so united by this ordeal. And for the first time it occurred to her, What if the baby had died? What if he'd come back and found the baby frozen stiff? It would have been a whole different story.

Teddy made a beeline straight to his room and shut the door. She saw the hem of light under his door blink off. *So this is how it's going to be,* she thought, feeling shut out. Part of her wanted to say, *Fine,* and go sit in the living room alone, drinking the rest of the bourbon, if Dan had left any for her. But the other part of her walked up the hall and knocked softly on Teddy's door.

"Go away," he said. "I'm sleeping." His voice was muffled in the pillow.

She opened the door and sat down on the foot of his bed. He buried his head under the pillow, as if the bright light from the hallway hurt his eyes. Or he didn't want to be seen. She slid her hand underneath his T-shirt — he hadn't bothered to change into his pajamas — and skated her fingernails over his thin bony back, something he usually loved. He was the smallest boy in his fourth-grade class. In the class picture this year they had placed him in the front row, next to the girls, most of whom were taller than he was. The Cornhuskers T-shirt his grandparents had sent swam on him. Giselle had suggested that he put it away for a couple of years, but he'd insisted on wearing it. At the touch of her fingers, he tensed his muscles, but she kept it up until she felt his body gradually letting go. Then she kissed him on the back of his head, smoothed the damp hair from his forehead, and whispered, "Good night. I love you." Still, she thought the missing word silently — *I* still *love you.*

As she stood up and tiptoed across the carpet toward the door, he turned his head in her direction. "Mom?"

"Yes, Teddy?" She paused and waited.

"Do I have to go to school tomorrow?"

She caught her breath. Monday morning. She hadn't gotten that far yet. The thought of school, the resumption of a day-to-day routine. "No," she said. "Don't worry about school right now. We'll explain to your teacher." Then she paused again at the doorway, struck by a new thought. "Unless you want to. Do you want to go to school tomorrow?" She thought maybe he needed to do the normal things, to get out of the house, into the rest of the world, where life would still be going on as usual.

"No way." He shook his head violently. "Everyone will know. Eric will tell them."

"They'll know it was an accident. We'll talk to Mrs. Shimono personally, and she'll explain that it was just an accident."

"She doesn't like me," he said dully. "Because my penmanship is sloppy. She only likes the girls with neat penmanship."

"She does too like you," Giselle told him. "Look at all those nice things she said about you on your last report card."

"I don't think so." He sounded unconvinced. "She just likes to be polite to the parents."

In fact, she had been less complimentary about Teddy than his previous teachers had, something Giselle had attributed to a certain quiet reserve. But maybe she was wrong. Maybe Mrs. Shimono didn't really like him, or boys in general. Giselle wished he still had Mrs. Honey, his third-grade teacher, whom he'd been crazy about. A woman just as sweet as her name. He was going to need all the sweetness he could get in order to swallow this bitter pill.

"Maybe you won't even go back to that school," she blurted out without thinking. "Maybe we'll move."

"Back to Nebraska?" Teddy sat up in bed and looked at her hopefully.

"No." She let out an exasperated sigh. He barely remembered Nebraska; he had been perfectly happy in California up until now. "Forget I said that. It's too soon to make plans. One step at a time, remember? And the first step is sleep."

He sank back under the covers, and she shut the door softly behind her. She stood in the hallway for a moment thinking, *Now what?* The door to Trina's room was shut. Usually they left it open so they could hear if she cried out in the night. The baby monitor had broken months ago, and they had never bothered to replace it. Trina liked the door open. She would cry, "Up!" — meaning "open" — if someone forgot and shut it. She had the general idea but still didn't quite have her bearings when it came to preposi-tions. Giselle had the feeling that if she opened the door softly, she would hear the little sleep noises Trina made in the back of her throat. Little burbles and gurgles. It still had not really sunk in yet. She had seen too many movies; she was still holding her breath, waiting to be saved in the nick of time. All those sappy, sentimental blockbusters. Until she'd taken Dan's class, she had thought that sentimentality was a good thing. He was the one who made her see that it was actually a bad thing, something that in-telligent, sophisticated people avoided at all costs. Of course, that was before his father's death.

When Dan's father died of a sudden massive coronary three years ago, they had been in bed together; she had been lying next to Dan, holding him, as his mother delivered the bad news. Before his father's death, Dan had been cautious about keeping his distance, not introducing her to his parents, not spending too much time with her son. He was thirty-five and had never been married. He said he liked his life the way it was; he liked the solitude, the freedom to spend all night reading and writing.

After his father's heart attack, he spent a week with his mother and brother. They had convinced their mother to sell the house and move into a condo, and they were busy with Realtors. But every night Dan would call Giselle before he went to bed, something he had never done before. There was a new sentimentality, a vulnerability about him that seemed to put them on a more equal footing.

When he got back from his parents' house in Los Feliz, he began spending more and more time at Giselle's cramped apartment. On the weekends the three of them — Dan, Giselle, and Teddy — would do typical family things together, like going to the beach or the zoo.

A month later they were married — a trip to City Hall — and two months after that she was pregnant. On purpose this time. She might have preferred to wait until she had finished her belated B.A., but Dan was eager to start a family of his own. Teddy was almost seven, and Dan thought if they waited, Teddy would be too old to relate to a younger sibling. Dan had this image of one happily integrated household — the Partridge family, only smaller and hipper. Giselle could see his logic. Plus, this was one area where she was the expert and he was the novice. She might not have a Ph.D., but she had given birth. She might not have been to Europe, but her uterus was as fertile as prime Nebraska farmland.

She heard the Buick sail into the driveway, scraping against something. She got up and walked to the kitchen. The Beemers' dog started barking. Dan shouted at him to shut the fuck up. As she was standing in the kitchen, pouring herself the last dregs of the bourbon, she could hear Dan muttering curses to himself, as if assessing some damage to the paint, and then he struggled to push open the warped kitchen door that they always had difficulty closing properly. She thought of Ed's do-it-yourself efficiency. She doubted that Dan would have the faintest idea how to plane a door. She walked over and tugged it open from the inside. Off balance, he stumbled into the kitchen, grabbing on to her for support. They clung together for a moment before he pulled away and walked over to the refrigerator.

"Did you find Teddy?" he asked, staring blankly inside. The kitchen was dark — she hadn't bothered to snap on the light. As she watched Dan standing in the bright circle of light from the refrigerator, she felt like a member of the audience, sitting out in the dark, waiting for the actor in the spotlight to speak his lines. It seemed suddenly as if nothing were normal and natural between them anymore. Their real life had been canceled. Or someone had flipped the channel. And now they were stuck in some godawful soap opera that could go on and on for years. *The Guiding Light*. *Search for Tomorrow*. Even before she met Dan, when she was just a college dropout with a baby, she had never watched the soaps.

She nodded. "He's in bed."

Dan pulled out a small box of Juicy Juice and stared at it as if it were a grenade he might hurl through the window. Then he set it back in the refrigerator, grabbed a can of Old Style, and flipped the top. He rarely drank beer, and when he did, it was Corona or Dos Equis. The beer was Giselle's, a vestige of her first marriage, her Midwestern heritage.

"So how does he seem?" he asked, taking a swig. He grimaced. "Why do you buy this cheap shit?"

She let that pass. "He's — I don't know how he is. He's upset. He's very upset. Naturally."

Dan nodded grimly. "Well, we've got the names of those therapists."

"Yeah. I guess I'll call someone in the morning. Make an appointment or something." Some social worker at the hospital had given her a list of names, which she had shoved into her pocket without a glance. "But mostly, I think, he just needs us." She looked over at Dan, to see if he was picking up on what she was trying to convey, but he was looking at his watch.

"It's only nine-fifteen," he announced with a bemused look on his face. "What are we supposed to do now?"

"You mean for tonight, or the rest of our lives?" she asked.

"Watch TV? Grade some papers? Rent a video? Get out the old home movies?" He shook his head, ignoring her. His stomach rumbled.

"You should try to eat something," she said, even though the thought of actually swallowing anything but alcohol made her gag. She opened the refrigerator and took out the bowl of potato salad she had made that morning and grabbed a bowl from the dish drainer. It was Trina's Beatrix Potter cereal bowl. She shoved it back — hoping he hadn't noticed — and grabbed a plain blue bowl. She spooned out a small serving and handed it to him. He was crazy about her mother's Swedish potato salad.

"I don't want any."

"You shouldn't drink on an empty stomach."

He took the bowl from her and shoveled the potato salad into his mouth mechanically, like a human IV. The sour smell of the vinegar turned her stomach. She covered the bowl with tin foil and stuck it back in the fridge, scanning the shelves. Nothing appealed to her. But she felt as if she should make the gesture, a show of eating with him, taking nourishment together. Finally she took one of the kids' fruit Popsicles from the freezer. She tore off the wrapper and walked over to the trash can. There was a note on the table she hadn't noticed before. In her mother-in-law's elegant, convent-trained handwriting. It said, *Your mother called. Call as soon as possible.* Obviously her uncommunicative brother had broken down and called them with the news. It had occurred to her that she should call them but figured it could wait until morning. Now she felt guilty. They must be going crazy. And below that: *Your sister Yvonne called.* Giselle wondered who had called Vonnie — Todd or her parents. The thought that they knew knocked the wind out of her. She grabbed a chair and sat down, crumpling the note in her fist. Soon everyone would know. And then there would be no way to undo it. Once people knew, that was that. It was real.

"What is it?" He walked over and knelt down beside her. She shook her head. She couldn't explain. She knew it didn't make any sense. He tugged the crumpled note out of her fist and read it.

"I don't want to talk to anyone," she moaned. It came out like a whine.

"My mother's going to take care of the arrangements. The service and everything. So you don't have to worry about any of that." He set his dish in the sink and ran water on it, something Ed could never remember to do no matter how many times she complained about his dishes sitting right where he'd left them. As if she had lodged some sort of protest, Dan added, "She'll check it all out with us beforehand. She's just trying to help."

"That's fine," she said. "Really."

She had never been to a child's funeral before. In fact, she had been to only one funeral in her entire life. Her aunt Loraine had died of lung cancer at age fifty-six, and at her funeral everyone had bemoaned her untimely death. Even though she'd smoked two packs of Camels since she was a teenager and already had two grandchildren. Giselle remembered her coffin — a long ivory-and-shiny-brass affair the size of a boxcar. Loraine had been a big, strapping woman before she got sick. Giselle wondered if they had special boutique mortuaries that dealt in children's coffins: a sort of Gap for dead kids.

"I really don't know what to do now," Dan said. He was standing at the window, looking out. "What do people do?"

She stood up and circled her arms around him from the back. He turned and rested his cheek against the top of her head. She brushed a strand of hair away from his eyes. A warm breeze ruffled the kitchen curtains that they kept meaning to replace with mini-blinds when they had the time. With two kids, one still in diapers, there was never any time. Maybe now there would be more time. It was a nice night after the rain. Any other night she would have gone out onto the back porch, but she knew that Trina's wading pool was still sitting out there. Like a black hole.

"Let's go to bed," she suggested. "Even if we don't sleep. We can hold each other."

He nodded and let her lead him back to their bedroom, as if he'd lost all will of his own. She sat him down on the edge of the bed and undressed him like a sick, tired child. His socks, tennis shorts, polo shirt, jockey shorts. They were damp and sweaty. They didn't smell like him. Usually she liked the smell of his sweat, but this was an unfamiliar, unpleasant odor. She threw the clothes in the hamper.

"Maybe I should take a shower," he said, not moving. It touched her to see him like this, so bewildered and listless. Usually he was energetic and decisive to a fault. He hated to shop with her because she took so long to make up her mind.

"I'll run the water for you," she said.

He followed her into the bathroom and waited with uncharacteristic patience while she adjusted the faucets to the proper temperature, somewhere between soothing and scalding. She liked the water hotter than he did. In fact, she had read somewhere that women could withstand hotter water than men could. When she turned around, he was staring at himself in the mirror.

"I was just getting used to myself as a father," he said. "I mean, it was kind of unreal at first. Having a daughter. And now this is just as unreal." He drew a question mark in the film of steam on the mirror. "It's hard to know what's really unreal."

She slid back the curtain, clear plastic with bright pink flamingos, and steered him into the shower.

The bed was still unmade from this morning. This morning. Sunday. Babies made no distinction between weekend mornings and weekday mornings. Trina's cries had woken them at six-thirty. They had a deal: Saturday mornings Dan had kid duty, and Sunday mornings were her watch. Yesterday Dan had fed the kids, then driven Teddy and Eric to soccer practice while Giselle had slept in (until eight o'clock) and then gone to the university library to do some research on Hawthorne for an upcoming term paper. But this morning Dan had slept in while she made pancakes — a special treat — and then dragged the kids to the grocery store (Teddy pouting the whole way, as if she were forcing him to undergo an unnecessary root canal) and then to the playground, where she turned him loose to work off some of his manic energy. She had sat on the edge of the sandbox reading *The Scarlet Letter,* trying to concentrate on Hawthorne's dry, long-winded introduction while Trina played with a little black girl, who immediately grabbed Trina's pink plastic shovel, whereupon Trina whacked the little girl on the side of the head with her pail. After both mothers had intervened and the girls had stopped crying, they settled into playing side by side companionably enough. Parallel play, the books called it. Meanwhile, Teddy was off on some climbing device, doing his best to break his neck. After an hour or so at the park, Teddy declared that he was bored and hungry. They had stopped for lunch at McDonald's and then returned home, where Dan was busy mowing the lawn. It was only twelve-thirty, and she was exhausted.

Against Trina's tired, feeble protests, Giselle put her down for a nap. She wound up the musical mobile hanging over the crib, and by the time it had tinkled out the final lilting notes of "Scarborough Fair," Trina was out cold. Teddy ran next door to play with Eric. Dan took off to play tennis. The house looked as if it had been ransacked by cops looking for illegal drugs, but she tried to ignore the discarded shoes, toys, books, and trails of cookie crumbs. The house would have to wait until the kids were in bed. She went into the kitchen and made the potato salad and marinated the chicken for supper. On Sunday evenings Dan barbecued. While she was making supper, her parents called, as they did every week. Her mother launched into a familiar diatribe against the condo management board, and Giselle tuned out, wishing she could get back to studying before Trina woke up. And then Trina did wake up and Giselle said she had to go, the baby was crying, and hurried into the baby's room, where she changed Trina's diaper and gave her a box of apple juice. Then she had dragged the wading pool out into the sun and run the hose into it and dumped in a pile of Trina's water toys, including the new Go Fish game. She had meticulously slathered suntan lotion over every inch of her daughter's warm, sleep-flushed flesh. Trina rubbed some in her eye and started to cry and then stopped when Giselle dangled the bright new fishing rod in front of her and showed her how to hook a yellow fish and then a purple one. She clapped her hands and grabbed for the rod, whipping it around wildly, laughing as she splashed herself. "Careful. Don't poke your eye out," Giselle had cautioned her as if she could understand. Giselle had thought about running inside for the camera but didn't have the energy. She had collapsed into the ratty lounge chair and opened her book.

Just this morning.

The shower clunked off and Dan emerged, still half wet, from the bathroom, a blue towel wrapped around his waist, and threw himself facedown onto the bed. She could see his shoulders shuddering; the pillow helped muffle his sobs. She didn't know whether she should go or stay. She felt guilty and helpless. When his father died, he had turned to her for comfort, and she had been glad to give it, secretly thrilled that he had turned to her. This was before they were married. But now she had her own grief. There was no comfort to give.

She put her hand on his back. "Honey," she said. He groaned. "Please, honey, turn over." She tugged at his shoulder. He rolled over but kept one arm flung over his eyes, which were shut. She sighed.

"I was going to take a picture of her," she mumbled. "Today, in the swimming pool. I actually thought about going inside for the camera — she looked so cute — but I didn't." Her voice broke. "I was afraid to leave her alone in the water. Afraid she might drown," she lied. She didn't want to admit she'd been too preoccupied with her studying. She wondered suddenly how much history she would have to rewrite now. "It would only have taken a second. Why didn't I get the camera?"

"Don't do that," he said. "Stop." He reached out and put his fingers against her lips. She grabbed hold of his hand. He still had his eyelids clenched against the harsh overhead light. Or maybe he just didn't want to look at her, to see her. The bedside lamp was still broken, and she didn't know whether they were ready for darkness just yet, but she got up and flicked off the overhead light. The light from the bathroom was still on, and that helped. He seemed to relax some.

"I think I have a couple of Valium if you want one," she told him. She didn't say they were from Lois, who had a perpetual stash of sedatives and sleeping pills. Every once in a while, when the kids and school got to be too much, Giselle would pop one, like a little vacation.

He shook his head. The towel had slipped down below his slim hips, and his arms were flung out, crucifix-fashion. With his dark beard and longish hair, he was a dead ringer for Jesus. She traced the thick scar just above his groin. An emergency appendectomy. His mother loved to tell the story. How when he was only three months old, she had seen blood in his diaper and rushed him to the hospital. The doctor had checked him over and found nothing. So he sent them home. But then when she walked in the door, the phone was ringing; it was the doctor telling her to bring the baby back to the hospital. The doctor said that as he was driving home, the baby's face had appeared to him, like a vision, in the rearview mirror. And he'd thought to himself, *That baby doesn't look healthy. Something's not right.* It turned out that the baby's appendix had burst. "It was a miracle," her mother-in-law always said at the end of the story, and made the sign of the cross. "If they hadn't operated immediately, he would have died."

He would not have lived to father a baby who died.

"I'm not going to sleep," he murmured. "How can I sleep?"

She got a blanket from the linen closet and spread it over him. He was sinking under from sheer exhaustion. His breathing deepened, but it wasn't a peaceful sleep. She could see his eyelids twitching, his lips moving. She walked around to her side of the bed, but suddenly she didn't feel like lying there next to him, thinking God knows what in the darkness.

"I need to brush my teeth," she whispered, just in case he was still conscious. "Be right back." She gave his hand a squeeze. It felt like a dead fish. She set it down gently on the blanket. She turned off the bright light in the bathroom. Moonlight was shining through the miniblinds from the backyard. She fumbled for the wand and shut them, then tiptoed across the hall and checked on Teddy, opening his door stealthily. He seemed to be asleep, his bedclothes tortured into a twisted knot with his feet sticking out. She shut the door. Then, as if some invisible leash were tugging on her, she walked next door to Trina's room, which she had been avoiding all afternoon and evening. Giselle turned on the carousel lamp that played "London Bridge" when you wound it up, and sat down in the rocking chair next to the crib. *Koko's Kitten* was lying facedown on the changing table where Dan had left it, as if he'd just jumped up — her adoring slave — to fetch her a cup of water and was planning to pick up where he left off. She could hear his expressive voice reading aloud the second paragraph: "Koko knows what birthdays are. When asked what she does on her birthday, Koko answered, 'Eat, drink, (get) old.'" Giselle shut the book and closed her eyes. With her eyes shut, inhaling the mixed bouquet of powder, urine, baby shampoo, and Ivory Snow, Trina's ghost turned to sweet, solid flesh.

She must have fallen asleep in the rocking chair. In the middle of the night she woke up stiff and startled. Teddy was standing next to her.

"I thought I heard her crying," he said.

In the master bedroom Dan let out a piercing yelp. Teddy flinched. Giselle assumed it was a nightmare until she heard him mutter, "Shit, I'm bleeding!"

She hurried to the bedroom and flicked on the overhead light. Dan was sitting on the side of the bed, trying to get a look at the sole of one foot. She could see blood on the sheet and floor.

"What happened?" She went into the master bathroom for the hydrogen peroxide and a towel.

"I stepped on a goddamned piece of the lamp."

Giselle felt a stab of guilt. She should have swept it up. She had meant to but forgot. "Let me see." She blotted the blood, appalled by how much there was. "It's deep," she said. "Maybe you need stitches."

"No fucking way I'm going back to that hospital," Dan said. She knew there was no use arguing with him and, anyway, she didn't blame him. She tried to pour some hydrogen peroxide on the gash. He waved her away. "Just get some gauze and adhesive tape," he snapped at her. "I can take care of it myself."

The first-aid kit was in the other bathroom. She turned and saw Teddy hovering in the hallway looking pale and scared. "He's going to be okay," she said. "It's just a cut." He seemed not to hear her. "Go get me the broom and dustpan from the kitchen, okay?"

He turned and ran down the hall. She heard him rummaging in the broom closet. He returned with the dustpan and brush. Without being asked to, he knelt on the floor and swept up the china shards, even crawling under the bed to retrieve a couple of bigger pieces. Dan was watching him as if Teddy were a bug he might suddenly crush underfoot. The expression on his face made her turn away.

"That was a really stupid thing you did," he said to Teddy, who was still kneeling at his feet, sweeping.

"I know," Teddy said. He dumped the swept-up shards into the wicker wastebasket. "I know that." He sounded calm and mature.

"You're lucky you're not my son."

"What's that supposed to mean?" Giselle shot him a murderous look.

Dan ignored her. He leaned closer to Teddy, practically in his face, and said, "Is that all you have to say for yourself?"

"What can I say?" Teddy looked almost dignified as he walked back to his room and shut the door quietly. For the first time all day she felt almost proud of him.

Dan looked at her and hung his head. "I don't know where that came from. I'm sorry."

She stood there in the doorway, speechless and motionless. She didn't know what to say. She didn't know where to go. She could hear Teddy crying in his room.

IT IS IN THE NEWSPAPER THE NEXT MORNING. AS *soon as the paperboy tosses the* L.A. Times *onto their front stoop, his mother opens the door and snatches it. She skims through the paper, finds the article, and then hides the paper in her desk. As if it's the only one, as if there aren't a million copies. He waits until she heads into the bathroom to take a shower, then finds the newspaper where she buried it under a pile of old compositions that Dan had graded, all marked A or A+ in green ink. The headline reads*

BOY KILLS BABY SISTER IN ACCIDENTAL SHOOTING
Two nine-year-old boys were playing with a .38-caliber pistol when the gun fired, fatally wounding a twenty-three-month-old girl.

The little girl died about 4:45 P.M. Sunday at Holy Angels Hospital after undergoing surgery for a gunshot wound to her heart. Joan Lufkin, a Western Ambulance spokeswoman, said the bullet entered the girl's chest, then exited.

Los Angeles County Attorney Angela Peralta said the girl's older brother was holding the gun when it discharged through the bedroom window and struck the sister, who was playing in a wading pool in the backyard. Initial police reports indicate the shooting was accidental. Peralta is awaiting results from the analysis of the gun, to determine how it functioned and whether it was working properly, before making an official report.

Both boys' mothers were home at the time of the shooting. Investigators determined that the gun belonged to the other boy's father, who had given it to his wife for protection following some recent burglaries in the neighborhood.

Teddy takes his time reading and rereading the article. Dan isn't home. He is at the funeral home, dropping off Trina's burial clothes. Nana had offered to take care of it, but Dan said he wanted to see the place for himself, to prepare himself. Trina is going to wear the red velvet dress she is wearing in the photograph of her that hangs in the dining room next to a photograph of Teddy in a white shirt and bow tie. His mother had dragged them both down to Sears during some two-for-one portrait special. The photographer liked Trina's portrait so much that he put it on display out front, where everyone at the mall could see it. He didn't put Teddy's up, which was fine with him. He didn't want the kids from school to see him on display looking like a dork. He'd wanted to wear his Jurassic Park *T-shirt, but his mom said no way.*

He puts the newspaper back where he found it and calls his real dad in Nebraska. He tells him about the article in the newspaper, and his dad seems upset by the news.

"They didn't even mention my name," Teddy says.

"That's because you're a minor, I guess." His father sighs.

"What's a minor?"

"It means you're not an adult. Is your mother there?" he asks. "I want to talk to her."

"She's in the shower. Gramma and Grampa are coming this afternoon. We're going to the airport to pick them up."

"That's good," his dad says.

"Yeah."

His dad doesn't say anything for a minute, and Teddy can't think of anything else to tell him, so he says good-bye and hangs up. He looks at the clock. It's not even nine o'clock yet, and his grandparents' plane won't get in until four-thirty. They are flying out from Florida. He's really glad they're coming. When he talked to them on the phone earlier this morning, they kept saying how much they missed him, how they couldn't wait to see him. They didn't sound mad at all. But he could tell Gramma was crying. They kept asking him how he was feeling. He knows that sometimes old people get things all confused. He hopes they don't think that he was the one who was shot.

GISELLE HAD NEVER REALIZED WHAT A WELCOME diversion a funeral could be. All the phone calls and travel arrangements helped distract her from focusing on the main event. Trina's name was on everyone's lips so often that it was almost as if she were there, taking a nap in her crib, and any moment now Giselle would go in and get her. She hated to wake her up. When she was left to wake up naturally, Trina was always in a good mood, bright-eyed and playful. But when her sleep was cut short, she could be cranky. Giselle remembered how right after Teddy was born, she would occasionally wake up (on the rare occasions when she wasn't awakened by Teddy's cries), and it would take her a minute before she remembered that she had a baby. The recollection would catch her by surprise. It was the same now, only in reverse. Brief moments of amnesia, and then the instant of remembering, which was so painful — it hit her anew with such undiminished force that it seemed like some cruel trick her mind was playing on her. It was like being knocked out over and over again. She had only two Valium left. Dan's brother, Greg, was a doctor, but she didn't want to ask him, and Lois was off-limits. Giselle was saving one pill for the funeral itself.

Her parents had arrived first, in the late afternoon, almost twenty-four hours to the minute since Trina had been pronounced dead. Her brother, accompanied by Teddy, had picked them up at the airport and brought them over for a quick supper — a pizza — most of which was still sitting in its box on the kitchen counter. Dan's brother's plane was scheduled to arrive at seven-thirty. His wife had stayed behind in Tucson with the three boys. They had thought the funeral would be too traumatic for them, and they never left them with sitters. Angela, Greg's wife, didn't believe in day care. She and Luisa were thick as thieves, like mother and daughter. Giselle was just as glad not to have to deal with her. The brother, at least under other, better circumstances, she had always liked. But she wasn't counting on anything.

Even though Greg had offered to rent a car, Dan had insisted upon picking him up and driving him over to their mother's place. He wanted to keep busy. And she couldn't blame him. But now she wished he were here. It was after ten o'clock. Her parents and Teddy were spending the night at Todd's apartment. Teddy had begged to go, and she thought maybe it was just as well. It would give Dan and her some time alone. She glanced impatiently at her watch. She was already in her nightgown, so exhausted that she could barely keep her eyes open, but she didn't want to get into bed alone. It was the night before they buried their daughter. Shouldn't they be comforting each other? She kept catching herself thinking in terms of "should" and "shouldn't," as if there were correct and incorrect ways they should be handling this. Was there a Miss Manners guide for grief-stricken parents that everyone but her had read? It made her worry that she was shallow, that somehow her grief was inauthentic if she could be worrying about whether she was doing it right — when who could tell her she wasn't? Who in the world had that right?

The phone rang. She thought maybe it was Dan, telling her he was just now leaving, but when she picked up the receiver, she was disappointed to hear her sister's voice asking how things were going. She missed Vonnie but didn't feel like talking right now. Giselle had told her not to fly out for the funeral. She thought it would be too much for her to handle. Vonnie's lover had died of ovarian cancer just this past winter, at Christmastime, and she was still estranged from their parents, who had not even bothered to send flowers. Giselle had assured her that she didn't mind, she really didn't, and in fact it was probably better this way. She felt pulled in enough directions without having to run interference between her sister and parents, even though Teddy was disappointed when he heard that she wasn't coming. He was crazy about her. Once, three or four years ago, when a friend of theirs asked him what he wanted to be when he grew up, he'd answered, "A dyke."

"I hope they're not driving you crazy," Vonnie said. "I still feel bad about not being there."

"It's okay," Giselle said. "It's good for Teddy to have them here. He's really perked up since they arrived." She didn't say that he'd seemed almost too cheerful, as if he'd forgotten all about the reason for the visit. At one point when he was roughhousing with her father, Giselle had snapped at them, and her mother had shot her a reproachful look.

"Yeah, well, as far as they're concerned, the sun rises and sets with their grandson. Their apartment looks like a fucking shrine." On her end Giselle could hear a doorbell chime and Vonnie shouting for whoever it was to come in. "They were still complaining about your taking him to California last time I was there."

Giselle sighed and waited while Vonnie put her hand over the receiver and made an aside to whoever had walked in. "Look, you've got company. You better go. I'll talk to you in a couple of days," she said hurriedly and hung up, anxious to end the conversation before Vonnie could really get going about their parents. Not that Vonnie didn't have legitimate grievances. Or that Giselle didn't have her own bone to pick with them. All evening they had made it clear, in subtle but unmistakable ways, that their primary allegiance was to their grandson, whom they had spent a lot of time with during his first four years, before Giselle moved out West and they moved to Florida. They had met their granddaughter only once, the Christmas before last, for a week. Mostly they just knew Trina through a succession of snapshots sent through the mail: a series of Piaget milestones. And now they would never have the chance to know her any better.

Giselle looked at the open pizza box lying next to the phone on the counter. A dead fly was stuck in the congealed cheese. She plucked out the fly and shoved the box in the refrigerator. Then she lay down on the couch and cried. It was the first opportunity she'd had to cry alone, in private, and she thought that if no one interrupted her, she might never stop.

In the middle of the night she jolted awake as if a doctor had attached cardiac paddles to her chest. Back from the dead. Her heart pounded. Her neck was stiff. She had heard a noise. She had been dreaming: she had heard Trina's voice half singing along with her favorite nursery rhyme. *The little mice are creeping, creeping / The little mice are creeping all through the house* . . . And laughing. This was the part where Giselle would creep her fingers across her lap and grab hold of Trina's chubby little leg, which was her cue to squirm away and put her fingers to her lips, pretending to chew, as Giselle continued to sing. *The little mice are eating, eating, eating* . . . She was standing up now, fully awake, and she could still hear it, crystal clear, coming from the back of the house. *The little mice are sleeping, sleeping, sleeping* . . . At this point they always closed their eyes and pillowed their cheeks against their hands. Giselle shivered. "I'm going crazy," she mumbled as she walked across the living room to the hallway — and stopped dead. She could see the light coming from Trina's room. *The old gray cat comes creeping, creeping, creeping* . . . She heard her own voice saying, "Do you know what comes next?" And then Teddy's voice yelling, "Mom! Hey, Mom, can I ride bikes with Eric?" Dan was sitting on the floor, leaning against the pink toy chest with the little cassette player in his lap. He must have come in while she was asleep. He was wearing his pajama bottoms. She looked at her watch; it was two-thirty. When he sensed her standing there, he looked up and punched the OFF button, then held out his hand to her. She braced herself against the doorframe and pulled him to his feet.

"Listen." He set the tape player on the little white bureau and pressed REWIND:

"Who's got the ball? Where'd the ball go? Where'd it go, Teeny?" Teddy was saying in his best big-brother voice.

"Me! Ball here!" Trina was shouting and giggling.

Dan hit the PAUSE button and shook his head. "I have to keep reminding myself what a good brother he was. I have to put the other thing out of my mind. I keep telling myself it doesn't matter how it happened." Giselle nodded and squeezed his hand tight. "I mean, when someone you love dies, does it really matter if it's a car crash or a plane crash or even, you know, cancer or whatever?" Giselle shook her head. "At least that's what I tell myself." He sighed and ejected the cassette. "But it's hard. I'm not sure I can do it."

Giselle let go of his hand. "What does that mean?"

"It means I want to, but I don't know," he said quietly, not looking at her.

"He's only nine years old."

"And she'll never be nine years old." Dan snapped the tape back into its case.

"She was my daughter, too, you know."

When he didn't respond, Giselle turned and left the room. "I'm going to bed," she said. "Are you coming?"

"In a minute." He was standing by the crib, staring into it, as if maybe if he stared hard enough, she would materialize out of thin air. Giselle went into the bathroom and took a Valium. There was only one left, and she planned to take it right before they left for the service. She wanted to behave with dignity. She flashed on photographs of Jacqueline Kennedy in her black veil, her expression of stunned anguish. Giselle hadn't even been born yet, but she had seen the footage of the funeral — who hadn't? — and her mother, an ardent JFK admirer, had an entire bookshelf devoted to Kennedy books. Giselle tried to imagine Teddy standing there in a suit, saluting his sister's casket, breaking everyone's heart, but she couldn't. He didn't even own a suit.

The funeral service was scheduled to begin at eleven. The first thing Giselle thought when she opened her eyes and looked at the bright sunshine was *I can't go through with this.* Dan was lying on top of the covers, his arms cradling Mookie against his chest. She imagined waking him and breaking the news to him — *I'm sorry, I know all the arrangements have been made, but I just can't do it* — like a bride with cold feet. But before she had a chance, the phone rang on his side of the bed and he answered it — perfectly alert, as if he had just been faking sleep. She could tell it was his mother, calling to iron out some last-minute detail. Giselle got up and went into the bathroom, popped the remaining Valium, then headed into the kitchen to start the coffee. The immediate family was going to meet here at ten so that they could all ride to the funeral parlor together. Luisa seemed to be orchestrating some huge, lavish affair — something just short of a state funeral. A Day of the Dead festival. If there was a funereal equivalent to eloping, Giselle would have opted for it. Already her head was pounding; she could feel her intestines clutching. What if she couldn't get through it? She had felt the same fear right before Teddy was born. What if she couldn't withstand the labor pains? But she had no choice then, and she had no choice now.

As the coffee perked, she looked at the wall clock hanging above the American authors calendar that Teddy had picked out for Dan's birthday last year all on his own. It was 8:15 A.M. Any other Tuesday she would be dropping off Trina at the day care center, then racing across campus to her Chicano lit class, which was a piece of cake. She had already read all the novels. This week they were discussing *Bless Me Ultima*. She wondered if tucked away in the barrio there was a *curandero* who could have saved

Trina with some concoction of herbs and spells. It seemed that no-body in these stories ever died for real unless they were ancient, and even then their spirit just entered some owl or wolf waiting right outside the door. Once she had tried to talk to Luisa about the books she'd been reading, tried to have a real discussion for once, but her mother-in-law had just looked insulted. She pictured Dan hugging Trina's stuffed monkey in his sleep as if her spirit had flown inside poor beat-up Mookie, who had been through the washing machine one time too many.

Giselle drank two cups of strong black coffee, but the caffeine seemed to have no effect. There wasn't enough coffee in the world to counteract the lethargy she felt. She set her cup in the sink and went in the bathroom to take a shower before the others arrived. Her parents were always early.

The next thing she knew, she was standing in the bedroom blow-drying her hair. She couldn't even remember being in the shower. This was the third or fourth little blackout she had experienced in the past two days. Suddenly she would just "come to." She had to look in the mirror to see if she had already put on makeup. A week ago she would have been worried about a brain tumor, but now she just attributed it to exhaustion, a short circuit caused by emotional overload. She wished she would black out and come to after the funeral was over.

She could hear voices in the kitchen. She heard her father asking if anyone wanted a jelly doughnut or a cruller, then a chorus of no, thank you's. Teddy, who loved doughnuts, was spending the day at her friend Ellen's house. She opened her closet and stared. Yesterday her mother had asked if her clothes were in order for today, if she needed anything from the mall, and Giselle had just shrugged as if to say that her wardrobe was the last thing on her mind. But now she realized that her only dark dress was a cocktail dress, too low cut to be appropriate. Even though it was already eighty degrees out, unseasonably warm for April, she put on a long-sleeved black sweater and skirt. She still hadn't lost the last stubborn ten pounds of the weight she'd gained during pregnancy, and the waistband wouldn't zip. She went into Trina's room and found a diaper pin with a little duck on the end and safety-pinned the skirt. With her sweater over it, no one would know the difference. She hadn't worn panty hose in months. The only ones she could find had a run in the foot, but she didn't care. As she sat on the edge of the bed, pulling on her panty hose, it was all she could do not to crawl between the sheets and pull the blanket over her head. Dan walked into the bedroom, dressed in the dark suit he'd bought for his father's funeral. She had only ever seen it hanging in the closet. He perched on the bed next to her. They clasped hands for a minute in silence, heads bowed. She wished that everyone would just vanish and leave them alone. But then Greg — a shorter, squatter version of Dan — appeared in the doorway and said, "The limousine's here."

From the moment she saw the black limo sitting in their driveway, it was as if the starship *Enterprise* had landed and beamed her to another galaxy. *It's not real,* she thought. *It's just a hologram.* The chauffeur, grave and dignified, even reminded her a bit of Captain Picard. She settled in to the plush gray seat between Dan and her father. Her mother, Luisa, and Greg sat in the seat behind them. Todd, for some reason, insisted at the last minute on following them in his own car. The smell of Greg's cologne overpowered her. She felt sick to her stomach and asked Dan to please lower his window.

"The air-conditioning's on," he said. "Are you sure?"

Her father patted her hand and lowered his window. She closed her eyes and focused on taking deep breaths the way she had when she was little and used to get carsick on family outings. Her mother snapped open her purse and handed her a stick of peppermint gum. Giselle obediently unwrapped it and folded the gum into her mouth. Her mother held out the pack. "Anyone else?"

The only other time Giselle had been in a limo was the night of her senior prom. Ed and the guy who was Laura's date — Giselle couldn't even remember his name — had rented a white stretch limo. Ed, who usually looked like he just rolled out of bed, was wearing a white tux. She remembered thinking, *This is the high point of your life,* addressing herself in the second person as if double-checking to make sure she was actually there.

The funeral home was crowded with strangers — friends and business acquaintances of Dan's parents mostly. Dan's father had inherited a small tile store in Silver Lake, which he had built into a million-dollar enterprise with shops in Santa Monica and Beverly Hills, selling beautiful, unique handmade Mexican tiles. His tiles adorned movie stars' pools and bathrooms from Bel Air to Malibu. Luisa designed most of the tiles herself. A number of people were speaking Spanish. In among the strangers she saw a few familiar faces. Friends, colleagues. She didn't want to talk to anyone. She huddled awkwardly in a little knot with her parents and brother, half hidden by a potted palm. Her parents stood there with solemn but friendly expressions fixed on their faces, waiting for people to offer their condolences, but everyone seemed to be avoiding them. They were all clustered around Luisa or Dan. Giselle saw her father remove his glasses to wipe away the perspiration that glistened on his face. Last year he had suffered a minor heart attack. His dark suit seemed too large, as if he had shrunk a size. His eyes, without his glasses, looked weak and vulnerable, and she felt bad, as if she were somehow responsible. If Trina had died of cancer or been hit by a car, Giselle suspected that things would be different. People would be behaving differently toward them. As it was, she sensed everyone whispering behind their backs, shaking their heads, blaming Teddy. And by extension, his flesh and blood. She looked around for Dan. He was standing beside the casket, talking with his friend Harvey and his wife. Then Stan Levine, a colleague who taught Shakespeare, joined them, resting his hand briefly, awkwardly on Dan's shoulder. Giselle had taken his Tragedies course and received a B+ even though she'd worked her butt off. At the time she had been crushed by the grade, which she thought was unfair, but now she realized that he should have flunked her. She didn't know the first thing about tragedy.

The coffin was small and white. Giselle was shocked by how small it was. Lying there against the pink tufted satin, Trina looked like a doll. A very beautiful, very expensive doll — too nice to play with. Giselle had been afraid to look, but once she did, she couldn't look away. She had never seen her daughter completely still before. Even in her sleep she was in constant motion. Giselle wanted to touch her but was afraid to. It was like being at a museum where some officious guard would hurry over to scold her. She could still see the faint scratch below Trina's eye caused by Giselle's belt buckle as she'd bent over and hoisted her out of the sandbox at day care last week. Trina had cried and cried, her lips trembling with innocent outrage, as if Giselle had hurt her on purpose. In the coffin a dark curl had sprung loose, as if it still had a life of its own, and was hanging in front of Trina's eye. Giselle was trying to work up the nerve to brush it back when they began paging the family to return to the limos. Dan's brother put his arm around her and turned her toward the door. "She's with the angels now," he whispered. Giselle shook him off. "You're a doctor," she said. "You know better."

At the church she felt even further disoriented by the service, the sights and sounds of the priest going through the familiar rituals of the mass. She had not been to church since she was fourteen. She half expected to see snow drifting down outside the windows, to feel her sister poking her in the ribs and pointing to some ridiculous hat in the pew in front of them. Once Todd had farted as he bent over to retrieve a missal he'd dropped on the floor, and Vonnie and she had dissolved into a convulsive giggling fit while their mother glared at them, mortified. "Just wait until you have children of your own," she had scolded them in the car on the way home. It was one of her favorite refrains.

Giselle sat dry-eyed while Dan wept noisily beside her. His mother handed him her handkerchief. Everything seemed muffled and blurred, as if her brain were experiencing poor reception. She was grateful for this. She clenched both fists in her lap. *Just let me get through this,* she prayed, through the next minute, the next hour. There was constant sniffling and nose blowing. She could feel the stares directed at the back of her head. *Look, she's not even crying.* She sat up straight and stared straight ahead. It reminded her of a wedding, with all the flowers. The groom's people on one side and the bride's on the other. Only there were hardly any people on her side. Maybe Teddy was right. Maybe they never should have come to California.

At the cemetery they all crowded into a small chapel sitting on a crest of green lawn. She had been relieved to hear that you didn't actually go to the grave. Apparently it was only in the movies that you saw the casket lowered into the ground and threw dirt on it. She thought they must have put an end to that because it was just too, too unbearable, but her brother said it was because of the weather. The weather was too unpredictable. It was hot in the small chapel, suffocating, and she was wearing a long-sleeved wool sweater. She broke out in a sudden intense sweat. She reached for Dan's handkerchief to mop her face — and the next thing she knew, she was lying in the backseat of the air-conditioned limo. Her mother was hunched over her, fanning her face with her missal.

"What happened?" Giselle asked.

"You fainted." Her mother rummaged in her purse and produced a bag of honey-roasted nuts from the plane. "I bet you haven't eaten anything in hours." She ripped open the little bag with her teeth and shook a few into the palm of Giselle's hand. It reminded Giselle of the little red boxes of Sunmaid raisins her mother always used to carry in her purse, along with Band-Aids, safety pins, and a roll of dimes in case she needed to make a phone call. Giselle sat up and dutifully ate a few peanuts. Up on the hill she could see a dark line of people straggling out of the chapel, like a flock of crows, blinking in the bright sun. She glanced impatiently at her watch and thought how Trina would just be waking up from her afternoon nap and that they were out of apple juice.

Her brother volunteered to drive Giselle back home. The others could go on to the catered lunch without her. Dan leaned into the limo and said he didn't know what to do, he felt bad about leaving her. He looked about to keel over himself. "Don't worry about me," she told him. "You have to go. I'm sorry." She started to cry. "I know I'm letting you down."

Outside the car she could hear people being directed back into the waiting limos. The whole event seemed to be as choreographed as the Academy Awards. "You go," she told him. "If I feel better, I'll come later." Dan nodded and kissed her cheek. Then his brother, the doctor, checked her pulse and handed her a couple of sedatives for later. "To help her sleep," he told her mother.

At the last minute her parents decided to go home with her. "We can go get Teddy," her mother said. She lowered her voice. "Besides, I'm worried about your father. He looks beat." She tapped her chest, as if to remind Giselle of her father's heart condition. "I'll make our excuses," her mother said. "They'll understand."

The cemetery was a half hour's drive from the house, during which no one said much of anything. Except for Todd, who kept fiddling with and cursing his air-conditioning, which seemed to be on the fritz. "I just had it fixed," he kept muttering. "I can't believe this." Finally their father suggested that he just turn it off and roll down the windows.

As soon as she got home, she peeled off her sweaty clothes, took a sedative, and crawled into bed. Her parents had taken Teddy back to her brother's place to swim, to give her time to recover. She was thankful to be alone. She shut her eyes and pictured Trina in her wading pool, laughing and splashing. It wasn't fair. She cried like a baby until the sedative finally kicked in.

The two days following the funeral were just a blur of commotion going on all around her while she stayed put, mostly in bed, mostly in a drug-induced haze. Teddy was shuttled back and forth between Todd's apartment and home. Even though her brother hated family gatherings, he rallied to the cause, chauffeuring them all over the greater Los Angeles area. Giselle was grateful to Todd for grasping the emotional complexities of the situation, for sensing what needed to be done without being told. Their sister's nickname for him was Data, like the android on *Star Trek*, but apparently, when the occasion demanded, Todd had all the necessary software to respond to human tragedy. He didn't even grumble when their mother would suggest the day's itinerary: the La Brea Tar Pits, Universal Studios, a matinee in Westwood. "You stay home and rest, dear," her mother said. "We'll take care of Teddy." And in the evenings they would return with supper — Kentucky Fried Chicken or Chinese — and Giselle would force herself to sit at the kitchen table and eat a few bites, mostly for Teddy's sake.

Sometimes Dan would join them, unfailingly polite and affable but remote. He didn't really know her parents, and Giselle could see that it was a strain on him being around them. She encouraged him to spend time with his mother and brother, whom he didn't get to see that often. The atmosphere in the house was lighter somehow with him gone. Teddy seemed to shrink and freeze, like a scared rabbit, whenever Dan was around, even though Dan went out of his way to be nice to him. He even bought Teddy a present, a rubber lizard he'd picked up at some toy store where Greg had gone to buy presents to take back to his own kids. Giselle suspected that Dan was putting on a show for her parents, but she wanted to give him the benefit of the doubt. At least he was making the effort. And she could see how exhausted he was. From across the room the dark circles under his eyes looked like charcoal smudges. She was already unconscious by the time he got into bed at night, and he was gone by the time she reluctantly came to in the morning. He didn't seem to be sleeping at all, and his stubborn refusal to take any pills annoyed her. It seemed like an implicit criticism of her own urge toward oblivion. She hated to think of her parents' and Greg's leaving at the end of the week. What she dreaded most was the return to daily routine, to real life. It seemed that for the rest of their lives they would simply be going through the motions.

THE DAY BEFORE HIS GRANDPARENTS LEAVE, HIS *mother tells him he can't go swimming at his uncle's, because they have an appointment with a family therapist. When he says he doesn't want to go, his mother presses her lips together and says he's going whether he wants to or not. "This isn't exactly our idea of fun either," she tells him. Something about the way she says this, the look on her face, makes him think the police are probably making them go.*

At the doctor's office they sit in the closet-sized waiting room for ten minutes before the doctor comes out to get them. There is no receptionist, just a small sign saying to please ring the bell to let the doctor know they are there. It doesn't seem like a real doctor's office. There are no other people waiting. Teddy thinks maybe she isn't a very good doctor, even though there are a lot of official-looking diplomas on the wall. His mother flips through a magazine. Dan slumps in his chair with his eyes shut, sighing loudly every few seconds. Teddy remembers once, at the grocery store, Dan's abandoning a whole cart of food in the checkout line because he got tired of waiting. Teddy and his mom had to drive back and get it.

Finally the doctor opens the door and invites them inside her office. She looks more like a movie star than a doctor. She has lots of poufy red hair and bright lipstick. Her name is Dr. Cole. She says to call her Hannah.

First she sees all of them together for half an hour. Mostly she just listens and takes a few notes while his mother tells her what happened and gives her some background information, like their ages and how long she and Dan have been married and where Teddy's real dad lives. Dan cries a lot but doesn't say much. When his mother tells the doctor that Teddy's nine, Dan interrupts and says, "Almost ten." The therapist mostly just nods. Sometimes she looks over at Teddy and smiles. Then she says she'd like to talk with him alone for a few minutes. Teddy doesn't want to be alone with her. Even though she's smiling at him, he feels as if he's being picked on. His mother didn't say anything about talking to the doctor alone. If Dan wasn't there, he'd beg his mother to stay with him.

Once he is alone with the doctor, they move over to a sandbox on legs filled with weird little figures he is supposed to feel free to play with, as if he were a little kid, like his sister with her Playskool people, who were always getting swept up in the vacuum cleaner. The doctor asks him some questions, which he mostly answers with a shrug or "I don't know." At one point she asks him if he has anything particular on his mind. He shakes his head and then thinks of his sister's empty room, how they keep the door closed now, and suddenly starts to cry.

The doctor takes his hand and looks him right in the eye, sadly, as if she might burst into tears herself. "You are going to have to forgive yourself," she says. "Do you think you can do that, Teddy?"

He shrugs and says, "It wasn't my fault." She doesn't say anything, which makes him nervous, like maybe she doesn't agree. "My mom says it wasn't my fault. She says that sometimes things just happen." He reaches into the sandbox and buries a whole little family in the sand. "If it was my fault," he adds, "I'd be in jail, right?"

The therapist pats his hand. "They don't put children in jail, Teddy."

What's that supposed to mean, *he thinks to himself, but he doesn't ask. He can see from the clock that the hour is almost up. He finds a little dog and buries him in the sand, too. Maybe if he just sits here for five more minutes, he can go.*

On the ride home no one says much. At one point his mom says she wishes that the doctor were older and more experienced. Dan just shakes his head and says she seems to have excellent credentials. "Why? Because she went to Stanford?" his mother snaps. Dan graduated from Stanford University. He was always telling Teddy that if he studied hard and got good grades, he could go there, too, someday.

Teddy is sitting next to his sister's car seat, which makes him feel bad. His mother suggested that they take the other car, but his step-father said it didn't have enough gas. Teddy figures that Dan just wants to make him feel bad. Dan hardly speaks to him, and when he does say something, he sounds too polite, the way he sounds when a student calls him at home with some lame excuse for why his paper is going to be late. Teddy can't blame him for being mad. He knows how crazy Dan was about Trina. He was always kissing and hugging her. Sometimes, in between classes, he would run over to the campus day care center and play with her for an hour. He liked to sit by her crib and watch her sleep. He even liked changing her smelly diapers.

Teddy is really glad his grandparents will still be there when he gets home. This afternoon they are going to the beach. He wishes they could stay forever.

His mother twists around in her seat and asks him, "So what did you and Hannah talk about?"

Dan turns down the volume on the radio.

Teddy says, "Nothing. It was stupid. She wants me to play with toys like I'm a baby."

"You have to give it a chance," his mom tells him. He can see her jaw jut out like it does when she's really mad. "I'm sure she doesn't think you're a baby. Unless you act like one." She turns back around.

He wishes she'd just yell at him and get it over with. He knows she wants to. He knows they both want to.

"I'm not going back," Teddy shouts, "and you can't make me!"

Dan turns the radio back up.

The next morning his grandparents have to leave. At the airport Teddy begs them to take him with them. He clings to his grandfather and bawls like a baby. He doesn't care who sees him. His grandmother pats his back and says, "I wish we could, honey, but your mother needs you."

"No, she doesn't," he argues. "They hate me!"

"No one hates you." His grandfather crushes him in a bear hug. "Don't even think that for a minute. Your mother loves you. She's just upset right now."

"Dan hates me," Teddy says. "He wishes I were dead."

His grandparents exchange one of those looks and shake their heads. "Here comes your uncle Todd," his grandmother says, sounding relieved. Todd had run off to the gift shop for some gum and a couple of magazines for the flight home. He hands Gramma a Redbook *and a pack of Big Red gum. He hands Grampa a* Sports Illustrated *even though he hadn't asked for a magazine.*

"I've got a subscription to this at home." Grampa frowns.

Gramma glares at him and makes a shhush *noise, which he ignores. "Why don't you take it and read it?" He hands the magazine back to Todd, who shrugs and tosses it onto an empty seat. As far as Teddy knows, the only sports his uncle is interested in are computer games.*

"You aren't just going to leave it there?" Grampa asks, worriedly.

"Oh, just forget about the damn magazine!" Gramma explodes. She hits him on the knee with her rolled-up magazine like he's a bad dog. "Honest to God! At a time like this." She shakes her head, disgusted. Then she turns to Teddy with a big smile. "We'll see about a visit later on this summer, when school gets out. I'll talk to your

mother." Sometimes he forgets that Gramma is his mother's mother. Usually they fight a lot, but not this time. They were all on their best behavior for the funeral. She opens up the pack of gum and hands him a stick. "Maybe your mother will come, too. We can go to Disney World." She hands him a second stick of gum. "For later."

"I'm going to Nebraska," Teddy says, "to see my dad."

"Well, there's no reason you can't do both, is there?" His grandmother winks at him as if it's their little secret. It reminds him of how he used to wink at Trina and watch her blink back. She was too uncoordinated to shut one eye at a time. It always used to make him laugh. He misses his little sister. No one ever seems to think that maybe he's sad, too. That maybe he doesn't want to be an only child again. The voice on the PA announces that the flight to Sarasota is now boarding. At the last minute Grampa picks up the Sports Illustrated *when Gramma isn't looking and sneaks it into his suitcase like a naughty child.*

After their plane leaves, Teddy drags his feet through the airport until his uncle finally yells at him to speed it up. Teddy dreads going back home. He would almost rather go to the dentist. At least the dentist isn't mad at him. Teddy asks his uncle if he can go back to his place and swim, but Todd says, "Sorry, buddy, I have to go to work." Teddy heaves a big sigh and tries not to cry. In the car — his uncle has a cool Mitsubishi Eclipse, black with a sunroof — Teddy distracts himself with the fancy CD player. His mother's old Honda doesn't even have a cassette player.

AFTER SHE SAID GOOD-BYE TO HER PARENTS, waved to them all scrunched up with their luggage in Todd's little sports car, she crawled back into bed. She couldn't think what to do with herself. Before she took off, her mother had cleaned the house and bought groceries. She had even left a macaroni and cheese casserole, Teddy's favorite, in the refrigerator for supper. And her father had bought some new videos for Teddy to watch when he got home from the airport. "To take his mind off our leaving," her dad had said, "and give you a little break." She could tell that they were worried about what she'd do once they were gone. They had offered to stay longer, but Giselle had declined their offer as diplomatically as possible. Although their presence was a comfort to Teddy, it was a strain on Dan. To her they were parents, but to Dan they were houseguests. She could understand not being in the mood for company.

Dan was off doing something with his brother, who was leaving soon — she'd forgotten just when. The sedatives seemed to be affecting her memory. Or maybe she just wasn't paying attention. A paperback copy of *The House on Mango Street* was lying on the floor next to her bed where she'd flung it yesterday or the day before — the days and hours blurred together — after trying unsuccessfully to concentrate on the opening pages. There was no way she could return to school. She couldn't even think straight. And already she regretted all the hours she had spent studying that she could have — should have — spent with her daughter.

When Teddy came back from the airport, she could see that his eyes were red from crying. She forced herself to get out of bed and make him a bologna and cheese sandwich even though he said he wasn't hungry. Todd had bought him a frozen yogurt on the way home. She set the sandwich on the coffee table in the living room, where he was already watching one of the new movies. She didn't know how they were going to get through the weekend. He was used to playing with Eric in his free time. On Monday, thank God, he would be going back to school. She sat down on the sofa next to him and watched *The Great Panda Adventure*. Followed by *Babe,* which they had both seen before. Then she heated up her mother's casserole for an early supper. It wasn't even six o'clock yet. Dan called and asked how they were doing, then said he was going to eat at his mother's, if that was all right with her. She told him it was fine. In fact, she was relieved. If Dan came home, she'd have to stay up, find something useful to do. This way she could just lie in bed and skim through the magazines her mother had left behind. Teddy was in his room playing Nintendo, another gift from Uncle Todd. "I'll be reading in bed," she told him, "if you need me." Teddy just nodded, eyes glued to the screen. She shut the door to muffle the sounds of bombs and sirens.

She couldn't remember when she fell asleep, but when she woke up, it was dark and the house was quiet. She checked on Teddy, who had apparently passed out on top of his bed, fully clothed. He didn't even stir when she pried off his sneakers. She had to pee. As she walked into the bathroom, she heard the murmur of voices through the open window. She peeked through the blinds and saw Dan and his brother sitting on the patio, drinking tequila. She was going to call out to them but didn't want to interrupt, and she wasn't in a sociable mood. Plus she looked like hell.

"I know he's just a kid" — she could hear Dan's voice through the open window — "and I want to forgive him, but every time I see him, I don't know, I just can't stand to look at him. I feel this terrible rage. I can't help it." The ice cubes clinked in his glass.

"Well, it's understandable," Greg said. "I don't think you should beat yourself up over how you feel right now. It's a tough situation, any way you look at it. You just need some time to sort things out." He paused and lit a cigarette. He was one of the few doctors she knew who still smoked. He was always trying unsuccessfully to quit. "What about Giselle? How do you think she feels?"

"Shit, I don't know. How *can* she feel? He's her son." Dan stood up and started to pace, something he used to do in class when the discussion heated up. "That's the worst part. I keep wondering if it would be different, I mean, if I'd feel different, if he were my son, too. I know it shouldn't matter. It makes me feel so petty or something. He's a good kid. I care about him. I thought, you know, until this, that I loved him. We were a family. But it's just not the same." His voice cracked. "What I felt for my daughter and what I feel for Teddy — it wasn't the same. It wasn't even in the same ballpark." He threw his glass against the side of the house. It shattered onto the concrete. The Beemers' dog went ballistic. "Fucking dog," he muttered. "I'd like to kill that dog."

"Take it easy," Greg said. "Take a deep breath."

There was a silence. Then his brother said, "Maybe you need to get away for a couple of days. Give yourself a little breathing space. We could go camping for a night or two. We haven't done that in years."

"I can't." She could hear Dan picking up the broken glass and throwing the shards into the metal trash can. "Are you crazy? What about Giselle? I can't just take off."

Greg heaved a sigh. "I know, I know, but I think it could be worse if you don't go. You need to get yourself under control. You're still in shock."

"I can't go," Dan repeated, but he sounded less certain about it. "They need me."

"You aren't doing them any good like this. You could do more harm than good."

"I don't know." Dan sank back in his chair and closed his eyes. "I don't know anything anymore."

"She'll understand," Greg said, leaning forward in his chair. "I'll talk to her."

"I just don't think I'd feel right."

"Well, it's up to you." Greg threw up his hands, as if to concede a lost cause, and poured himself another shot of tequila.

Giselle hesitated, her heart pounding in her ears. She didn't want to admit she'd been eavesdropping. But she thought that maybe Greg was right. He was the doctor, after all. Dan looked so miserable sitting there. She didn't know if she had the strength to deal with both Dan and Teddy right now. Maybe if he got away for a couple of days, sorted some feelings out, like Greg said, things would be better when he got back. They would all be a little more rested and levelheaded. She walked down the hall and slid open the screen door. They looked startled to see her standing there. And a little guilty. Dan walked over and put his arm around her. "Hi, honey," he said, "we thought you were sleeping."

"I hope we didn't disturb you." Greg glanced at his watch and stood up. "I should be getting back to Mother's."

"Listen," she said, clearing the rust from her throat. "I heard what you said about getting away for a couple of days. Going camping." She tried to sound strong and positive. "I think it's a good idea." She turned to Dan. "You should do it."

"I don't know." He shook his head, not meeting her gaze. She could tell he was wondering what else she'd overheard.

Greg smiled at her and nodded his encouragement.

"I don't know either," she said, "but I think maybe Greg's right."

Dan shrugged helplessly and looked at his brother, who shrugged back, as if to say it was up to Dan. Greg seemed anxious to be off. He gave Giselle a quick hug and then turned back to Dan, waiting.

"Okay," Dan mumbled, "I'll go."

Giselle squeezed his hand. Dan gave her a kiss on the cheek and walked his brother to the door. They stood on the porch, talking for a minute, making plans, and then Dan came back inside. He looked like a lost soul, and it occurred to her that it was going to be up to her to get them through this.

The next morning when she woke up, he was already gone. There was a note lying on the kitchen table, a few lines scrawled on the back of a sympathy card. She skimmed it.

> Dear Giselle,
>
> I really appreciate your giving me this time to think and grieve and, hopefully, begin to heal a bit. Somewhere green and peaceful. I hope you understand and I think you do. Which is why I love you, or at least part of why. I'm struggling to rise above my small, base feelings — to take the larger view. I think you know what I mean. I feel like a heel leaving you right now, even for a couple of days, but I hope, in the long run, to be there for you. And for Teddy.
>
> Love, D.

When they were first married, he used to leave her notes twice that long telling her he'd gone to the 7-Eleven for a loaf of bread. She had saved them in an old heart-shaped candy box in her bureau drawer. It looked as if the "And for Teddy" had been added as an afterthought, squeezed in above the signature. She tossed the card in the trash. As if to confirm the fact of his absence, she opened the garage door and stared at the space where his car usually sat. Then she looked at the metal shelves crammed with junk and saw that the camping gear was gone. The tent and sleeping bags that he had bought last fall for the soccer team's father-son weekend. Teddy had been so excited, he'd slept in his new orange sleeping bag for two nights before they left. At the last minute Dan had come down with a bad cold that he'd probably caught from Trina, who'd had a runny nose all week. Giselle had felt a little guilty watching him pack up when she knew that all he wanted to do was lie in bed and drink hot tea. But Dan knew how much the trip meant to Teddy. He had fortified himself with vitamin C and Contac and never complained once. They had ended up having a great time. "Nothing like a little male bonding," Dan had joked when they returned, "right, Ted?" Teddy grunted in agreement and beat his fists against his chest. This would be the first time that Dan had used the tent since then. She hoped it would jog his memory. She shut the garage door, fished the card out of the trash, and read it over again more slowly. Then she gravitated back to bed.

Monday morning Giselle woke up before the alarm clock rang. She was anxious about Teddy's going back to school. Their first step back into the old routine.

"Time to get dressed," she said in a transparently too-cheery voice. Teddy was lying in bed, staring at the ceiling, already awake. Usually he slept so deeply that she had to call his name and tickle his arm to wake him for school. Giselle knew he didn't want to go. Or rather, he was afraid to. But he couldn't much like being stuck at home with her either. All weekend, after Dan had left for the mountains, they had moped around the house like two invalids, watching TV and eating canned soup. She walked over and opened his blinds. Bright sunshine flooded the room. The weather seemed cruelly oblivious to personal tragedy. It was depressing to be depressed in California.

Teddy got up and started to dress without a word.

"You want cereal or frozen waffles?" she asked him.

"I don't care." He shrugged as he pulled on his socks.

"Well, I'll go make your lunch," she told him brightly. "How's

PB and J?" He shrugged again. She walked into the kitchen and opened the cupboard. Shit, they were out of grape jelly. There was a jar of marmalade in the refrigerator, but she knew Teddy wouldn't go for it. She found an ancient jar of Marshmallow Fluff, left over from a weak moment at the Safeway when Teddy had pleaded with her to buy it. But when she took a closer look at the bread her mother had bought, she saw that it was some sort of healthy multigrain stuff that Teddy would never eat. She tossed the Fluff and the bread into the trash and sighed. She couldn't face going to the store. She wondered if there was any place that delivered.

"You're going to have to buy lunch today," she told Teddy, rummaging in her purse for a couple of dollars, as he trudged into the kitchen and sat at the table. She tucked the dollar bills into the pocket of his polo shirt.

Teddy poked a spoon at his Cheerios. "I have a stomachache," he complained.

Giselle nodded sympathetically. She took a sip of coffee and said, "There is absolutely no reason you should feel embarrassed or ashamed, honey. Kids might ask you a few questions — kids are naturally curious about things — but a week from now they'll have forgotten all about it."

Teddy looked skeptical. "What about when Zoe Kozak's sister was kidnapped and killed last year? Our whole class made cards for her. And the school psychologist came to talk to us. Twice." He looked glum. "And the principal even made an announcement on the loudspeaker."

"That was different," Giselle told him emphatically. "That was a terrible, violent crime. You all saw it on TV. This is completely different. There's no comparison between an accident and a crime. And this was just an accident." She washed an aging apple and dropped it into his lunchbox along with a couple of Oreos she found in the cookie jar. Her parents had stuffed him so full of treats, he hadn't even bothered to raid the cookie jar. "Accidents happen every day. Unfortunately."

He seemed to think about that for a minute and seemed reassured. "Yeah, I wasn't on TV," he said, as if this proved it couldn't be all that serious. He ate a couple of spoonfuls of Cheerios and looked a little less spooked.

Giselle let out a small sigh of relief. She set the lunchbox on the table next to him. "For a snack," she said. "Since you didn't eat much breakfast." Yesterday she had moved the high chair out to the garage, but in the merciless sunlight she could still see a spattered halo of dried food on the beige linoleum surrounding the spot where the chair used to sit. She plucked her car keys out of a basket of miscellaneous junk — stamps, coupons, spare change — and clenched them in her fist so hard that it hurt. "Come on. You don't want to be tardy, do you?" She wanted to get him off to school while he seemed to be feeling more confident, before some new worry hit him and his mood took a nosedive. Usually he took the school bus that picked them up right at the corner. But today she was driving him herself. At least he wouldn't have to endure the neighbor kids' blatant stares or third degree. He stood up obediently and even wiped off his milk mustache without her having to remind him.

"Hey, you forgot your snack." She picked up the lunchbox and handed it to him.

"What about your book bag?" He pointed to the leather shoulder bag Dan had given her for their first anniversary. "Aren't you going to class?"

"Not today," she said. She was surprised by his question; she'd thought it was obvious. She was still wearing the sweatpants and T-shirt she'd slept in.

"Why not?"

She was about to say that she wasn't in the mood for school when it occurred to her that Teddy would probably shoot back something to the effect that he wasn't in the mood either. "It's dead week," she said, blurting out the lie before she realized how it would sound. When she saw the stricken look on his face, she hurried to explain. "Dead week's the week before final exams. You're supposed to stay home and study."

"Oh." He looked skeptical but turned toward the garage without further comment.

She noticed that his hair was sticking up funny in the back. He obviously hadn't bothered to brush it. "Wait," she said, fishing through her purse for a brush. As she bent over him with the hairbrush, he smacked her cheek with his lips. She was so stunned, she burst into tears. He pushed her away and ran out to the car, slamming the door behind him. She called after him, but he ignored her. *Shit,* she thought. She climbed into the driver's seat and leaned over to give him a peck on the cheek. He whipped his head away. She couldn't remember the last time he had spontaneously kissed her, and now she had gone and ruined it. "Thank you anyway," she said, backing out of the garage.

They didn't say much during the short ride to the elementary school. Teddy fiddled with the radio knob, something that normally drove her crazy, but today she refrained from slapping his hand away from the tuner. When they pulled up to the curb, her eyes blurred with tears as she watched him walking toward his classroom. He looked so small and defenseless with his red backpack strapped to his bony shoulders, like a tiny Sherpa trekking up a huge snowcapped mountain. She fought off an urge to call him back to the car. At the doorway to his classroom he turned back and waved at her, a limp halfhearted wave, and she had to clutch the steering wheel with both hands to keep from beckoning him back.

She looked at her watch. 8:25. As she watched Teddy disappear inside his classroom, she felt a sudden pang. A week ago at this time she would have been rushing to drop off Trina at the campus day care center in order to make it to her American lit class on time. If you came in late, Dr. Diller would stop mid-sentence, frown, and glare at you. He was one of the few professors, an Ivy League antique approaching retirement, who resisted the new student-centered teaching methods — the meandering class discussions, the small groups, the soul-baring journals — in favor of old-fashioned imparting of knowledge. Giselle was one of the few students who seemed to appreciate his style. Walking out of class one day, she had overheard two students, frat guys with baseball caps turned backward, referring to him as Dr. Duller. She didn't feel much in common with the younger students, who acted as if going to class were a giant imposition; she had loved all her classes.

But instead of Dr. Diller, she had an appointment with Dr. Cole, the family therapist, this morning. Or rather, she and Dan had an appointment. Giselle had debated whether to call and cancel since Dan was gone — what was the point? — but then she'd decided to go alone. She needed to talk to someone. Although she would have preferred someone older, dowdier, and grayer. A cross between Aunt Bea and the Dalai Lama. But this was southern California, where the doctors looked like actors playing doctors.

WHEN TEDDY ENTERS THE CLASSROOM, ALL THE kids stare and whisper until Mrs. Shimono orders them to get out their math workbooks and do the problems on page 95. It is the first time he has seen Eric since the afternoon it happened. Their families have been avoiding each other. At recess Eric walks over to him standing alone by the fence and says, "My mom and dad haven't stopped yelling at me. And they took away my new bike." Teddy knows that Eric is trying to get him to feel sorry for him. "How about your parents?" Eric asks. "Do they yell at you?"

Teddy shakes his head. He wants Eric to go away. He doesn't even want to look at him. For the first time it occurs to him that it was really Eric's fault. He wasn't supposed to touch that gun in the first place. And he had practically shoved it into Teddy's hands.

"No shit? They don't yell at you at all?" Eric asks as if he can't believe it. Teddy shakes his head again. "Goddamn, that's not fair!" He sounds just like his father, who likes to cuss a lot. Eric frowns and kicks at the gravel. "You're the one who shoots her, and I'm the one who gets yelled at. Go figure."

Teddy walks away. He goes back to the empty classroom, sits down at his desk, and turns to the next set of problems in his workbook. He likes math. He's good at it, and it takes your mind off every-

thing else. He is trying to divide 1,640 by 20 when he feels a soft tap on his shoulder. He looks up and sees Chandra Patel, the prettiest, smartest girl in the class, standing next to him. Last year they were both in the Bluebirds, the top reading group in Mrs. Honey's class. On field trips her mother always accompanied them wearing a sari and a red dot on her forehead. Her father is a surgeon. Dan saw him parked in front of the school once in his silver Jaguar and said, "You could feed a thousand Biafran families for a decade on what that car cost." Chandra stares at him with her big brown eyes like melting chocolate.

"My father operated on your little sister," she tells him. "He felt very bad. He said it was a very sad accident. I know you didn't mean to do it." She smiles a sad, sweet smile. Her dark eyes and long lashes remind him of Trina's.

He feels his lip trembling and bites down hard. "How do you know?" he says and turns his back on her as she bursts into tears and runs back out to the playground.

GISELLE SETTLED BACK IN THE SOFT BLACK LEATHER chair — Italian, no doubt — and waited for the doctor to ask her where Dan was. Although the doctor had asked them to call her Hannah, Giselle was having a hard time feeling comfortable with that — even though they were probably the same age. Maybe that was why. It seemed too much like girlfriends. And what she wanted, at $130 an hour, was sage counsel — not girl talk. When the doctor didn't ask where Dan was, Giselle felt compelled to state the obvious. "Dan couldn't come," she said. "He's out of town." And then realizing how odd that must sound under the circumstances, she added, "He went camping with his older brother for a couple of days. His brother lives in Arizona. He thought Dan needed to get away, you know, just for a couple of nights."

Hannah nodded. She seemed to be waiting for Giselle to say more.

"His brother's a doctor," Giselle explained, as if that explained everything.

"And how do you feel about that?" she asked when Giselle didn't continue.

"About his going camping?"

This time the doctor didn't even bother to nod.

Giselle shrugged and gazed at the bright Haitian paintings on the stark white walls. At their first appointment she had assumed they were children's paintings and was relieved that she hadn't said anything about them when Dan, standing up close to one of the larger paintings, had asked the doctor if she had been to Haiti. And Hannah had replied yes and steered the conversation back to more pressing personal matters.

"I think it's a good idea. I mean, it's a very difficult situation." She picked up a ceramic lizard sitting on the table next to her, next to the Kleenex box, and examined it. "He has some mixed feelings about Teddy right now, understandably. He's trying to sort them out. These things take time," Giselle said, as if she were the doctor. She set the lizard back down and looked at Hannah expectantly, thinking that it was her turn to hold up her end of the conversation. She could at least do that much if she wasn't going to proffer any brilliant solutions. But the doctor just waited. Rattled by the silence, Giselle said, "I like your dress." It was a loose bronze Moroccan caftan cinched by a wide studded copper belt. Giselle felt dowdy in her jeans skirt and tank top. She was just as glad that Dan wasn't there to note the physical contrast between them. Then she felt a twinge of guilt for imagining that Dan would be so shallow. He wasn't like that at all.

Finally, ignoring the compliment, Hannah said, "So you don't feel any resentment?"

"Not really." Giselle shook her head. "I understand." She pulled a card out of her purse and passed it to Hannah. "He left me this note."

Hannah looked at the card and then back at Giselle, clearly confused. The card was white with silver hands clasped in prayer: WITH OUR HEARTFELT SYMPATHY IN YOUR TIME OF SORROW. It was from some couple down the street whom they barely knew and had been slipped into their mailbox during the night. It was signed "Chip and Phyllis (yellow house on corner)," as if they realized that Giselle and Dan might not have a clue who they were, which had touched Giselle and made her like them more. "The other side," Giselle prompted. "On the back."

Hannah turned it over and read the brief note. Then she

handed the card back to Giselle. They had a whole basket full of cards sitting on the kitchen counter. She especially hated the religious ones. All except for her sister Vonnie's card. It had a picture of Jesus on the front, but inside she had crossed out the pious sentiments and printed GOD SUCKS in Magic Marker. Giselle could see that the doctor was waiting for a response. She had, in fact, forgotten the question. Something about how she felt when she read the note. She figured Hannah could see the card had been in the trash; she could probably smell the coffee grounds and week-old banana peels. Giselle didn't know why the note had initially pissed her off; she was the one, after all, who had convinced him to take the trip. And when she reread it, she had found it perfectly tender and sincere. After all, what could he say? That it didn't matter that Teddy had killed their daughter? *Hey, it's no biggie, don't sweat it.*

"Well, I suppose I felt a little abandoned at first. But also sort of relieved," Giselle mumbled. "I told him he should go."

"Relieved?" Hannah pounced.

Giselle shrugged. "Not to feel his anger and resentment." She sighed. "I know Teddy feels it. And I know Dan can't help it. That's why he took off. It's not his fault. I mean, can you really blame him?"

"So you blame yourself instead."

It wasn't exactly a question. Giselle shrugged. "I feel guilty. I don't know if that's the same as blaming myself, exactly."

"If you don't blame yourself and you don't blame your husband, who do you blame?"

Giselle heard Teddy's voice asking her, *How can something be no one's fault?* echoing off the dark garage walls.

"What makes you think I blame anyone? It was an accident. Shit happens." The office suddenly felt stuffy. Giselle fanned herself with the sympathy card. "Hasn't anyone ever heard of an accident before?"

It was the therapist's turn to shrug. "It's human nature to want to blame someone."

It had taken two days for the Los Angeles County Attorney's Office to complete its investigation and officially declare it an accident. No charges would be filed. Up until that point Giselle had been so outraged, so fiercely protective of Teddy, so indignant that anyone could even fleetingly consider holding him legally culpable, that once she was able to breathe a sigh of relief on that front, something dark and debilitating had crept in through the back door. Her rock-hard clarity had crumbled to dust. Her brain felt like the inside of one of those cheap snowglobes.

"I blame the Beemers," she shot back defiantly. "It was their goddamned gun." She felt Hannah's eyes on her, still waiting. Silent. Impassive. Waiting. "And I suppose maybe, sometimes, I blame Teddy," she mumbled. Then she shut her eyes and slumped in her chair, head hanging. All along she had insisted, *insisted,* that she didn't blame Teddy.

Hannah was nodding, almost smiling, as if Giselle were a slow pupil who had at long last, after much coaching, blurted out the right answer to a difficult question.

At the funeral service the priest had spoken about accepting God's will and about sharing their common bond of grief. They had all cried together, but somehow you could feel the subtle undertow, the crosscurrents of grief. Always, at the back of everyone's mind, was the awareness of how Trina had died, the knowledge that *this didn't have to happen.* Giselle could feel Dan's family thinking it every time they looked at Teddy. Lying in bed the night after the funeral, she thought about human accidents versus what she termed "pure accidents." Accidents with no human error involved. Acts of God. There weren't that many. And if you took away natural disasters — lightning, tornadoes, earthquakes — she was hard-pressed to think of any scenarios that did not involve some degree of human negligence. It had never occurred to her before that what *accident* meant was *unintentional.* It didn't mean *blameless.* No matter how hard you tried to pretend it did.

After leaving Hannah's office, she drove home and lay on the sofa, paralyzed. Her life had been so hectic, so scheduled, running from person to person, from place to place — trying to be a good mother, wife, and college student — that she didn't know what to do with this sudden yawning vacuum of hours until it was time to go pick up Teddy at school. She knew that she should call her professors and negotiate extensions or incompletes or whatever, but she just couldn't stand to talk about what had happened, to endure the awkward expressions of sympathy. She knew that her professors would bend over backward to help her complete the semester, but the idea of just continuing on as if nothing had happened made her sick. She felt as if she deserved to fail. She had always been so intent upon getting A's. Flunking a couple of courses seemed like the least she could do — a small penance, a shabby sacrifice.

There were dishes in the sink, unmade beds, groceries to buy, bills to pay — but none of that seemed compelling enough to evict her from the sofa. Since she'd run out of the sedatives that Greg gave her, she hadn't been sleeping much. She was exhausted, yet she knew she wouldn't fall asleep. The phone rang, but she didn't answer it. There was no one she wanted to talk to, except maybe Dan. She heard the answering machine click on in the kitchen and the caller hang up without bothering to leave a message. For a moment she worried that it had been the school nurse calling to inform her that Teddy was sick and needed to come home, but then she realized the nurse would have left a message. She clicked on the remote and lay there listening to a Spanish soap opera with her eyes closed. Despite her Spanish tapes, she could recognize only a word here, a phrase there. She remembered painting Trina's room with Teddy when she was seven months pregnant, enjoying those last few intimate weeks before her son would cease being an only child. She clicked off the TV. Tomorrow Dan would be back.

They had buried Trina in a cemetery in Los Feliz, next to Dan's father. It was a beautiful plot on a hill with palm trees. Still, Trina had never known Dan's father; Giselle had never even met him. He was dead before she'd married Dan, and now Trina was up there all alone next to some strange man. It didn't seem right. When Ed's

Great Dane, Dinky, had died at the age of sixteen, the vet had given Ed a choice: he could leave the body to be disposed of or he could take the body home. Ed had hauled Dinky home in the back of his pickup, wrapped in an old Indian bedspread from their dorm days, and buried him in a field, underneath a huge oak tree, behind his grandparents' farmhouse. It was April and the ground was still frozen. It had taken him hours to dig a grave big enough. Giselle had sat there, five months pregnant, drinking mulled cider from a thermos his Granma Rose had provided, offering moral support. She wished they could have buried Trina in the backyard so that she would be near them, so that she would know they hadn't abandoned her. But it was against the law, and they were only renting anyway.

Soon after their marriage, they had made out wills, in which they both stipulated their wish to be cremated. They had also appointed Dan's brother as Trina's legal guardian should anything happen to them. Giselle had hated the idea of splitting them up, her son and daughter, but there seemed to be no compromise available. Teddy would, of course, go to his father. It had been her first inkling of the biological fault lines running beneath their little family. But everyone in California lived with the threat of an earthquake every day and didn't dwell on it. It was Midwesterners who loved to talk about the Big One, as if to console themselves for six months of shoveling snow. Dan and she had never actually discussed where or how the children should be buried or whatever — who would? who could? — and in the end neither of them could bear the thought of reducing Trina's sweet, fresh body to ash.

At two o'clock she peeled herself off the sofa and drove to Teddy's school, arriving there twenty minutes early. Usually she was rushing to get there on time. She used to complain that there were too few hours in the day, too much to do. If she could have her old life back, she would never complain again, not so much as a murmur of protest. Her stomach rumbled although she had no appetite.

She remembered the emergency rice cakes she kept in the glove compartment for Trina. They were sealed in a plastic Baggie, only slightly worse for wear. She choked one down penitently, methodically chewing and swallowing the tasteless cardboard disks. They reminded her of communion wafers from her childhood; they had tasted disappointingly bland even on her First Communion, when she still believed in God. As soon as she spotted Teddy emerging from a throng of kids and trudging toward the car, she could tell that it had been a rough day. Even the flashing lights on the heels of his sneakers seemed dimmer. He climbed in the car and slammed the door without bothering to say hello. As kids ran by the car, he slumped down in his seat, striving for invisibility. "Let's go," he grouched. "What are you waiting for?"

She pulled away from the curb, into a caravan of school buses. Lois Beemer, of all people, was in the lane next to her, with Eric in the passenger seat of her Jeep Cherokee. They hadn't spoken since the day of the accident. When Lois glanced over and saw them, her face blanched. Giselle nodded to her; she couldn't really muster up all that much hostility toward Lois personally. When Giselle nodded at her, Lois looked abjectly grateful. Then the car behind her honked impatiently, and Lois made a belated left turn, nearly colliding with an oncoming minivan.

"Did you talk to Eric today?" Giselle asked.

"He's a jerk," Teddy said.

She wanted to ask more about his day but could sense that he wasn't in a receptive mood. "Want to stop at Baskin-Robbins?" she asked. It was just a couple of blocks away. He shrugged. "Is that a yes or a no?"

"It's a yes or a no," he said like a little smart-ass.

She took a deep breath. *You're the adult, he's the child.* She flicked on her turn signal and pulled into the strip mall parking lot.

At Baskin-Robbins they sat silently at a small round table, listlessly licking single-dip ice cream cones. She remembered the last time they'd come here. She had picked up Trina at day care, then picked up Teddy at soccer, and he had wheedled her into stopping for ice cream even though it was too close to dinnertime. Giselle had ordered a small cup of chocolate ice cream for Trina, who kept grabbing for Teddy's cone. He had held it to her mouth and let her take licks, mouth open like a baby bird.

"Dan's coming home tomorrow," Giselle said.

Teddy looked at her, alert to subtle nuances, waiting for her to go on.

"He just wanted to be by himself for a little bit while he's feeling sad. Some people are like that. Some people like to go off alone when they feel bad. Other people like lots of attention."

"Like cats and dogs," Teddy said.

"That's right." She smiled and leaned over to wipe a glob of mint chip off his T-shirt.

"What are you?" he asked. "A cat or a dog?"

"I'm a mother," she said, and suddenly wondered what she would have done if she'd had the option, the luxury, of choosing to stay or go. The long night stretched ahead of them. "How 'bout we get a pizza and rent a movie," she said, forcing a little doggy smile as she imagined herself sprawled in catlike independence on a king-size bed in some soothingly blank hotel room somewhere.

"If you want to," Teddy said, as if he were doing her a big favor.

She tossed the rest of her cone in the trash.

When they arrived home with a frozen pizza and a video, the light on the answering machine was blinking. Her first thought was that it was Dan calling to say he wasn't coming back.

"I bet it's Dad," Teddy said, punching the PLAY button. Ed had been calling every day. The phone cord was extra long, and Teddy would carry the phone to some place private — the bathroom or back stoop. When she'd asked him what they talked about, he just shrugged and said, "Stuff." And when she'd asked Ed, his response hadn't been much more enlightening.

Sure enough, Ed's deep voice rumbled self-consciously, too

loud, into the kitchen. "Hi there, it's your dad. Just wondered how school was. Give me a call. I'll be home." Giselle thought he always sounded like a foreigner with limited English skills whenever he left messages. A throwback to an earlier generation, Ed got stage fright talking to machines. Dan was at the other extreme. Before they had moved in together, he would sometimes call and leave a poem or some passage he'd just read that had struck his fancy. Coming home and turning on her machine was like finding a bouquet of wildflowers on her doorstep.

"It's too early for supper," she said. "Why don't you call your dad back while I watch the news."

As Teddy carried the phone out onto the back stoop, she went into the living room, flopped down on the sofa, and reached for the remote. Back in Nebraska they had watched Tom Brokaw, a fellow Midwesterner, but Dan had converted her to CNN. Wolf Blitzer was standing on the lawn of the White House, looking and talking like a college professor. She clicked to NBC and felt a sudden rush of comfort as Tom's clean-shaven face and prairie vowels — his solid presence — soothed her. She hadn't realized how much she'd missed him.

After a few minutes Teddy appeared in the doorway holding the telephone to his chest. "Dad wants to talk to you."

She sighed, muted the volume on the TV, and stretched out her hand for the receiver. Maybe it was the nostalgic background murmur of Brokaw's voice, but as she listened to Ed asking her how they were doing, she found herself crying. Teddy hung his head and then disappeared down the hall to his room. On the other end, Ed fumbled for some magic words of comfort.

"I can't believe that guy just took off," he said. He never referred to Dan by name. His voice sounded indignant. "What about you and Teddy?"

"He's coming back tomorrow." She tried leaping to Dan's defense, but her voice didn't quite make the leap. *Damn Teddy,* she thought. *He would have to go and tell Ed that Dan was gone. It wasn't any of Ed's business.*

"Camping!" Ed snorted. "What is this — the Boy Scouts?"

"He's the sort of person who needs to work through things alone. I can respect that."

"I thought you said you needed to work things through as a family. That's why Teddy couldn't come stay with me. Now this clown's off sitting around a campfire somewhere in the redwoods feeling sorry for himself."

"I don't want to talk to you about this," she said stiffly. But, in fact, she felt better listening to Ed berating Dan, saying aloud the things she couldn't help thinking to herself. "Teddy's upset. I better go check on him."

"You sure you don't want me to come out there? I hate to think of you and Teddy going through this alone." He sounded as earnest and genuine as Tom Brokaw.

"He's coming back tomorrow," she repeated. "We're not really alone. It's just . . ." — her voice trailed off — "oh, never mind." It was too much effort to speak. Or think.

Ed waited. Someone else would have prodded her, but he seemed prepared to wait indefinitely. Finally she said, "I have to go."

"I just want you to know I'm here for you," he added quickly, before she could hang up. "Teddy and you."

"I know," she said.

"He's my son. You're his mother. Nothing can change that."

He had said the same thing, word for word, when she'd left for California. Standing in the driveway next to their packed car, sad and angry. At the time his words had struck her more like a curse than a comfort. But this time she felt a wave of gratitude wash over her. "Thank you," she said meekly.

"Tell Teddy I'll call tomorrow." He waited until she hung up.

The news had ended. She slipped the video into the VCR. *The Land Before Time.* Teddy had seen it countless times when he was much younger, but she didn't have the heart to argue with him at Blockbuster, even though she was worried that it was a sign of regression. The therapist had warned her this could happen — one of her only useful insights to date. As she slid the frozen pizza into the oven, she wondered whether there was a support group for parents whose child had killed a sibling. SADS. Sibling Accidental Death Society. There seemed to be support groups for everything these days. It was human nature, apparently, in this era of increasing specialization, to form a herd of fellow sufferers in the particular area of your tragic expertise. Although she had never been a joiner, she could understand the appeal of such a group. A safe place where you could admit your ugliest thoughts, reveal your worst self, and have others nod their head in recognition. A therapist might have heard it all before, but that was a far cry from having felt it. Like labor pains. No amount of talk or reading could prepare you for the real thing. There were doors that no amount of imagination or empathy could open. You crossed the threshold, and you were in a new country. On another planet. Repatriated. If you were lucky enough, that is, to stumble across a settlement of your own kind. She didn't know how you went about finding such settlements, the appropriate support group. *Oprah*? The Internet? Word of mouth? Maybe you didn't have to do anything. Maybe if you just waited, a representative would knock on your door, teach you the secret handshake.

While Teddy picked at his pizza and watched the movie, Giselle sat out on the back porch drinking vodka and tonics. She thought that Dan might have taken the bottle of vodka with him, but he hadn't. She imagined he saw this time alone as a sort of purification ritual — that sort of thing appealed to him, appealed to his literary sensibility. It was a warm, clear night. She could hear the Beemers' dog whining and scratching at the back door to be let inside. The faint circular outline of the wading pool was still visible even though her father had attempted to rake it away. Her parents had been calling every day. She couldn't bring herself to tell them that Dan wasn't there. She could imagine their silent consternation across the wire if she told them he'd gone off with Greg for a couple of days. As she got up to refill her drink, the phone rang.

"Just let it ring," she said to Teddy as he skidded across the linoleum in his socks and made a lunge for the receiver.

"But what if it's my dad?" he said.

"It's not going to be your dad. You just talked to him."

The caller hung up the instant the answering machine clicked on. No message.

"See. It was probably just someone trying to sell us something." She imagined shouting at the unsuspecting solicitor: *Look, you asshole, my daughter just died and we're not interested in any life insurance just now!*

"I'll be on the back porch, reading," she told Teddy as she carried her book back outside, although she knew she wouldn't bother to open it. She still couldn't seem to focus her mind. She'd had to read the cooking directions on the frozen pizza three times. The book she was carrying around was *Billy Budd,* the next novel on the syllabus after *The Scarlet Letter,* even though she had already made up her mind to drop her classes.

As she was rereading the same paragraph for the third time, she heard the phone ringing in the kitchen again. Four rings and then the machine picked up. After the beep she heard her friend Ellen's voice: "Hi, it's me. We're taking Zack to the zoo tomorrow afternoon and thought maybe Teddy'd like to come along. Give you and Dan a little time alone. We can pick him up at school — it's on our way. Just let me know. Bye." Giselle sighed. She still hadn't thanked Ellen for baby-sitting Teddy the day of the funeral. She didn't even have the energy to talk to her friends. Then almost immediately the phone rang again. Vonnie. "Hey, Gigi, it's your sister. I know you're there. I'll count to ten. One, two, three, four, five . . . Okay, be that way. Six, seven —" Just as Giselle was about to give in and answer it, Vonnie hung up — which was just like her, not even bothering to count all the way to ten.

On the way back to the patio, she glanced in the hallway mirror and noticed that her face was wet with tears. She hadn't realized she was crying. Too much vodka. She screwed the lid back on the bottle. Someone switched on the floodlight Bill Beemer had installed as an antiburglar device. It lit up their backyard like a movie set. Dan had resented it even before the accident. The light was harsh and glaring. He said it made him feel as if he were living in a combat zone. She tried to picture Dan somewhere dark and quiet, sitting by a small flickering campfire. Maybe smoking a joint. Probably wishing he had never married her. She peered at her watch and went inside.

The television was off. The house seemed unnaturally quiet. "Teddy?" she called out.

No response. She sighed and opened his door a crack. The room was empty. Trying not to panic, she checked the windows and saw the screens were undisturbed. You had to walk down the hallway to leave the house. She didn't think he could have slipped by her. She checked the master bedroom, the bathroom, and then reluctantly opened the door to Trina's room. He had climbed into her crib and was curled up in a fetal position hugging her stuffed bunny. He was sleeping soundly, but she could see a trail of dried tears on his cheeks. She reached out to touch him. Her hand hovered in the air above his head. Suddenly she wasn't sure if she was going to stroke his cheek or slap it. The hand seemed to belong to someone else. It was trembling. His eyes flew open, and he stared at her, holding his breath, as if he knew what was going on inside her. Her hand dropped to her side. She felt incapable of coping with this. All of it. It was just too much. She had coped with an unplanned pregnancy, divorce, single parenthood — you name it — but this, this was too much. She turned and headed toward the door. "It's time for bed," she said. "Your bed." She knew he needed something more from her, but this was the best she could do. Trina's absence was like a crown of thorns encircling her heart. Each breath seemed to stab her in a fresh tender spot.

After Teddy had completed his bedtime ritual, she wandered back out to the living room. It was still only nine-thirty. She wished she had rented a movie for herself at Blockbuster. The idea had occurred to her, but as she skimmed over the various sections — COMEDY, DRAMA, FAMILY ENTERTAINMENT, HORROR — nothing seemed appropriate. She thought they should have them arranged like greeting cards: WEDDING, BIRTH, CONGRATULATIONS, SYMPATHY. She walked into the kitchen and wrapped the leftover pizza in foil and stuck it in the refrigerator. She could nuke it for Teddy's dinner tomorrow. She hadn't eaten any herself. She pulled out a butterscotch pudding and a juice box. For the past few days the only thing she could stomach was kiddie food — pudding, Cheerios, rice cakes, applesauce, SpaghettiOs. She had even eaten an old jar of Gerber's strained carrots that she'd found in the back of the cupboard.

The answering machine was right there, the red light blinking. She knew she should call Ellen back and say yes, Teddy would love to go to the zoo with them, but she didn't really feel like talking to her. Or worse yet, her husband, a shrink, who always made Giselle nervous. He had this habit of echoing the ends of your sentences as if to ask, *Did you really mean to say that?*

She thought maybe she'd call her sister back. At least Vonnie was depressed, too, still mourning her lover. Giselle had met Bev only once, shortly before Trina was born, when Vonnie and Bev had flown out to L.A. for a training seminar — something to do with computers — Bev had to attend. They went to Zuma Beach. Bev wore a black crocheted bikini and had a body that made Jane Fonda look like Roseanne. She worked out with weights, she had explained, flexing a perfectly sculpted arm. Vonnie had been homecoming queen before she'd gone off to college and written her parents a letter informing them she was gay. Included in the brief letter was a snapshot of Vonnie with her shoulder-length blond hair reduced to a buzz cut. In a postscript she had bequeathed all her teenage cosmetics and jewelry to Giselle, who had been both thrilled and bewildered, not quite understanding the whole deal.

The thing that had originally brought Giselle and Ed together, that had helped them cross the line from friendship to intimacy in high school, was the fact that they both had gay siblings. In Nebraska. Ed's older brother Brice had come out and was active in gay politics, always giving speeches and getting his picture in the *Daily Nebraskan,* the university paper. The guys in high school used to give Ed shit about it. He would blush and look as though he wanted to sink into a hole. No one except Giselle's best friend, Laura, knew about Vonnie because she was far away, at the University of Wisconsin, and never came home for holidays. But Giselle knew how Ed must feel. So one day when she noticed him looking particularly miserable after a bout of macho razzing, she took him aside and confided in him about her sister. "But Yvonne was a cheerleader!" he'd exclaimed, completely shocked. "She went steady with Bo Larsen." He shook his head. "Are you sure?" It was the most they had ever talked, even though they had known each other since third grade. A couple of weeks later Ed called and asked her to one of his wrestling matches. They started going out together. Ed's brother gave him a key to his apartment in a peeling white Victorian, and they used to go there to make out on Brice's king-size waterbed when he wasn't home.

Giselle tossed the empty butterscotch pudding into the trash and was skimming through her address book to find her sister's new number — Vonnie had moved back to Lincoln, to a smaller, cheaper apartment, after Bev died — when she noticed Ed's number written in on the automatic dial list so that Teddy could just press a button and get his father. A sudden impulse made her finger punch the number 1. After a couple of rings Ed picked up the phone, his voice froggy with sleep. She imagined him nodding off in the ratty velour armchair, a half-empty beer in hand, with a *Star Trek* rerun on the crummy thirteen-inch TV. Although he'd probably bought a new and better TV set by now — it had been five years, after all; she'd give him the benefit of the doubt. He seemed surprised to hear her voice. She never called him.

"I'm afraid," she said without any preamble. "I'm afraid Teddy thinks I blame him. That I don't love him anymore." She'd had too much to drink; her voice sounded boozy and tearful.

"Do you?" Ed asked.

"It's hard," she sighed. "I don't know."

"You don't know if you love him?" Ed cleared his throat nervously. She could visualize him chewing on his thumb, something that had always driven her crazy.

She didn't say anything. She felt suddenly nauseous; the butterscotch pudding had not mixed well with the vodka. Or maybe it was what she was saying. She felt her skin break into a cold sweat.

"I love him. Of course I love him," she said, trying not to sound impatient. "I'm his mother." She sighed. "But I was also her mother. No matter what I do, I feel like I'm being disloyal to someone." What she wanted to say is how much easier it would be — well, not easier exactly, but more manageable somehow — if Dan were Teddy's real father. Then they would be in the same boat at least. They might handle it differently, but at least they'd be handling it in the same boat. But even half drunk she knew better than to say this to Ed. Instead she said, "I was just remembering when Dinky died and you dug his grave."

To her amazement, Ed started to cry. Hoarse, shuddering sobs. She couldn't remember ever hearing him cry before, not even when she left him and took his son with her halfway across the country. To a place Ed had never even been to.

"Oh, Ed," she said, at a loss, "I'm sorry," and hung up.

She stumbled to the bedroom and lay down on top of the rumpled quilt, keeping one foot steady on the floor to prevent the room from spinning. There was a cheap plastic light fixture on the ceiling. They had never used it before Dan broke the bedside lamp. The bottom of the plastic shade was littered with dead insects. It was disgusting. She hauled herself up and turned off the light. Darkness was better anyway. She had always preferred making love in the dark. Ed had never seemed to mind, but Dan insisted that they leave a light on, or at least burn a candle. He seemed to view sex in the dark as something for unenlightened people, people who found oral sex perverse — which she had to admit she had until Dan educated her on the subject. At first she had felt annoyed with Ed for being such a pedestrian lover, but later, in rare nostalgic moods, she would feel a certain tenderness for their white-bread, puppylike gropings. They had both been virgins. Dan, on the other hand, had revised and polished her style in bed just as he had on paper. After the first time they made love, she had gone into the bathroom to pee; when she turned on the light, she'd half expected to see comments in green ink scrawled on her naked body: *A little more here. A bit awkward. Great! Nice work, Giselle!* Before Dan, sex was something she could take or leave, something she desired in theory more than in practice. But with Dan, she daydreamed about sex while she was grocery shopping or sitting in traffic jams. When Trina was a baby, before she slept through the night, she seemed to have a sixth sense. On the rare nights they weren't too exhausted to attempt to make love, Trina would wake up crying the moment they started to fuck. (Dan had taught her to say the word *fuck*. She and Ed had never much graduated from their high school vocabulary; they referred to sex as *it*.) If they tried to ignore her, her crying would escalate from a lovelorn whimper to a jealous wail of betrayal. But now the loud silence coming from her room would be even harder to ignore, impossible to quiet. Now she wondered if they would ever make love in the same way again.

Suddenly she had to know for sure what Dan was feeling. Not what she thought he was feeling, but his actual thoughts in his own words. She rolled over to his side of the bed and slid her hand underneath the mattress, searching for his journal, which she knew he hid there. He had been keeping a journal for years and required all his students to keep journals for class, something else they all grumbled about. His old journals he kept locked in a file cabinet in his office, but the current journal he kept at home so he could write in it at night, usually after she was asleep. Until now she had never looked at it, although she had been tempted. She knew how appalled he would be at this violation of his privacy. And she was worried that if she read something that disturbed her, she wouldn't be able to keep it to herself. But this was different. Everything had changed. She ran her hand back and forth several times until she gave up. He must have taken it with him. Of course he would. She pictured him hunched in his small dome tent, writing by flashlight. She remembered his telling them the first day of class that writing was easy: you just opened up a vein and let the blood drip onto the page.

She rolled back over to her side of the bed and lay there for a moment with her eyes closed. Then she got up and went into the bathroom to hunt for some over-the-counter sleeping pills she had bought ages ago. They were in the back of the medicine chest. She swallowed two pills. They had never worked very well, but she supposed they were better than nothing. As she passed by Teddy's room, she heard an odd noise and stepped inside. He was grinding his teeth in his sleep, something he hadn't done for a couple of years now.

Those first weeks in California, when she was plagued by anxiety attacks in the night, she used to crawl in bed next to Teddy, who slept on a flip-out futon. When he ground his teeth, she used to slip her finger between his baby teeth and he would suck on it like a pacifier. Then she tried using her relaxation tapes on Teddy. They seemed to help. Together, they would drift off to sleep listening to soothing bells and rippling surf. She walked over to Teddy's toy chest and rummaged around until she found a couple of the old tapes. The Walkman Dan had given him for Christmas was lying on the dresser. She snapped a tape in and slipped the earphones over Teddy's head. Then turned the tape on. Himalayan bells. He sighed as a ripple of peace washed across his face.

IN THE MORNING HIS MOTHER DOES NOT GET OUT *of bed. She says she doesn't feel well, he'll have to take the school bus. She tells him to call the Walshes and say he wants to go to the zoo with them after school.*

"But I don't want to go," he protests. *The last time he went to the zoo was with Dan and Trina while his mother was writing a term paper. When they passed the gorilla cage, Trina shouted and pointed, "Koko!" Every time they tried to move on to see some other animals, his sister threw a fit. They must have stood by the gorilla cage for an hour. Teddy wanted to go to the reptile building, but Dan wouldn't let him wander out of his sight. "Your mother would kill me if anything happened to you," he said. He gave him a five-dollar bill and told him to go over to the concession stand, only a few yards away, and bring back three soft ice cream cones. Teddy had tripped on his shoelace and dropped one of the cones on the way back, but Dan hadn't yelled at him. Just handed him his own cone, saying he wasn't really hungry.*

"Why not?" *his mother asks, exasperated.* "You'll just be bored here."

He shrugs. She picks up the receiver off the nightstand and dials the number and hands the phone to him. When Ellen answers, he says, "This is Teddy. My mom wants me to go to the zoo with you." His mother glares at him as he slams down the phone.

"You better get dressed," she tells him. "And eat some breakfast."

"We're out of cereal," he informs her. "I told you."

"Then have some cookies." She rolls over and covers her head with the pillow.

He can't believe she actually told him to eat cookies for breakfast. They are out of milk, too. He eats three Oreos and drinks a Diet Coke.

On the ride to the zoo Ellen asks him how his mother and father are doing.

"My mom's sick in bed," he says. "Dan's camping in Big Sur."

"Really?" Ellen says and exchanges a look with her husband. Dr. Walsh shakes his head and tugs at his dark beard.

"When's he coming back?" Ellen asks, frowning at Zack, who is kicking his feet against the front seat, until he stops it.

"Probably tonight," Teddy says. "Maybe."

Zack says, "Now you're an only child. Like me." He sounds as if Teddy should be glad about this.

Ellen sighs and rubs her forehead as if she has a headache. "What's your favorite animal?" Zack's father asks Teddy.

"Komodo dragon," Teddy says.

Zack's father nods and turns on the radio.

At the zoo Teddy is bored. Zack's father stops and reads every sign aloud to them — all the vital statistics about emus and eagles — determined to make it a real educational experience. There is a big wooden statue of bald eagle wings with inches marked off, and kids are supposed to stand in front of it with their arms outspread to compare their arm spans with that of the bald eagle's wingspan. Zack's father makes them do it, and Ellen snaps a picture. She snaps two of Zack and one of Teddy. He knows they don't really want a picture of him, but they don't want to make him feel left out. When Dr. Walsh takes Zack to the men's room, Ellen sits down beside Teddy on a stone bench and says, "You look so sad, Teddy. Is there anything I can do?"

"I'd like to go to the reptile building," he says.

She nods, and when the others come back, she tells them that she and Teddy are going to the reptile house; they'll meet at the front gate in half an hour. Zack whines that he wants to see the Kimono dragon, too. "Komodo," Teddy mutters under his breath. Ellen pats Zack on the head and tells him to stay with his father. Dr. Walsh drops his large hairy hand, like a bear paw, onto Zack's shoulder and gives him a fatherly squeeze. Zack pouts as they walk off.

At the reptile house he is surprised when Ellen goes inside. His own mother is afraid of snakes and always waits outside for him. He makes his way over to the iguanas and Komodo dragons and presses his face against the glass. He wishes he could crawl in there with them, camouflage himself under a nice big rock. When he and his mother were living alone in the apartment, when they first moved to California, his mother had bought him two anoles in a Plexiglas cage. He missed their dog in Nebraska, and you weren't allowed to have real pets in their apartment complex. The only good thing about the place was a swimming pool in the center, but since he was only four years old, he wasn't allowed in it unless his mother was holding him, even though he knew how to swim. At first they bought just one anole. He set it in a patch of sunlight in his room and decorated the cage with sticks for it to climb on. Twice a day he spritzed it with his mom's plant mister and fed it live crickets from a Baggie. After a couple of days he complained that the anole, which he'd named Rocky, never did anything. It just clung to the side of the cage and never bothered to climb on the twigs. Teddy's mother thought that maybe it was depressed, being all alone in there. So they went back to the pet shop and bought a second anole, which he named Stoney. Stoney seemed a little peppier than Rocky. There was more activity to watch. But two mornings later Teddy woke up to find Rocky gone. He searched the whole cage until he found part of Rocky's tail. Stoney had eaten him. His mother was so outraged that she flushed Stoney down the toilet. "I refuse to have that monster in my house," she said.

Teddy pounds his fist on the glass until the Komodo dragon looks up at him, puffing out his chest. They stare, eye to eye, not blinking. A guard walks over and warns him not to touch the glass. The guard has a holster strapped to his hip.

"What are you going to do? Shoot me?" Teddy says.

Ellen apologizes for him, making it clear that Teddy is not her son.

AFTER TEDDY LEFT FOR SCHOOL, GISELLE JUST lay in bed feeling simultaneously leaden and jittery. She hadn't heard a word from Dan since he'd been gone — three days — and he'd said they would be back sometime on Tuesday. Today. The thought made her stomach cramp. What if nothing had changed, if he still felt the same way about Teddy? She threw off the covers and ran to the bathroom. As she was flushing the toilet, she heard the phone ring. The answering machine picked up, but she couldn't hear who it was. She hurried into the kitchen and played the message: "Hi. We're back to civilization. If you can call the IHOP civilization. Be back by suppertime, maybe sooner. I miss you." His voice sounded surprisingly normal. Almost like his old self.

Her Daily Planner was lying open on the kitchen counter next to the answering machine. Feeling a removed sense of curiosity, she flipped through the past few days to see what she had missed, back in her old life, which already seemed like some vivid dream in fast-forward: rushing here, rushing there. She saw that she had missed, completely forgotten about, the first meeting of her women's investment group, which Heidi, a fellow soccer mom, had asked her to join. Giselle had hesitated at first, thinking she was too busy and too ignorant about stocks — didn't know Dow Jones from Dow oven cleaner — but then realized that was the point, wasn't it? Heidi worked in a bank but assured Giselle that the other five women had no background in finance. They were just going to read, study, consult with some so-called experts, and start up investment portfolios. When Giselle had told Dan about the women's group, he said it sounded like a great idea. He was even vaguer about money matters than she was. When they got married, he had handed over all that to her. "You'll be great at it," he'd said when she sounded doubtful about the group. "God knows, I'm never going to make us rich, so I guess it's up to you." And suddenly she had been full of resolve. At the grocery store that afternoon she had spotted a *Money* magazine sandwiched in a rack between *Family Circle* and *Bon Appétit* and tossed it into the cart. She realized that money was another area, like childbirth, where she could be the expert. You didn't need to know Shakespeare to make a killing on the stock market. In fact, it was probably a liability. She had read the magazine cover to cover and taken copious notes. She had always been a straight-A student. Only instead of making a 4.0, she would make piles of money. Enough for a new car — make that two new cars, her tuition, and a trip to Europe.

According to the Daily Planner, she had also missed an appointment with a financial aid officer at UCLA. The thick catalog of courses, bigger than the Lincoln phone book, was sitting on the kitchen table along with her letter of acceptance. Dan had not been all that keen on her transferring, concerned about the longer commute and more complicated day care routine. But she had insisted, arguing that it would help her get into a decent law school. And once she was admitted for the fall, Dan had seemed to accept it with good grace. Giselle had even overheard him telling his mother that it wouldn't be the end of the world; they would manage just fine. "Don't worry about it," he had said into the phone. "You know Giselle. The efficiency experts could learn something from her." The remark had surprised her. She had never thought of herself as particularly efficient. Or known that others thought of her that way. Mostly she just felt overwhelmed. Spread too thin. Not that it mattered now. That Giselle was gone for good. And in her place was this paralyzed slug who couldn't even muster the motivation to take out the smelly garbage. Or wash the dishes.

She flipped the Daily Planner shut and replayed Dan's message, feeling more hopeful than she had been feeling about the prospect of his return, but this time his upbeat voice struck her as manic. As if he were being held hostage and forced to read a message to prove that he was still alive. She wished he had left a longer message. Still, the main thing was, he was coming back. She could tell by the relief she felt that part of her had been afraid he would just take off, disappear, like Wakefield, a character in a Hawthorne story they had just read in her American lit course, who — for no apparent reason — decides to hide from his wife for a few days, which turn into twenty years. And it's not as if Dan didn't have a good reason to want to disappear.

For the first time in the three days since he'd been gone, she washed all the dishes in the sink and threw out the trash. The trash cans were in the side yard next to the Beemers' house. As she dumped the plastic bag in the can, she heard loud music, Marvin Gaye, and knew that Lois was at it again, working out to keep her husband from playing around. Giselle hurried back inside and stood in the laundry room, a tiny utility nook off the kitchen, staring at the overflowing basket of dirty clothes. She knew that Trina's clothes were mixed in with the others: little sunsuits and dresses and nighties she had worn just a few days ago. It wasn't so much washing them that Giselle dreaded. She could just dump the whole basket into the washer, set the dial, and walk away. It was what to do with them once they came out of the dryer, warm and fragrant. She would fold them — and then what? Put them back in her drawer? Donate them to the Salvation Army? What if someday she saw a little girl at the playground or grocery store dressed in Trina's clothes? When Dan's father died, Dan had tried to persuade Luisa to let the doctor take out his pacemaker and send it to some Third World country where people who needed pacemakers

couldn't afford them. He had read about the program in the newspaper. But his mother had balked. Dan, who carried an organ
donor card in his wallet, thought her refusal was irrational. But
Giselle had stuck up for Luisa. She had understood her mother-in-
law's resistance.

It occurred to her that maybe the ancient Egyptians had the
right idea, burying everything alongside the body. But not so
much to preserve it as to get it out of sight. Out of sight, out of
mind.

After dumping the clothes in the washing machine, she went
and stood in the doorway to Trina's room. She felt a sharp surge of
energy and could see herself stripping the room bare and boxing
up everything. The only problem would be disassembling the
crib. She even fantasized about slapping a coat of blue paint over
the pink and lavender, restoring the room to its original state, leaving not a trace of evidence that it had ever been a little girl's room.
The fresh paint would overpower the scent of baby powder and
wet diapers. But Giselle was afraid of Dan's reaction. Once when
she had, on the spur of the moment, rearranged their bedroom
furniture, Dan had objected to her making what he referred to as
"a unilateral decision." She had been surprised that he cared; Ed
had never noticed when she made decorative changes around the
house. She used to have to point them out to him and ask him what
he thought, and he would invariably say they were fine with him.
Sometimes, although she appreciated Dan's more refined aesthetic
sensibility, she missed the autonomy. But she knew that clearing
out Trina's room went far beyond interior decoration. It had to do
with rearranging their internal furniture, reupholstering their
minds and hearts, remodeling their vital organs. She shut the door,
took a set of fresh sheets from the linen closet, and stripped the old
sheets off their king-size bed. Dan always liked crisp, clean sheets.
He said they reminded him of being a child, safe and coddled.
When he was growing up, they had a housekeeper who used to
wash and iron the sheets every other day.

As she was changing the sheets, it occurred to her that things might go more smoothly if Teddy weren't there when Dan first got home. They could have a couple of hours alone together, to get off on the right foot, just the two of them, before having to complicate the equation. The past few days she had felt as if they were all in suspended animation. When she thought of Dan's return, she yo-yoed between cautious optimism and despair. In more hopeful moments she imagined Dan's anger smoldering itself out, reduced to ash along with the campfire, leaving only a pure, unadulterated grief. The grief, she thought, they could handle. They could share. It was the other stuff that would tear them apart. And in her hopeless moments, she imagined Dan raging through the house like a wounded, enraged bear, swatting her aside as he lumbered down the hall to Teddy's room.

She glanced at her watch. She hated to ask Ellen for another favor, but Ellen had told her not to hesitate. *What are friends for?* she had said. *People want to help.* Giselle picked up the phone and dialed Ellen's number. She knew that if their positions were reversed, and something had happened to Zack, Giselle would be eager to help out. Still, she hated having to take advantage of people's sympathy. Their pity. Their relief that it had not, in fact, happened to them. Ellen answered right away and said that it would be no problem to keep Teddy through suppertime. "Are you sure?" Giselle asked. "Really?" When she hung up, she felt almost light-headed with relief. Then she felt bad when it hit her just how relieved she was to get Teddy out of the way. After all, he was part of the family. She couldn't keep Dan and Teddy apart forever. *But just for a couple of hours,* she told herself. *What's wrong with that?* Discretion was the better part of valor. It couldn't hurt to have a little time alone together. She headed for the shower. For the first time in days she was going to wash her hair. Afterward, maybe she would even venture to the market for some steaks and a bottle of wine.

At five o'clock she was watering the plants — the spindly brown-edged ferns and anemic spider plants — when she heard Dan's car pull into the garage. Her hand shook; she splashed water onto the top of the bookcase and quickly blotted it with the hem of her dress. She tried to strike a normal pose, but she didn't know what felt normal under the circumstances.

Dan called out her name as he walked through the kitchen into the living room. He was still wearing his dark glasses. When he saw her, he took them off and set them on the coffee table. She set the watering can down beside them. He held his arms open. He hadn't shaved in days; his face scratched against her cheek as they kissed.

"I should take a shower," he said. "I stink. The drive back was long and hot." He raised his arms above his head and stretched his back. "I thought we'd never get here."

"You want some iced tea?" she asked politely, as if he were a guest.

"Okay." He followed her into the kitchen. She took the pitcher out of the refrigerator and poured him a glass. She had thrown out the last of the Juicy Juice boxes that morning even though Teddy would have drunk them.

"Thanks." He took a long sip. "Where's Teddy?"

"At Ellen's." She shut the refrigerator door, then opened it again and grabbed a Dos Equis she'd bought at the store earlier in the day. "He'll be back after supper." She watched him carefully, looking for signs of relief or disappointment, but his expression remained neutral.

"How's he been?"

She shrugged.

"I did a lot of thinking," he said. "Up there."

She didn't say anything. He reached out and placed his palm flat against her chest. "Breathe!" he commanded. "You're not breathing." Obediently, as if he were a doctor, she took a deep breath. "That's better." He took his hand away and scratched at his stubble.

"Are you growing your beard again?" she asked. He'd had a beard as long as she'd known him, then suddenly shaved it off one weekend a couple of months ago. She was shocked when he emerged from the bathroom; she had wanted to protest this unilateral decision but could tell that he was feeling self-conscious and vulnerable, so she had assured him it looked good, even though the skin underneath looked like overcooked pasta. Less of a diplomat, Trina had cried when she climbed onto his lap and touched his bare chin. She liked to nestle her fingers in his beard.

"Do you think I should?" He scratched at the stubble underneath his chin. "It itches like hell."

"I always liked the beard." She had missed its softness against her cheek. She turned away and looked out the window as two kids she didn't recognize rode by on their bikes.

The phone rang. She willed him not to answer it, and he didn't. Which she took as a good sign. A hopeful sign. Usually he couldn't resist answering. There was Dan's taped, well-modulated voice telling the caller to please leave a message, and then Ed's voice boomed into the room, too loud as usual. "Hey, Ted-head, it's your dad." Long pause, as if to give Teddy time to pick up the phone. "Guess you're not there. Just checking in. Bye."

Dan was frowning. She sighed and bit her lip, irritated with Ed's bad timing.

"Has he been calling a lot?" Dan asked.

"A couple of times." She poured the beer into a glass.

"I thought about you a lot," he said, startling her as he pulled her toward him. "I know I was an asshole to take off like I did, but —"

She put her hand over his moving lips. "Don't say that." She felt limp with relief. She hadn't realized until this moment just how afraid she'd been that he was going to announce that he was leaving. And they'd both pretend it was "just for a little while," even though they'd know better.

"I know I let you down. You and Teddy." He paused and looked at her. "I thought you might be really angry."

She shook her head. It had never even occurred to her that he might be worried about what she was thinking. What right did she have to be angry?

"But I have to say," he sighed, "that having some time to think and talk with my brother helped. I'm not saying I'm entirely okay with it." She knew that *it* referred to Teddy. "But I think I've got a little better perspective on things."

She nodded and gave him a hug. "We need you so much," she said, "Teddy and I. I know how —" Her throat clamped shut. *Don't cry,* she told herself, *don't cry.* She understood that he was making an effort to be strong. She owed it to him to be strong, too. "You want some more iced tea?"

"No, thanks." He clapped his hands together, suddenly businesslike. "I should unpack the car," he said. "There's stuff in the cooler."

"I'll help," she offered, starting to follow him into the garage. Then the phone rang again. She was about to ignore it when she heard Ellen's voice. She could hear crying, Zack's jagged wails, in the background. "There's been a little trouble here." Ellen spoke fast and nervously. "I was thinking I'd bring Teddy back now, but I guess you're not home, so —"

Giselle picked up the receiver.

She was furious with Teddy on the drive over to Ellen's to pick him up, and even more furious with him on the way home as he slumped silently in the passenger seat, refusing to speak. Everything had seemed to be going okay, better than she had hoped for, and now this. She had seen the way Dan's face seemed to shut down when she told him she had to go get Teddy. It seemed that he'd whacked Zack in the stomach with a croquet mallet for no reason.

When she arrived at the Walshes' house, Teddy was sitting alone on the curb. The front door was open, and Ellen was keeping an eye on him — she assured Giselle that she hadn't told him to go outside, that he'd simply refused to come back inside the house. Zack was still sniffling. When he caught sight of Giselle, he burst into fresh outrage, clutching his stomach and moaning, "It hurts! It hurts!" Ellen patted his head, trying to soothe and shush him. Giselle apologized profusely and ordered Teddy into the car.

"Why did you do it?" she kept asking him. "What got into you?" But he maintained a stony silence, picking at a scab on his knee until it started to bleed.

"Leave that scab alone!" she snapped at him and then sighed. In a more civil tone of voice she asked, "Did Zack do something that made you mad?"

Teddy stopped picking at the scab but ignored her question.

The therapist had warned Giselle that Teddy might start acting out. And to try to view such behavior as a cry for help. But Giselle was too upset for psychology. It was easy when you were being paid a zillion dollars an hour and it wasn't your kid.

She could see what sort of an evening the three of them had ahead of them. Teddy sulking in his room, tension seeping out from under his door like napalm, spreading through the house. Not exactly the reunion she had hoped for. She tried not to think it, but she couldn't help it: how much easier it would be if Teddy were the one who was gone. Or maybe not, she realized as soon as the forbidden thought skulked its way into her mind. Most likely she would resent Dan for not feeling the loss she was feeling; she would hold it against him that in his heart of hearts he was relieved that it was Teddy and not Trina. It seemed that no matter what, they would not be in the same boat. No matter what, they were up shit creek without a paddle.

When they pulled into the driveway, Giselle said, "Dan's back." She felt Teddy tense up. "Look —" She turned to him. He looked away. She took hold of his chin and tilted his face toward hers, pleading with her eyes. "We all have to make a special effort. We all have to try our best. Can I count on you?"

He started to cry, shaking his head no and then yes. She plucked a tissue from the box underneath the dashboard and dabbed at the tears, then tugged his skinny braid. "I love you," she said. "Dan loves you."

Teddy blew his nose in the Kleenex and tossed it on the floor instead of into the trash box.

"Pick that up," she snapped.

He picked it up almost cheerfully and placed it in the trash, then unbuckled his seat belt and opened his door.

"Where's your backpack?" she asked, checking the backseat.

"I don't know," he mumbled. "I guess I left it in the Walshes' car."

"Great."

"I didn't mean to," he protested, slamming the car door.

"I know that. I didn't say you did, did I?"

Dan was standing in the doorway, holding the screen door open for them. "Look who's here!" He had a welcoming smile pasted on his face. She could see that he was making an effort. He tried to give Teddy a high five. Teddy slapped his palm against Dan's cautiously, as if testing a stove burner. "I saw this big snake up there. Humongous." Dan held his hands about a yard apart. "I wasn't sure what type it was. I thought maybe we could look it up in one of your reptile books."

"Okay." Teddy brushed past him into the kitchen. Dan looked over at her still standing on the garage steps, as if to make sure she saw that he was trying.

Teddy marched over and pushed the blinking button on the answering machine. "Hey, Ted-head, it's your dad." Dan walked abruptly into the other room. Teddy smiled to himself as he listened to the message. Giselle shut her eyes and counted to ten. If she'd had a croquet mallet handy, she would have smashed the machine to bits. She only hoped she'd have enough self-restraint to stop there.

Teddy grabbed the phone off the counter and started to carry it out to the back stoop.

"Don't call him now," Giselle said. She grabbed hold of the cord so he couldn't take another step.

"Why not?"

"Because I said so."

He slammed the phone down on the counter, ran back to his room, and slammed that door. She heard the shower running in the bathroom. The wall clock said 6:15. She couldn't imagine how they were going to make it through the evening. She wished she could run next door and bum a Valium from Lois, but those days of easy neighborliness — along with everything else — were gone for good. Maybe she should run out and rent a video, something they could all watch. And make some popcorn. She was still sitting at the kitchen table attempting to summon up the energy to drive to Blockbuster or the grocery store, which was closer and sometimes had a decent selection, when Dan walked out with his wet hair slicked back, dressed in fresh khakis and a coffee-colored T-shirt that matched his eyes. He had shaved off the stubble.

"I'm going to school to check my mail," he told her. She nodded, understanding his desire to get out of the house even though he had just returned. "I might stop by Harvey's on my way back. If you don't mind."

Of course she minded, but what could she say? *I think you should stay here so we can all spend a miserable evening together.* She shook her head and tried to look and sound pleasant. "Say hello to Harvey for me. Thank him again for the flowers."

"I'll only be an hour or two," he said, stooping to give her a peck on the cheek. He reeked of shaving lotion. Up close she could see a couple of little cuts that hadn't quite stopped bleeding.

As soon as he was gone, she grabbed another beer from the fridge — the last one — and headed for their bedroom. There was dead silence as she passed Teddy's room. She supposed that she should attempt to smooth things over, soothe his ruffled feathers, but she didn't know how long Dan would be gone. Maybe he would have second thoughts and turn the car around. His blue backpack was slumped in the corner by the closet. A dingy mound of dirty underwear was on the floor near the hamper. She knelt down and reached into the backpack, feeling around for the hard edges of the blank book he used as a journal. He always bought the same kind — black with thin-ruled pages about the size of the missal she had received for her First Communion. There were a couple of paperbacks but no journal. Curious as to what he would have felt like reading, she pulled them out. A well-worn, yellowed copy of *Siddhartha* by Herman Hesse and a heavily underlined copy of Thoreau's *Walden*. She had never read anything by Hesse. Her senior year of high school they had read *Walden*, but she never actually made it through the whole book; she had just skimmed it for the final exam. When she complained to Ed, who was in the same class, about how boring it was, he had surprised her by saying that he actually kind of liked it. Ed wasn't much of a reader. She would have thought he was just saying it to impress her, but she knew he wasn't the type. Even without reading the book, she had aced the exam while Ed ended up with a B–. Instead of feeling guilty, she had just felt superior.

She opened the large front flap and there it was. Surprised that she'd actually found it, she sat down on the edge of the bed and started to flip through it. Her hands trembled; she sloshed some beer onto the sheets. His handwriting was even more illegible than usual. She grabbed a pair of his jockey shorts from the floor and blotted the spilled beer. She was afraid, but she had to know. Desperate times required desperate measures. She flipped to the last entry, about two-thirds of the way through the book. It took her an instant to register that it was in Spanish. She flipped back a few pages. The rest of the journal was in English. Right up to the April 24 entry, the last entry before Trina's death. She could make out a word or phrase here and there, but her one semester of Spanish wasn't up to the task of translation even under less fraught circumstances. Besides, the shock of it was too much for her. The fact that he had deliberately switched to another language, a language he knew she didn't know, seemed to confirm her worst fears. It was as if she had found a one-way ticket to South America.

Down the hall she heard Teddy flush the toilet. She put the journal back where she'd found it and looked at her watch. The poor kid hadn't even had any supper, not that he had much appetite. He picked at whatever she set in front of him as if he suspected she was trying to poison him. "Hey!" she called out to him as soon as the bathroom door opened. He ignored her. She reached out and grabbed his T-shirt just as he was about to slip back into his room. It was a hideous tie-dyed lime green and purple Goosebumps shirt with a grotesque tarantula on the front. Compliments of Uncle Todd, who actually had a matching one, although on him it looked as if it had shrunk a size or two. "How about McDonald's?" she asked. His favorite. She couldn't just let him starve.

"Okay." He shrugged but seemed to perk up.

Then she remembered that she didn't have any cash. She had been meaning to get to the bank for days. The simplest errands seemed like arduous missions. "Hey, I just remembered. I don't have any money. You think I could borrow five dollars?"

He sighed and rolled his eyes but seemed pleased to help as he ran off to get his stash. "I'll be warming up the car," she called after him. She hoped that Dan wouldn't come back while they were out. She thought about leaving him a note, but the thought of composing it seemed like too much work. Trying to strike the right tone. Cool, wounded, apologetic, conciliatory, matter-of-fact. She took a final swig of her beer and tossed the bottle into the trash. To hell with recycling. To hell with the environment.

She must have fallen asleep. It was after midnight when she finally heard someone at the front door. She was lying on the couch, a book open on her chest like a prop. Since the accident she had been unable to make her way through a single page without her mind wandering off. She hadn't heard the car, and she wondered why Dan would be using the front door. For a moment she was afraid that it was someone breaking in. She leaped up and looked out the window. She could see Harvey sitting at the curb in his vintage Volvo, watching as Dan fumbled with the lock. When she opened the door, he practically fell inside. Harvey pulled smoothly away from the curb.

"Sorry." Dan looked sheepish. "We had a few drinks. Didn't realize how late it was."

His voice sounded warped. He looked green around the gills. She had never seen him drunk before. He preferred smoking pot. And even thoroughly stoned, he was always perfectly articulate. In an abstract, elliptical way she sometimes found annoying. But never pathetic.

"I don't feel so good," he mumbled. "Couple aspirin." He veered off in the general direction of the bathroom.

"Shit," she muttered to herself. A minute later she heard him cursing at the childproof cap and then the pitter-patter of pills spilling all over the tile floor. When she walked to the doorway, he was on his hands and knees scooping them clumsily, like a kid in a sandbox. His helplessness touched her. She knelt down beside him. "I'll do it," she told him. "Go lie down."

He didn't protest. He patted her on the head in what she took to be a gesture of wordless gratitude and lurched toward the bedroom. When she arrived with a glass of water and two aspirin, he was already passed out cold. She set the glass and pills on the table beside him, pulled off his shoes, loosened his belt, and turned off the harsh overhead light. The lights in the hall and bathroom she left on in case he suddenly woke up nauseous. She figured he would sleep better alone. He was something of an insomniac even under normal circumstances. When they first started sleeping together, it used to bother her when she would wake up occasionally in the middle of the night and find him watching her sleep or reading a book in the other room. She thought all men were like Ed, who conked out the instant his head hit the pillow and slept like a log until the alarm rang.

It was a nice night and she suddenly felt like taking a walk, getting out of the house. In Lincoln she wouldn't have thought twice about it, but here it wasn't safe. A teenage girl had been raped walking home from a baby-sitting job just half a block from her parents' house.

Giselle took some sheets and a pillow from the linen closet and made up a bed for herself on the sofa. A bag of Teddy's half-eaten french fries was wilting on the coffee table. She nibbled a couple of cold fries as she gathered up the paper sack and paper cups and tossed them in the kitchen trash. At the last minute they had decided on the drive-through window instead of going inside. They both seemed to shrink from crowds these days. As if everyone were looking at them, whispering behind their backs. And to add insult to injury, everywhere they went, the world seemed populated by little girls Trina's age, smiling and crying and full of life. She turned out the lights in the kitchen and living room.

In the bathroom she heard a stray aspirin crunch underfoot as she brushed her teeth and washed her face. She hadn't bothered to floss since the accident. She could see the reproachful look in her dental hygienist's eyes. Fuck her. She would gladly lose all her teeth to have her daughter back for one hour. Just one more hour to cuddle her and tell her how much Mama loves her. How if anything ever happened to her, she doesn't know what she'd do.

In the middle of the night Teddy woke up, shouting and trembling. She held him close until he quieted down, rocking him like an infant. She asked him what the nightmare was about. He said he couldn't remember, but she knew he was lying. Dan slept through all the commotion. As she turned off the light in Teddy's room, he said, "Mom?"

She paused in the doorway but kept the light off, sensing the confessional hush of the darkness between them. "Yes," she said softly.

"Zack said when I grow up, I'm going to prison. He said the police are just waiting for me to finish school first." His voice quivered. "Is that true?"

"Oh, honey," she sighed. "No. The police know it was an accident. I explained all that, remember? They know you didn't mean to do it. The police are never going to bother you again."

"Even when I'm not a kid anymore?"

"Never," she said firmly.

"Are you sure?"

"Positive." She walked over and picked up his Walkman off his bureau. "How about some waves?" she asked.

"Okay."

She rewound the tape and settled the headset over his ears. As she bent over to kiss him good night, she could hear the surf lapping against the shore, faint and far away.

In the morning Dan was sheepishly hungover. As if to make amends, he surprised her by suggesting that Teddy stay home from school. "It's a beautiful day," he said, squinting valiantly out the sunny window. "Let's drive to the beach." He even insisted on running out for Danishes. Without being told, he brought Teddy his favorite: a maple-iced long john. Teddy said thank you, but only picked at it. He seemed quiet and pale. When she pressed her hand to his forehead, he jerked away, saying that he felt fine. Across the kitchen table she sent him a telepathic message, pleading with him not to throw cold water on Dan's heroic and fragile enthusiasm.

They changed into their bathing suits and drove to Santa Monica. The beach was crowded but not mobbed; it was a mild day, not particularly hot. They lucked out and found a parking spot a block away. *This is how life works,* she thought. *You lose a child, you find a great parking space.* She kept this observation to herself. As they trudged across the sand to the water, Giselle kept feeling that she was forgetting something; she was used to carrying the heavy diaper bag loaded with diapers, juice, crackers, toys. The two of them sat on the sand for a couple of hours while Teddy sloshed around in the surf. The water was too cold to actually go swimming. Dan told her that he was planning to get back to his book project — a critical study of the confessional novel that he had more or less abandoned after Trina's birth, claiming that he had no time. He thought, if he really focused, he could finish the Fitzgerald and Conrad chapters by the end of summer. Talking about the book, he sounded energetic, confident, almost like his old self. Giselle took this as another good sign. When Teddy finally emerged from the water, blue-lipped and shivering, they bought hot pretzels on the pier. Then Dan helped Teddy build an elaborate sand castle. Normally they would have argued over who was chief architect. It broke her heart to see them being so polite and accommodating. For supper they stopped off at Taco Bell on the way home and picked up a video. No one argued over what to rent. They were all on their best behavior. They were all pretending to be enjoying themselves. She thought maybe if they pretended long enough, they might start believing it. When they got home, she made popcorn. Then they discovered that the girl had given them the wrong video. Instead of *Iron Will,* she'd given them some kung fu movie with subtitles, made in Hong Kong. They watched it anyway. Afterward Teddy was so wound up, he kept leaping around, faking kung fu moves, just like any nine-year-old boy. And when Teddy crashed into the coffee table, Dan yelled at him to knock it off. "Watch what you're doing!" Just like any irritated father. *So this is how normal life resumes,* she thought hopefully, as she picked at the tiny kernels left in the popcorn bowl.

TWO

A T THE MALL HE EATS A SLICE OF PIZZA AT THE *food court while his mom drinks a coffee Julius. She barely eats anymore. But unlike Eric's mother, she doesn't stand on the scales twice a day, frowning at the black lines. She doesn't seem to care. When Dan asked her how much weight she'd lost, she shrugged and said she didn't know. For the past couple of weeks they have been looking for a new house to rent. Every morning she reads the classified ads, circles one or two, and makes phone calls to the landlords or rental agencies. So far, nothing decent has turned up. He has heard her complaining on the phone to his dad and his aunt Vonnie back in the Midwest about the rents in southern California. She doesn't complain to Dan, because he doesn't care whether they move or not. He has agreed to move if she finds a nice place, but he said it would only depress him more to drive around looking at tacky houses in iffy neighborhoods and make him more resentful of how underpaid he is, "of how little society values education."*

Teddy doesn't think that a new house is going to be as big a deal as his mom thinks it is. She seems to think everything will be just like it used to be once they move. It's all she can talk about. And even though he's just a kid, he knows that's impossible. Everyone is really trying, but it's as if they're all trying too hard, like they're all laughing too hard at a joke that isn't really funny. He's worried his mom will die of disappointment if they finally move to a new house and they're all just their same old selves. Sometimes he can't believe it hasn't even been a month since the accident. It seems like something that happened years and years ago, when he was just a little kid.

This morning Teddy and his mom looked at two places. One was too small, even though they only need two bedrooms now, and the other was too run-down. It had stained gold carpeting and reeked of cat pee. After they got back in the car, his mother rested her forehead against the steering wheel and moaned as if she were in pain. He thought maybe she was going to cry, so he said, "I'm hungry. It's past lunchtime," hoping his whining would distract her from crying. He'd rather have her mad than sad.

"What do you feel like?" she asked him.

"Pizza." They were only a block from the mall and Sbarro's, which has the best pizza. His mother used to love pizza. He thought maybe if they went there, she would eat something for a change. But she just nibbles on his leftover crust as she drinks her coffee Julius, looking sad and preoccupied.

"Can I go to the toy store?" he asks.

"I'll go with you," she says. She drives him crazy these days, always worrying that something's going to happen to him. He'll get hit by a car or kidnapped or fall off his bike and get brain damaged. She gets nervous when he's out of her sight. Or maybe she's just afraid he's going to do something really stupid again, like shoot someone. When he saw his sister's room all emptied out, he wished he were dead. Every time he walks by it, he feels sick. Last week he saw this documentary on the Discovery Channel about India. It showed how when people died, their bodies were laid out on rafts and set on fire and floated down the river. In the old days wives used to throw themselves on top of their husbands' burning bodies. Teddy wasn't sure if the wives wanted to or they had to, but it didn't happen anymore. Nowadays they weren't allowed to. He could see how maybe they'd wanted to. But he didn't think he'd be brave enough to throw himself on top of the flames like that. It seemed like a pretty awesome thing to do.

His mother walks off without bothering to clean up their trash. He dumps their stuff into the bin and sets his plastic tray on top, then runs to catch up with her. He would rather go look at toys alone — he has his own money in his pocket — but he's afraid she'll cry if he says so. She cries at the drop of a hat these days when Dan's not around. She doesn't cry in front of him. But he's mostly at his office, working on his book, until late at night. He says the only time he feels energetic is when he's sitting at his computer. At home he mostly paces around or watches old movies late at night on the classic station.

They take the escalator down two floors. It's the weekend and the mall is crowded. His mother tries to take his hand, but he shoves his hands in his jeans pockets. He spots the toy store at the end, next to Sears. It's not his favorite toy store, but it's the only one in the mall. And mostly he's just trying to kill time so they don't have to go home. He hates the weekends. He'd rather be at school. He misses playing with Eric. A couple of times they have messed around outside together, but they haven't gone inside each other's houses, which they know, without even asking, are off-limits. Suddenly his mother stops dead and he bumps into her. She lets out a little cry and puts her hand to her mouth. There are maybe a dozen framed color portraits hanging on display at the Sears photo studio. She is staring at Trina in her red velvet dress, who is not just smiling but laughing. Thanks to him. Teddy remembers standing behind the photographer making funny faces, pretending to strangle himself with his dorky bow tie. When you look at the picture, you can practically hear her laugh.

"Wait here," his mother snaps at him. "Don't move." Then she marches into the photo studio. He knows she is going to yank the picture off the wall, shout at the photographer, make a big scene, cry. He doesn't want to see it. While her back is to him, he darts next door to Toy Town.

The store aisles are clogged with kids and their parents. Babies in strollers crying. Kids whining for toys. Parents arguing. "It costs too much." "You don't even play with the one you have." "It's too old for you. Maybe next year."

He manages to weave his way down the aisle past the Star Wars stuff and the kid computers to some cheaper electronic toys. He thinks maybe he'll buy a Quiz Master. Chandra has one at school. It asks you questions, and you answer them. He knows he doesn't have much time. He keeps glancing toward the door, expecting to hear his mother's voice yelling for him. Instead of the Quiz Master he picks up something called a Talkboy Jr. The package says you can record messages and play them back. You can make your voice sound fast or slow, and there are special effects, too. He tries out the buttons and hears a couple of satisfyingly loud screechy wailing and bonking sounds. It seems like something his uncle Todd would like. There's also another brand called a Yak Bak that's supposed to play what you say backward. The instructions on the package tell you that if you record "muss ha," it will play back as "awesome." Teddy tries it, but the sound comes out all muddy. Unimpressive. He glances toward the door and sees his mother. The clerk is busy ringing up stuff at the cash register. Teddy grabs the Talkboy Jr. and slips it under his T-shirt, tucking it into the waistband of his jeans. The package is pretty small and his T-shirt is big, like most of the clothes his grandparents in Nebraska send him. His mother says kids are bigger in Nebraska and they turn into fat adults; he should be glad he's skinny.

His heart beats fast as he walks through the crowded aisle to the front of the store, where his mother is standing. He expects her to yell at him, but she just says, "Thank God," and pulls him out of the store behind her. As they walk past the portrait studio, he notices that there is another picture hanging in the space where Trina's was. Twin blond girls dressed in identical blue sailor dresses holding each other's hands, smiling fake smiles. They look exactly alike except that one has a tooth missing on the top and the other has a tooth missing on the bottom. He wonders if that's how their parents tell them apart. He slides his hand under his shirt as if he's scratching an itch on his belly and fingers the plastic molded package the Talkboy Jr. comes in. He *has never stolen anything before. He feels excited, like running and jumping. By mistake he presses one of the special effects buttons. A siren blasts. His mother looks around in alarm. "What's that?" she asks. "Did you hear that?" He shakes his head and tries to look innocent.*

THEY RETURNED FROM THE THERAPIST'S OFFICE in a good mood. Dan had been back almost a month, and things, they said, all things considered, were going as well as could be expected. There was a lot of cautious, qualified language, but that was only natural, under the circumstances, wasn't it? On the ride home they made fun of Hannah's therapist tricks. The way she always turned everything you said into a question.

"Is anybody hungry?" Dan asked.

"Are you saying that you're hungry?" Teddy asked.

"Are you asking me whether I'm saying that I'm hungry?" Dan turned to Giselle. "And what about you? Are you hungry?"

"I had a dream I was hungry," she said.

Teddy snorted and laughed.

"I dreamed I was eating blue hamburgers," she said as Dan turned into the Burger King parking lot.

"That's what I want!" Teddy shouted. "A blue hamburger with green french fries."

"Ah!" Dan exclaimed. "The Dr. Seuss Special!"

Teddy and Giselle groaned. And then a pall fell over the car as they sat waiting at the drive-through window, thinking about how Trina had loved *Green Eggs and Ham*. About how, after *Koko's*

Kitten, it had been her favorite book. When they pulled into their driveway, Teddy burst from the car and ran inside to his room. He spent most of his time closeted in his room with his computer. Dan looked at his watch as he turned off the engine. "I'm going to play racquetball with Harvey. Then I think I'll stop by my mother's for a while. Is that okay?"

"Sure. Whatever." She followed him into the house, carrying Teddy's half-eaten kid's meal. She put it in the refrigerator for later.

"Do we have any clean towels?" Dan asked.

"In the dryer," she said.

He walked into the utility room and fished out a couple of faded blue towels, leaving the rest of the load for her to deal with. One of Trina's tiny pink socks was clinging to the towel. It fell onto the floor. They both looked at it lying there. Dan picked it up and held it to his nose, inhaling as if it were a wilted rose petal. His shoulders started to shudder, and she knew it was just a matter of seconds before he would be sobbing convulsively. It didn't take much to set him off.

She grabbed a couple of shopping bags stuck between the refrigerator and the wall. He was blocking the doorway. She shoved past him and strode down the hall to Trina's room. The door was shut. She flung it open and slammed it behind her. Then she yanked open each bureau drawer and stuffed Trina's clothes into the shopping bags as fast as she could, without stopping to think. That was the key — not thinking. As she was moving on to the toy chest, Dan opened the door.

"What do you think you're doing?" he shouted.

She ignored him, dumping a pink plastic telephone and some stuffed animals into the larger of the two bags. Trying not to think of Trina on the toy phone: *Hi, Mommy, Mookie talk,* shoving the receiver into Mookie's face, making monkey chatter.

He stepped into the room and grabbed hold of her wrist.

"Let go!" she snapped, struggling to shake him off. "I'm putting her things away. We can't live like this."

He let go of her so abruptly, she lost her balance and stumbled into the crib. The bright mobile hanging overhead tinkled and chimed.

"I'll do it," he said. "Just leave it. Let me take care of it. Please."

"When?"

"Tomorrow. Tomorrow morning." He glared at her. "Do you think you can wait that long?"

She glared back, then hung her head, feeling the tears threatening to spill. It wasn't her fault. They really couldn't live like this. No one could. There should be a rule that no child was allowed to die before his or her parents. Everyone died in chronological order, according to his or her age. No exceptions.

He reached up, unhooked the mobile, and gently set it down on the crib mattress. "I just want it to be done right."

He was as good as his word. The next morning before she even woke up, he had everything all packed away in brand-new boxes he had picked up at some packing store. Each box was neatly labeled: TOYS, STUFFED ANIMALS, CLOTHING, BOOKS. Giselle remembered how when they had moved in to this house, all his books had been precisely cataloged while hers were thrown together haphazardly. In the early-morning sunlight the walls glowed a rosy pink like the inside of a conch shell. He was sitting on the floor with a screwdriver in hand, disassembling the white crib. The crib was brand-new. They had bought it together at Baby World. She had been glad that all Teddy's baby stuff was back in Nebraska, stored in Ed's grandparents' attic. She had wanted to start fresh. No hand-me-downs. She remembered how cheerfully Dan had gone about the task of assembling the crib even though normally he hated that sort of thing. He had no mechanical aptitude and would curse at the instructions. It had taken him hours to assemble Teddy's computer desk, and the desk still wobbled whenever you bumped against it. Ed would have put it together lickety-split, and the thing would have been rock solid. But the night they had brought the crib home in its big box, it was as if Dan's hands were graced, as if some carpenter's spirit had entered his body. He had hummed to himself as the pieces snapped together. But now he was muttering to himself, cursing at a recalcitrant screw. His back was to her, for which she was grateful. She didn't want to see the expression on his face.

He barely spoke to her for the rest of the night. *Well, so be it,* she told herself. No pain, no gain. The first step was putting away Trina's things. The second step was finding a new place to live. She wasn't a fool. She knew that it would take more than a new house to create a new life, but she also knew, sure as shooting, they couldn't do it in this house. In the middle of the night she got up and stood in the empty room for a long time. Such a long time that the birds started to chirp and the light filtered through the blinds. Even without a stick of furniture, the room was full. The only emptiness was inside of her.

She knew that Dan felt it, too — the emptiness — but they seemed to fill it in such different ways. She didn't want to go anywhere or talk to anyone, whereas Dan couldn't sit still and couldn't keep quiet, at least to others. He didn't have much to say around the house, to his wife or stepson, but he seemed to have plenty to say to total strangers. She had seen the handful of letters in his briefcase — yes, she was snooping again. Letters from mothers or fathers in Texas or Massachusetts or Oregon who had also lost a child. Giselle wasn't sure if he had contacted them first or they had contacted him, but the letters were all the same. Giselle couldn't understand how Dan, who had always sneered at sentimentality, could be so open to all this communal gush. The sappy little poems and photos. She couldn't believe he actually felt a bond, a rapport, with these people. Always before, he had been the elitist, gently criticizing her more populist enthusiasms. But over the past few weeks it was as if he had been brainwashed by Hallmark. And she had seen the books, too. A growing library. *When Good-Bye Is Forever: Learning to Live Again After the Loss of a Child. The Mourning Handbook. Beyond Endurance: When a Child Dies.*

Jonathan: You Left Too Soon. What did he possibly hope to learn from reading these books? It seemed that he felt close to everyone, coast to coast, except for the two people living in the same house with him.

Last Saturday they'd had a fight about it. Dan had dropped Teddy off at soccer practice as usual and told him he'd be back to pick him up at noon. But he forgot. The phone had rung and it was Teddy, holding back the tears, saying that he was waiting for Dan. One of the other fathers had offered to give him a ride home, but he was afraid that Dan would show up late, wondering where Teddy was, and be mad at him for going off with someone else. Giselle stormed into the bedroom, where Dan was busy answering one of his pitiful letters. "I'm going to pick up Teddy," she'd announced grimly.

A stricken look crossed his face and he said, "No, I'll go." He stood up abruptly, knocking his chair over. "I'm sorry. I just lost track of the time."

"It seems to me you've lost track of more than that," she shot back at him as he hurried out to the car.

When they had pulled into the driveway half an hour later, Teddy was holding a new toy, some gruesome-looking alien — one of those Skeletors or whatever they were called. And he seemed all recovered. But Giselle wasn't. She was tired of pussyfooting around, hoping things would get better. She was tired of being afraid to rock the boat. The goddamned boat was sinking anyway.

"What is all this shit?" she had shouted at Dan, throwing one of his stupid books against the wall. Just the sort of attack-mode opening that the therapist cautioned against. She could hear Hannah's voice: *Try to couch things in terms of what you're feeling.* "It's like you've joined some crazy fan club."

"It's not like that," Dan said in his calm-and-rational voice. "People grieve in different ways. You and I are each coping, or attempting to cope, in our own way. If you'd take the time to read any of these books you're so contemptuous of, you'd learn that."

He picked up a small paperback, flipped through it, and started to read, "In the early weeks following Christopher's death, both Mairi and I saw that we were dealing with our tragedy very differently. For the —" Giselle slapped the book out of his hands.

"I don't give a fuck about Christopher," she said. "I'm sorry. But I think this whole thing" — she gestured to the piles of books and envelopes sitting on the small desk in the corner — "is sick. Pathetic. Creepy."

He'd sat on the edge of their bed and held out his hand to her. Tears spilled down his face. She sighed and shook her head. She was tired of his tears. Sometimes she felt as if they had been allotted a finite pool of tears to get them through this tragedy, and he was using up her share as well as his own. She was tired of this public exhibition of grief, this national network of bleeding hearts. Maybe it was her Midwestern heritage, all those pioneer families who lost child after child, crop after crop, and endured — without support groups listed in the back of self-help books. Sure, maybe the neighbors brought them some home-baked bread or helped raise a barn, but that was different. She had seen the lists of organizations: the Compassionate Friends, Parents of Murdered Children, Inc., Candlelighters Foundation (for parents whose children had died of cancer), National SIDS Foundation. She didn't want any part of them. Maybe she was being a bitch, but she didn't care. She had her son's feelings to consider; she didn't have the luxury of publicly proclaiming and analyzing every little nuance of grief.

She grabbed the letter he was writing and thrust it at him. "I suppose you're telling everybody how hard it is to look at your stepson every day, alive and well, after he shot your daughter, your precious little girl."

He flinched. She knew she'd hit a bull's-eye. "That's part of it, of course," he said, "but just a small part. There's so much more to it than that." He rested his head in his hands, as if he didn't have the energy to explain. Or she was just too dense to understand.

"Look, there's a meeting of the Compassionate Friends next month. I thought I'd go, check it out. We could go together. Just once, just give it a try, that's all I ask."

She shook her head. "I'm sorry, I just can't."

"Is it so much to ask?"

"I don't know. I guess not." The anger had suddenly leaked out of her. She felt deflated and depressed. She felt as if some shrew had taken possession of her momentarily and then departed. "But I don't think I can do it."

"Well, there we are." He shrugged. "I don't think I can *not* do it. So where does that leave us?"

She didn't like the sound of that — it sounded so final. An alarm rang in the back of her brain, signaling her to find a compromise. "I'm sorry I sounded like such a bitch," she said. "I won't blame you for doing what you have to do." She sighed. "I mean, it's not like I'm right and you're wrong. I know that. There is no right and wrong here."

He put his arms around her, and they sat there holding each other for what seemed like a long, calm moment, as if all the angry words had finally cleared the air, and the storm had passed over them. She breathed a sigh of relief.

The next weekend was a holiday. She had forgotten all about it. She was cleaning out the refrigerator on her hands and knees, removing rotted, smelly things from the vegetable bin. Her interest in housekeeping, never that keen, had dwindled to nothing since the accident. She waved a fuzzy, caved-in cucumber in Dan's direction and wrinkled her nose. "I couldn't take the smell anymore." She tossed the mutated cucumber into the trash can, followed by some limp, dessicated scallions that resembled seaweed.

"That was Joe and Martha," he said, "on the phone." As if maybe she'd think they had come and gone in person without her seeing them. She could tell from the tone of his voice that he was going to try to get her to do something she probably didn't want to do. Which was pretty much everything these days. "They're having this little get-together for Memorial Day — just a few people — and they want us to come. Tomorrow afternoon." He took the garbage bag out of the can, tied it up, and put in a fresh one. "They said to bring Teddy. The kids will be swimming." Joe was a former student of Dan's, an ex-Marine who had become a high school English teacher. His wife was a returning student like Giselle. Dan set the full bag by the garage door. "What do you think? I told them I'd talk it over with you." *Gee, thanks,* she thought, *make me the heavy.*

"I take it, you want to go." She sat on her heels and stretched her back. Her body felt tight and achy, like an old woman's. She hadn't exercised in weeks.

"Well" — he shrugged — "it's not like I'm really in the mood for small talk, but I suppose we can't live like hermits forever. And we've always felt comfortable with Joe and Martha. And Teddy likes their kid, what's-his-name."

"Marky."

"Right." He reached past her and grabbed a Diet Coke. "It's up to you. I don't know."

"I don't know either," she sighed. "We'd probably just cast a pall over their party. They'd have to warn everybody in advance — like prep them — and either everyone would be saying how sorry they were or avoiding the topic, hoping nobody put their foot in their mouth."

Dan nodded his head as if she'd made a reasonable remark, but she could tell he thought they should go. At their last therapy session they had talked about the danger of becoming shut-ins. At least Dan and Hannah had discussed it. They always seemed to be on the same wavelength, some Stanford alumni vibe that made Giselle feel like a third wheel.

"Well, we don't have to decide right this minute," he said. "You can think about it." He shoved open the sticky garage door and picked up the garbage bag. "I thought I'd cut the grass."

She was impressed by how low-key he was being. Had he been pushier about it, she'd probably have dug in her heels, but his being so nice made her feel guilty about saying no. She supposed they had to go out sometime. Joe and Martha were about as relaxed and unpretentious as you could get. And Teddy would enjoy it. They had a pool with a slide. She walked out to the driveway, where Dan was bent over the old lawn mower, trying to coax some life into it, cursing to himself as he yanked on the cord over and over again, only to get a feeble whine that picked up steam and then sputtered right out. She tapped him on the shoulder. He was spending so much time on his book that he hadn't been playing tennis lately; she noticed his tan was fading. "Okay," she shouted as the motor abruptly roared to life. "We can go." He smiled and gave her a thumbs-up sign.

Sitting in the backseat, Teddy wasn't saying much, but he seemed happy to be going to a barbecue at the Goodmans'. He had insisted upon wearing his hideous tarantula T-shirt over his red plaid swim trunks. Scrutinizing him in the rearview mirror, Giselle saw that he needed a haircut. His hair was hanging in his eyes.

The traffic was even worse than usual — holiday traffic. Except for the funeral, she hadn't ventured more than five miles from home since the accident. A radius circumscribed by the supermarket, bank, post office, and Teddy's school. The traffic scared her. She kept reaching for the dashboard to brace herself, telling Dan to watch out, even though she had never had any complaints about his driving before. She'd always felt perfectly safe with him at the wheel, unlike with Ed, who loved motorcycles and drove like a bat out of hell, as her mother used to say. Dan reached over and clasped her hand. He gave it a little squeeze, as if to say, *Be brave*.

"The freeway's so narrow over here," she said. "It feels as if the cars are right on top of you."

"Look at that cool 'vette!" Teddy pointed to a flashy silver convertible up ahead.

"It's a '69," Dan said, sounding equally smitten.

Giselle shook her head. It never ceased to amaze her that even the most un-guylike guy seemed to be up on cars. She thought about how different it was with a daughter. Even though Trina was only two, already they'd had this "gal thing" going. Trina loved to go clothes shopping with her. She would point to various items and say, "Pretty!" And whenever Giselle painted her toenails, Trina had insisted upon having hers painted, too. Giselle worried about the sexist stereotyping, but it all felt so companionable. And she made sure to instill some early feminist principles as the two of them stood in the dressing room at May Company. "It's nice to look pretty," she would tell Trina, "but it's more important what's in here." She would reach over and tap Trina's forehead and heart, and Trina would tap Mommy's forehead and heart solemnly, to show that she understood. Then she would shake her head at the red dress — "No!" — and point to the black dress — "Yes!" Already she had good taste in clothes. And now that Trina was gone, Giselle wouldn't have a daughter to do those mother-daughter things with, ever. Just a son with his ugly Power Rangers and Hot Wheels. She clenched her eyelids shut to dam the tears.

"You doing okay?" Dan asked. "You're awfully quiet."

She shrugged.

He squeezed her hand again. He was looking a little shaky himself. "We don't have to stay long," he said.

The moment she saw all the cars parked in front of the Goodmans' house, edging both sides of the narrow tree-lined street, she felt like turning the car around and going home. If she had been alone, she would have driven right past the house and kept going, but Dan was already attempting to parallel park in a tight space bracketed by two jaunty red sports cars. She held her breath, waiting for the sound of scraped metal, smiling tensely at Teddy in the backseat, as Dan somehow managed to maneuver them into the space without mishap. "Is that an awesome feat of parking, or what?" he asked, clearly pleased with himself.

"Too bad parallel parking isn't an Olympic event," she joked, trying to sound convivial and lighthearted, like someone on her way to a party.

Dan put his arm around her as they walked up the flagstone steps to the house, a graceful old pink stucco two-story that Joe had bought with a six-figure settlement of a long, involved lawsuit from a motorcycle accident he'd been in years ago, before Dan had ever even met him. Teddy was trudging along in front of them, dragging his gaudy beach towel on the grass. As they followed the buzz of voices around back to the pool, Dan reached down and flipped the beach towel over Teddy's head. "Hey!" Teddy protested, pretending to stumble around like a blind zombie. Dan laughed even though it wasn't that funny. He seemed to be wired, in an aggressively upbeat mood, but she didn't trust it. All it would take was someone with a toddler or even a familiar toy, and he'd fall apart. Earlier in the week he'd broken down in the post office parking lot watching a father bending into a Volvo station wagon to unstrap his child from her car seat.

At the gate to the backyard she froze at the sight of twenty or thirty people milling around the pool or standing on the lawn by the barbecue grill, talking and laughing, drinks in hand, voices raised to be heard over the shrieks of the half a dozen kids splashing in the water. Even Teddy seemed to shrink back until Marky Goodman caught sight of him and hollered out his name, motioning for Teddy to jump in. As Teddy peeled off his T-shirt, Dan leaned over and whispered in Giselle's ear, "How you doing?"

"Okay," she lied. Already she knew that this had been a terrible miscalculation on her part. She wasn't ready. She couldn't imagine what she could say to anyone. There was only one couple she recognized from another get-together. They were very nice, just recently transferred to the West Coast from Tulsa. Giselle remembered having a pleasant conversation with the wife about the Midwest and California public schools. She was trying to remember the woman's name when Martha pushed through the screen door carrying a tray of condiments, which she set down on the picnic table before hurrying over to where they were standing.

"Dan, Giselle!" She hugged them each hello. "I'm so glad you could make it." Giselle saw her hesitate, no doubt debating whether to make a direct reference to Trina, and was relieved when Dan had the presence of mind to step in and ask where Joe was. Martha looked over at the grill and pretended to frown like an exasperated schoolmarm. "He was supposed to be cooking hamburgers, but he's probably showing off his new pool table." She pointed to the garage, and Dan took off. Giselle noticed he was holding a Dos Equis that she hadn't seen him take from the ice chest. "You want a glass of wine?" Martha asked her. "A gin and tonic?"

"A gin and tonic sounds good," Giselle said. She followed Martha into the kitchen and tried to look relaxed as she leaned against the counter, waiting for her drink. Martha looked terrific, she thought. She had finally got her long, dark hippie hair cut to shoulder length. "I like your hair," Giselle told her.

"God, talk about trauma," Martha laughed. "I think I'm still suffering phantom hair syndrome. I actually cried on the way home from the beauty parlor. I hadn't had my hair cut more than an inch since tenth grade." She sliced a lime into quarters and shook her new, bouncier hair. "Joe thought I was nuts. He didn't see what the big deal was. But I swear I went through the five stages of grief." A stricken look flitted across her face as she handed the drink to Giselle, who forced an oblivious smile as if the gaff had flown right past her.

"I'm the same way about my hair," Giselle said. "A complete coward." She took a swig of gin and wandered back out to the pool area to see how Teddy and Dan were doing. She was afraid to drink too much. She didn't want to end up making a tearful, boozy public spectacle of herself. But she knew that if she didn't drink, she'd remain uptight and silent. There was some old acronym about the stages of drunkenness — something about jocose, bellicose, morose, lachrymose. She couldn't remember the exact order. Teddy pounded the ball over the net and let out a whoop. They were playing water volleyball. He looked happy. She didn't want the sight of her standing there like a wallflower to dampen his mood, so she edged over toward the fence, where the nice woman she'd recognized earlier was talking to a handsome older couple dressed in expensive-looking white tennis outfits and athletic shoes. She glanced at her watch, wishing she could go wait in the car, like a dog, until it was time to go home. But Dan was probably enjoying himself for a change. The husband of the nice woman from Tulsa walked up to Giselle and said hello. He was holding a half-eaten hot dog and kept dabbing self-consciously at a tiny spot of mustard on the front of his white shirt. He was pale and overdressed, obviously not yet socialized to California.

"So, how are you all adjusting to the big move?" she asked him.

"Well, I can't say I missed the winter," he said. "All those people who go on about the four seasons can have them."

Giselle nodded and smiled, almost relaxed. "I hate to admit it, but I love to watch footage of people shoveling snow on the news." She'd had this conversation a thousand times; she could hold up her end on automatic pilot. But then a little girl, about six or seven, ran up in her bathing suit and tugged on his hand. "Daddy," she whined, dripping water on his canvas shoes, "Gavin pushed my head underwater and wouldn't let go. He tried to drown me." Her lip quivered indignantly as she wiped her runny nose with the back of her hand.

"Excuse me a moment," the man sighed, and rolled his eyes at Giselle. He took the little girl's hand and let his daughter lead him away. Giselle took another swig of her drink and sidled over to the food table. She was munching a carrot stick, trying to look absorbed in the array of chips and dips, when Dan walked up to her, looking as if he'd been mugged.

"You were right," he said. "I'm not ready for this." He gestured to a small knot of people talking and laughing. He looked at his watch. "This is my third beer and we've only been here fifteen minutes." He took a final swig and tossed the bottle into a bin. "I'm ready to take off. How about you?"

"What about Teddy?" she asked. They both looked over to the pool, where he was splashing around like a madman, obviously having a great time.

"Yeah." Dan heaved a sigh and bit into a minitaco. A woman standing by the grill in a spandex halter dress burst out laughing, snorting beer down the front of her dress, screeching, "Look what you made me do!" The guy she was talking with made a big show of patting her boobs with his napkin. Dan shook his head. "Who are these people? Were conversations always this stupid?"

"Maybe we could go somewhere — a coffee shop or something — and pick up Teddy in an hour or so." She felt torn. Dan looked so depressed, she wanted to get him out of there, but Teddy seemed to be having real fun for the first time since her parents had left. It seemed cruel to yank him away so soon.

"What about Joe and Martha?"

"They'll understand," she said. "I'll tell Teddy we'll be back in an hour or so."

She had to wave her arms and shout to get Teddy's attention. She could feel people's eyes on her, watching. *There's the woman whose son shot her little girl. Can you imagine?* Finally Teddy waded over to the side of the pool. She knelt down and told him they'd be back for him in a little while. "Okay," he said, eager to get back to the game. She had the feeling she could have told him they'd be back for him in ten years and it would have been okay with him. As she was opening the gate to leave, someone tapped her on the shoulder and said, "Giselle?" She flinched and turned around. It was the woman from Tulsa.

"I'm sorry we didn't get a chance to talk," the woman said. Her eyes managed to convey the fact that she knew. "I know this must be so hard for you." She leaned over and kissed Giselle lightly on the cheek, catching her by surprise. Although she felt the tears welling up, Giselle also felt a flash of gratitude. She mumbled a thank-you and walked out front, where Dan was pacing up and down the driveway, waiting for her.

Neither of them was familiar with Pasadena. They drove around until they found a funky little coffee shop called the Kozy Korner or the Comfy Cafe. It even had booths with jukeboxes, something she hadn't seen in years, and they ordered slices of coconut cream pie, something she hadn't tasted in years, and spent a surprisingly soothing hour playing music, eating pie, and drinking coffee. They were both so relieved to be away from the party, to be alone with each other, that they just sat there holding hands, not even bothering to talk. Then they drove back for Teddy. When Teddy whined about leaving, Dan told him to knock it off. Which Giselle took as a good sign, a sign that Dan was treating him like a regular kid again. Tired out from the sun and excitement, Teddy nodded off during the long ride. She felt calmer; the traffic didn't bother her. Dan punched in a cassette and they listened to old Linda Ronstadt songs, humming along more or less on key, glad to be going home.

Later that night they made love for the first time since the accident. Not because they'd had a good time, but because they'd had such a miserable time — together. She had been worried that she would suffer through the whole ordeal while Dan somehow managed to enjoy himself, and the whole outing would only serve to widen the gulf between them. But it hadn't worked out that way.

"Well, at least Teddy seemed to have a good time," Dan said as they lay there holding each other in the dark.

She stroked his hair. She kept meaning to buy a new lamp for the night table, but she always forgot when she was out. Her mind never seemed to focus anymore. Dan readjusted the pillows. "Comfortable?"

She nodded.

"I felt like a total alien," he said. "Like we were from another planet, you know?"

She nodded again and snuggled closer to him.

"I know it's unfair, it's uncharitable to be so critical." He blew out a long stream of air. "We can't expect everyone to go around with a long face, talking philosophy, just because of our situation, but shit, I don't know. I just don't know anymore."

"You don't have to know," she said softly. "It's all right." She was glad to hear him using the word *we* again.

"That's why I wanted you to go with me to this Compassionate Friends meeting. They're people who know what it's like. We wouldn't have to feel like aliens." He turned to face her in the dark. Her heart sank as she felt him waiting for her to say yes: Yes, now she understood. Yes, she'd go. She kept her eyes shut and tried pretending she was drifting off. "What are you thinking?" he prodded.

"It's just that, to me, it's such a private and personal thing. Maybe they've lost a child, too, but they haven't lost our child. We're all different. I guess I've just never been much of a joiner."

"Oh, and I suppose I am?" His voice had an edge to it now. She'd offended him. "Whose the elitist now? You want to feel you're unique, that no one in the history of the world has ever felt your pain. Not even me." He rolled over with his back to her. "Well, fine with me."

She sighed, on the verge of tears. It was the first intimate time they had shared in so long, and now suddenly it had degenerated into this. "Okay." She couldn't stand it. "I'll think about it. Maybe you're right."

He groped for her hand, raised it to his lips, and planted a kiss in the center of her palm. It was something he used to do with Trina when she hurt herself. She would come running to him, palms extended, and say, "Bad boo-boo. Kiss better!" And he would. Maybe he was right. What did she know? He was the teacher, after all.

"Martha told me about a house for rent over near Palms Park," she said, anxious to change the subject. "She happened to be driving by and saw the FOR RENT sign."

Now it was his turn to pretend to be drifting off. She could see his eyelids twitching. "She said it had a nice little yard with fruit trees." She shook him lightly. "Hey!"

"Ummm," he murmured. "Ummhmm."

She lay there, tired but not sleepy, running her hands over her naked body, feeling his naked thigh pressed against her own. It had been a long time since they had slept naked. In the past few weeks they seemed to wear more and more clothes to bed, even as the temperature outside got warmer, with summer approaching. The clothes were like layers of protection, a shield against intimacy or the lack thereof. The sex per se had not been that good in the technical sense — passion still seemed a long way off — but she didn't care, the intimacy was enough.

After Trina was born, they were usually too tired for sex when they got into bed at night, but they had always tried to make time to snuggle and read together for a few minutes before turning out the light. Dan liked to read poetry aloud to her. He was a wonderful reader. In college he had majored in drama, thinking he would be an actor, before a favorite professor had influenced him to switch to literature. She remembered the afternoon they bought the Neruda book. *Il Postino* had just opened, and Dan was dying to see it. So they took the afternoon off — Dan played hooky from his office hours — and went to an early matinee in Westwood while Trina was still at day care. They had the theater practically to themselves. They held hands and ate popcorn, as if they were on a first date. And then they walked over to a bookstore and bought *Selected Odes of Pablo Neruda*. She remembered lying in bed smiling to herself as Dan read aloud "Ode to the Artichoke" — "Ode a la Alcachofa" in Spanish — and thinking how this was it: the life she had always wanted. Before she moved to California, she had never eaten an artichoke, let alone read Neruda.

She got up slowly, careful not to rock the bed, and took the book from the night table, where it still lay. There was a particular poem she remembered, "Ode to a Couple." She sat on the sofa and turned on the lamp, leafing through the pages until she found it, one stanza in particular:

> If snow falls
> upon two heads,
> the heart is sweet,
> the house is warm.
> If not,
> in the storm, the wind
> asks:
> where is the woman you loved?
> and nipping at your heels
> will press you to seek her.
> Half a woman is one woman
> and one man is half a man.
> Each lives in half a house,
> each sleeps in half a bed.

The rest of the poem blurred on the page. She shut the book. The Beemers' dog was barking halfheartedly, more, it seemed, to see if anyone was listening than to protect his territory.

The next day she drove over and looked at the house. It was in a different school district. But now that school was about to let out for the summer, it occurred to her that changing schools in the fall would probably be the best thing for Teddy. It was a white stucco bungalow with a tile roof and had a tidy little yard with hibiscus bushes and lemon trees. She walked around and spied through the miniblinds on tiptoe. She couldn't see everything, but what she saw looked nice. Bright and clean. She copied down the landlord's phone number from the sign and stuck notes to both the front and back doors saying that she was definitely (desperately) interested in renting the house. She would have camped out in her car until someone showed up, but Teddy would be getting home from school in an hour.

Even though she was anxious to move, she knew she would miss house hunting. It gave a focus to her otherwise aimless days, a mission. Dan had urged her to go back to school, but it still didn't seem right. It didn't seem right somehow to just pick up where she had left off. It seemed unseemly, like a widow remarrying too soon. It was different for Dan, who had returned to his teaching and research with a vengeance. She wasn't sure how or why it was different, she just felt that it was.

Heading back toward the freeway, she took a wrong turn and got lost in a maze of streets named after fruit — Orange Grove, Lemon Tree, Peach Blossom, Plum — pleasant stucco houses with well-tended yards. As she wended her way closer to the exit ramp, the houses seemed to shrink into concrete cubes and the lawns grew ragged. There were wrought-iron bars on the windows and doors. She made a mental note to avoid this route when she brought Dan. She had pinned all her hopes on moving. Even though she knew, rationally, that what ailed them couldn't be left behind like an old chair or carpet. It would ride along in the U-Haul with them — their heaviest, most cumbersome possession. As she merged into the thickening sludge of traffic, the pre–rush hour rush, she thought how ironic it was that Dan's father's death had brought them together, while their daughter's death had driven them apart. At least until last night. She hoped that maybe last night had closed the gap, the widening gulf, at least a little.

As she neared her exit, she noticed suddenly that the generator light was on. She cursed under her breath. The last thing they needed was car trouble. She remembered a phone conversation with her cousin a few months after Ruth's daughter had been killed by a car. "It's the little things that set you off," Ruth had told her. "If I break a glass washing the dishes or burn the toast or stub my toe on the bathroom door in the middle of the night, I might burst into tears and cry for an hour. You lose all sense of proportion."

When she heard about Trina, Ruth called her. A week or two after the funeral. And Giselle had felt a rush of relief when she heard Ruthie's voice, thinking that maybe Ruth could tell her something to help them get through this. Something that no one else would know. But she hadn't. They just cried together long distance for a couple of minutes, and then Ruth said she had to go — her older daughter was hollering for help in the kitchen, where she was baking cookies. After the phone call Giselle had felt even lower. It had seemed blindingly clear that there was nothing anybody could tell her. No secret words of wisdom to be passed from one survivor to the next, no underground network of comfort. No Compassionate Friends. She cringed as she remembered telling Dan that she would go to one of their meetings. She imagined it taking place in some drafty modern church with people sitting in rows of metal folding chairs, like an AA meeting. They would introduce themselves: "Hi, my name is ———, and I have lost a child."

It was just past two when she got home. The first thing she did was check the answering machine to see if anyone had left her a message about the house for rent. They hadn't. There was only one message, and it was from Dan saying he wouldn't be home for dinner. He was going to work on the book. She felt a twinge of disappointment. The three of them had been managing to coexist more or less peacefully, mostly by going about their separate business. The therapist said this wasn't necessarily a bad thing. But Giselle had hoped that after yesterday, last night, they might start spending more time together. Well, maybe in the new house.

She called his office number, but there was no answer. She left a message on his voice mail, "Hi, it's me. Got your message. Call when you get a chance." Then she lay down on the living room sofa to rest before Teddy got home and began moping around the house, complaining that he was bored. On occasion she had almost suggested he go over to Eric's; they used to keep each other entertained from morning till night. But Dan had forbidden him to have anything to do with the Beemers. Sometimes, despite everything, she missed chatting with Lois in the backyard. Since the accident it was like having a vacant house next door, only worse. There was an even emptier feeling.

"What do you do with your time?" her sister had asked her the last time she called. Giselle didn't remember what her reply had been. But whatever it was, she could tell that Vonnie hadn't been satisfied by it. "You should go back to school," Vonnie had told her in her big-sister tone of voice.

Apparently Vonnie's grief had not taken the form of pure exhaustion. Even with the sleeping pills Greg had prescribed for them, it seemed as if neither she nor Dan ever really slept anymore. The exhaustion just accumulated; each sleepless night she felt as if she were gaining weight, another five pounds to drag around. This heaviness that was always with her, as if Trina's dead body were inside of her, a two-year-old mummy in a snuggly, pressing against her lungs and heart. On her last visit to the pediatrician, just a week before the accident, Trina had tipped the scales at thirty-one pounds.

Giselle reached over, picked up the remote, and clicked on CNN. *TalkBack Live.* Then she muted it and closed her eyes. She couldn't believe they were still doing postmortems on the Simpson case. Her sigh stretched into a yawn. *What do you do with your time?* Before the accident it seemed as if she did, in fact, do things with her time. She organized her time. She made time for the various activities in her life, although it seemed there was never quite enough time to go around. But now time had the upper hand. She felt like a dog being dragged through time on a leash. She was straining with all her might to go backward while Time kept dragging her forward. She wanted to go back to the morning of the accident. Or barring that, maybe further, maybe back to the night of Trina's conception. Instead of turning off the VCR halfway through *Bullets Over Broadway* and making love, they would watch it all the way through, then have an argument over whether it was a good movie, and go to bed miffed at each other. If you weren't born, you couldn't die. Life was full of trade-offs.

She used to think nothing could be more exhausting than keeping up with a toddler — the terrible twos — until she didn't have one to keep up with anymore. After Teddy was born, and then again after Trina was born, there was that fog of exhaustion that all new parents know so well. Getting up night after night to nurse the baby. Wearing a path in the carpet as you pace and croon the fussing infant back to sleep. Then waking up at the crack of dawn — who needs a rooster when they've got a baby? — to a full day of being at baby's beck and call. Where did the energy come from? But that was nothing compared with this. That was child's play compared with this. There were all those bright moments that lit up the fog. The baby's smile. That look of wonder on her face as you dangled a new toy. The feel of her tiny fingers with those sharp little nails exploring your nose and eyes and mouth. The scent of her sweet belly as you bent over to kiss it after whisking away the dirty diaper. The taste of her pudgy thighs as you pretended to eat her up. And, last but not least, it was only temporary. When you collapsed into bed at nine o'clock, you knew that in less time than it takes for all the cells in your body to renew themselves, she would be walking and talking and pushing you away. It was only temporary. Whereas this, this was forever. From now on, she was always going to be dead. Trina was never ever going to grow out of being dead. No matter how much time passed.

Giselle envied Dan his book, his ability to concentrate so deeply, to blot out everything else. She couldn't really blame him or begrudge him this. She was relieved, actually, that he had found a way to cope. It was better than the two of them sitting around making halfhearted conversation. As the silences lengthened between them, she marveled, once again, at life's little ironies. She had left her first marriage largely because of the silence that descended upon Ed and her once the baby stopped crying or the TV was turned off. They had nothing to say to each other, it seemed.

Or rather, she had things to say, but Ed never had anything to say back. Spending her days cooped up with a baby, she was ready for some adult conversation in the evenings, and when Ed failed to hold up his end of the conversation, her resentment and frustration grew. She began to see him as dense and thoughtless (as in "without thoughts"), whereas she'd seen him as strong and reserved before. She had fantasies of holding a gun to his temple and shouting, *Talk! Talk, you dolt! Talk to me as if your life depended on it!*

So, naturally she had been attracted, even a bit dazzled, by Dan's articulateness, his almost feminine (she'd thought) desire to communicate his ideas and feelings. Talking with him was like talking on the phone to a close girlfriend, only better. His conversation was more witty and stimulating. Maybe, as her old friend Laura had pointed out, he was a better talker than listener, but that was still a big leap forward from what she had been used to. And there were times, mostly when they were alone, when he did seek out her thoughts, when he did really listen to her. But lately it was becoming more and more obvious to her how much of the conversation between them had always relied upon Dan's verbal energy and agility. Whenever he withdrew into silence, she felt as tongue-tied as poor Ed. If you don't have anything nice to say, don't say anything.

And now there was Teddy with this Talkboy gizmo, driving her berserk. He refused to converse normally anymore. He had to record everything and then play it back to her at slow speed or fast speed so that he sounded like a zombie or a munchkin. It had become an obsession. She had tried taking it away and hiding it, but then he refused to speak, period. He even took it with him to the therapy sessions. The therapist admitted that it was a troublesome sign; however, she theorized that if they didn't make too big a deal out of it, it would probably phase itself out. But ever since he'd got the damn thing, the only time he spoke normally was on the phone with his dad.

Some days, like yesterday, she thought maybe they would make it. Other days she thought no way. No way in hell. One of the worst days was Trina's birthday, last Tuesday, what would have been her second birthday. As the day approached, Giselle had felt her panic mounting. How did you celebrate a dead child's birthday? She wasn't sure Teddy would remember the date, but she knew there was no way that Dan was going to forget. She even went so far as to look up "Birthdays" in *The Mourning Handbook,* which she had filched from Dan's bookcase. The author's suggestions had ranged from bad to worse, from donating toys to a children's hospital in your child's name to releasing a helium balloon inscribed with your child's name at the gravesite. Giselle threw out the book. Dan had found it in the trash and yelled at her about her attitude. He had ended up going to the cemetery without her.

Teddy was eating his supper at the coffee table in front of the TV, watching old reruns of *Kung Fu,* when the landlord called about the house. The rent was fifty dollars a month over their upper limit, but ever since she'd stood on tiptoe and peeked in the back windows, she'd had this image of the three of them eating in the sunny breakfast nook, joking around like the old days, that seemed worth any amount of money. She made an appointment for them to see the house at seven o'clock. Then she called Dan again at his office. She knew he wouldn't appreciate his evening's work being interrupted, but he had to see the house. It would be snapped up right away, and she didn't want to lose it. She had been tempted to tell the landlord on the phone that they would take it, but she was afraid of Dan's reaction to such a major unilateral decision.

This time his officemate, Lou Trujillo, answered the phone. He said that Dan had just run over to the union for a sandwich. She started to ask Lou to tell Dan to call her, then said, "No, tell him we'll be by for him in half an hour." It was already six o'clock and the university was more or less on the way to the house. She didn't want to take any chances that he'd get caught up in his work and be late. Or forget.

She took Teddy's empty bowl and set it in the sink. Lately she had taken to making him ramen noodles every night, since she and Dan weren't much interested in real meals. Teddy seemed content to eat his bowl of noodles in front of the TV. Before, when they used to all eat together, he hadn't been allowed to turn on the television set during dinner.

"You want a Popsicle?" she asked him.

He nodded, engrossed in some conversation David Carradine was having with an old monk. She didn't bother to ask him what flavor, which was just as well, since there turned out to be only one flavor left in the box.

"We've got to go look at a house," she told him as she handed him the Popsicle. It was lime, his least favorite. He ate the grape ones first, then the cherry, then the orange, and left the lime for last. "A really nice house I saw earlier today. You'll like it."

He held the Talkboy to his lips, pressed the RECORD button, and said, "I don't want to go." Then he played it back at slow speed. "I dooonnn't waaannnt tooo gooo." He sounded like a stroke victim.

"Well, you're going," she said. "You can't stay here alone. And we're going to pick up Dan at his office." She looked at her watch. "So put on your shoes, please." When he didn't make a move, she added, "Now."

Teddy grumbled to himself as he tied his sneakers. In order to free both hands, he set his Popsicle down on top of a magazine on the coffee table, the June issue of *Harper's,* which Dan hadn't even looked at yet. She snatched up the dripping Popsicle. "What's wrong with you?" she sighed. "Go wash your face."

Teddy trudged back to the bathroom, not bothering to turn off the TV. As Giselle wiped off the magazine cover, all she felt was irritation. Then suddenly she remembered noticing Trina's sticky handprints all over the sliding glass doors — just a day or two ago — when the bright sun hit the glass at a certain angle. Trina was gone, but there they were, like fossils — too precious to wipe away. There was no double standard quite like that for a living versus a dead child.

"I'm sorry I snapped at you," she said when he returned. He looked at her suspiciously and clicked off the remote control just as the phone rang. Chances were, it was Ed. She raced over and turned the volume down low before the message could start to play. If it was Ed, then Teddy would want to talk to him and sulk if he couldn't. Before the accident Teddy could take or leave talking to his dad. The phone calls tended to be short and monosyllabic unless Teddy was really wound up about something in particular — a movie he'd just seen or some kid throwing up on the school bus or a soccer match his team had won. But now it was as if the phone calls from Ed were the high point of his life. Suddenly it was as if his dad were the only one in the world who was really on his team.

Teddy frowned but refrained from making a comment. His face was cleaner, but his tongue was still a sickly shade of green.

"We have to go," she said, ushering him out to the garage. "It was probably just someone trying to sell us something."

During the ride to the campus, he read aloud into the Talkboy all the personalized license plates he saw whizzing by on the freeway: NU PONY, ISU4U, SHEGOES, XWIFE, GASHOG, DONT SIN, PEARL HARBOR SURVIVOR #472. He snickered to himself as they passed an old purple VW whose license plate said, A GRAPE. Then he played back the list over and over again at fast speed as they were walking to Dan's office. He had wanted to stay in the car, but she refused to let him. The thought of him alone made her nervous. She didn't have a clue what was going on in his mind these days.

The campus was at its most peaceful, in between day and evening classes. It was no ivy-covered citadel, but she had always loved the feel of a college campus. One of her most vivid early memories was sitting with her father in the midst of a sloping green expanse on the KU campus, eating a picnic lunch her mother had packed. It was her father's tenth reunion. Her mother had been too pregnant to make the trip, so her father had taken her along instead. Vonnie had a test and couldn't take the day off from school. Giselle was only in the first grade, too young for tests, so she got to go. She had felt special being alone with her father, like a little wife. The campus was very hilly — the first place she had ever seen that wasn't flat — and she had imagined coasting down the steep hills on her new two-wheel bike. Her father took her into the library, a huge stone building like a cathedral, hushed with sunlight streaming through the large windows. Standing there looking at the stacks of books, she felt a shivery thrill and didn't know how she would ever make it through all those years before she was old enough to go to college, which she knew, suddenly, was where she really belonged.

When they got to the English department, housed in an unprepossessing building, she hurried past Dr. Diller's office, tugging her reluctant son down the corridor behind her. She had not talked to any of her professors since dropping their classes. The door to Dan's office was ajar, but the office was empty. She hoped that Lou had remembered to give Dan her message. Lou's desk was a blizzard of papers strewn in haphazard drifts. An old *Venceremos* poster of a clenched fist hung above his desk, the edges yellowed and curling. Dan's desk was neat and organized. There was a smaller version of Trina's portrait in the red velvet dress sitting on his desk, along with a photograph of Giselle with a hibiscus tucked behind one ear, her face flushed with sun and mai tais, taken in Hawaii on their honeymoon. There was no picture of Teddy, and nothing hanging on the wall above his desk — he didn't like anything to distract him while he was composing at his computer. She noticed a scrap of paper lying on top of some papers weighted down by a stapler and thought it might be a note he'd left for her. She walked over and read it. *Lunch today? J.* It was written in lavender ink. The single initial, written with a feminine flourish, struck her as intimate. But before she could absorb the emotional impact of this discovery, her attention was snagged by an open book marked with a profusion of yellow sticky tabs. *The Gun Control Debate.*

She flipped it open to one of the marked pages. The underlined phrases leaped out at her: "88 children's deaths in California from 1977–83 . . . 24% of the cases the shooter was a sibling . . ." She picked up the book and held it closer. "70% of the cases the shooter was a boy aged ten to fourteen . . . 69% were shot in the head or neck; wounds to the thorax . . ." Jesus Christ. She flipped to the next page. "Serious long-term effects are not limited to those killed or injured. At least 52 of the 53 shooters in deaths inflicted by others were family members . . . They are almost certainly at increased risk for acute and chronic emotional and behavioral disturbance; to our knowledge, this hypothesis has not yet been evaluated." No shit. You didn't have to be Freud to figure that out, but still, seeing it in print, in black and white . . . Her hands shook as she bent over to retrieve a letter that had fallen out of the book onto the floor. It was typed on Doubleday letterhead. She skimmed it, her heart pounding out each word like an old daisy wheel printer:

We are all very excited about *Johnny's Got Your Gun.* While I agree that some discussion of the Brady Bill and the debate over gun control have a place in the book, it is important that you keep in mind that the personal, intimate account of your daughter's death has to be the main focus of *JGYG.* Unfortunately, the times are such that people see these tragic events on the evening news with numbing frequency; your book will have the power to bring it closer to home, to make them feel as if they've lost their own son or daughter. Little Jennifer or Jason.

The letter was signed by Annabel Dixon, senior editor. There was a P.S. that said, "Give Harvey a kiss for me."

She felt faint. She fell into the desk chair. Teddy stopped rearranging the pushpins in the little bulletin board outside the door and looked at her. Giselle dimly remembered some dinner conversation about a sister-in-law who worked for a publishing house in New York. Something about her dating someone famous, a painter or musician whom everyone but Giselle had heard of.

"What's the matter?" he asked, forgetting for once to use his Talkboy. "Is something wrong?"

The sound of Teddy's natural voice, young and timid, brought tears to her eyes. Then, as the shock turned to anger, she stood up. The confessional novel. Well, this was it, all right, the real thing. Forget Fitzgerald and Conrad. And here was the true irony: the author was too cowardly to confess that he was writing it. What was he planning to do? Wait until she stumbled across it in Barnes and Noble? Until she turned on *Oprah*? Of course it wasn't enough that he just read everyone else's book. No, of course not. He had to write his own book. All the other stuff was just research. She should have known. She should have seen it coming. He was an academic, after all, and he would deal with his loss academically. It put a new spin on "publish or perish." How about "perish and publish"? Suddenly she felt stronger than she had in weeks. A mother bear ready to defend her cub. She ripped up the letter and scattered the pieces, like ashes, over his desk.

"What are you doing?" Teddy asked, eyes wide with surprise.

"Come on," she said. "Let's go." Her fist clamped onto his skinny arm above the elbow. As she steered him down the corridor, he protested that she was hurting him. Derek Jackson was just unlocking his office, juggling a cup of coffee and a briefcase in one hand as he fumbled with the key in the other. He was the most recent recruit, fresh from some Ivy League school. She had met him at a party, and he'd reminded her of an actor playing a college professor. She had the feeling that if she whisked off his horn-rimmed glasses and looked through them, they would be nonprescription, a prop. She was hoping he wouldn't remember her, but he flashed her a big smile. "It's Giselle, right?"

She nodded and tried to smile. She wanted to get out of there before Dan got back. She didn't want to confront him in public. And she knew he wouldn't go off and leave his office open for more than a few minutes.

"How's it going?" he asked. She saw him flinch and knew that he'd just remembered about the accident and was kicking himself. "What's that you got?" He pointed to Teddy's Talkboy to change the subject.

"It's called a Talkboy Jr.," Teddy said into the mouthpiece, then played it back at fast speed.

"Hey, that's cool." Derek grinned. "Maybe I should use it for my lectures. Can I try it out?"

"I'm afraid we're late," Giselle broke in. "Good to see you." She gave Teddy a little shove forward. He glared at her but kept his mouth shut and his feet moving. They trotted back to the parking lot in silence.

The car was hotter than hell. As she rolled down the windows, Teddy asked, "Are we still going to look at that house?"

She had forgotten all about the house. She looked at her watch. The landlord would be waiting for them. "I don't know," she sighed. It suddenly seemed pointless. They weren't going anywhere. Who was she kidding? "I think I'll just drive to a pay phone and call the landlord and tell him something came up. Okay?"

Teddy shrugged. Two students in an orange VW convertible sailed into the parking place next to them, blasting rock music from the car stereo. She turned the key in the ignition. Nothing. She checked to make sure the car was in PARK and tried again. Stone cold dead. She looked at the dashboard and saw the generator light. "Shit!" She pounded her fist on the dashboard. Teddy groaned. She started to cry with her face pressed against the steering wheel. A flimsy whimper that escalated into a loud gasping wail. She thought of her cousin Ruth saying that it was the little things, as if coping with her daughter's death had sucked up all the patience and forbearance allotted for this lifetime. When the convertible driver suddenly switched off the motor and the music stopped, they looked over to see what all the racket was. But she was too far gone to care. Teddy slumped down low in his seat, mumbling into his Talkboy. The parking lot was filling up with students arriving for their seven o'clock classes.

When the fit subsided, she grabbed a Kleenex from a box on the dashboard and blew her nose. "We have to call Triple A," she told Teddy. "Have them send a tow truck."

"Are they going to tow the car away?" He looked mildly interested at the thought of witnessing this.

"Probably." She sighed. "And then we'll need a ride home." She cursed Los Angeles for having such lousy public transportation. The last thing she wanted to do was drag herself back to Dan's office and ask him for a favor. She thought about calling a cab, even though it would cost a small fortune, but she didn't have enough cash on her. Ellen was out of town, visiting the in-laws back East, and no one else she knew, except Lois, lived anywhere near them. She couldn't even think of any other friends. Surely, before the accident, she'd had friends, hadn't she? She couldn't remember the last time she'd just gabbed on the phone. If her brother was around, she would have called him. But Todd was in Tokyo working on some new monster movie. He had been sending Teddy funny Japanese postcards of indoor beaches and ski slopes with strange bits of cultural lore on the back. On the last card he'd said you could rent dogs by the hour in Tokyo, since people thought dogs were relaxing but didn't have the space to own one. Later she had heard Teddy on the phone with Ed joking about taking Beowulf (Dinky's replacement, a scruffy malamute) to Tokyo and setting up their own Rent-A-Dog. She took out her wallet and flipped through the packet of credit cards, making certain the AAA card was there. And not expired. Thank God.

"Come on," she said to Teddy. "We've got to go back to Dan's office."

"I want to wait here," he spoke into the Talkboy. As he pressed the PLAY button, she reached over and grabbed the gadget out of his hand and threw it out the car window onto the asphalt.

He shouted, "Nooo!" and then scrambled out of the car to retrieve it, darting out in front of a Jeep, which screeched on its brakes just in time. She sat frozen for an instant and then leaped out after him. The Jeep's driver, a middle-aged man, blasted his horn and shouted, "Jesus Christ, kid, watch where you're going!" Then he glared at Giselle and shook his head. She ignored him.

Teddy's lip was trembling. He wouldn't look at her. "I'm sorry," she said, trying to lasso her arms around him in a hug. "I was just upset about the car not starting. I'll get you another one. I promise."

He bucked away from her, slugging her in the stomach, kicking her shins with his sneakers. "Leave me alone, I hate you!" he yelled, pushing her away as he bent down to pick up the broken Talkboy. There were a couple of plastic shards lying on the ground; he tucked them into his pocket. When he pressed the buttons, nothing happened.

She leaned against the side of the car and tried to think. She needed some time to cool off, Teddy needed some time to calm down, before they saw Dan. When she confronted him, she wanted to be in control. She wanted to make herself clear. She wanted to make him see just what a disaster this book would be, what an act of disloyalty. She looked at Teddy, who was watching a blind girl and a Seeing Eye dog make their way across campus, the girl's cane tapping against the sidewalk. He looked as if he'd just lost his best friend.

"Let's go to the student union and have a Coke," she said. "We'll call Lois and see if she can give us a ride home." She knew that Lois would leap at this opportunity to help. Maybe the cold war had lasted long enough. She knew that Lois was suffering, too; she could see it in her eyes on the few stiff occasions when they had bumped into each other at the grocery store or in the driveway by the mailboxes. She had lost the five pounds and then some, but she didn't look good. Giselle had heard them fighting next door on a couple of occasions. One night Bill had roared off in his Corvette, taking the corner so fast that he plowed into the neighbor's chain-link fence and broke a headlight. It was one of the few times in recent memory that she had seen Dan crack a spontaneous smile.

Teddy looked surprised at the mention of Lois's name. He didn't knock her arm off when she rested a hand on his shoulder.

The path to the student union led past the day care center where she used to leave Trina. Looking straight ahead, Giselle tugged at Teddy's hand, dragging him as quickly as possible past the gaily painted jungle gym that dominated the small fenced-in yard. She remembered dropping off Trina there for the first time. She was so little. Giselle had steeled herself to hear heartrending wails as she walked away, but Trina was sitting in the corner sandbox with two other toddlers, poking at the sand with an orange plastic shovel, seemingly amused and content. Giselle had felt relief at first, followed by a swift descent into self-doubt. Shouldn't a child cry and cling to her mother's skirt? She remembered Teddy's first day of kindergarten. How he'd thrown up in the car and then clung to the chain-link fence, screaming at her not to leave him. She had slunk away feeling like a murderer. But that was preferable to feeling so dispensable. This was like leaving your lover at the gate — a long tender embrace, the slow shuffle down the Jetway — then turning back for one last tearful look, only to see him chatting blithely to some stranger. When Dan called to ask how it had gone, she found herself fibbing. "Not too bad," she had said, "only a few tears."

The student union was brightly lit but deserted. Only a handful of solitary figures sitting at small tables, drinking coffee and munching hamburgers or burritos, with books lying open in front of them. She had never seen it like this before, only during the day when the lines were long and tables hard to come by amid the deafening dissonance of a hundred conversations going on at once.

"I want an ice cream cone," Teddy announced, daring her to just say no.

"Okay." She walked over toward the ice cream stand, eager to make amends for the broken Talkboy. She imagined his telling the therapist what she had done, his voice quivering with righteous indignation. "One chocolate cone and one small Diet Coke," she told the young woman behind the counter, who looked vaguely familiar, as if she had been in a class with Giselle. But then, from the vantage point of age, most of the students looked alike to her. This girl was more striking than most, though, with deep-set brown eyes and glossy blunt-cut platinum hair straight out of a Vidal Sassoon commercial. Giselle immediately felt frumpy and certain that the girl could see her red-rimmed eyes through the lenses of her dark glasses. Ray•Bans, a birthday gift from Dan.

"Aren't you Professor Trias's wife?" the girl asked as she handed Giselle Teddy's cone.

Giselle nodded, taken by surprise.

"I was in his Fitzgerald and Hemingway seminar. We had a party at your house, you know, for the last class." Her face lit up. "It was a really great class."

Teddy tugged at her purse, and Giselle handed him his ice cream with a wad of paper napkins. She could tell that the girl was about to launch into a little speech about what a prince Dan was, praise that she was in no mood to hear, so Giselle snatched her Diet Coke, mumbled a thank-you, and beat a hasty retreat.

She settled Teddy at a table where she could keep an eye on him while she used one of the pay phones next to the candy counter. She looked up AAA in the Yellow Pages. To her surprise, someone answered right away and said a tow truck should be there within twenty minutes. Then she dropped a second quarter into the slot and dialed the Beemers' number, which she still knew by heart. Her palms were sweating. She prayed that Bill wouldn't answer. Maybe it was unfair, pushing all the blame onto Bill, but that was how she felt. His Corvette hadn't been around for the past several days, so she figured he was probably away. The phone rang and rang. She counted six rings and was about to hang up when Eric answered. "Beemer residence." Like some sort of child butler.

"Hi," she said. "Is your mother there?"

"Mom!" Eric shouted, dropping the receiver with an unceremonious clatter. "Hey, Mo-omm!" After a minute he picked up the receiver again and asked, "Who is this? She's in the bathroom."

Giselle almost hung up, but she knew if she did, then she would have to talk to Dan. She felt caught between a rock and a hard place, a familiar feeling these days. They couldn't sit in the parking lot all night. "It's Giselle," she mumbled and was about to add that he shouldn't disturb his mother if she was busy, but he was already shouting, "It's Teddy's mother!"

From the phone booth she watched Teddy licking his ice cream cone methodically to catch any drips. She tried to imagine how a stranger would see him, whether he looked like a normal nine-year-old. When she looked at him these days, she was reminded of news footage of children in refugee camps, staring at the camera with a world-weary distrust. He avoided eye contact. And when, on occasion, she would turn his face toward her, it gave her the creeps. What paramedics called "doll's eyes," that fixed glassy stare that signaled the end was in sight.

"Hello?" Lois sounded breathless and tentative. It occurred to Giselle that Lois might be afraid she was calling to berate her, to unleash the full force of her smoldering anger at long last.

"Hi, I was, uh, just wondering if —" A group of rowdy students jostled past her, shouting and laughing, drowning her out.

"What?" Lois shouted. "I can't hear you."

"I was wondering," she began again, "if I could ask a favor. Teddy and I are at the university. Our car broke down and —"

"Of course!" Lois jumped in eagerly, before Giselle could even finish the request. "Where are you? I'll be right there."

"We'll be waiting in the parking lot, but you don't need to

rush. Triple A said it would be about twenty minutes. And they tend to be optimistic."

"It's no problem," Lois said. "Just give me directions."

As Giselle told her the quickest way to get there, she thought about how Dan's pride would never allow him to ask Lois for a favor. Giselle knew that he would rather crawl home on his hands and knees. A couple of attorneys had called them right after the accident, offering a free consultation to discuss a possible cause of action against the Beemers. Giselle had been adamant; she did not want to pursue it. A lawsuit would only spark more publicity and drag things out. For Teddy's sake they needed to move on. What would they gain from a lawsuit anyway? But Dan was more ambivalent. It wasn't revenge, he argued, to want them to admit responsibility. But, at her urging, he told the first lawyer no. Then when a second lawyer called a few days later, Dan couldn't help himself. He went to his office for a consultation. When he got home, he refused to say anything about it beyond the fact that the lawyer was willing to take the case. Giselle had met this bit of news with tight-lipped silence. She prepared herself for a major battle. But, for whatever reason, he decided not to pursue it. A couple of days later when the lawyer called back, she overheard Dan telling him that he didn't want to proceed any further. The lawyer must have tried to argue with him. After a brief silence Dan snapped, "Yes, well, but you aren't in my shoes, are you?" and hung up. She had breathed a huge sigh of relief. Maybe they weren't exactly in the same boat, but they were at least steering the same course. And she felt as if she'd just got her first glimpse of dry land. But now there was this book. Which he had been working on in secret, knowing damn well what her reaction would be. The full depth of the betrayal had yet to sink in fully. She supposed she was still in shock. She couldn't believe it. She flashed on an image of him communing with Oprah. And Teddy's new school friends saying, "Hey, I saw your stepdad on TV yesterday. What's it feel like to shoot someone? So how come you're not in jail?"

When she hung up, she bought Teddy a roll of Life Savers from the candy counter. She still felt guilty about the Talkboy.

"Let's go back to the car and wait for the tow truck." She handed him the Life Savers, which he accepted without comment. As he was busy unwrapping them, she took a quick swipe at his mouth with the wadded napkins. He frowned and ducked his head so quickly that she ended up poking him in the eye. "Ow!" he protested in a shrill, aggrieved tone, as if she had hurt him on purpose. She glanced back at the ice cream counter to see if Dan's former student was watching. The girl was wiping off the machines, getting ready to close up. "Okay then, do it yourself." She handed Teddy the napkins.

As they walked across the campus to the parking lot, her stomach grumbled. Teddy snickered. She supposed she should have grabbed something to eat. Teddy kicked at stray stones. She had noted a new aggressiveness in his movements that worried her. He slammed drawers, punched the buttons on his computer, stabbed at the paper with his pencil, yanked on his clothes in the morning, crunched his cereal as if he were chewing gravel. The other night he had brushed his teeth so hard that his gums bled, whereas before, he had merely waved the brush in the general vicinity of his teeth. And Mrs. Shimono, his teacher, had sent home a note recently saying that Teddy had broken Chandra Patel's new fountain pen. When Giselle had asked him why he'd done such a thing, he claimed it was an accident. He had just pressed down so hard, the metal point snapped off. He hadn't meant to break it. Giselle believed he was telling the truth. Even so, she had made him write a note of apology to Chandra and give it to her along with five dollars from his own private stash in the Band-Aid box. "But it wasn't my fault," he'd grumbled. "You said sometimes things are nobody's fault, remember?" He had stood there gripping the Band-Aid box, staring straight at her, waiting for a response.

"I never said that," she lied, and walked out of his bedroom.

Sometimes she couldn't believe what a lousy mother she was. It seemed as if, in some sick way, she derived a certain pleasure from reminding herself just how low she could go. Then, later, her con-science would bother her and she would try, unsuccessfully, to make amends. When she was kissing him good night, she had said, "It's true that sometimes some things aren't really anybody's fault. But if you have it within your power to make up for it, like Chan-dra's pen, then you should. Even if you didn't mean to do anything wrong. Understand?" She had smiled down at him as if he were lit-tle Timmy and she were June Lockhart. As she turned off the light, she could almost hear Lassie wagging her tail in the dark.

"It's your fault for leaving my dad," he'd mumbled. "If you didn't get a divorce, we'd still be in Lincoln and I'd never of shot Trina."

The smile died on her face. "That's a stupid thing to say," she snapped. "If we hadn't got a divorce, Trina wouldn't even have been born."

"See?"

She'd slammed his door shut and walked away.

In the parking lot, while they were waiting for the tow truck, Teddy found a red Bic lighter lying on the asphalt next to a beau-tifully restored black GTO. She noticed something flicker out of the corner of her eye and saw that he was playing with the flame. She sighed. After the Talkboy incident she didn't feel like getting into a hassle over the lighter. But she couldn't very well sit by and let him incinerate himself. She had seen a terrible thing on one of the newsmagazine shows the other night. A young couple had bought a defective crib monitor that caught on fire. The baby had died and their other child, sleeping in the same room, had been badly burned. Giselle had to shut her eyes when they showed a close-up of the disfigured boy. Since then she had thought of the couple often, when she was lying in bed at night not sleep-ing. They had seemed genuinely close, united against a common enemy: the negligent crib monitor manufacturer. At the same time that she could not imagine how they could endure such loss, she envied them this enemy outside the gates. Someone they could blame with all their single-minded wrath. Someone they could point their finger at on national television. She was sure that it was the only thing that saved them. She sighed again, then got out of the Honda and walked over to Teddy. "Give me that, please?" she said as affably as possible.

"Why?"

"Because it's dangerous. You know that."

"It doesn't even work," he said.

"Let me see." She held out her hand, palm up.

"I won't light it," he pleaded, changing his tack. "I promise."

"I don't know," she said, wavering. "I don't think it's a good idea, Teddy." But even though she knew it wasn't a good idea, she was about to weaken, anything to preserve peace, when he said, "You broke my Talkboy Jr." Pissed off, she grabbed the lighter out of his hand and shoved it into her pocket.

"I hate you," he informed her calmly.

She stuck out her tongue at him, something that used to make him laugh even when he was in a bad mood, but he didn't crack a smile. She sighed and massaged her temples. She felt a headache coming on. There was aspirin in her purse but nowhere to get any water to take it with. She remembered the time she was sitting in the car in front of Teddy's school, waiting for him. Trina was throwing a tantrum, shrieking in her ear, and Giselle's head was pounding. She'd been up half the night studying for an exam. She popped two Tylenol into her mouth and then grabbed the juice bottle away from Trina, who shrieked even louder. Giselle was sitting there sucking on the plastic baby bottle, attempting to swallow the two pills, when Teddy and his friends appeared. One of the boys elbowed him in the ribs and shouted, "Look, your mom's drinking from a baby bottle!" Teddy's face had flushed bright red, and he'd stalked over to the car and hissed, "Don't do that! It looks stupid." Laughing, she had handed the bottle back to her fussing daughter, then turned to her sulking son and said, "Oh, lighten up! It's not the end of the world." And that evening at supper

Teddy had related the whole incident to Dan, giggling so hard that he could hardly get the words out.

She sighed again and looked at her watch. The tow truck was behind schedule. Big surprise.

"There's Lois." Teddy pointed to the Jeep Cherokee turning into the parking lot. "Eric's with her!" He perked up and waved.

Giselle could see that Lois was smoking. Last New Year's Day she had made a resolution to quit, and she had. She was worried about gaining weight, but Bill had quit smoking the year before and was hounding her to quit, too. She had gone to the doctor and got a patch. On April Fool's Day Bill had surprised her with a diamond bracelet as a reward for having kicked the habit. Giselle and Dan had been invited for dinner, and as Bill presented Lois with the velvet box, Dan and Giselle had rolled their eyes at each other behind his back while Lois oohed and ahhed and Bill went on about what a great deal he'd got on the bracelet in Bangkok.

She was glad when the tow truck rumbled into the lot right behind Lois. The awkwardness of the reunion, of sorts, was smoothed over by the sudden bustle of activity. The two boys buzzed around the tow truck driver, asking him questions while Giselle signed the charge slip and told the driver where to take the car.

While they were waiting, she turned to Lois and said, "I appreciate your coming. Dan's teaching." Which wasn't true, of course, but she thought Lois must be wondering where he was.

Lois just nodded. "I'm glad to help. You must know that." Her eyes filled with tears, and she turned her head away and called out something to Eric. Giselle noted, with some satisfaction, that Lois did not look good. Her hair was too blond and her eyes were too green, a startling emerald. Tinted contact lenses that glittered in her pale face like stoplights.

"Bill's moving out," she said abruptly. "He's rented an apartment in the Marina."

Giselle replayed the sentences in her mind, attempting to get a fix on Lois's tone. Did she catch an undertone of resentment?

Was Lois somehow blaming her for the inevitable demise of her crummy marriage? As if reading her mind, Lois said, "He blames it on you. I mean, on what happened. It makes me sick." She took a deep drag on her cigarette and exhaled. "He never could accept responsibility for anything. He's just an overgrown child with pilot's wings."

Giselle didn't know what to say. She watched as the tow truck driver, a tall blond surfer type in a faded pink Maui T-shirt, hopped into the cab of his pickup and drove off with her old Honda trailing behind like a hooked fish. The boys ran over, and the four of them climbed into the Jeep, the two boys in the back. Giselle turned around and smiled at Teddy, to make sure he was doing okay with Eric. They were huddled over some Gameboy that was giving off little beeps. For a moment he seemed just like his old self. Then, feeling her eyes on him, he looked up at her, a wary expression on his face as his smile faded. She turned back around. A Chieftains tape was playing sprightly Irish music at full volume, too loud for conversation.

Giselle was remembering how Lois used to fuss over Trina, bringing her presents from their travels — a plaid tam from Scotland, a tiny aloha shirt from Honolulu. Lois had always wanted a daughter. Bill, of course, had wanted a boy. When Eric was born, Lois had consoled herself with the thought that their second child would be a girl. But then she'd had two miscarriages and a hysterectomy. Even though Bill wasn't keen on the idea, Lois had been looking into the possibility of a private adoption. But now that Bill was leaving, that was that. Giselle thought it was only fair. Imagine how she'd feel if Lois and Bill had a baby girl. Maybe that was mean and irrational, but she didn't care. After all, she was paying $130 an hour to be reassured, once a week for fifty minutes, that such irrational anger was perfectly normal.

"I've really missed talking to you," Lois said. "But I understand." She reached over and tentatively touched Giselle's hand. "I still can't believe it happened." Giselle nodded. Her hand flinched involuntarily and Lois pulled hers back. She needed both hands on the wheel to make the turn onto their street.

The front door was open and Dan was standing there, looking out through the screen, as the Jeep pulled into the Beemers' driveway. Giselle was surprised, although she supposed she shouldn't have been. No doubt, he'd returned to his office and found the ripped-up letter, then hurried home to make sure she wasn't going to do anything really crazy. Like slash his clothing and burn his books. Her stomach knotted.

He opened the screen door and stepped out onto the front stoop as she was thanking Lois for the ride. Eric asked if Teddy could come inside, he wanted to show him some new toy. Giselle hesitated and then shrugged. What did it matter anyway? "Half an hour," she said, trying to sound in control. She glanced at her watch. "Be home by eight-thirty."

"I'll make sure he is," Lois said, glancing nervously in Dan's direction. He was wearing black pants and a black V-necked sweater over a white T-shirt. From a distance he looked like a priest.

As Giselle cut across the weedy, neglected lawn to her own front door, Dan retreated inside, letting the door bang shut behind him. She paused on the front stoop for a moment to concentrate again on her anger, the pure outrage, a moment of clarity before it all got twisted and muddled. Sometimes she almost missed Ed's stubborn silence, his refusal to get into it with her when she was mad. He would just sit there, his face turning red, until he blew his stack and stomped off, muttering curses, grinding the gears of his old motorcycle as he peeled away from the curb. In high school Dan had been a star debater. The instant she stepped inside the house, he confronted her. "What were you doing with *her?*"

"The best defense is a good offense," she snapped, brushing past him to the kitchen, where she poured herself a glass of water and just managed to swallow two aspirin before he appeared in the doorway, glaring at her. Immediately, she felt herself in the wrong and had to remind herself that she was the one who had a legitimate right to be angry.

"Where's Teddy?" he said, although he knew perfectly well where he was. He had seen him get out of the Jeep and go inside the Beemers' house with Eric.

"What do you care?" She slammed her glass down on the counter and looked him in the eye, forcing herself to stare him down. "You want to interview him for your book?"

"I was going to tell you about it," he said, looking away. "Nothing's definite yet. I figured there was no use bringing it up until I had something solid to show you. To see what you thought."

"Right," she snorted. She could feel the dry aspirin burning the back of her throat. Her pulse raced. She took another sip of water to calm herself. "Since when do you require my editorial input?"

He shrugged. "You're not rational. I knew you wouldn't be able to talk about this rationally."

"Fuck you, you self-righteous asshole!" It felt good to shout even if he only chalked it up as further proof of her irrationality. Score one point for his side.

"I'm not doing this to hurt anyone, believe me." He lowered his voice and took a step closer to her. "God knows, we've all been hurt enough." There were tears glinting in his dark eyes. He held out his arms, and part of her wanted to fall into them. Receive his priestly absolution. She could feel her body weakening, like rigor mortis in reverse, her jaw and fists unclenching. And then he said, "I honestly think it will be good for Teddy. To get it all out in the open."

She shoved him back against the counter. "You make me sick," she hissed. "You don't know the first thing about being a parent, you arrogant bastard."

"Yeah, well maybe I would've learned if your son hadn't killed my daughter."

"It's not something you learn. That's your problem." She bulldozed her way past him as he tried to block her, to put her in her proper place with some brilliant comeback. Like a child, she clapped her hands over both ears and ran. She ran right smack into Teddy, who was standing in the hallway. "What are you doing here?" she demanded, startled.

"I used to live here," he replied in this eerie grown-up voice. "When I was a kid."

I T IS THE MIDDLE OF THE NIGHT. A NIGHTMARE, *or maybe just hunger, has jolted him wide awake. It feels like a small animal is gnawing away inside his stomach, maybe hollowing out a spot to nest. He thinks about tiptoeing to the kitchen for a snack — a handful of mint Oreos or a couple of slices of prewrapped American cheese — but he doesn't want to risk waking up Dan, who is sleeping on the sofa after the big fight. Chances are, he isn't asleep either. Teddy imagines that all three of them are lying in the darkness all alone and wide awake, hating each other. He knows how Dan feels about him. And he's pretty sure his mother hates him, too, but isn't allowed to say so, because she's his mother. If he were his mother, he'd hate him. He wouldn't have any choice. It would be confusing probably, because he knew you weren't supposed to hate your own kid. But the other day on Oprah he'd heard some parents talking about how they wanted to divorce their kids because the kids were so bad. One of the ladies in the audience asked one of the mothers on the stage if she still loved her son, and the mother on the stage just shook her head and started crying. And then there was that mother on the news who drowned her two little boys, pushed the car into the lake with them inside. Then she lied to the police and said someone had stolen them. She was crying into the microphone as if she really missed them, pre-*

*tending that she really loved them, just like his own mom was pre-
tending that she still loved him.*

*Before he fell asleep, he'd heard her crying in her bedroom. She
used to cry that way sometimes in their old apartment before Dan.
Because she was just lonely, she said, when Teddy would ask her what
was wrong. A lot of nights she would crawl into bed with him. If he
woke up, they would fall asleep together. She smelled good, like flowers. When Dan started staying overnight, Teddy missed his mother's
crawling into bed with him. Even on the nights Dan wasn't there, she
didn't do it anymore. But he was glad she didn't cry at night anymore,
even though he wanted to move back to Nebraska. Sometimes his dad
sounded sad on the phone. The happier his mom was, the sadder his
dad sounded.*

*Before they moved to California, his mother had slept on the sofa
in the living room for a long time. In the morning she would fold up
the sheets and blankets and shove them into a straw hamper in the
corner so that he could sit on the sofa and watch cartoons while he ate
his cereal. Most mornings his dad was already gone by the time Teddy
woke up. Now probably Dan would move out. His mother would get
lonely again and cry herself to sleep. Only this time it will be worse.
Teddy knows that this time she won't want to crawl into bed with
him.*

*He remembers his mother talking with Eric's mother about how
the lady who pushed her kids into the lake had done it because of her
boyfriend. The boyfriend didn't like the kids, and she wanted to be
with the boyfriend. Teddy knows for sure that Dan doesn't like him
anymore. He heard what Dan said about his killing Trina. And probably his mother thinks that if Teddy weren't around, if he were dead
or something, Dan wouldn't have to sleep on the sofa. He would still
love her. She has to know that it is all Teddy's fault, even if she is
his mother. He can see it in her eyes when she looks at him when she
doesn't think he is looking at her. He wishes he were dead. Like Trina.*

*He wishes the Beemers still had that gun. If they did, he would
sneak over there and shoot himself with it. He'd wait until Eric was
at school and Mrs. Beemer was at the store or something. Then he*

would sneak out of the playground at recess and run back here. He knows where the Beemers hide their spare key, under a flowerpot on the back deck. When they found his dead body, his mother would probably cry and feel bad for a while, but then Dan would put his arms around her to make her feel better. He would stop sleeping on the sofa. And they would start thinking about how brave poor Teddy was to shoot himself like that, and they wouldn't be mad at him anymore.

He could run away — he has some money saved up — but how? He doesn't think they would sell a bus ticket or a plane ticket to a nine-year-old boy. And he is afraid to hitchhike. His mother has told him over and over how cruel, sick people pick up little kids and do terrible things to them before dumping their bodies in the woods. Even though Teddy doesn't mind the idea of being dead, he doesn't want to be tortured and mutilated first.

His stomach grumbles underneath the covers. He feels trapped. He can't go back to sleep and he can't go to the kitchen. He feels he is going to spend the rest of his life lying there wide awake in the dark, starving. Which, he knows from watching the Discovery Channel, is a very painful way to die, unlike freezing to death, which is not supposed to hurt. You just get numb and sort of float away. But it is impossible to freeze to death in California. He could freeze to death in Nebraska if he could figure out how to get there and if it were winter. He would walk out into a deserted field and lie down in a soft white bed of snow and drift off to sleep and never wake up. But it is the beginning of June. There won't be any snow for another five or six months. And he can't wait that long.

He thinks of other ways to kill yourself. He knows there is some way where you sit in the car in the garage, but he isn't exactly sure how it works, and Dan would be sure to hear him anyway. Then he remembers that his mother has a bottle of Nytol in the medicine cabinet. She got it just recently; he'd heard her complaining to Dan that it didn't work nearly as well as the pills she used to get from Lois. He knows that some really famous blond movie star killed herself that way, because he remembers his mother watching a movie on TV not so long ago. The movie star was lying on her bed in her pajamas, trying to call the president.

He pushes back the covers and climbs out of bed. At his doorway he pauses, making sure that no one is up. He doesn't hear anything except a low mumble from the TV set, which is on in the living room. Then he creeps into the bathroom, shuts the door, and turns on the light. He stands on his old footstool, which he doesn't need anymore — he used to have to stand on it to brush his teeth — and opens the medicine chest. He freezes up as the mirrored door squeaks open. His reflection, so big and close, startles him. He waits a moment, avoiding his face in the mirror. If he looks into his own eyes, he might chicken out. When he doesn't hear any noise from the hallway, he snatches the small bottle of Maximum Strength Nytol, which is half hidden behind the calamine lotion. Then he slips the bottle into the pocket of his jeans — he hasn't bothered to change into his pajamas — and makes his way quietly back to his room.

SHE WAS COLD IN THE SKIMPY TOP SHE WORE TO bed, one of Dan's old white undershirts. She got up and turned off the air-conditioner. It went into a noisy convulsion, rattling and shuddering to a halt. It was not really hot enough to need air-conditioning, but she had turned it on to screen out sound from the rest of the house, to create a cocoon of white noise.

After the argument they had gone to their separate corners of the house like two boxers waiting for the next round. Only it was worse than that. The gloves were off now. She could feel it. Whatever civility they had been clinging to, by some silent mutual agreement, had been knocked out cold. They were free to hit below the belt. She was scared but at the same time exhilarated. She could feel the adrenaline pumping. Alert, wary. On her toes.

In the sudden quiet she pressed her ear to the door, straining to hear the mumble of the television from the living room. The house felt too quiet. Some tension had lifted. She could feel it. A tug-of-war gone slack. She slipped on a robe, for greater dignity, and tiptoed down the hall.

The living room was empty, the television screen blank. The comforter was neatly folded on top of the pillow at the end of the sofa. She looked at her watch. *Where could he have gone at 12:15?*

The kitchen light was on. She found a note stuck to the refrigerator with a banana magnet. *Couldn't sleep. Gone to the office. Want to go out for breakfast? Give me a call. D.* She let out her breath. She realized she had stopped breathing the instant she spied the note. She had been expecting something more along the lines of *Good-bye and good luck, you'll need it.*

She poured herself a shot glass of bourbon, a nightcap, and deconstructed the note. It was curt, but the invitation to breakfast encoded a whole lot of their past. Before Dan had begun spending the night at her apartment, he used to get up and leave before Teddy woke up. Then, after Teddy was off to school, she would meet Dan for breakfast at the Buttercup, a shabby, classic coffee shop not far from campus. The waitress was a dead ringer for Ethel Merman with dyed red hair in a hairnet. She called them "kids," as in "You kids want the usual?" "The usual" — Giselle loved the phrase — it made them sound like an old married couple. Maybe by California standards six months was a golden anniversary. They would sit in a booth and talk and laugh and hold hands. She would be floating on air for the rest of the day. Not long after Trina was born, the Buttercup went out of business. One day she drove past it and it was closed. The next time she drove by, the place had a face-lift and a new sign: SAMURAI SUSHI GRAND OPENING!!!

On her way back to the bedroom she pushed open Teddy's door to check on him, to see if the covers needed straightening or the window needed to be shut. She was gratified to see that he was sleeping peacefully. As she walked over to pull up the covers, she stepped on something hard in her bare feet. She was used to stepping on Legos all over Teddy's floor, tired of nagging him to sweep all the stuff into the toy box when he was done playing. Later, she would remember how she was about to toss the thing into the toy box without looking at it when something — she remembered it clearly — some maternal something made her walk out into the lit hall and look at it. And then she saw what it was. The bottle of Nytol from the medicine chest.

She panicked and dropped the bottle and ran back to the bed

and shook Teddy by the shoulders, calling his name. "Teddy! Teddy! Teddy! Wake up, Teddy!" He moaned and flopped like a rag doll. But he was breathing, thank God. She ran back out and picked up the bottle and read the fine print on the label. IN CASE OF ACCIDENTAL OVERDOSE, SEEK PROFESSIONAL ASSISTANCE OR CONTACT A POISON CONTROL CENTER IMMEDIATELY. She was torn between calling the Poison Control Center — the number was on a list of emergency numbers stuck to the refrigerator — or just dialing 911. Or just throwing him in the car and driving to the emergency room. *Immediately* — she stood there paralyzed by indecision, thinking she had to act *immediately*. She thought about Ed, about the time that Teddy swallowed the backgammon piece and couldn't breathe. While she was on the phone calling the ambulance, Ed had performed the Heimlich maneuver. The checker popped right out. She wished Ed were here now. But he wasn't. She grabbed the phone off the hook and dialed the number for Poison Control. A woman answered on the first ring. "My son took a bottle of Nytol pills!" Giselle screamed into the phone. "I can't wake him up!"

"How old is he?" The woman's voice was calm and businesslike.

"Nine. Almost ten."

The woman asked how long ago he had taken the pills and how many. Giselle glanced at the kitchen clock. "Sometime after ten o'clock," she said. She looked at the bottle again. "There were sixteen pills, but I took some myself" — she tried to remember how many. "Maybe four, maybe six, I don't know. Not that many. Oh, God —"

The woman's voice interrupted her. "The over-the-counter sedatives contain diphenhydramine hydrochloride, which generally isn't that harmful." A car sped by outside, windows down, blaring loud rap music. Giselle held the phone to her ear more tightly, concentrating on the woman's instructions. "But you should take him to the emergency room. Since it has been less than four hours, they can still pump his stomach. After four hours, the pills are absorbed and it's too late for that. But if you think it has been only about two hours —"

"Yes, I'm sure," Giselle cut in. "He went to bed at ten. I'll take him to the hospital. It's close, just a few blocks." She slammed down the phone as the woman was requesting her name and address, grabbed her purse and key ring, then ran back to the bedroom and half carried, half dragged Teddy to the garage door. She still had her robe on, but she didn't care. Teddy was limp, a dead weight in her arms. When she opened the garage door, she was shocked for a moment to find it empty. Then she remembered the tow truck. Christ! She couldn't believe it. Of all the times to be without a car. As she dragged Teddy into the living room and propped him up on the sofa with some pillows, she cursed Dan for not being there. Then she ran into the kitchen and dialed 911.

After throwing on a pair of jeans and a sweatshirt, she paced around waiting for the paramedics, wishing she had asked the Poison Control woman if she should put him in the shower — run cold water over him. Or force some coffee down his throat. Or Coke. Caffeine. In the movies they always made the person walk. She put her arms around Teddy and dragged him up onto her own feet and sort of walked him around the room. She remembered this life-size rag doll she'd had when she was about his age. It had stirrups on its feet that you could slip your own feet into so you could dance together. The doll had yellow yarn pigtails and a red-and-white polka-dot dress. She had forgotten all about her until now. Suddenly it occurred to her that she hadn't called Dan. Or Ed, of course. But Ed was too far away to do anything. She didn't want to worry him until it was all over. She would call him from the hospital or when the paramedics assured her that Teddy would be fine. She was still thinking about calling Dan, wondering why she should even have to think twice about it, when she heard the siren's wail screaming in the distance, homing in on them. It was déjà vu. She felt faint, short of breath. She covered her ears with her hands. A sickening thought hit her. *What if they were the same paramedics who had come for Trina? What kind of mother will they think I am?* Involuntarily she looked out the glass doors toward the backyard. The Beemers' dog was howling and barking at the commotion as the ambulance wailed into the driveway. In the darkness the glass doors reflected her own image back at her.

At the hospital they pumped his stomach and assured her that Teddy would be fine. Different doctors, a different floor, but the same smell, the same fear like a boa constrictor wrapped around her vital organs. She wanted to get out of there as soon as possible. The doctor said a couple of hours of rest and observation. He seemed sympathetic. And young, with a ponytail and tiny octagonal glasses so small that she wondered how he could see through them. It worried her. You would think a doctor would want the best possible vision. Then that small, niggling worry was interrupted by a bigger worry when he told her that a psychiatrist would want to talk with her shortly. She must have looked blank. "It's routine procedure," he added, "in cases like these."

"But we already have someone, a psychologist," Giselle said.

He patted her shoulder and left her in the waiting room.

She had been so focused on the pills themselves, on making sure he was going to live, that she hadn't really taken in the larger implications of how the pills had ended up in Teddy's stomach. Now it hit her that her nine-year-old son had tried to kill himself. Her nine-year-old son, whose birthday was next month, July 4, had tried to commit suicide. She had managed not to cry all night, but now she couldn't help herself. She had been thinking she could go call Ed now and tell him that everything was fine. No need to worry. She had thought about not telling him at all, but she was worried that Teddy would tell him; then Ed would be angry with her, demanding to know what was going on "out there." But now it hit her just what she would be telling him. As if only now that she knew Teddy was going to be okay, at least physically, could she begin to think about the rest of it. It occurred to her at that point that she should call Hannah Cole. For all she was worth, with her Stanford diploma. Giselle's anger suddenly flared up and raged toward the therapist. Her perfect hair and clothes and tastefully decorated office with its Haitian paintings. Giselle had felt all along in her gut that Hannah was too young, too inexperienced, but Dan had been impressed by her credentials. And after all these weeks, what had she accomplished with Teddy? Obviously not a whole fucking lot. Incensed, Giselle fumbled in her purse for a quarter and marched over to a pay phone. She tried to insert the quarter into the slot but dropped it. Her hands were trembling. The quarter rolled away, under the vending machine. "Shit!" She was on her hands and knees, cursing, when the psychiatrist walked up. "Mrs. Trias?" he asked tentatively. If he had slapped a straitjacket on her and thrown her into a locked ward, she would have been grateful. Instead, he led her to a tiny neutral office, not much larger than a confessional. As she babbled on, he listened quietly, his hands folded the way they did when they were kids — Here's the church and here's the steeple; open the door and see the people! — his chin balanced precariously on the tip of the steeple. Giselle hated to think what he must be thinking.

The divorce agreement stipulated that Teddy spend a month each summer with his father. So when Ed demanded that Teddy come to Nebraska immediately, Giselle said okay, "since he would be going soon anyway — there was only a week of school left." She was trying to save face. In fact, she was eager to get Teddy away from home, into a new environment, but she didn't want to admit to Ed just how bad things were. How helpless she felt. How hopeless. She continued to blame Dr. Cole, who kept leaving messages. But Giselle refused to talk to her or let Teddy talk to her. It felt good at last to have a target for her anger, someone to blame. Dan said she was being irrational. Even the psychiatrist at the hospital, Dr. Krings, said Hannah couldn't be held responsible. But Giselle didn't care; she didn't want to hear it.

It had been only two days. Thursday and Friday. Dan was staying at his mother's place. Giselle was furious with him as well. She
didn't want to lay eyes on him. At the hospital she had called a cab
to take her and Teddy home. Then she had called Dan at the office,
told him about Teddy, and suggested that he stay with his mother
for a while, to give them both a break, a little time to cool off. He
hadn't offered any resistance. He seemed relieved to be out of
the house. Teddy was leaving on Saturday morning. Giselle had
wanted a couple of days with him before he took off. A couple of
days to mend or bond or whatever. To talk heart to heart. But although Teddy was uncharacteristically agreeable, almost cheerful — visibly relieved to be going fifteen hundred miles away —
he remained politely remote. Like a guest. His suitcase sat in his
room, already packed. Seeing him so upbeat, she wanted to shake
him. It hit her that maybe he had orchestrated this whole thing,
manipulated her into sending him away. Away from the scene of
his crime. And then she felt guilt-stricken for thinking such a
thing. After all, he had tried to kill himself. He was just a kid.

Lately it occurred to her more and more that maybe she was just
a kid, too — only older. Maybe you never really grew up at all.
Maybe adulthood was a myth, except for those few obvious exceptions like Mother Teresa and Ralph Nader. The rest of us were
all a bunch of scared, desperate imposters. Children in adults'
clothing. Although, more and more, especially in California, she
had noticed that adults didn't even bother to dress like adults. You
saw fifty-year-old women in skimpy sunsuits, sixty-year-old men
in T-shirts and dungarees. Her father wore a suit and tie to work
every day, and to restaurants, school plays, cocktail parties. Her
mother wore nylons and heels. They at least acted the part. They
had always managed to convince her that they were adults and
that one day she, too, would be an adult like them — like it or not.
Even if maybe inside they felt confused or needy. There was a lot
to be said for just dressing the part.

It was odd, but her marriage to Ed had felt somehow more real or adult, despite the stupidity of it, than her marriage to Dan. Every day she woke up knowing that she was a wife and mother, even if she hadn't chosen to be, whereas with Dan it had always felt a little like playing house. She didn't know why exactly. She had always felt a bit like the ingenue. With Ed, even though they were both barely drinking age, she used to brood about growing old together. She could see it all too clearly, like time-lapse photography. Ed would be on his third or fourth La-Z-Boy, replaced every few years during a blowout sale at Nebraska Furniture Mart. He would look exactly like his father with a thatch of white hair and a face as lined, leathery, and all-American as an old baseball mitt. Somehow she had never pictured Dan grown old, maybe because he was older when she met him, already in his mid-thirties. Or maybe because she had never met his father. Or maybe because some part of her knew that he would already be long gone. Till death do us part. Well, Trina was dead and now they were apart.

The night before Teddy left for Nebraska, they went to the movies, just the two of them — the way they used to, before Dan. Giselle hated sitting in a movie theater alone, even though she knew it was silly — she didn't like for anyone to talk to her during movies anyway — but there was something about being in the dark in public. She wanted a familiar body next to her. And she loved the movies, ever since she was a kid. She still felt guilty about the way she used to drag Teddy out into the frigid winter when he was a baby, bundled up in blankets, and shush him when he started to fuss during the movie. Or the times he had to sit through boring and inappropriate movies as her "date." "Let's go on a date," she'd say, and bribe him with popcorn and huge, overpriced boxes of candy. Junior Mints, Raisinets, Good & Plenty. The poor kid would sit there squirming or napping — ruining his teeth — through *The House of the Spirits* or *Sommersby*.

But this time it was Teddy's choice. Even he knew what she was up to, trying to ingratiate herself before he went back to his dad, so he would say nice things about her, think nice thoughts. Maybe even miss her. One last desperate attempt to make things right.

At the food court of the mall, next to the movie theaters, she bought him pizza and an Oreo Blizzard. They had time to kill before the movie started. A new *Star Trek* movie. She couldn't even remember the title. Teddy was kicking his feet under the table, anxious to get going. He had already kicked her in the shins twice, and she'd told him to quit it. Since the sleeping pill incident — she flinched whenever Ed referred to it as the "suicide attempt" — Teddy's listlessness had been replaced by this restless, manic energy. Yesterday she had stood at the window as he raced his bike around the block in circles, peddling like a person possessed. After a couple of laps she had started counting, and finally after his tenth time around the same block, she had gone out and ordered him to come inside the house. She had attempted to talk with him about the pill incident, but he clammed up whenever she mentioned it. When she'd asked him to promise her he'd never do anything like that again, he had shrugged and said, "Okay, I promise," in a tone of voice she hadn't found the least bit reassuring.

At the next table there was a little dark-haired girl in a high chair eating lo mein with her fingers. She was Asian but from the back looked just like Trina. The mother and sister were deftly shoveling away their noodles with chopsticks, smiling and chatting. The brother was eating a hamburger and fries. Every so often he would feed his little sister a french fry, dangling it just above her mouth, and she'd leap for it like a fish taking the bait. It struck Giselle as slightly sadistic, but the mother seemed oblivious. Giselle watched Teddy watching them. She couldn't read the look on his face. She was about to suggest that they go, "in case there's a line at the theater," when Teddy looked at her and said, "You never talk about Trina." It sounded like an accusation. "If you think that makes me feel better, it doesn't. 'Cause I know you're thinking about her all the time."

Giselle didn't know what to say. He'd caught her by surprise. She was struck dumb by the truth and perspicacity of his statement. She took a sip of her coffee. He seemed to be waiting, expecting her to say something adult. She shrugged and nodded her head. "That's true," she said. "You're right, you're absolutely right."

Her response seemed to mollify him. He sucked on his straw, raucously draining the dregs of his Blizzard. She wanted to keep him talking. She leaned across the table and said, "When you come back, things will be better."

"Why?" He looked dubious.

"Because these things take time. They say time heals all wounds. Like when you cut your finger. It takes time to heal. The deeper the cut, the longer it takes."

"I don't think so," he said.

"What do you mean, you don't think so?" The Asian family scraped their chairs back and stood up. The mother pointed, and the boy obediently carried their trays to the waste receptacle.

Teddy shrugged. "I don't really want to talk about it. Okay?"

She sighed and looked at her watch. "We might as well go."

They walked down the mall to the theater complex. As she was paying for their tickets — she still couldn't believe the price of movies in California — he tugged on her purse and asked, "Can I get popcorn?"

"You just ate," she said.

"But it's my last night." He stood stubbornly in front of the popcorn machine.

She knew that he knew she didn't want to get into a fight with him, that she didn't want anything to ruin their last night together. The little blackmailer. She shook her head. "Come on, let's get a seat."

"No."

The smug look on his face infuriated her. Her hand whipped out and smacked his cheek. Right there in the bright lights of the concession stand in the midst of a small throng of people. He looked more shocked than hurt. She couldn't believe what she had done. Mortified, she dropped to her knees and kissed him and mumbled how sorry she was, she didn't mean it. They were creating a scene. She was aware of the murmur of voices surrounding them, but she didn't care. She had never struck him before, except maybe once or twice on the butt, a tap really, when he was small.

"Mom," he said, "Mom" — he was tugging on her jacket sleeve — "it's all right. Get up. It's okay."

A couple of older women clucked and shook their heads, glaring at her as they walked by. Giselle could feel the hot blood scalding her cheeks. Teddy took her hand. She couldn't remember the last time he had voluntarily slipped his hand into hers. "It's not her fault," he announced to the clucking, glaring women. "You don't know what I did."

At the airport the next morning Giselle was surprised that she passed through the security checkpoint without a second glance from the guard. She felt like a crazy woman. A domestic terrorist. Racing pulse, sweaty palms, dry mouth. A fanatic of some sort. A seeker of vengeance. She had not slept all night, tortured with shame and remorse over her violent outburst at the movie theater, even though Teddy seemed to harbor no grudge. He seemed almost grateful for the slap. These days she could only guess at what was going on inside that head of his. Maybe he felt it evened the score between them. The ledger of guilt and blame. Maybe he craved some sort of tangible punishment. It must seem odd to him how you got punished for the minor infractions. A "time out" for talking back. No Popsicle for coming home late. No TV for breaking your sister's busy box. But for the major crimes, there was no punishment. How much "time out" for shooting your little sister?

At the gate Teddy stood by the large windows, watching the jets take off and land. He did not seem the least bit nervous about the prospect of flying alone for the first time. He was wearing his red backpack loaded with stuff to do on the plane — books, puzzles, gum, M&Ms, Life Savers, raisins. She had insisted on the raisins even though he didn't want them. "I don't want your father to think you only eat junk," she'd said. Ed was going to meet Teddy at the gate in Omaha since you couldn't fly directly to Lincoln, then the two of them would drive back to Lincoln, an hour away. As she looked out at the tarmac, she wished she were going, too. She had thought about it but knew she would be a third wheel. Teddy needed to get away from her, and from Dan, who had surprised her by calling while they were at the movies. He had left a message asking whether they needed a ride to the airport and offering his services if they did. When Giselle called him back to say it was okay, the car was out of the shop, she ended up talking to his mother. A quick and cool conversation. She knew that Luisa blamed her for everything. Maybe she should have taken Dan up on the offer. She dreaded going back to an empty house. An empty weekend. She couldn't even remember the last time she had spent a weekend alone.

What she couldn't help remembering was the last time they were at the airport. She had arrived early to give Teddy time to watch the planes and to give herself time to get lost, since she had never driven to LAX before. She was still intimidated by the California freeways. Dan had gone to the Modern Language Association convention in New York, and they were picking him up. Trina was fussy and feverish from teething. Giselle was exhausted from four days alone with the kids, but she had showered and changed and put on makeup. She could still remember the feeling of happy anticipation as his plane landed and passengers started flooding through the gate. It was their first family reunion. Teddy spotted him. "There he is!" They were all smiling and waving. Trina squealed and lurched forward, nearly somersaulting out of Giselle's arms. Dan caught her just in time. "How's my main man?" He slapped Teddy's palm in a high five. "And my best gals." He squeezed his wife and daughter in a big bear hug. "God, I missed you guys," he said as they joined the stampede to the baggage claim. "Mi familia. I'm never going away again."

On the way home they ran out of gas. Dan didn't yell at her, but she knew it was her fault. She burst into tears. "What are you crying for?" he said. "I can see the gas station from here." Fortunately, they were near an exit ramp. But she knew her carelessness had ruined the perfect reunion. She would have preferred that he cuss her out the way Ed would have done. *How could you be so damn dumb,* Ed would have blustered, shaking his head. And she would have shot back, "Yeah, why don't you try taking care of two kids for four days. See what happens to your brain." But instead, she kept apologizing and Dan kept assuring her it was all right. In that voice he reserved for his densest students, the hopeless cases, the ones he had diagnosed as lost causes. The Flatliners, he called them. He liked to shock people by saying he believed in pedagogical triage: "You can't save everyone from their own stupidity," he would say. "You've got to save your energy for the ones who can be saved."

Teddy walked over to Giselle and asked her how much longer. The gate was crowded now. A large, extended Indian family had seated themselves all around her, urgently conferring with one another in Parsi or Urdu or whatever. They had enough carry-on baggage for a platoon. A curry-scented cloud seemed to envelop them. Giselle's stomach rumbled. She hadn't eaten anything. Teddy made a funny face at a little girl sitting on her grandmother's lap. She stopped sucking her thumb and broke into a huge smile. The little girl had glossy black ringlets and dark eyes like Trina's. Giselle shut her eyes and sighed. Another reason to go back to Nebraska, the Aryan nation, headquarters of the American Nazi Party, a place where all the children were blond and blue-eyed and looked nothing like her daughter. Little latter-day Vikings.

The loudspeaker crackled. *Flight 482 is now ready for early boarding. First-class passengers and children traveling alone . . .*

"That's me," Teddy said.

Giselle nodded and followed him over to the line of early boarders, old and young. She wanted to say something important, to take advantage of this last chance to wipe the slate clean. But all she could think to say was "Don't forget to call me when you get there." Teddy wasn't paying attention anyway. He was telling the ticket agent that his father was going to meet him at the airport in Omaha. "She's not going with me," he told the woman, referring to Giselle. His voice clearly did not contain the faintest pang of regret. The ticket agent smiled at Giselle and said, "We'll take good care of him. Don't worry."

HE LINES UP HIS PEANUTS IN STRAIGHT ROWS
on the fold-down tray in front of him and pops them into his
mouth, one by one, left to right, as if he is eating words on a page. The
nice blond stewardess gave him an extra packet and some pilot wings
that she pinned to his sweatshirt. He already has a bunch of them at
home from his uncle Todd, who is always flying to New York or
Japan, but he didn't tell her that. At his sixth birthday party a kid
from school had given him a Don't Spill the Beans game he already
had. When he ripped off the wrapping paper, Teddy had said,
"Thanks. This is a cool game. I've already got one." He thought he
was being polite. But later his mother told him you shouldn't say if
you already have something, because it makes the person feel bad. "I
was just being honest," he'd protested. "You always say to tell the
truth." And his mother had said it was okay to tell "little white lies"
to make someone feel better. For days after that he had gone around
thinking up sample lies and asking if they were black or white. If I say
I brushed my teeth and I didn't, is that a white lie? How about if I
say I can't eat vegetables because I'm an alien from Mars?

He takes a sip of his Coke and looks out the window at the clouds.
It looks as though you could step out of the plane and walk on them

like white stepping-stones. The plane isn't very full. He is in the front row by himself. When they aren't busy, the stewardesses take turns sitting next to him for a minute, as if they feel sorry for him. He has spread his Goosebumps books out in the empty seat next to him so that they can see he isn't a baby who needs to be entertained. He is content to be left alone. Both stewardesses, the blond one and the black one, asked him the same questions in the same order. How old are you? Where are you going? Do you have any brothers or sisters? He said no. He didn't know if that was a lie or not. If it was a lie, he figured it was a white lie. Because it would make them feel bad if he said his sister was dead.

He is the only kid on the plane who is traveling by himself. He checked it out on his way to the bathroom. There aren't a lot of kids on the plane, period, and none who are his age. They're probably all still in school. He would be sitting in school right this minute if he hadn't taken the pills.

He doesn't remember much about the hospital. All he really remembers is lying in bed waiting to see what it felt like to be dead. On TV he'd seen people talking about this beautiful white light, like a bright tunnel, with dead relatives smiling and waving at them. He could remember wondering if he would see Trina and if she would be mad at him for shooting her. He doubted it. She wasn't even old enough to understand. She would probably be thrilled to see him, just like she was in real life. He doesn't remember any white light. He must have fallen asleep before anything happened.

His father was mad at him when he found out. Everyone else was tippytoeing around him, speaking slowly and softly. But when he picked up the phone receiver, his father shouted in his ear, "Jesus Christ, Teddy, how could you pull such a dumb-ass stunt?" His mother, who was eavesdropping, tried to yank the phone away from him, but he wouldn't let her. He liked hearing his dad yell and cuss. He was tired of everyone trying to be nice when they didn't mean it anyway. By the end of the phone call he and his dad were joking around, laughing. His dad asked him what it felt like to get your stomach pumped, and Teddy said how should he know, he was asleep, but his throat hurt from the tube. And his dad said he'd kill him if he ever tried anything like that again.

His mother just shook her head and rolled her eyes at what she could overhear, which was probably everything, since his dad had a loud voice on the phone, as if he thought long distance meant you were in the next room. Teddy knows that his mother doesn't think his father is all that smart.

The black stewardess picks up his empty Coke can and asks him if he would like anything else. She smiles at him with bright teeth and purple lipstick. She is wearing silver hoop earrings so big he could pass his fists through them. Teddy says no thank you. As she walks away, he wonders if someone in her family was ever shot. A brother or sister. On the news black people are always getting shot and killed. Every day. He thinks maybe if they were black — his mother and stepfather and sister and him — they wouldn't have fallen apart. They would have handled it better. On the news black people are always singing in church. His family doesn't go to church. They don't even believe in God. When he asked his mother what religion they were, after Chandra Patel had informed him that she was a Hindu, she had said they weren't really anything. At the time it had bothered him. He didn't like being nothing. But now he is glad. Now that he'd killed his baby sister. He doesn't want to go to hell or be reincarnated as something disgusting like a rat or cockroach. Which is what Catholics and Hindus believe happens to you when you die if you've done something bad. If you are nothing, nothing bad could happen. You just turn into air, he thinks, looking out the window of the plane. They are flying through a thick white fog. It looks like they are flying through nothing, flying through some huge white lie.

ON THE WAY HOME FROM THE AIRPORT, ON IM-pulse, Giselle went into the Family Cutters in the strip mall. It was next to Drug Fair, where she had stopped for toothpaste. She had packed off the last of the Crest with Teddy, as if Ed wouldn't have toothpaste — even though Ed had perfect teeth, big and white like toy piano keys. He always kept a yellow box of baking soda by the bathroom sink; he swore by the stuff years before they started putting it in toothpaste. Unfortunately, Teddy had inherited her teeth. Twenty-one cavities by the time she was ready for braces. The name, Family Cutters, struck her as ironic. She pictured a family of paper dolls being scissored apart.

"Just a trim," she told the anorexic receptionist with the platinum crew-cut. Giselle held up her thumb and index finger about a quarter of an inch apart. Seeing the look of skepticism on the receptionist's face, Giselle widened it to half an inch. All the beauticians sported short, spiky hair in various unnatural hues. To give herself courage, Giselle thought of Martha Goodman's new haircut, how much younger and lighter she'd looked — unburdened somehow. Giselle's own hair hadn't changed since junior high school, when she had insisted on growing it out of the ugly pixie to down past her shoulders, where — as if at the end of its rope —

it refused to grow any longer. Her mother had insisted that Giselle's light brown hair was too fine, too tangle-prone, and should be kept short and neat. "Yvonne's hair is different," she had told Giselle, whom she knew was just copying her older sister. "It has a completely different texture. Plus Vonnie has a wider face." All of which made Giselle even more determined never, ever to cut her hair, no matter what.

But something came over her as she sat in the chair with her hair dripping wet and the pink plastic cape draped like a gigantic bib. She was so tired of being herself. "I'm ready for a change," she heard herself telling the hairdresser, who hardly looked old enough to be playing with such sharp scissors. "What do you think?"

The hairdresser, Cindi, said, "Great. Just leave it to me." As she snipped away, she chattered on about this trip she just took to Club Med in Belize. She asked Giselle if she'd ever been to a Club Med, and Giselle shook her head.

"Please keep your head still," Cindi chided her, frowning.

It was like at the dentist when the hygienist insisted upon asking you all sorts of questions with her hands stuck in your mouth. The stylist switched the subject to her stepdaughter, Noelle, who was visiting from Bakersfield for the month, and suddenly Giselle's stomach clutched. A lump swelled in her throat. She knew what was coming next. She wanted to rip the plastic cape off and run out of there with her hair half cut.

"Do you have any kids?" Cindi asked her as she casually unclipped another clump of Giselle's hair and began snipping away. Giselle knew that if she answered yes, the next question would be "How many?" She thought about lying, just saying no, but she couldn't bring herself to do it, as if it were bad luck. As if it could cause Teddy's plane to fall out of the sky.

"I have a nine-year-old son," she said. "He's on his way right now to visit his father in Nebraska."

"Oh, really?" Cindi shook her head as if coincidences never ceased to amaze her. "My brother-in-law's from Omaha. His name's

Jim Leggett, maybe you know him?" Cindi looked surprised when Giselle shook her head, as though everyone in Nebraska was on a first-name basis.

"Omaha's a big city," Giselle said. "Relatively speaking."

"He thinks Nebraska's great. Clean air, no crime, great place for families and all that. He keeps trying to get my sister to move back there." Cindi rolled her eyes. "Me personally, I'd rather die of emphysema in California."

Giselle smiled and nodded. She knew she was off the hook. She marveled at how easily the crisis had been averted. Then, just as the lump in her throat began to subside, she said, "I had a twenty-three-month-old daughter, Trina, but she died. In April."

Cindi's face crumpled as if Giselle had punched her in the gut. "Oh, my God, I'm so sorry. Really, I'm so sorry." In the mirror she could see that Cindi actually had tears in her eyes, which made Giselle feel both better and worse. She fished into her jeans pocket and handed Cindi a tissue. Cindi thanked her and blew her nose. Still sniffling, she unclipped the last clump of Giselle's hair. "Was she sick?" she asked in a meek, reverent voice. Underneath her burgundy hair and skin-tight minidress, she was actually a sweet, tenderhearted girl. Giselle felt bad for having ruined her day.

"No," she said. "It was an accident."

Later that evening when her brother arrived to take her to dinner, he didn't even recognize her at first. She was outside watering the moribund flowers that edged the front of the house; she had planted them herself with great enthusiasm just the spring before last, thrilled to be living in her first house, even if it was only rented. "Geez," he said, "I thought you were the baby-sitter." Annoyed, Giselle didn't bother to point out that there was no one to baby-sit for. He knew that Teddy was in Nebraska. "It looks good. You look like Tinker Bell. You know, in *Hook*."

He took her to dinner at Ed Debevic's, a hip diner with valet parking, where they avoided talking about anything heavy, and she was home by ten o'clock. She was surprised to find a message on her machine from Ed. Teddy had called her that afternoon to say that he had arrived safely and that everything was fine. They were watching a movie and waiting for a pizza to be delivered. When she heard Ed's voice, her heart stopped — she thought something must have gone wrong — but as if reading her mind long-distance he said, "Everything's A-OK here. I just thought you might be feeling lonely, so I called to say hey. And to say what a great kid he is." Ed paused for a moment and picked up again at lower volume. "He seems to be doing okay, you know, considering. He looks kind of pale. We're going fishing tomorrow. Take care of yourself."

Despite herself, she was touched by his thoughtfulness. She supposed he knew better than she did what it felt like to miss Teddy. When she had first noticed the blinking light, she thought the message was probably from Dan. They were going out to dinner tomorrow night. She had thought maybe he was calling to cancel. Or calling to say he couldn't wait, he wanted to come back tonight. She didn't really know what was going on. In the past couple of days they'd had a couple of decent conversations on the telephone. He had apologized about the book, admitted he'd been wrong not to tell her, and said he was reconsidering the whole project, although he wasn't making any promises.

She walked into the bathroom and stared at herself in the mirror, trying to get used to her new hair, wondering whether Dan would like it, then thinking, *So what?* Why was she so eager to forgive him? If she had been as eager to forgive Ed his failings, they'd probably still be married. But then she had never worshiped Ed from afar, felt honored when he bestowed a smile upon her, or imagined various scenarios of bumping into him outside of the classroom. The first time Dan had touched her, held her hand in the dark, crowded parking lot at the Hollywood Bowl, she felt her whole body light up like a neon sign. Most of Dan's toiletries were still neatly arranged on his shelf. She opened the bottle of Grey Flannel, closed her eyes, and inhaled. Surprised by a twinge of lust, a quick power surge from the vicinity of her womb. It had been a long time since she felt horny. Not that she felt exactly horny now. It was more like a nostalgia for sex, a desire for desire. She slipped out of her dress and ran the water in the tub. A warm bath was about as much sensuality as she could take these days. She didn't really want to feel that much. Her emotions were all connected, like a complex switchboard with no circuit breakers. The very thought of an orgasm terrified her. All those fuses blowing out in the dark.

As she eased herself into the warm water, she wondered if it was different for Dan. All her life she had been told that men were different. Ed had certainly seemed to be. His penis had seemed to be totally lacking in introspection, like a big friendly dog always ready to play. It was Dan who had educated her to the idea that men and women weren't really all that different. For several weeks after his father's funeral, Dan had trouble sustaining an erection. He seemed to crave physical affection — lying in bed holding each other's naked body — but not sex per se, which was what she had been led to believe was all that men were really interested in. Fucking. The first couple of times his hard-on wilted, she had been alarmed. She had taken it as a sign of his flagging ardor. The beginning of the end. But in fact the opposite was true. It was the beginning of the beginning, as if a pane of glass that she hadn't even known was there suddenly slid away.

And now it had slid back again.

The next morning Dan did in fact call, bright and early, before she was even awake. Although she had gone to bed early, she had not fallen asleep until dawn. He wanted to know whether they could push back dinner to 7:30. Something about the racquetball court schedule. She was too groggy to protest. But now, as she drank her coffee, it occurred to her that she didn't know how she was going to fill up all the empty hours until dinner. She felt as if she were in suspended animation. What would she do if the marriage was truly over? Where would she go? Who would she be? In September she would turn thirty. A two-time loser. But maybe there was still hope. There was still time to salvage the marriage. The dust had barely begun to settle. Even her brother, Teddy's loyal champion, had said to cut Dan some slack. It was too soon to give up. A thought that made her feel even more hopeless since it seemed to require some action on her part, some energy. When all she wanted to do was sleep. And she couldn't even do that. At night the demons stood in line to shake her hand.

It was unseasonably hot for early June. She dragged a decrepit chaise longue into the backyard and lay in the sun. When she was younger, a teenager, she had elevated tanning to an art form. Applying suntan lotions of various strengths, rotating at precise intervals, ever vigilant against unsightly strap marks. But now she didn't care. It was only skin.

On the plastic end table next to the chaise was a bottle of sparkling water and the cordless phone. On Sunday mornings her parents called. She didn't feel like talking to them, but she would have to answer the phone if it rang. It might be Teddy, saying he was homesick. Then she remembered they were going fishing; they would have been up and out by sunrise, hours ago. Once Ed had taken her fishing when she was pregnant with Teddy. The rocking of the small boat and the smell of fish had made her nauseous. Ed rowed her back to the shore, where she spent the afternoon lying on the grass, slapping away gnats, wishing she had brought something to read, wishing she weren't pregnant.

They had considered abortion, at least she had. Her best friend, Laura, had urged her to do it and offered to make the arrangements. All she had to do was go to Planned Parenthood on O Street. "It's like going to a matinee," Laura said. "Two hours." Thinking back, Giselle really couldn't remember why she didn't do it. It certainly wasn't her religious faith; she had stopped going to mass as soon as she moved into the dormitory. Even before that, she would sometimes convince her parents to let her attend a later mass and then spend the hour browsing through fashion maga-

zines at the drugstore. Her thinking was confused and contradic-
tory, as if scrambled by hormones. As far as she could recall, it
wasn't so much a decision to have the baby as indecision about
doing something else.

And Ed seemed easy either way. They could have been discussing what movie to see, what restaurant to go to. It irked her,
she remembered that much. She remembered yelling at him. "This
is a baby we're talking about. A lifelong commitment. It's not a fish
you can throw back." The only opinion he had ventured was that
he wasn't keen on adoption. "Why not?" she'd challenged him.
"What's wrong with giving your baby to a good family?" She remembered clear as day how he had closed his eyes as if searching
for the right answer cribbed on the insides of his eyelids. Finally
he shrugged and said, "It's like Oedipus." She knew he was referring to the play they had read in English 101 the year before, their
freshman year of college. "It has to do with destiny." She had
snorted and rolled her eyes and scoffed, "You think the kid's going
to come back and sleep with me?" "Never mind," he had told her,
the picture of wounded dignity, "just forget it."

She heard someone call her name. She opened her eyes. Lois
was standing at the fence in her bathing suit. "I was wondering if
you felt like company."

Giselle stood up too quickly. The blood rushed to her feet in a
dizzying swoosh. "Are you okay?" Lois asked her. Giselle nodded
and walked over to help Lois drag one of their fancy padded
chaises across the stubble of lawn. "Do you want the other one?"
Lois asked, pointing to the matching padded chaise. Bill's chair.
Giselle shook her head. She liked the way the frayed plastic webbing of the cheap lawn chair mortified her flesh.

"I guess you saw," Lois said as she positioned herself to catch
the rays. "Bill moved out."

"I saw the U-Haul truck," Giselle admitted. She had, in fact,
watched from the kitchen window as Bill and a big burly guy
made several trips back and forth between the truck and the
house, loaded down with stuff. She knew that Eric was at soccer

practice on Saturday mornings, conveniently out of the way. She had watched, mesmerized, as Bill carried out the fancy stereo, bought for a great price in Singapore, followed by his buddy holding aloft a pair of skis and ski poles.

"How are you doing?" Giselle asked.

"It's a relief, to tell you the truth." Lois offered her some Bain de Soleil, which Giselle declined.

"Really?"

"Really. I feel as if I've spent the past ten years trying to postpone the inevitable."

Behind the fence Ninja's whine escalated into a shrill yelp as he dug frantically, trying to tunnel his way into the neighboring yard. "Stop that!" Lois barked at the dog. "I wish to God that Bill could take the damn dog. No pets allowed in his new apartment complex, naturally." She sighed. "But I suppose Eric would miss him. Especially now."

Giselle nodded. The cordless phone rang. She was 99 percent sure it was her parents, but for some reason she felt compelled to pick it up anyway.

"Hello, dear," her mother chirped. "How's the weather there?" Her mother had adopted this relentlessly upbeat voice ever since the accident.

"Fine, nice. I'm sitting in the sun, in fact. How's Dad?"

"He's fine. Chipping away at the putting green. I can see him from here. How are you doing?"

"Okay. Nothing much new. Todd and I had dinner last night. He seems like he's doing great. Did he tell you he met Steven Spielberg?"

"We heard all about it. How about your sister? Have you heard from her lately?"

"No," Giselle lied. Vonnie had called a couple of nights ago, but Giselle didn't want to get into it. Her sister still refused to speak to their parents. "Look, Mom, Lois just stopped by. Could I call you back later?"

"Lois." She heard the undertone of disapproval and thought

her mother might be about to offer some advice or criticism, but then her Pollyanna voice kicked in again. "Well, could I talk to Teddy for just a second?"

"He's at soccer."

"Oh. I thought he had soccer on Saturday."

"They switched it," Giselle improvised. She hadn't told her parents about the sleeping pills incident and didn't intend to. She knew her mother, who had a mind like a steel trap when it came to dates, knew that school wasn't out yet; if Giselle told her that Teddy was in Nebraska, she would wonder why he had left before school ended. "We'll give you a call when he gets back from soccer. Okay?" She'd just have to think of something later, some excuse. "Give my love to Daddy," she added hurriedly, before her mother could say anything, and hung up. Exhausted.

During the brief phone call Lois had run next door and returned with two Michelob Lights. Giselle accepted one gratefully.

"Parents," Lois said. "I dread telling my mother about Bill's moving out. She'll blame me. She thinks everything's my fault. The Great White Pilot can do no wrong." She took a swig. "I thought parents were supposed to be on your side. Especially mothers."

Giselle had met Lois's mother — a brittle, blue-haired widow whose favorite expression was "I don't like to complain but . . ."

"How's Eric taking his father's move?" she asked.

"I think he's relieved, too. All that tension." Lois let out a huge breath. "I think all that macho father-son stuff just made Eric nervous. Maybe when he's older, but not now."

Giselle let out a soft, yeasty burp. "Excuse me." She waited for a second burp to pass before saying, "Teddy's in Nebraska. Ed's taking him fishing today, speaking of father-son stuff. He left yesterday."

"Oh," Lois said. "I didn't realize he was leaving so soon."

Giselle could see the look of surprise on Lois's face and appreciated that she didn't ask. If Lois had asked, Giselle probably would have lied. But suddenly she found herself telling Lois about the sleeping pills.

"Oh, my God" was all Lois said, shaking her head speechlessly, when Giselle was through. Something that Giselle also appreciated. What could you say? In general people tried to say too much: words of comfort, advice, sympathy. A big, unappetizing casserole of words.

Trina had just been learning to talk. A handful of new words every day. *Juice! Ice cream! Music!* All commands or exclamations. By now she would have been forming her first complete thought. Giselle would have written it in the baby book under BABY'S FIRST SENTENCE. Teddy's first sentence had become a family joke: "Give me more noodles!" She had a feeling that Trina's first sentence would have been something more feminine and eloquent, something about flowers or clouds.

The sympathy cards were the worst. They were still receiving a belated trickle from distant friends and relatives who had just heard the news. She couldn't imagine who they got to write those verses. Imagine being paid to compose such earnest, empty doggerel. Years ago, on their trip to KU, her father had pointed out the Hallmark headquarters just outside of Lawrence, Kansas. She could just picture them sitting at their computers, reading the verses aloud, snickering. A room full of cynical advertising majors whose résumés weren't impressive enough to land them a job in New York. Twentysomethings who wouldn't know a coffin from a tanning bed.

"I'm getting thirsty," Lois said after a while. "How 'bout another beer?"

"Sure." In the hot sun she felt drunk already.

Five minutes later Lois reappeared with a small cooler and a bag of tortilla chips. Giselle passed on the chips but accepted a beer.

"Look how thin you are," Lois said. "I'm jealous."

"I'm on the Steady Misery Diet," Giselle shot back, annoyed that even now Lois was worrying about her weight, as if it mattered.

"When I'm miserable, I eat even more." Lois crunched on a handful of chips. "You should put on some lotion, you're getting burned. Here." Lois squirted some lotion into the palm of her hand and squatted down beside Giselle, massaging the sun-warmed Bain de Soleil across her chest and stomach, then down her arms and legs, grunting a bit as she stretched to reach the extremities.

It felt soothing to be touched. Giselle was sorry when it was over. "Thanks," she said quietly.

Lois settled back in her chaise and closed her eyes. "I wonder how Eric's doing. Mostly he seemed thrilled to death that there's a pool at the complex. I don't think the whole thing's really sunk in yet." She sighed and looked over at Giselle, as if waiting for her to say something. As if it were her turn. Giselle knew that Lois must be wondering about Dan, his conspicuous absence, but she didn't ask and Giselle didn't volunteer anything. She flashed on Dan moving his things out. Dan and his faithful friend Harvey carrying armloads of clothes, boxes of books, out to a U-Haul, and her heart seemed to sink in her chest. No matter what he'd done, Dan was Trina's father. If they split up, it would be like losing some last vestige of her daughter.

"Of course, Bill was away so much anyway," Lois said. "Sometimes I wonder if he was ever really here."

Every so often Giselle sneaked a glance at her watch.

By four o'clock the creeping shadows stole the last remaining patch of sunlight. Giselle gave up and went inside the house. Lois had left about an hour earlier to do some grocery shopping. She had invited Giselle over for supper, but Giselle had declined without bothering to give an excuse. When Lois looked rebuffed, Giselle had relented enough to say, "Dan and I are going out to dinner." She didn't want Lois to think she was saying no because of the accident. Although it would have been the first time she set foot inside the Beemers' house since that day. And she wasn't, in fact, quite sure how she felt about it.

Three and a half hours until seven-thirty. And Dan was always late, a manifestation of his Latin heritage. She showered and put on her kimono. Then, even though it was too early to dress, she sat on the edge of the bed, staring into the open closet. Dan's few clothes hung neatly on one end, hers crowded together at the other. The garments looked familiar, but she felt no emotional attachment. She recognized them only from snapshots: the red sheath she had worn on the first night of their honeymoon in Lahaina, the embroidered turquoise blouse she had bought in Rosarita Beach one weekend when they drove across the border for a cheap lobster dinner. The next morning she had woken up sick, thinking she had food poisoning, but it had turned out to be morning sickness. Even the nice things she had worn only once or twice looked tawdry and unappealing, as if she were browsing through a rack of clothes at a Salvation Army store. She looked at the clock on the night table. Four-thirty. There was still time to drive to the mall. It was as good a way to kill time as any.

In the dressing room at Contempo Casuals, stripped down to her dingy white bra and panties, she examined her reflection in the three-way mirror, surprised by how good she looked. She hadn't been this thin since her freshman year in college. She remembered crowding into the dressing room at Miller & Paine with Laura, trying on clothes for college in the fall. They were both going to the University of Missouri at Columbia, which was known for its journalism program. They had it all planned. After college they would get jobs as reporters at some major metropolitan newspaper — they hadn't decided whether it would be the East or West Coast yet, but definitely not the Midwest — and lead lives straight out of some stirring commencement speech, with a touch of Danielle Steele thrown in for good measure. Laura's life had pretty much gone according to plan, except that she was working for a paper in Providence, Rhode Island, waiting for the chance to move to the *Boston Globe* or *Washington Post*. They still talked a few times a year but had drifted apart after Giselle punked out at the last minute by deciding to stay in Lincoln and go to UNL to be near Ed.

The first dress she tried on was too big. Giselle had to ask the clerk to bring her a size 6. The clerk, who was grossly overweight, snatched the size 8 away as if Giselle had deliberately insulted her, and then seemed to take a certain satisfaction in informing Giselle that they didn't have the dress in a size 6. Giselle mumbled a meek thank-you. Laura would have managed to put the girl in her place, subtly but firmly.

Stuck in Nebraska, Giselle hadn't really wanted to talk to Laura; the contrast between their lives had been too stark. But once Giselle had mustered the gumption to leave — to move to California — she'd turned to her old friend for moral support. When she felt lonely and scared in her tiny, tacky apartment after Teddy was asleep, she would call Laura long-distance so that Laura could assure her she'd done the right thing in leaving Ed, in moving to California. And Laura, knowing that Giselle couldn't afford big phone bills, would always pretend to have something on the stove or someone at the door. "I'll call you back in five minutes," she'd say, saving Giselle's pride.

Laura had been skeptical about Dan, cautioning Giselle not to get hurt, as if she thought a professor couldn't possibly be seriously interested in a college dropout with a kid. Even though she thought the same thing herself, Giselle had felt insulted, and the phone calls had tapered off. Plus, she wasn't so lonely anymore. When Dan asked her to marry him, the first person Giselle had called was Laura — like a kid saying, "Nah-nah, see? You were wrong."

But maybe she wasn't. One of the maddening things about Laura was that she was almost never wrong about anything. Including clothes. Giselle was having trouble deciding between the peach linen shift and the violet flowered sundress. Laura wouldn't have had an instant's doubt. "That one," she'd say, "definitely."

But who could have predicted something like this? They were doing fine before the accident. A happy family. Or at least as happy as families get these days. Ozzie and Harriet didn't need two incomes to buy a house. They didn't live across the street from drug dealers. They didn't need to worry about drive-by shootings and

paroled sex offenders. They had never even heard of radon or attention deficit disorder. Of course, as Ed frequently pointed out, it
was still like that in Nebraska. You could still live The Good Life,
as the state welcome sign proclaimed.

She just couldn't make up her mind. Even though they were
broke, what the hell, she decided to take both dresses. It seemed
like a luxury to feel guilty about something as trivial as money.

Dan arrived at seven-thirty sharp. She didn't know whether this
was a good sign or a bad sign, whether he was eager to see her or
eager to get it over with. Although he had been gone less than a
week, there was an awkwardness to his arrival. She noted how he
knocked on the front door as he opened it and called her name.
"Wow, your hair," he said, "you look so different." He didn't like
it, she could tell.

At the mall she had picked up some wine, cheese, and crackers.
But he seemed anxious to get going. "Nice dress," he said. "Sexy."
Instead of feeling complimented, she felt embarrassed. She knew
that he must realize she had bought it specially, as if this were a
first date and she wanted to make a good impression. She felt awkward and vulnerable and wished she had worn jeans, like him,
fresh from racquetball, his dark hair still damp, shiny as patent
leather. He was growing out his beard. It always grew fast. After
only a couple of days he was already looking romantically swarthy,
like Antonio Banderas in *Desperado*. Despite Lois's best attempts
with the suntan lotion, Giselle's skin radiated a Day-Glo pink. It
hurt. She had flinched when he hugged her hello.

His matching Honda Civic was parked at the curb. She waited
as he moved a pile of books into the backseat. In the car he said,
"Arturo's?" It was a restaurant they had eaten at often, although
not so much in the past two years. With two kids, one in a high
chair, it was easier to eat at home. In fact, she couldn't remember
the last time they had gone out to eat like this, just the two of
them. She thought the fact he'd suggested Arturo's was a good

sign. They had gone there for an early supper, to celebrate, after the ultrasound that had revealed to them the baby's sex. Dan had been jubilant at the news; he had been hoping for a girl. They had ordered a pitcher of tequilaless margaritas and debated girls' names, working their way through the alphabet: Amelia, Amanda, Aviva, Bianca, Bonita, Catrina.

The restaurant was a good fifteen-minute drive. They didn't say much. The weather, the traffic. Always the good discussion leader, he brought up something in the news, something President Clinton had said about the future of education in America, and they discussed it as long as they possibly could, discussed the hell out of it, relieved to be talking about something three thousand miles away that didn't concern them personally. She wished that she had a cigarette. She had been a sporadic smoker but had given it up when she got pregnant with Trina and hadn't started up again because she knew that Dan didn't like it. Back in Nebraska all her friends smoked cigarettes. There wasn't that much else to do. Dan reached over and punched the cassette player, then rested his hand on the edge of her thigh. Self-consciously, she cupped her hand over his. Some tape she didn't recognize started up at loud volume. He slid his hand out from under hers to adjust the volume and then put it back on the steering wheel.

"What's this?" she asked.

He looked startled, as if he didn't understand the question for an instant, and then smiled. She had forgotten how white his teeth looked against his beard. "One of my students recommended her. You like it?"

She shrugged. They had never shared the same taste in music, hers being the more pedestrian — although she in fact had a slight edge in classical music, thanks to her mother's insistence on piano lessons. She had no discernible talent, but at least she'd learned something about music theory and history. Vonnie, on the other hand, was clearly gifted. She had majored in music at Wisconsin before switching to women's studies; she now played keyboard in a lesbian rock band called Shebang.

Giselle spotted the empty CD case and examined it. The clock on the dashboard said 7:46. Nine forty-six in Nebraska. Teddy would be in bed. She wondered if he was grinding his teeth. The fact that he was in a different time zone made her miss him more. She hated the thought of their daily lives being out of sync. The CD cover was a psychedelic swirl of sensual colors. Deep purples and blues. For some reason it brought to mind the note she had seen on Dan's desk at school. *Lunch today? J.* Written in swirling lavender ink. Usually Dan listened to cool jazz or old sixties rock.

At the restaurant, seated in a booth, they sipped their margaritas and commented on how everything was just the same — the sombreros on the walls, slick bright oilcloths on the tables, fake cacti sculptures, Mexican blankets tacked to the ceiling. The same greasy menus with the same typos. Chilli. Tortila. Burritoes. They used to joke about Buried Toes — the house special — a plate of toes smothered with bloody salsa and melted cheese. Even the same waiter, who recognized them and spoke to Dan in Spanish. Giselle had learned just enough from her one semester of Spanish to get the general drift. The waiter said it had been a long time. He asked Dan how they were. Dan nodded and smiled. "Bueno, bueno." Giselle marveled at how convincing he sounded, how normal. Seeing them sitting here drinking their margaritas, no one would guess what they had been through. As soon as the waiter left with their order, Dan leaned forward and caught her hands, which were fidgeting with the silverware. He looked into her eyes. It was the first time they had made direct eye contact all evening. She felt a disturbance in the pit of her stomach, as if she had swallowed a hot chili pepper.

"This all seems so unreal," he said. "Sometimes I wake up in the middle of the night and can't believe any of it." He sighed. He was squeezing her fingers so hard that it hurt, but she didn't want to pull away. "Then other times . . . I don't know —"

"I know," she said. "I know what you mean." And she did. Sitting there across from him, she felt the unreality of it — or maybe it was a sort of heightened reality that felt like unreality. She was listening so intently, with such focus, that she could almost see the words coming out of their mouths. She noted each gesture, like stage directions: *He bites his lip and turns his head away from her. But the tears come anyway. He unfolds his napkin and blows his nose.* It gave her the creeps. She gulped her drink down quickly. Maybe if she were a little drunker, it would go away. His touch felt so good, she just wanted to lie down next to him somewhere quiet, to hold each other. She thought if they could do that — take a time out — it was possible that everything would somehow realign itself and they could be back on track again, the same track. Maybe now that Teddy was gone for a month, they could start over, ease their way into a new routine; and when he returned from Nebraska, it would be all right.

"I read that Kübler-Ross book, the one about when someone dies," he continued. "I can't believe I'd never read it." She nodded to show that she knew what he was talking about and to encourage him, even though inside she was thinking, "Oh no, here we go, more goddamned books." His voice was uncharacteristically tentative, halting. "My mother had it, you know, from when my father passed away." Giselle noted the euphemism. In class he had always instructed them to avoid such euphemistic phrases. "Anyway, it would appear I've still got a ways to go. I can't accept it. At least not yet. I'm sorry."

She was following him, nodding, but suddenly his apology set off an alarm. An internal warning light blinked on inside her brain: "Caution! Go Slow! Dangerous Curve Ahead!"

She points to her empty glass; the waiter whisks it away with the flourish of a matador.

"Excuse me," she said. "I think I'll go to the ladies' room. Back in a minute." She had to do something. Maybe if she interrupted his train of thought, he would forget it. It happens sometimes. You are on the verge of saying something, even something important, and then there's an interruption of some sort and the moment passes and it's gone for good.

He looked surprised but didn't comment as she slid to the end of the red tufted booth and stood up. In the ladies' room she stalled for as long as she could — washing her hands, brushing her hair, applying fresh lipstick, picking at a spot of salsa on her new peach dress — all while trying to avoid her reflection in the mirror. She didn't want to see the fear in her own eyes. It would only scare her more. Why was she acting like such a scared rabbit? That was one of her mother's favorite expressions: "You look like a scared rabbit." She had been planning to confront him about the book proposal, to find out whether he had really dropped the project, but now somehow she didn't have the courage to issue an ultimatum. She didn't want either of them to say anything that couldn't be unsaid. Maybe it was being back in this familiar place where they'd had so many good times, where they had actually chosen their daughter's name. She couldn't believe they couldn't work things out if they gave themselves enough time.

When she got back to the table, her second margarita was waiting for her. She slid into the booth across from him, smiled, and took a sip — concentrating on holding her hand steady.

The waiter brings them their food. "Be careful, the plates are hot," he cautions them.

Later that night she lay in bed trying to remember exactly what he had said. Not the gist of it, which left room for misinterpretation, but his actual words. But the four margaritas that she had downed in quick succession had blurred the sharp edges, diffused her focus. She had cried steadily on the ride home, clutching her damp, shredded napkin in her hand. Instead of fighting back, Dan had mumbled a series of lame apologies and retreated into his shell. In the dark interior of the car, his shoulders hunched with tension, his head poked forward to see the road, he looked like a large, silent turtle. The gist of it was that although he wants to make it work, he doesn't think he can. Although he tells himself that it was just an accident — he knows it was just an accident — he can't help feeling this resentment. Toward Teddy. The fact that he is still alive. Toward her. The fact that she still has a child. He hates himself for feeling this way, but this is what he feels. Moreover, sometimes when he's alone, he can sort of scroll back, erase the past three years — Giselle, Trina, the whole shebang — and feel almost okay. Almost as if his life isn't over. But when he's around them, Giselle and Teddy, it's always there. He can't get beyond it. He can't accept it. At least for now. Maybe, after some time, who knows? He can't predict how he is going to feel a month or a year from now. For the time being, he thinks he needs to be alone. He knows this isn't much help in the present. He's sorry.

Or words to that effect.

At 4 A.M. she was still lying there wide awake, playing the evening over and over again in her mind. She hated this time of night. She had come to think of it as the Earthquake Hour. They had been sound asleep when the earthquake hit. The first tremors jolted them awake, and they waited for a split second — to make sure it was real, not some dream — and then all hell broke loose. It sounded like the end of the world. Teddy was already out of bed, crawling toward the door. Dan scooped him up and handed him to her. The three of them huddled together, crouched, under the doorframe. The floor was shaking as though it were going to crack apart and send them crashing into the ground-floor apartment. She was relieved that there was no one above them. It seemed to go on forever. The noise was deafening. Like all the glass in the world being shattered at once. Like bullet trains colliding head-on.

When it was over, the worst of it, they had surveyed the apartment in a daze, shell-shocked. They were in the process of moving to the house on Buena Vista, and all their stuff was packed in boxes. The walls were bare. As luck would have it, Dan had just moved a carload of pictures, dishes, and lamps over to the new house the evening before, so they didn't have pictures crashing down or books flying off shelves. Everything was still just sitting there in boxes. It was almost as if they'd hallucinated the whole thing. Until Teddy said, "Look!" and pointed to a huge crack spreading down the dining room wall. They watched in amazement as a chunk fell out of the ceiling, sprinkling them with plaster dust. Dan walked over and turned on the TV, which didn't work. There was no electricity. A fact that somehow brought home the extent of the disaster. Giselle was five months pregnant. Dan walked back over to where she was standing, knelt down, and pressed his ear to her big belly. "Everything okay in there?"

The next day the electricity was still out. Desperate for news, they drove around the streets and saw for themselves the crushed cars, caved-in buildings, buckled pavement, the fires and floods from the broken mains. There was a postapocalyptic friendliness in the air. Everyone waved and greeted one another, stunned and elated by the mere fact of their survival. She and Teddy had just moved into Dan's fourplex in Sherman Oaks a couple of months earlier, after the wedding. Otherwise, they would have still been living in their little apartment just off of Balboa Boulevard, a few blocks from the Northridge Apartments that collapsed, killing sixteen people. When Giselle finally saw the news footage, she couldn't believe it. They might have been killed! As it turned out, after looking through all their cartons, the only damage that she could see was a box of cheap, shiny Christmas ornaments with a couple of shattered balls. She couldn't believe how lucky they were.

In the aftermath, Teddy became obsessed with earthquakes. They went to the library to check out books on earthquakes, but they were too late. They were already checked out to other frightened kids. Dan scouted around and found one lone copy of *Volcanoes and Earthquakes* at a used-book store. Teddy insisted upon reading the book so often that she could still, two and a half years later, recite the facts from memory — the various types of faults: reverse faults, thrust faults, transcurrent faults, strike-slip faults, dip-slip faults, oblique faults, and normal faults. Teddy could match each type of fault with its illustration. The San Andreas was a strike-slip fault, whereas the Sierra Madre was a thrust fault. Teddy was particularly anxious about hidden faults; the Northridge earthquake had been the result of a hidden thrust fault, only discovered after the fact.

The term *fault line* suddenly struck her as odd. She had never before thought of it in terms of "fault," as in someone's "fault," pointing the finger of blame. Lying there staring at the ceiling, she wondered what sort of fault line had been lurking underneath the surface of their lives. Oblique? Reverse? Normal?

Every morning as soon as the sun was out, she flopped into the chaise and lay there until the sun disappeared. By the end of Teddy's first week in Nebraska, she looked like a piece of bread that someone had forgotten to flip over in the toaster oven. Her back was a sickly white with deep ridges from the plastic webbing that was unraveling further every day, her butt sinking lower and lower toward the burned, unkempt grass. Before Teddy left, she had made out a list of projects. But now she didn't have the energy. She couldn't even remember what they were. Or where she'd put the list. Yesterday she had unearthed a video from underneath a stack of unread newspapers. *The Indian in the Cupboard.* They had rented it two nights before Teddy left for Nebraska. Without her kids, without her husband, her life had no structure. It was as if her skeleton had dissolved, leaving only an empty bag of skin.

Sometimes Lois joined her in the backyard. Two emotional cripples. Although Lois wasn't quite so bad off. An emotional quadriplegic and an emotional paraplegic. Lois still had Eric to keep her going. She had to get up in the morning to prepare his lunch and get him off to school. Dentist appointments to keep track of, chauffeur duties. Lois still had enough energy or vanity to roll over onto her stomach and get an even tan.

In a week's time they had graduated from beer to orange blossoms and Bloody Marys. Lois was cleaning out Bill's liquor cabinet. Giselle had taken to bumming Carletons from Lois, who had started smoking again now that Bill was gone. They were like two unsupervised teenagers run amok.

She had received two postcards from Teddy. One of the Huskers' stadium and the other of a field full of hogs. Neither particularly informative. The gist of his pithy, block-printed messages seemed to be *Having a swell time, don't wish you were here.* Talking to him on the phone was even worse, like a game of Twenty Questions punctuated with monosyllabic grunts. Usually Ed would get on the phone afterward and fill her in on what they'd been doing. He sounded happier than she could ever remember him. His grandmother had moved into a retirement home and left Ed the old farm off Old Cheney Road. Ed was turning it into a kennel. He had always dreamed of being a veterinarian, and she supposed that this was the next-best thing. He was busy building the dog kennels; he wanted the place to be the best one in the area. A five-star hotel for your pet. His brother Brice was working on the advertising. He was calling it Ed's Animal Farm. What did she think? She said it sounded great. Last night he had invited her to visit: "We're having our grand opening July fourth, Teddy's birthday," Ed told her.

She bit her lip. They hadn't yet discussed a return date for Teddy's visit, but she had anticipated having him back by his birthday. She didn't say anything, since she knew that Teddy was listening in on the extension.

"It's going to be really neat, Mom," Teddy had broken in, as if sensing trouble on her end. "There's going to be free pony rides, and Aunt Lou is going to bake this giant Milk-Bone — how big's it gonna be again, Dad?" For a minute he sounded like his old self. A kid again. It broke her heart.

"Ten feet," Ed said. "I don't know how she's going to do it, but I've got faith."

Aunt Lou had baked their wedding cake. Even though it was just a small affair, she'd gone all-out. Five layers. An architectural wonder.

"Why don't you come?" Ed said, catching her by surprise. "It's going to be a real blast."

"I don't think I —"

"We'd love to have you. Right, Ted-head?"

"Ummhm," Teddy said without much conviction. That mechanical Talkboy voice she recognized from the past two months.

"Well, you think about it," Ed said.

She had made some excuse and hung up, then walked into the kitchen and fixed herself a fresh gin and tonic. Two days ago she had run out of limes and hadn't made it to the market yet, although it was on the top of her short list of things to do.

Dan had left a couple of messages on the machine saying he wanted to come pick up some books he needed. She had been there — she had barely left the house since their dinner at Arturo's — but she hadn't picked up the receiver. She vacillated between anger and pain, between fantasies of revenge and reconciliation. Out the kitchen window the gray, overcast sky seemed to mirror the fog in her brain. She walked out into the backyard and stared disconsolately at the mass of dull clouds that didn't show any sign of breaking up anytime soon. From her kitchen window Lois waved at Giselle and motioned her to come over. The dog jumped up as she opened the gate, wagging and groveling. Lois hurried out and dragged him off by the collar. "How about some coffee?" she asked. Giselle nodded and followed her inside. Coffee was also on her short list of things to buy.

"Shitty day," Lois said as she handed Giselle a mug of steaming coffee that smelled wonderful. She ground her own beans fresh every morning, some gourmet blend she bought at a coffeehouse. "Any news from Teddy?"

Giselle nodded. "I talked to him last night. He sounds good." She poured a splash of milk into her coffee. "They invited me to visit. Ed's having a grand opening party for the kennel on Teddy's birthday."

"Are you thinking of going?"

"I don't think so."

"Why not?" Lois shoved a pile of Eric's Goosebumps books aside to clear a spot on the table for their coffee mugs.

Giselle shrugged. "It was Ed's idea. He feels sorry for me. It's not like Teddy's dying to see me. May I?" She plucked a cigarette from the pack on the counter.

Lois handed her a cloisonné lighter from a trip to China. "You talk to Dan yet?"

Giselle shook her head and sputtered out a cough as the first drag of smoke hit her lungs. She knew that Lois thought she should be more aggressive about trying to save her marriage. "It's not like Bill and me," she'd told Giselle a couple of days ago. "You had a good marriage. You love each other. You're just going through a terrible time." She was right about the terrible time; Giselle wasn't so sure anymore about the rest of it.

"Well, I think you should call him," Lois said. "He's like a cat who can't make up his mind to go in or out. You've just got to give him a push in the right direction."

Giselle was standing by the window looking out into her own backyard. She could still detect a faint circular depression where Trina's wading pool had sat. Shutting her eyes, she saw Trina splashing in the water, her plump tummy protruding over her ruffled plastic pants. "Buddha belly," Dan would call her, kissing her belly button and making loud "belly farts," as Teddy called them. She set her mug down on the counter and said, "I'm not feeling too well. I better go." As if sensing her mood, the dog left her alone as she cut back across the yard.

The days blurred by. She told herself she was just waiting for Teddy to come back. A month at the most. She told herself she deserved a month to vegetate, to wallow in self-pity, if that's what she felt like doing. She had lost a daughter. She seemed to have lost a husband. She was entitled to a nervous breakdown. She wasn't ready to think about the future. She didn't want to have a future; she wanted to have the past back. Once Teddy returned, she would snap out of it.

More often than not, it seemed, the weather was bad. On those days, she lay on the couch with the television on — mostly talk shows — alternating between fascination and boredom. She couldn't believe such people existed; she couldn't believe the things they said on national television. One night she had a dream — a nightmare, really — that she was on *Sally Jessy*

Raphäel with Teddy sitting next to her. He was holding a gun, demonstrating how he shot his sister. She woke up sweating. It was 2 A.M. An eternity until daylight. Since Teddy took the pills, she couldn't bring herself to buy any more Nytol or Sominex. She dragged herself into the kitchen to look for something, anything that might help her get back to sleep. She had finished off the gin earlier in the evening. In the back of the cupboard she found a half-full bottle of rum, but she was out of Coke. And some crème de menthe that Luisa had brought over. The sight of it turned Giselle's stomach. In high school she and Laura had made themselves violently ill on Grasshoppers one summer night when Laura's parents were away. Giselle stuffed the crème de menthe in the trash can, which she hadn't bothered to empty in days, and opened the refrigerator. No wine or beer, but there was a bottle of champagne hidden in the back. *What the hell,* she thought. They had bought it last New Year's Eve and then ended up nodding off before midnight, exhausted from a day with the kids, both of whom were sick — Teddy with strep throat and Trina with an ear infection. After the kids were finally asleep, they had set the champagne out in an ice bucket — a wedding gift from Harvey — along with some brie and crackers and strawberries. They had fallen asleep watching David Letterman.

She twisted off the little wire contraption holding the cork in place. It seemed, for an instant, that nothing happened — and then the next thing she knew, it felt as if a bullet had struck her in the eye. She let out a startled yelp and dropped the bottle. Half the champagne fizzed over the linoleum before she grabbed it and set it on the counter. Then she ran to the bathroom and examined her eye in the mirror. Fortunately, the cork had just missed. There was a livid mark below her eyebrow. The tender skin already seemed to be swelling. And throbbing. She wet a washcloth and folded it into a neat square. Pressing the cold compress to her eye, she walked back to the kitchen for the champagne. *Some celebration,* she thought grimly as she carried it into the living room and turned on the television. And it wasn't the cheap stuff either, like

Eden Roc or Tott's. They had splurged on real French champagne to start the New Year off right. There was an infomercial for something called a Fitness Flyer. Giselle had never seen anything like it. You put your feet in these suspended stirrups and swung your legs back and forth. Some former astronaut was saying it was the next-best thing to walking on the moon.

That night she dreamed that she and Trina were astronauts, the first mother-daughter team to be sent into space. A mission to Mars. The interior of their spaceship looked like a cross between their living room and a beauty parlor. Cindi was part of the crew, dressed in a silvery bodysuit. The mission director, Tom Brokaw, told them it was time to step outside onto the surface of the planet and collect dirt samples. Everyone back home on Earth was watching them on the evening news. Giselle held up Trina to the camera, and together they waved to Dan and Teddy. Teddy had been so mad because he didn't get to go along, but NASA wanted only mothers and daughters. They said that boys were too rambunctious. Giselle and Trina climbed the silver ladder, like a swimming pool ladder, and floated out into the atmosphere. They were attached by an umbilical-like cord wrapped around Giselle's waist and Trina's wrist, like the ID bracelets babies wear in the hospital. Trina was turning somersaults in the air and giggling. "Look, Mommy, watch me!" Giselle smiled and waved. Trina squatted down and started digging in the powdery white dirt. She had her pink plastic pail and shovel with her, as if it were a day at the beach. Giselle was reading the mission manual, attempting to comprehend the technical instructions, when she heard Trina shout, "Mommy, help!" The cord had snapped. Giselle looked up to see Trina floating away, floating off into space.

She couldn't run. Her moon boots were magnetized to the surface of the planet. She woke up screaming. She lay in bed panting, letting her heart rate return to normal. Her mind sent a message to her legs that it was time to get up, but her legs lay there like iron girders, too heavy to move. Pinned down by the full force of Earth's gravity. Until she heard Lois pounding on the back door, calling her name. *Go away,* Giselle thought, but she knew if she didn't respond, Lois would probably call the police, sure she'd killed herself. She got up and dragged herself to the door.

"My God!" Lois gasped and took a step backward. "What happened to your eye?"

At first Lois seemed suspicious, as if Giselle were some battered woman making up a half-cocked story about a champagne cork, until Giselle fished the bottle out of the trash and waved it at her.

"You sure you don't want to go to the doctor and have that eye checked?" Lois kept asking on the drive to the supermarket. But Giselle insisted that she was fine. Lois had made it her personal mission to see that Giselle had food in the house. At the store, wearing her dark glasses, she trailed Lois up and down the aisles, talking earnestly about this new exercise machine she'd seen on the infomercial the night before. "Do you want skim or two percent?" Lois butted in as Giselle went on and on, describing how this string of ordinary people had testified as to how the Fitness Flyer had changed their lives. She had copied down the 800 number, she said, and was thinking of ordering one. What did Lois think? Lois said she thought Giselle ought to wait a few days, think about it a little longer. Later, Giselle couldn't find the scrap of paper on which she'd jotted down the 800 number. She thought Lois must have hidden it. Or taken it for herself. After all, Lois was the exercise fanatic. But she decided not to confront her about it. She knew that Lois meant well. Giselle could tell that Lois was worried about her. A couple of times she had sent Eric over with a plate of dinner for her. Pizza or Kentucky Fried Chicken.

That night Dan appeared at the door about suppertime. She offered him a piece of fried chicken, which he declined. From the look on his face you'd think she'd offered him a dead bird. "Jesus Christ," he said, "what did you do to your face?" She thought about saying she'd been mugged, something to make him feel bad, to make him feel guilty for not being there to protect her, but she just shrugged and said she had walked into an open cupboard door. She didn't want to mention the champagne. He looked skeptical but didn't pursue it. He apologized for barging in unannounced; however, he had no choice, he said, since she hadn't answered the phone or bothered to return his messages. He looked uncomfortable and nervous. There were some books he needed, he said. "Fine" — she shrugged — "go get them. Help yourself. Be my guest." He hurried into the back of the house and returned several minutes later with a couple of suitcases full of stuff, which he set by the front door. Then he sat on the edge of the armchair opposite the sofa and tried to strike up a conversation. "How are you doing?" he asked. When she didn't answer, he picked up an empty glass and sniffed it, then shook his head.

"So, how's the book going?" she asked, perky as a talk-show host. She knew she looked like a slob. If she'd known he was going to show up, she'd have changed her clothes and done something with her hair.

"I told you, I stopped working on it."

"For good?"

"Look, Giselle, you've got to pull yourself together," he said, ignoring her question. "This is bad. The place looks like a dump. It stinks in here." He walked over and opened the sliding glass door, then the window behind her. "When's Teddy coming back?"

"Why? What do you care?" She picked up the remote and snapped on the TV.

"Giselle" — he raised his voice — "I'm trying to talk to you."

She muted the volume and turned to him. "Do you have anything to say to me?" Her tone was belligerent, but her voice cracked and she turned away so he wouldn't see the tears.

He shook his head helplessly.

"That's what I thought." She upped the volume on the TV. He shrugged and walked out with his heavy suitcases balanced in each hand, like the scales of justice. When she heard the car door slam, she leaped up and ran to the window. She stood there watching him drive off, thinking of all the things she already wished she had said. Such as, *Please stay. Don't go.*

It seemed like later the same night, although it could have been the next night, that Vonnie called her. Giselle had given up answering the phone — it was mostly wrong numbers anyway — but when she heard her big sister's voice shouting, "Pick up the goddamned phone!" she reached over and picked it up.

"That bastard called me," Vonnie announced without preamble. "He says he's worried about you. Not worried enough to stick around, obviously, but worried enough to call me."

"You mean Dan?" The alcohol seemed to have numbed her brain. The synapses moved sluggishly.

"Yeah, you know, your husband. Hell of a guy."

Vonnie and Dan hadn't really hit it off on Vonnie and Bev's visit to California. But Giselle hadn't taken it too much to heart since Vonnie didn't have much use for men in general. She had always held it against Ed for impregnating her little sister and turning her into a college dropout. As if he had tied her down and forced himself on her.

"You don't know what he's been through, Von. You can't know what it's like."

"Why are you defending the slime? He walks out on you, and you make excuses for him. It's sickening. Where's your backbone?"

"Leave me alone!" Giselle started to bawl like a baby, great boozy sobs. She whimpered a couple of things into the receiver, which had slipped down to her chest. She could hear her sister saying, "What? I can't hear you," and calling her name, "Gigi? Gigi! Are you there?" Her voice sounded tinny and far away, like some angry alien munchkin. "Are you there, Gigi?"

She must have passed out then. When she woke up, it was nearly midnight. *Nightline* was on the TV. The phone had slipped between her body and the sofa cushion, beeping like a cricket. She couldn't remember who she'd been talking to. She shut off the phone and set it on the coffee table. Then she got up and, for form's sake, hung up the phone and stumbled into the bedroom. As if it made any difference where she slept. Or when.

The next morning the phone beside the bed rang. Still asleep, out of habit, she answered it. It was her sister.

"I've made you a plane reservation for this afternoon," Vonnie informed her in a no-nonsense tone of voice. "Do you have a pen and paper?"

"To where? What are you talking about?" Her head was pounding. She hoped this wasn't something they had discussed, something she had agreed to and then forgotten about in an alcoholic haze.

"Here. To Lincoln." Vonnie sighed impatiently. "It's United, flight —"

"Are you nuts? This afternoon? Forget it. I can't just pick up and leave. Even if I wanted to, which I don't." She sat up and tweezed an opening in the miniblinds to peer out of. Another overcast morning.

"Why not? Give me one good reason you can't go." When Giselle didn't answer right away, Vonnie continued in a less belligerent tone. "Look, you shouldn't be alone. I'd come out there, but I really can't be away from the bar right now."

"How's business?" Giselle asked, trying to change the subject, trying to give herself a minute to think. She couldn't seem to focus. She knew there must be some reason — reasons — she couldn't just take off, but she couldn't think of any just now. Only half awake and hungover. She didn't even have a cat to feed. But there was Trina to consider. She couldn't just go off. Someone had to be here. Sometimes in the middle of the night she'd felt something, some presence.

"Business is good," Vonnie said. "Don't change the subject. Now, do you have a pen and paper? I'm going to give you this information. Okay?"

"Okay. I guess." She dutifully scribbled down the flight times that Vonnie dictated. She had never been able to stand up to her big sister, who could be something of a bully, always sure she knew what was right. Now she'd taken the money that Bev had left her, twenty thousand dollars, and sunk it all into this gay bar on O Street. Orlando's Hideaway. Her parents would die if they knew. Right in their hometown. Giselle could just hear her mother: *What will our friends think? Is she trying to humiliate us? What did we do that was so bad?*

"So, okay," Vonnie said. "I'll be at the airport at seven-fifty." Daring her to object.

Giselle didn't say anything. She was still busy protesting inside. "For how long?" she asked finally.

"Two weeks. But you can change it."

"I can't be gone that long. It's impossible."

"I told you, you can change it. I'll pay the penalty. Don't worry about it, for chrissakes. Just get your butt on the plane, and we'll worry about the rest later. All right?"

"I don't know. I guess."

"Good." There was a slight pause, as if Vonnie were debating whether to get into it. Then she said, "I saw Teddy yesterday. Bumped into him and Ed at Pioneers Park. With that dog, the malamute."

"Beowulf," Giselle said. "How did they seem? I mean, did he seem okay?"

"Yeah. They looked like they were having a good time. Throwing the Frisbee around. Very family values."

"That's good," Giselle mumbled. "That's good." It *was* good, but somehow it made her feel like shit. Clearly, Teddy was doing better without her. She should just stay away. But maybe if she stayed away too long, she would never get him back. He'd be gone for good.

"I've got to run," Vonnie said. "We're interviewing for a couple of new bartenders. Hey, how about you? You think you could mix a decent martini?" She laughed. "Just kidding. Seriously, though, we'll have plenty of time to talk when you get here."

"Yeah." Her head was killing her. She thought she might throw up. She hung up as Vonnie was saying good-bye, then raced into the bathroom and stood over the toilet, poised to retch, until the nausea passed as suddenly as it had arrived. She splashed cold water on her face and brushed her teeth. Nebraska. The Good Life. She didn't know how she felt about going, about leaving. Two weeks seemed like a long time. Maybe she would stay a week. Maybe a week would be a nice break. Maybe she could persuade Teddy to come back home with her. They could move into a nice apartment. Maybe they could find a nice complex with a swimming pool. Teddy would like that. Who knows, maybe Dan would realize how much he missed her — missed them. And by then the bad weather would have passed. Nothing but sunshine. Like the license plates said: The Golden State. A billion cars couldn't be wrong.

THREE

TEDDY FEELS JUST LIKE ONE OF THE GUYS. HE *loves it here. He never wants to go back to California. At his dad's place it's like camping out, a constant party, even though it's hard work. They are remodeling the old farmhouse, turning the lower floor into the kennel offices and the upper floor into an apartment to live in. His dad's buddies, Mac and Frito, don't even bother going home at night. After they knock off work for the day, they all cook up hot dogs or spaghetti or chili and drink beer and watch TV. Mostly they're all dead tired after a long, hard day of work — sawing, hammering, plastering, painting — and they hit the sack early, curled up in sleeping bags on the two sofas like big slugs. They are behind schedule for the grand opening. Sometimes they fight. They curse and storm off. Yesterday his dad made some comment, and Mac threw down his screwdriver and yelled, "Quit bossing me around! You ain't paying me enough to put up with this fucking shit." He got into his old pickup and tore off in a cloud of dust and gravel. When he saw Teddy looking worried, his dad told him it was no big deal. "He'll be back," he said. "Hell, we've been friends since kindergarten." And an hour later Mac came back with a bag full of tacos for everyone, just like nothing had happened.*

Nobody looks at him funny or treats him special. Sometimes he forgets about it, the bad stuff, for hours at a time. If they know he killed his sister, which he figures they must, they seem too busy knocking down walls and arguing over whose turn it is to go to the building-supply store to give it much thought. Even his dad seems to have sort of put it out of his mind. At first Teddy could tell that his dad was thinking about it all the time, treating him kind of like he was sick, always asking him how he was doing, but now he's treating him like a normal kid. Last night he even yelled at him for leaving the hamburger out where Beowulf could get at it. They had to drive to Food 4 Less and buy more meat for supper. His dad was tired and cranky the whole way there and back. Later, as they were getting into bed, his dad apologized, but Teddy didn't mind. It felt kind of good to be scolded for something dumb. He wanted to tell his dad, but he didn't know how to explain it.

He and his dad sleep in twin beds in the guest room because his dad doesn't want to sleep in his grandparents' old four-poster bed. Granma Rose has left a lot of her stuff just as it was. Frito says the place looks like a museum. China knicknacks and family photographs in fancy frames. Flowered wallpaper, hooked rugs, lace curtains. The other night Frito said, "Better get rid of this shit or everybody's gonna think you're gay like your brother." His dad just shook his head and said to Teddy, "Don't listen to him. He's a moron."

There are photographs clustered on a small round table in a corner of what is going to be the new living room. In one picture, Teddy recognized his father and his uncle Brice and another, taller boy who looked a lot like his dad standing in the snow in front of a huge snow fort, looking proud of themselves. "Who's that other kid?" Teddy had asked his dad the first night he arrived.

"That was my older brother George. He was killed in a car accident when he was seventeen."

"How old were you?" Teddy asked.

"I was about your age. Well, no, actually a couple of years older. Eleven. I'd just turned eleven. It happened the day before my birthday. I remember because we canceled the party and nobody said any-

thing about opening my presents even though there were a couple of boxes sitting on the buffet all wrapped up. I got up after everyone was asleep and opened them by myself. Afterward I felt real guilty. I tried to sort of wrap them back up, but it didn't work."

Teddy walked over and put his hand on his dad's shoulder. His dad stopped looking sad and whipped him off the ground in a big bear hug. His dad was on the wrestling team in high school. One of Teddy's few clear memories of before California was wrestling on a gold shaggy carpet with his dad. His dad has already shown him a couple of basic moves, like the half nelson and the hammerlock, and has promised to teach him how to wrestle for real when he's older. "How old?" Teddy asked him, and his dad thought for a moment and said, "Thirteen."

Tonight Mac is the chef — they take turns — and they are having Spaghetti Mac for supper. Mac makes a big deal out of it, saying it's his special secret sauce he learned from his Italian ex-girlfriend, although when Teddy sneaked into the kitchen for a Coke, he saw a jar of Ragú in the garbage. When Frito complains that the noodles are still hard, Mac says, "They're al dente. You're just used to Franco-American in a can, you hillbilly." Frito winks at Teddy and says, "Al who?" While they eat, they watch a documentary on Japanese sumo wrestlers on the Discovery Channel. Frito makes a lot of jokes about their naked flabby asses. Then he and Mac suddenly leap up and start butting bellies, sloshing their beers onto the hooked rug, but nobody cares. Mac is skinny, but Frito has a beer belly that hangs over his Huskers' belt buckle, and he sends Mac flying across the room, where he crashes into a sawhorse and lands on his butt. Beowulf skitters around him, barking nervously. Everyone laughs like lunatics. Teddy laughs so hard, he almost wets his pants. Then Frito turns to him, suddenly serious, and tells him, "Hey, man, you should've seen your old dad here in his glory days. He was a real champ. Fast Eddie." Teddy nods, waiting to hear more, but Frito just says, "Got to take a piss," and ruffles Teddy's hair on the way to the john. Both Frito and his dad have ponytails and one pierced ear. His dad wears a small turquoise stud, and Frito wears a small gold hoop. Teddy thinks maybe he'll let his hair grow and ask for an earring for his birthday. July 4. The same day as the grand opening.

He remembers going to the mall with his mother and Nana to get Trina's ears pierced. They went to some booth in the middle of the mall called the Earring Pagoda. His mom bounced Trina in her lap, and Nana tried to distract her by jangling her key ring while the girl who worked there took this staple gun sort of thing and punched a hole in Trina's ear. His sister let out a loud, terrified wail and tried to squirm out of his mother's lap. His mom closed her eyes and looked white as a sheet. "That's enough!" she shouted, standing up. "Let's go." The ear-piercing had been his nana's idea in the first place. It was some Mexican custom. "But she can't have just one pierced ear," his nana protested, although she sounded shaky, too. "It'll be over with in a second." And she motioned to the young girl, who just looked bored, to do it quick.

On the ride home he'd sat in the backseat with Trina in her car seat crying at full volume the whole way. She had tiny gold posts in her ears. His mother and grandmother weren't speaking to each other. He kept patting her chubby knees and kissing her wet cheek, trying to comfort her, feeling helpless. And a little offended that she was ignoring him. Usually he had the magic touch. Everyone always said so.

An hour later, by the time Dan came home, Trina seemed perfectly happy playing with her soft blocks. She seemed to have forgotten all about it. When his mom launched into this big tirade about how awful it was and how she should never have listened to Luisa, Teddy could tell that Dan wasn't really listening. He said, "Don't you think you're overreacting a bit?" Then he knelt down and picked up Trina. She was all smiles now. His mother stormed into the kitchen and slammed the cupboard doors. "Was it really that bad?" Dan had asked him, man to man. Teddy had shrugged and said, "I don't know. I guess she'll live."

His dad looks over at him and says, "What's the matter? You okay?" The sumo documentary is over, and Frito is flipping through the channels, looking for something else worth watching. Mac is in the kitchen dishing up some ice cream. Suddenly Teddy wonders what his *mom is doing at this very moment. He kind of misses her, but he wouldn't want to be back there.*

"Thanks," he says when Mac hands him a dish of fudge brownie ice cream. He would just like to know what she's doing now, at this very moment he's eating his ice cream.

IT WAS DUSK WHEN THE PLANE LANDED. A CLUSTER of lights on the prairie. A lonely blip of civilization. It always depressed her to fly into Lincoln. It always raised existential questions, such as, Why am I here (as opposed to there)? Or, What's more important: good restaurants or clean air? Her sister was waiting at the gate chatting with a handsome pilot in uniform who reminded Giselle of Bill Beemer. Pilots all seemed to have that same look. Sky cowboys.

Vonnie was wearing what had become her uniform for the past several years: a black T-shirt, jeans, and black cowboy boots. Summer and winter, the only thing that changed was the earrings. She had an extensive collection dating back to high school, when she used to hang them in neat rows on a strip of lace tacked to her bedroom wall. Over the years she had graduated from ladylike pearl posts to eclectic, mismatched ear sculptures. Her dark hair, shorter and spikier than that last time Giselle had seen her, looked like she'd zipped over to Paris on the Concorde for a quick cut. Giselle couldn't imagine where in Lincoln you could go and come out looking like that. When they were growing up, their mother used to drag them to a husband-wife team (June and Frank) who ran a barber/beauty shop called His & Her Hair. After Frank died, June redecorated all in pink and rechristened it the Crowning Glory Salon. It was clear that Vonnie's haircut was not June's handiwork, even if she were still alive. As soon as her sister spotted her straggling off the plane, she extricated herself from conversation with the pilot, who, completely clueless, was obviously trying to hit on her. He looked so crestfallen, Giselle almost felt sorry for him. Guys had always fallen all over Vonnie.

Vonnie's first words to her were "That fucking bastard. How could he?" Confused, Giselle turned to look behind her and then realized that Vonnie was referring to her eye. The shiner. It had swelled and darkened to the size and hue of a small plum. On the way to the parking lot she did her best to disabuse Vonnie of the notion that her younger sister had been the victim of domestic violence. But Vonnie wasn't buying it. As she waited for her change at the toll booth, she looked over at Giselle and shook her head. "Why are you protecting him?" she asked. "He doesn't deserve your loyalty."

"What do I have to do to make you believe me?" Giselle said. "Shit. Give me a break, why don't you?" She reached over and punched the tape player. She already regretted coming. It was always like this with Vonnie. The know-it-all big sister. "Who's this?" she asked, referring to the woman singing, hoping to change the subject.

"Enya," Vonnie said as if she couldn't believe that Giselle didn't recognize the voice.

"Nice," Giselle said.

The ride from the airport to the Near South, where Vonnie lived, took all of maybe ten minutes. The town was laid out like a grid — alphabetical streets intersecting with numbered streets. Flat and square, in both senses of the word. But the trees and flowers were in bloom. After L.A., the lawns looked invitingly green and shady. The flight had been delayed more than an hour in Denver, and Vonnie was speeding, clearly in a hurry.

As she pulled up in front of an old gray Victorian duplex, Vonnie said, "I thought we'd have a little time to get you settled," glancing at her watch. It was large and plastic with a red band; she had sent Teddy one just like it. "But I've really got to get back to the bar. Why don't you come with me? I want you to see the place."

Giselle shook her head. "Not tonight. I want to see it, too, but I'm beat. Tomorrow, okay?" She opened the car door and reached for her suitcase in the backseat of Vonnie's sporty magenta Tracker, which she'd inherited from her dead lover.

"Are you sure?" Her sister seemed reluctant to leave her alone. "You can just sit in a booth and have a drink or two. It wouldn't require that much energy."

"I'm just not up for it." Giselle sighed and faked a yawn. "Sorry."

"Okay, well . . ." Vonnie shrugged, her earrings jittering impatiently. A small silver airplane dangling from one ear and a mini-globe from the other. Giselle was still wearing the boring little posts she'd switched to after Trina was born. The baby thought dangly earrings were toys to be grabbed and yanked. All Giselle's dangly earrings were in a box on her dresser. There was no reason not to wear them now.

"There's a key under the geranium pot next to the door. The door on the left. It's the upper floor. You sure you'll be all right?" Vonnie asked as she raced the accelerator.

Giselle smiled and nodded. "I'll just take a bath and go to bed early." She turned and headed up the walkway before her sister could get in the last word. But she wasn't quick enough.

"Hey Gigi!" Vonnie shouted, loud enough to make the elderly couple on the porch swing next door turn and stare at her. "Don't let the cat out!"

Walking into her sister's apartment, Giselle felt like a time traveler. It could have been their old apartment, Ed's and hers, on B Street, the apartment they had inherited from Ed's brother, the apartment where Teddy was born. Vonnie's place was, in fact, only one block away, on C Street.

There were two bedrooms. One was obviously her sister's room. A queen-size bed covered with a red Mexican blanket and a flurry of bright pillows and throw rugs. The guest room was smaller and more austere, bare except for a narrow futon on the wooden floor covered with crisp white sheets and a single pillow. Giselle liked the looks of the small room, suitable for a nun. The people in the downstairs apartment, probably college kids, were playing music too loud. Just like their downstairs neighbors on B Street used to. Once, Ed had marched downstairs to complain and returned an hour later, stoned out of his gourd. Giselle had been so pissed off that she made him sleep on the sofa, which was several inches too short for him. She used to worry about the noise from downstairs waking up Teddy, but it never seemed to bother him. In those days he could sleep through anything, the sleep of the innocent.

She went to the kitchen and opened one cupboard after another, looking for some liquor to help her relax. On the plane she'd had a couple of vodka and tonics. The cupboards were mostly bare, a teetotaler's dream. In the refrigerator she found an almost empty bottle of white wine. Maybe working in a bar took away your desire for alcohol. In high school she had worked in a bakery one summer and developed an aversion to sweets that lasted almost a year. She had started out gaining five pounds and ended up losing ten. When she was pregnant with Teddy, Ed had worked two part-time jobs until he landed a full-time job at the Kawasaki factory and, later, a better job as operations manager of a grain elevator. Afternoons he had bagged groceries at Hinky Dinky and evenings he delivered pizzas for Domino's. At first she craved pizza, her version of pickles and ice cream, but by the time Teddy was born, the mere sight of a pizza box made her gag. They used to joke that the baby would be born clutching a pepperoni in each tiny fist.

Giselle carried the wine bottle into the guest room and began unpacking. When she opened the closet door, she saw that there was a built-in bureau, just like the one in their bedroom on B Street. It had served as Teddy's changing table. She would set him

there to change his diapers, and sometimes when he was crying —
had been crying all day, it seemed — she had to fight the impulse
to slam shut the closet door and walk away.

The windows were wide open, but the room felt hot and stuffy
anyway. She had forgotten the feel of Midwestern summer nights.
There were wet half-moons under her armpits. She could smell her
own sweat, taste it in the back of her throat. She peeled off her
T-shirt and opened her suitcase to find a fresh tank top. She hadn't
put a lot of effort into packing — just dumped a few things from
her drawers into the suitcase, grabbed some toiletries from the
bathroom, not really caring whether anything matched. Not like
the old days. She remembered packing for their honeymoon trip to
Hawaii, laying out on the bed each outfit complete with acces-
sories — jewelry, belts, sandals — as she imagined herself sipping
a mai tai in the red silk and silver sandals, walking on the beach at
sunset in the white linen with the black espadrilles dangling from
her hand. This time she'd stuffed everything into a squashy suitcase the size of a microwave. Lois, who drove her to the airport,
couldn't get over how little she was taking. "It's only for a week,"
Giselle had said, although she had left a message on Dan's voice
mail at the office saying two weeks, just to be on the safe side.
He was supposed to mow the lawn and check the mail. During
the long flight out here, she couldn't help hoping that maybe her
absence would serve to knock some sense into Dan, make him
realize what he was losing, although she told herself not to get her
hopes up.

She dumped out the clothes on the futon and rummaged
around until she found a gray tank top, which she yanked over her
head. Then she peeled off her damp jeans and stepped into some
white shorts. She felt better but she still stank. Vonnie had left
some towels out for her in the bathroom, a large room with a mo-
saic tile floor and claw-foot tub. Their old bathroom on B Street
had been remodeled, unfortunately, with linoleum and fiberglass,
and a real shower. This place had one of those jury-rigged, hand-
held contraptions that sprayed water all over the bathroom if you

weren't careful. She was too tired to deal with it. She wet the washcloth and scrubbed her underarms, sniffing to make sure they were clean, then flapped her arms like chicken wings to dry off as she walked back to the guest room for her deodorant.

The deodorant wasn't in the cosmetics bag where it was supposed to be, even though she was almost certain she had packed it. She stuck her hand into the larger satin pocket on the inside of the suitcase and pulled out two stray Tampax and a Chap Stick. Then she tried the zip pockets on the outside. She felt something in one and pulled it out. Trina's pink pacifier. She let out a small cry, shut her eyes, rammed the pacifier into her own mouth, and sank down on top of the heap of clothes scattered across the futon, arms and feet contracted into a fetal position. She was glad that her sister wasn't there to see her acting like a big baby. Or Teddy, thank God. She had planned to call him as soon as she unpacked, but now she decided to wait until morning. She wasn't sure he'd be all that glad to see her anyway. And maybe if she were completely honest with herself, she wasn't sure how much she wanted to see him. But she couldn't afford to be completely honest with herself. She was his only mother.

This element of ambush was the thing that she found hardest to take. Day after day you accustomed yourself to the dull, lulling ache of loss. But nothing could accustom you to the sneak attacks, the sudden brutal trip wire — a pacifier, a knitted bootie stuck between sofa cushions — that set off a fresh explosion of grief. Not long ago she had seen a woman on some talk show, an amnesiac, who had lost her memory as a result of a head injury. A car wreck. The woman couldn't even remember her own son. She said she had to look at baby pictures and even demanded to see the birth certificate. Giselle had listened in fascinated disbelief. She couldn't imagine such a thing. And it had occurred to her to wonder what she would do if she could just snap her fingers and forget. Forget she ever had a daughter. Forget the pain of losing her. She was afraid that in a weak moment she would give in to the temptation. A snap of the fingers! Sweet oblivion! But she knew that somehow, someway the loss would find her. Even if she couldn't name it, she would feel it. A woman weeping at an unmarked grave, the name of her loss forever on the tip of her tongue.

No, it was better to remember. To remember how she had packed the pacifier, a spare, last October when they had driven up to Palo Alto for the weekend. They had stayed with Dan's old college roommate, newly divorced, in a spectacular wood-and-glass house in Portola Valley. Even though the friend, a lawyer, had lots of money and an Italian sports car, Dan had seemed to feel sorry for him. As she sat on the back porch nursing Trina while the men watched a football game on the big screen TV in the rec room — complete with an antique billiards table — Giselle had overheard Dan telling the friend, "You know, I've never been happier." She had smiled to herself, sitting there in the pale sunshine on the deck; and seeing her smile, Teddy had waved at her from the branches of a big tree he was climbing. *Look, Ma, no hands!* And for the moment she had felt such a sense of well-being, she wasn't even worried about Teddy falling and breaking his neck.

Giselle had been lying there on the rock-hard futon, drifting in and out of a thin sleep, when she heard Vonnie come home. Her cowboy boots echoing on the bare wood floors. There was just enough light from the moon or streetlamp to make out the time on her wristwatch: 2:15. She debated calling out to her sister versus pretending to be asleep as she heard Vonnie brushing her teeth in the bathroom. On the ride back from the airport, Vonnie had told her that she felt wired after she got off work. She found it difficult to come home and fall asleep. So she ended up sleeping half the day. On the one hand, Giselle felt too worn out for a midnight chat, but on the other hand, she felt lonely. For the past several days, ever since Teddy left, the emptiness of the house had weighed on her as she lay there in the darkness. The sounds of her sister's nightly bedtime routine were comforting. The *thunk* of the old water pipes, the toilet flushing. Vonnie gargling. The cat, who had hidden herself as soon as Giselle opened the front door, mewing softly in the hall.

Giselle got up and flicked on the bright overhead light. The heap of clothes she had been lying on top of was mashed and wrinkled. She tossed everything into the corner and pulled back the sheet so that it would look as if she had been sleeping under the covers like a normal person. Her sister was neat and energetic. She didn't have much use for slothlike self-pity. When they were growing up and Giselle skinned her knee or got stung by a bee, she would try not to cry in front of her big sister, who was famous for her stoic bravery. Giselle would hold it in until she saw her mother's face and then run into her arms, sobbing, while their mother ordered Vonnie to fetch the Mercurochrome and Band-Aids. Giselle always loved Band-Aids, the bigger the better. Her sister, the cheerleader, once pom-pommed and cartwheeled through an entire football game with a broken toe she didn't even mention until the final touchdown was scored.

Giselle tiptoed down the hall to the bathroom. She was about to knock on the door when she heard her sister's voice. At first she thought Vonnie was talking on the phone, but then she heard a second voice. Surprised, she hurried on toward the kitchen, as if she had just woken up thirsty. A minute later Vonnie emerged from the bathroom wearing what looked like their father's old maroon bathrobe.

"Hey," she said when she saw Giselle, "what are you doing up?"

"I needed a drink of water." Giselle rinsed out her glass and set it on the counter. "I guess I was dehydrated from the plane."

The bathroom door opened again and a pretty young blond woman walked up behind Vonnie and smiled at Giselle. She was wearing an oversized tie-dyed T-shirt and looked familiar. Before Giselle could place her, Vonnie said, "You remember Jess, don't you?"

Giselle stared. At the look on her face, the other two burst out laughing. Jessica Foley. The last time Giselle saw her, she'd had braces on her teeth and was wearing a Brownie uniform. The Foleys had lived in the big Tudor house down the street, the nicest house on the block. Giselle used to baby-sit for Jessica and her little brother, Carlton, who was deaf. They were her least-favorite kids to baby-sit for — spoiled brats — but their parents paid the best. Back then Jessica had long blond braids and expensive Kate Greenaway dresses and the most extensive collection of Madame Alexander dolls Giselle had ever seen. Just after Giselle started high school, the Foleys had moved to Denver to be closer to some famous school for the deaf. Giselle hadn't thought of them in years.

"I know I was a real pill," Jess said.

"She still is." Vonnie gave her a big squeeze and Jess wriggled free, pretending to be offended. She was thin and pale and delicate. Giselle did some quick arithmetic and figured she must be about twenty-four, but she looked more like sixteen. And the complete opposite of Bev, who had been dark and muscular, a body builder, although not grotesque like some of the women who competed in competitions Giselle had seen on television. She wondered what Jess thought of all the photographs of Bev that were all over the apartment.

"Jess is in law school," Vonnie said.

"Really." Giselle nodded, feeling old suddenly. She saw Jess looking at her and felt self-conscious, remembering her black eye. She wanted to explain about the champagne cork but knew how lame it would sound. She wondered how much Vonnie had told her. About Trina and everything.

Vonnie and Jess sat down on the sofa. Vonnie picked up the remote and clicked on the TV. The fluffy gray cat leaped onto Vonnie's lap. Jess leaned over and petted her.

Seeing the two of them sitting side by side on the sofa, Giselle felt a little left out. "I think I'll go back to bed," she said, yawning.

"Okay," Vonnie said. "Holler if it's too loud." The guest room was right next to the living room.

"I'm sure it won't bother me," Giselle lied. There was nothing she hated more than the mumble of a television when she was trying to sleep. It was something she and Ed used to squabble over all the time. As she walked back to the spare room and crawled underneath the sheet, she was thinking about Ed. About how odd it was to think of him being only ten minutes away, with her son. Their son. And their not even knowing she was here.

The next morning, before anyone else was up, Giselle called the farm. She felt nervous, like a party-crasher, as the phone rang and rang. She could picture the expression on her son's face as he recognized her voice: *Who invited you?* For no logical reason she felt pissed off at Ed, as if he were obscurely to blame for the difficulty of the situation, as if he had somehow poisoned Teddy's mind against her, even though the few times she had spoken to Teddy since he'd been away, she could hear Ed in the background coaching him to talk to her, to tell her about this or that. *Did you tell her about the deer?* she'd hear Ed prompting in the wings. *Did you tell her about soccer?* As if she would be pleased that Ed had found a soccer team for Teddy to play on so he could be with kids his own age. Well, she supposed she was pleased — she knew it was a good thing — but what would happen when it came time for Teddy to leave? To go back home to California? He never mentioned that. Ed was never big on thinking ahead.

After maybe a dozen rings, just as she was about to hang up, a groggy-sounding male voice, not Ed's, answered the phone, making no attempt to disguise his irritation at having been woken up. She almost hung up, but she couldn't stand the thought of waiting any longer than she had to.

"Hello," she said, "is Teddy there? This is his mother."

"Gigi?"

"Yes?"

"This is Mac. How the hell are you?" Then he groaned as he caught himself. "I'm real sorry about — you know — what happened out there."

"Yeah," she said. "Thanks. How are you doing?"

"Good, you know, hanging in there. It's been kind of a good time working on the kennel and all with Ed. It's really going to be something. How's California?"

"Actually, I'm here. In Lincoln." She paused as Mac hacked away, a smoker's cough he'd had ever since high school. "Can I speak to Teddy?"

"They're not here. There's a note here saying they went to do some errands. Should be back by noon."

Giselle sighed. It was only eight-thirty. "Well, tell them I'm at my sister's. You got a pencil?"

"Shit, just a minute." Mac disappeared for a minute and came back on the line. She gave him Vonnie's number. "Got it," he said. "Hell, it's real good to hear your voice. I know Teddy'll be real excited."

"Yeah," she said. "Thanks, Mac." She hung up and stood there looking out the window at the square green lawns and flowering redbud trees. She didn't know what she was doing back here. It was like being trapped inside her high school yearbook. Mac Mackey. They had gone out on a few dates before she started seeing Ed. All through junior high, she'd had a big crush on Mac. He'd played lead guitar in a garage band whose name changed every year but whose members remained constant. Ed played the bass. Then Mac's longtime girlfriend, Ginny Brantley, decided she wanted him back, and that was that. Mac had been real nice about it, but Giselle still felt crushed. It wasn't until months later she found out that Mac had put Ed up to asking her out. She had fallen for Ed on the rebound.

Just hearing Mac's voice made her crave a smoke. She saw a half-full pack of Camel Lights lying on the makeshift coffee table. They must be Jess's. Her sister had quit smoking when Bev was diagnosed with cancer. For a moment she fought the urge, remembering what an ordeal quitting had been, but then she thought, *What the hell?* and walked over and sneaked one. She lit it with the Zippo lighter lying next to the pack. As she inhaled, she felt dizzy, and it flashed through her mind that it was really over with Dan.

Her marriage was really over. She felt some superstitious sense that if she smoked this cigarette, that was that. There would be no going back. It was practically a felony to smoke in California. She grabbed the ashtray and stubbed out the cigarette, then went into the bathroom and turned on the shower. She wasn't ready to burn any bridges yet.

It had been years since she drove a stick shift. Giselle knew it was a real act of generosity on her sister's part to loan her Tracker. It was obvious Vonnie took great care of the car. It was spotless outside and inside. As she drove down Thirteenth Street, heading for the highway, Giselle thought of her old Honda sitting in the garage back home. A rolling Dumpster cluttered with soft drink cans, candy wrappers, old homework of Teddy's, discarded clothes, beach blankets, crinkled-up maps of places she'd probably never pass through again.

It was only eleven o'clock, but she was too anxious to wait any longer. Maybe they'd be back earlier than noon. She plucked a cassette blindly from Vonnie's tape carrier, afraid to take her eyes off the road even though there was almost no traffic by California standards, and slid it into the tape player. After a hazy morning, the sun was shining. The air, she had to admit, smelled fresh. After L.A., the sky seemed too blue to be real, the color of a crayon. Music blasted from the tape deck. *You seem very well, things look peaceful | I'm not quite as well, I thought you should know . . .* "Christ," Giselle muttered, "not this," and punched the tape out again. Just hearing a few bars had ruined her mood, which had improved dramatically once she got out of the apartment and into the car. It was 9 A.M. in California. Dan was probably driving to his office at this very moment, listening to this very tape. She bit her lip to keep from crying as she turned west onto Old Cheney Road.

It was amazing how quickly the city petered out and you were in the country. The prairie. Nothing but sky and fields and the occasional house. She remembered their friends in L.A. — Dan's friends, really — discussing some harebrained idea, a proposal they had read about in *The New Yorker* or someplace, to turn the Great Plains states into a buffalo commons. One big Yellowstone or Yosemite. Everyone except her, the only Midwesterner, seemed to think it was a fine idea.

It had been years since Giselle had been out to the Bedford farm, and she was worried she would miss the turnoff, but she spotted it right away. She recognized the mailbox that Granpa Bert had fashioned from an old duck decoy. From the outside the old white farmhouse looked just as she remembered it. She rolled up the window as the little jeep bounced up the long gravel drive, whipping up a cloud of dust. The malamute burst out of the screen door at the side of the house and lunged against the side of the Tracker, barking and wagging his tail. All bark and no bite apparently. Giselle yelled at him to get away, afraid he would scratch the shiny magenta paint. "Hey there, Beowulf," she called out, climbing out of the jeep. "You were just a puppy last time I saw you." The dog stopped barking and eyed her curiously, as if he'd just figured out who she was and had decided to reserve judgment.

There were three vehicles parked in front of the barn, including a white van. On the phone Ed had told her he'd traded in Granma Rose's Buick for a used Dodge Caravan he thought would be handy for transporting dogs and cats. He planned to offer a door-to-door taxi service. She figured they must be home. But then just as she was collecting herself to go knock on the door, Mac rounded the corner of the house holding a paintbrush, a big smile on his face.

"They aren't back yet," he hollered. She glanced down at her watch as if she didn't know what time it was. Right behind Mac was another familiar face, maybe thirty pounds heavier but unmistakable. Leverett Johnson, aka Frito. One Halloween about two decades ago he'd dressed up as the Frito Bandito, and the name had stuck. That's what she hated about small towns: everything stuck. She knew that Frito held it against her, leaving Ed and taking off to California with Teddy. He had tried to talk her out of going.

Giselle cringed inside and kept her gaze on Mac as they walked toward her. Mac gave her an awkward hug, careful not to drip white paint all over her. Frito just nodded and offered a neutral-sounding hello.

"I guess I'm a little early," she said, wishing she had waited until she knew for sure they were home. "I'm anxious to see Teddy."

"Nice little car," Mac said, looking inside the Tracker.

"It's my sister's," she said.

"How's she doing?" Mac asked.

"Fine. She opened a new bar."

"Yeah," Frito said. "We heard."

Mac shot him a don't-get-into-that look.

While she was pacing around Vonnie's apartment, it had occurred to Giselle that maybe it would be better to catch Teddy by surprise. Before he had time to build up any resistance to the idea of her being there. But now she wasn't so sure. Maybe it would have been better to meet on neutral territory. A McDonald's or Denny's. She was considering just taking off when they heard the crunch of tires on gravel and turned to see a big black motorcycle skimming up the long driveway.

"That's them," Mac said.

The dog's ears perked up and his tail beat the air in anticipation.

F ROM HALFWAY DOWN THE LONG GRAVEL DRIVE, *Teddy recognizes his mother standing there even though she is wearing dark glasses and her hair is different. Cut short and fluffy, almost to her ears. His arms cinch themselves tighter around his dad's waist. He yells, "My mom's here!" but the words are pushed back at him by the wind, and his dad just yells, "What?"*

Teddy is holding on to a small sack of drill bits and screws and half a dozen candy bars that they bought at Payless Cashways. On his feet he's wearing some new black cowboy boots with red stitching, which his dad just bought for him at The Fort. They are almost identical to his father's boots except that you could fit three of Teddy's inside one of his dad's. He loves riding on the motorcycle, an old Harley-Davidson his dad bought from a real Hell's Angel. Everywhere they go, he begs his dad to take the motorcycle, but more often than not they need to take the van in order to cart stuff.

The motorcycle skids to a halt, kicking up a cloud of pebbles, and they both remove their helmets. Teddy leans forward then and whispers into his dad's ear, "It's Mom." He can feel the shock zap through his dad's body as he looks over at her and smooths down his mussed hair.

The boots feel stiff and slippery — he feels as if he's walking on ice as he follows his dad across the dirt to where his mom is standing with Mac and Frito. When he first recognized her, he felt glad. But then it hit him that she must've come to take him back to California. Why else would she be here? And he doesn't want to go. Not now. Not ever. But definitely not now. He kneels down and lets Beowulf lick his face, a big slobbery hello, stalling for time. He can feel his mother watching him. He can feel her waiting for him. Let her wait, *he* thinks, I'm not going anywhere. *He can see her smile tremble and fade as he dawdles with the dog until his dad hollers, "Teddy! Get your butt on over here and say hello to your mother." Trying to make it sound like Teddy hasn't yet recognized her. He doesn't know why his dad is always worrying about hurting her feelings when she didn't care about his feelings. She didn't care whose feelings she hurt when she left his dad and dragged Teddy all the way to California. If they hadn't gone to California, nothing bad would've happened. They would all still be happy. Alive and happy. And he isn't the only one who thinks so. He heard Frito saying so to his dad after Teddy was in bed the other night. "It's a fucking tragedy is what it is," Frito said. "If she'd've just stayed put, everything would've been cool. You'd've worked things out." Teddy hadn't been able to hear what his dad said. Or maybe he didn't say anything. His dad doesn't really talk all that much.*

He knows his mother doesn't really think his dad is all that smart. Not like Dan, who is a college professor. In third grade when Teddy got stuck in the Robins reading group for slow readers — actually, medium slow, the real slow group was the Sparrows — his mother said she hoped he wasn't taking after his father. "Your father was never much of a student" is what she said. After a week in the Robins, Teddy got promoted to the Bluebirds, the best group, and his teacher sent home a note saying it was all a mistake, and his mother kissed him and seemed so happy to find out he wasn't a bad student like his father, after all. But his father is smart. The other evening before supper he was watching Jeopardy! *and calling out all the answers while he chopped onions and fried up some hamburger for the chili. He knew everything — sports, the Bible, presidents, science.*

Even Mac was impressed. He said, "You should go out to Hollywood and be a contestant." His dad just looked embarrassed and stopped saying the answers out loud.

Teddy can see his mom biting the inside of her cheek the way she does when she's nervous. He walks over and says, "Hey, Mom, fancy meeting you here." It's an expression his dad likes to use.

His mom smiles and nibbles at her lip. He can't see her eyes, but he has the feeling she might be about to cry. He can feel the new boots pinching his toes. It suddenly occurs to him that they left his old sneakers at the shoe store. Left them lying in a paper sack on the counter. He wants to tell his dad they need to go back, but he doesn't want to let his mother know they went off and forgot them. He knows she'll blame it on his dad, who gives him a little push toward his mom. Teddy takes a step closer and gives her a hug.

"So!" His dad smiles and rubs his hands together. "You want to see what we've been doing to the place?"

His mother nods her head, and they all tromp inside the house except for Frito, who says he's got work to do. Seeing it through his mom's eyes as his father leads her around the downstairs, pointing out the office and the grooming area and the indoor kennels and dog run, Teddy can see they've still got a lot of work to do. The grand opening is supposed to be in two weeks. But his mom smiles and nods and seems impressed. At least she oohs and aahs politely. Then his dad leads them upstairs to show her how they've turned the upper floor into a separate apartment. Teddy's boots clatter on the wooden stairs. He places each foot carefully, afraid he might slip and fall.

After the tour of the living quarters, his dad asks if she'd like a Coke or something. His mom says okay and sits down on the edge of the sofa that's covered with an old paint-spattered sheet. Teddy hesitates, then sits down next to her. He thinks maybe if he's really nice, she will see what a good environment this is for him and let him stay. He knows that Hannah was always talking about good and bad environments. His mother gave his dad the name of a shrink here Teddy is supposed to see, but they haven't got around to calling him yet.

Even though the living room is kind of dark — his dad's planning to put in a skylight — his mother is still wearing her dark glasses. It bugs him. Teddy says to her, "Why don't you take off your sunglasses?"

She takes them off just as his dad comes back into the room, holding a couple of Diet Cokes and a Sprite. His dad stops in his tracks and stares. Her hand flies up and covers her eye.

"It's not what you think," she says. "I got hit with a champagne cork."

His dad doesn't say anything, just kind of shakes his head.

"It's true," she adds defensively. "You want me to swear on a Bible?"

"I didn't think you had that much to celebrate these days," his dad says as he hands her a Coke.

She glares at him and slides her dark glasses back on. His father winks at Teddy as he hands him his Sprite. Mac has disappeared.

"So, how long you staying?" his dad asks, getting right down to it.

His mother fiddles with the buttons on her shirt and says, "A week. Possibly two." She takes a sip of Coke. "It was all sort of spur of the moment."

His dad seems to relax a little. He leans back in the rose velvet armchair and rests his head on the lace doily. At least she isn't planning to leave right away. Like today or tomorrow. They have some time to work things out. At least this is what Teddy thinks his dad is thinking. Sometimes he thinks he can read his dad's mind — they're so much alike. Then other times his dad seems like he's off in his own world. He doesn't even know you're there.

"I like your hair," his dad says.

"Thanks," his mom mumbles, and bites her lip.

"Mine's longer than yours now." His dad laughs and waves his ponytail.

"I'm growing my hair," Teddy tells her. He reaches up and tries to gather it into a stubby ponytail. He knows better than to bring up the earring.

His mother turns to him. "I thought maybe you could spend the night at your aunt Vonnie's. We could rent a movie and order a pizza." She smiles brightly. "What do you say?"

"You mean tonight?" Teddy shoots a look at his dad. Help me!

His mother sees the look on his face and says, "Well, not necessarily tonight. Whenever's good. Tomorrow maybe. Or the next night. I don't want to interfere with your plans."

"Okay," Teddy says. What else can he say? He doesn't want to make her feel bad. He's kind of glad to see her, but seeing her reminds him of all the bad stuff he'd just as soon not think about. And he doesn't want to piss her off. If she gets mad, she could drag him back to California. Just the other night his dad explained to him how custody works. "Maybe Thursday."

His dad nods agreeably. Teddy knows that his dad doesn't like "to make waves." It's another one of his dad's expressions. But he does have a temper he lets loose every once in a while. The other morning he cussed out Frito for starting a fire in the toaster oven and nearly burning the place down.

"Okay then. Thursday it is." His mother sets her nearly full Coke can on the floor and stands up. "How 'bout we say around dinnertime?"

His dad stands up and walks her down the stairs. Teddy stays on the sofa. He hears his dad saying, "I can drop him off. Save you the trip out here." His mother's voice is too soft for him to hear. Teddy leaps up and walks over to the window facing the front of the house, where the cars are parked. From here the little magenta Tracker looks like a Matchbox toy. He watches as his father walks his mother to the car, opens the door for her, and shuts it after she's climbed inside. She starts the engine right away and turns the car around. She seems in a hurry to leave. His father stands there, scuffing the dirt with the toe of his boot, watching as she bumps down the gravel drive to the main road. Teddy knows if he tried, if he concentrated, he could read his dad's mind, but he doesn't really want to.

SHE HAD TWO DAYS TO WAIT BEFORE TEDDY'S overnight. It felt strange knowing that he was in the same town, just minutes away, but not with her. Maybe it was just being back in the place where she grew up, but she felt like a junior high school girl mooning over some boy who didn't give her a second thought. It was all she could do not to drive by the house. When she was a teenager, she used to ride her bike by Tommy Harms's house at least once a day. And a couple of years later, she would drive by Ross Rosowski's house every evening, half hoping, half fearing he'd be outside washing his car or mowing his parents' lawn. In this instance it wasn't really a triumph of maturity. Ed's place was too far off the road to see anything.

She was reluctant to go out of the house and bump into people she knew, people she hadn't seen in years. There would be that awkwardness of wondering what they had heard through the grapevine. And beyond that there was something else. Being home again reminded her of who she used to be, who she thought she would be when she grew up. At the grocery store yesterday she had glimpsed Mrs. Van Dorn, her old English teacher, sorting through the cantaloupes with the same look of rapt concentration with which she diagrammed sentences on the blackboard, and

Giselle had ducked down another aisle. It had been an instinctive reaction of guilt, of shame, as if she were cutting school. Mrs. Van Dorn had been the yearbook adviser the year Giselle had been editor, and she had expected Giselle to go on to become a successful journalist. At graduation she had given Giselle, who was salutatorian, a biography of Margaret Bourke-White inscribed, "To a future White House correspondent. Don't forget us. Fondly, Mrs. V." Later, after she left the grocery store, Giselle felt terrible. She had heard from Laura that Mrs. V had undergone a double mastectomy last year. Giselle should have gone up and asked how she was doing. The whole world didn't revolve around her own problems. Mrs. V probably had more to worry about than a former student's defaulting on her youthful promise, which was probably more the norm than not. Still, on the way back to the apartment, Giselle had made it a point to stop by the main library and get a library card and an armful of books. She supposed that one of these days — she didn't know when exactly — she would be ready to go back to school.

That night Vonnie dragged her to the bar. Vonnie and her partner, Val, had done a nice job of redecorating, tearing out the old booths and dark paneling in favor of small, brightly painted tables and chairs and hanging plants. The walls were painted a deep womblike pink. It was like sitting inside a Georgia O'Keeffe painting.

Once she got there, Giselle actually enjoyed herself, sitting at the bar drinking free tequila sunrises and chatting with the bartenders. She could see that her sister was in her element — the perfect hostess — somehow managing to oversee the kitchen and mix drinks and greet people all at once. Giselle was happy that her sister had created such a congenial niche for herself; she wished that their parents could put aside their prejudice and embrace their daughter's entrepreneurial success. But she didn't think that was likely to happen anytime soon. Come Sunday, Giselle didn't know what she would do. She would have to call them, but she wasn't sure she would tell them she was staying at Vonnie's. She didn't want to get in the middle. She wasn't here to broker peace negotiations. It might just be simpler to lie. She would have to ask Vonnie what she thought.

In the meantime Val set down another tequila sunrise in front of her. They made small talk about California, where Val had lived for a year after college. Nothing heavy — just the weather, the traffic, the smog, the beach, the usual pros and cons. Giselle noticed a book called *A Woman's Guide to Investment* sitting underneath the cash register and asked Val if it was hers. When Val said yes, Giselle told her about the women's investment study group she had joined back in California. Val thought it was a great idea. She called Vonnie over and made Giselle tell her about it. Vonnie said she could think of at least four other women she knew for a fact would be into it. In the time it took for Giselle to drink her second tequila sunrise, Vonnie made a few calls and organized the whole thing. "We're on for next Sunday evening," she informed them. "All right! Way to go!" Val and Vonnie slapped hands. Giselle smiled. She could feel her spirits lifting — a combination of the tequila and the thought of making a bundle in the stock market. She could definitely use some money, some financial independence.

Ever since her near encounter with Mrs. V, she had been brooding over just how it was that she had allowed her life to stray so far off course. First there was Ed and the unplanned pregnancy and marriage. Okay, that was one major detour. But then, finally, she had found the will to leave for California, to start over, and what had she done? Fallen for a professor and — *wham!* — the next thing she knew, she was changing diapers again. Okay, so he was a professor this time, but what was she? When Giselle told Laura she was getting married again, expecting to hear congratulations, there had been a brief silence on the line and then Laura had asked, "But what about you?" Giselle had bristled and said, "What do you mean, what about me? I'm in love." As if being in love were a vocation or livelihood.

Later on, when the place got busier, Val recruited her to stand behind the bar and serve beers. "Keep the tips," Val told her, tying a forest green apron around Giselle's waist. It was hectic and fun. She loved the weight and jingle of the heavy coins accumulating in her apron pocket. It reminded Giselle of the lemonade stands she used to set up by the curb when she was little. For the first time in ages she didn't have time to brood. At first she was surprised and a little uptight when some of the women customers flirted with her, but pretty soon she warmed up to it and flirted right back. Every so often Vonnie would bop over and joke around, like an outraged guardian. "Hey, quit hitting on my little sister!" Or, "Forget it. She's straight." It felt good to laugh. Every time she laughed, she felt lighter, as if she were taking in great gulps of pure oxygen. When Val hollered out, "Last call!" Giselle was surprised so much time had passed. She was sorry to close up and go home.

That night Giselle slept better than she had since before she could remember. There was a sudden storm, the sort of storm that used to send her scurrying into her parents' bedroom when she was a child. Burrowing into her mother's arms and covering her head with a pillow. But now she lay on the futon, listening to the rumble of thunder and crack of heat lightning, feeling pleasantly tired. She fell asleep to the steady swoosh of rain drumming on the roof. It helped to be in a place where Trina had never been. A place with no associations.

In the morning she made coffee and curled up on the sofa with one of her library books even though there were floor-to-ceiling bookshelves in the living room of Vonnie's apartment. Her sister had always been a great reader. In Madison she had managed a women's bookstore called A Shop of Her Own. After a couple of pages Giselle's mind had taken a detour. She was thinking about Dan and feeling lonely, debating whether to pick up the phone and call him, when it rang. Since Vonnie was still asleep, Giselle leaped up and answered it. She said hello, hoping to hear either

Teddy's or Dan's voice on the other end, but it was her cousin Ruth's voice that she recognized instantly. Giselle hoped that her disappointment wasn't audible. Ruth said that she'd heard Giselle was in town and wondered if she would like to have lunch. Giselle hesitated, trying to imagine the scene — two mothers who had lost their little girls in tragic accidents, chatting over chicken salad — and then said yes, okay, she'd like that, even though she wasn't really sure if she would. Nicole, Ruth's seven-year-old daughter, had been Rollerblading on the sidewalk in front of their house when an elderly neighbor had suffered a heart attack at the wheel and lost control of his car. The driver died instantly, but Nicole had lingered in a coma for a week. Giselle remembered talking to Ruth shortly after Trina's death, hoping that Ruth would have some wisdom to impart, and feeling even more hopeless when she hung up. But maybe in person it would be different. At any rate, it was nice of Ruth to call, to extend herself. And Giselle couldn't very well say no. Ruth said she'd pick her up at noon.

Vonnie emerged from the bedroom, yawning and stretching, her short hair bristling unsymmetrically. "Who was that?" For the first time Giselle noticed a small tattoo just above her sister's left breast, a butterfly or hummingbird fluttering at the edge of the skimpy tank top — Giselle couldn't quite make it out from across the room.

"Ruth," Giselle said. "We're having lunch today."

"Oh, God." Vonnie wrinkled her nose. "Better you than me." She sniffed the air and walked into the kitchen, where she poured herself a mug of coffee. "I know that's mean. I guess I should be more charitable under the circumstances."

Giselle shrugged and sighed.

As kids they never got along, forced to endure family holidays in one another's company. Ruthie, an only child, was boring and well behaved and liked to sit with the adults. She was always tattling on Vonnie and Gigi. "Aunt Ruth," she would announce in a prissy, pompous tone of voice, "Vonnie called me a bitch!" or

"Gigi took her clothes off in the swimming pool!" To their mother's credit, even she thought Ruthie was "a little drip." Once, after a particularly tiring afternoon in Ruthie's company, their mother took two aspirin for her headache and said, "I'm sorry that little drip is named after me."

When Teddy was born, Ruth befriended Giselle. It was the first time they had ever had anything in common. On a few occasions they took the babies to a park or a lake. Ruth already had a toddler, Marissa, as well as the baby, Nicole. Although it was pleasant enough — at least, Ruth seemed content — sitting there in the sun chatting about diaper rash and colic, Giselle felt as if she were going to go crazy. She felt like screaming and yanking out her hair. *This isn't my life,* she thought. *What happened to my life?* Being around someone who seemed so serene and satisfied only made her feel more crazy. So she started to make excuses whenever Ruth called. And then Ed got busted for pot — no big deal, really (first offense, probation) — but Ruth's husband, Kip, wouldn't let her have anything more to do with them. And since Giselle's parents moved to Florida about that time, there were no more family holidays together.

At the restaurant Ruth insisted on ordering for them both in Japanese. In the car, a new silver Acura, Giselle had been surprised when Ruth suggested going to a Japanese place. The old Ruthie had been a picky, xenophobic eater. Pizza was the outer limits of her taste for exotic cuisine. And the only ingredient she liked on her pizza was hamburger. Now, as Ruth attacked the sushi, Giselle smiled to herself as a clear picture of ten-year-old Ruthie methodically picking olives and mushrooms off her pizza flashed in her mind. From the look of disgust on Ruth's face, you would have thought they were slugs and maggots. But apparently the year that they spent in Tokyo, where Kip's corporation had transferred him to start up some new branch office, had transformed Ruth into a sophisticate.

Her taste in clothes had also improved. Growing up, she'd had an unfortunate penchant for frilly and dainty garments completely inappropriate for a tall, large-boned girl. Behind her back, Vonnie used to say that Ruthie looked like a transvestite. But today she was wearing a flattering beige linen pantsuit.

"It was the best thing that could have happened," she said as she tweezed a piece of pickled ginger into her mouth. "I didn't want to go, but we had no choice. Kip wasn't about to quit his job, and he refused to leave Marissa and me behind. I was too depressed to pack. Kip's mother came over and did it all. I had insisted upon leaving Nicole's room just the way it was. Hadn't touched a thing. I thought it would kill me to see it all packed away." She paused to signal the waiter for some more water. "But in a way, it wasn't so bad, because we were all packing. It was almost as if Nicole were just going along with us. Least that's what I pretended to myself."

Giselle nodded to show that she understood. The sushi seemed to stick in her throat. She was amazed by Ruth's appetite.

"Anyway, to make a long story short, the complete change of culture just snapped me out of it. Suddenly everything was just so strange and different, and nothing reminded me of Nicole. Whereas here, everything reminded me of my baby. It was just all there was every minute, every second, every breath. I don't know what would've happened to me if we hadn't gone to Japan when we did." She shook her head and speared a shrimp tempura.

Although they were supposed to be commiserating, Giselle bit her lip in annoyance. What was she supposed to do? Move to Japan?

"How's Teddy doing?" Ruth asked, reaching across the table and cradling Giselle's hand in hers.

"Well, you know" — Giselle sighed — "he's had a rough time. It's been difficult, to say the least."

Ruth's eyes welled up with tears, and she blotted them with her napkin. "I just can't believe it. He was such a sweet little boy."

Giselle gritted her teeth. "He's still a sweet boy," she snapped.

Even though she didn't know if this was true or not. She just resented Ruth's talking about him as if he were dead or deranged. "It was an accident."

"Of course." Ruth nodded vigorously. "And God knows, accidents happen."

To change the subject, Giselle asked about Marissa, then more or less tuned out as Ruth warmed to the task of describing her remaining daughter's virtues and victories under the most trying of circumstances. "I think it has just made her a stronger person," Ruth concluded, picking up the check and reaching for her purse. "I think it was God's way of making all of us stronger."

"Excuse me," Giselle said, throwing her napkin onto her plate. "I'm not feeling too well. I'll just wait outside."

It was true: she really wasn't feeling well. And the air outside didn't help. In the mid-nineties with 100 percent humidity. The restaurant was in one of the small new strip malls that seemed to have sprung up everywhere. Ed referred to it as the "Californication of America." Giselle paced down the sidewalk and entered what appeared to be a big new sporting goods store that looked like it would be crisply air-conditioned. The first thing she noticed, standing to the right of the doorway, was a huge stuffed lion, ready to devour her. Startled, she walked quickly past it and found herself standing in front of a long glass display case full of guns. All sorts of handguns of various sizes. She caught her breath and took a step forward. A clerk, a young clean-shaven blond man, asked if he could help her. He had a shy, pleasant smile and seemed eager to be of service. Like a pharmacist or florist. She stared at the row of small guns on top, neatly labeled. She had never seen the gun. Had no idea what it looked like. The police report said it was a .38 Colt. The clerk slid open the case in anticipation of her request.

"I'd like to see a Colt .38," she said, amazed by how normal she sounded. Businesslike.

The clerk — his nametag said DAN — handed her a small

silver-and-black gun. As an aesthetic object, it was surprisingly pleasing. She held it in her palm, weighing it.

"My husband's name is Dan," she said.

He smiled, waiting for her to elaborate, then turned his attention to the gun in her hand. "Is it for self-protection?" he asked.

Before she could answer, Ruth burst through the door and said, "My God, Gigi, what are you doing in here?" She grabbed Giselle's arm as if to drag her away. Giselle thought of Eric's grabbing Teddy's arm and the bullet firing. She could almost hear the explosion as she dropped the gun onto the glass counter. The clerk's smile had faded; he was looking confused and concerned, slightly apprehensive, then relieved as Giselle turned and followed Ruth out of the store, back out into the oppressive heat of high noon.

When Giselle returned home after lunch, she found Jess ensconced at the kitchen table, studying. A yellow highlighter in one hand, a Bud Light in the other, and a Camel Light burning in the ashtray. The table was littered with dark, heavy law books.

"Can you spare a beer?" Giselle asked.

"Sure. Help yourself."

The apartment felt like a sauna. A breeze from an old box fan riffled the pages of Jess's book as she paused for a drag from the cigarette. She was wearing a black athletic bra and jockeys. She looked like some prepubescent waif in a Calvin Klein ad. Giselle opened the refrigerator, tore a can from the six-pack, flipped it open, and took a long swig.

"You look like you need that," Jess said, swinging her feet off the other chair so that Giselle could sit down at the little table wedged into a sunny corner.

There was a pungent odor of sweat, and Giselle wondered why Jess didn't study in the bedroom, the only room with an air-conditioner. "What is torts exactly?" she asked, reading the title off the spine of the book Jess was underlining in.

"A civil wrong, not including a breach of contract, for which the injured party is entitled to compensation," Jess rattled off by rote.

Giselle smiled. "Sounds like catechism."

"Yeah, only the law professor is God." Jess sighed and stretched. Her torso was thin and pale. You could count her ribs. "Don't ever go to law school."

"Really?" Giselle sat down in the empty chair. "That's funny because actually I was planning to. You know, before." She picked up a lime green Magic Marker, uncapped it, and took a whiff. The smell made her nostalgic. She missed school. She missed feeling smart. She missed being asked questions she knew the answers to. These days she just felt out of her depth. When Teddy asked her, *How can something be nobody's fault?* what could she say? *Sorry, son, I didn't read that chapter.*

"You could still go," Jess said, "couldn't you?"

Giselle shrugged. "I don't know. I just don't have the energy to plan that far ahead right now."

She had, in fact, been wondering lately about the law, in the abstract. According to the law, were there cases where no one was to blame? There was a lot of talk these days about "victimless crimes." Was there such a thing, in the eyes of the law, as "crimeless victims"? Where do you draw the line between fault and guilt? If X is your fault, are you necessarily guilty of X? These were some of the questions she mulled over on sleepless nights.

"*Torts* is also Latin for 'twisted,'" Jess added. "As in 'twisted conduct.'" She sighed and flipped the book shut. "Brain-twister is more like it. After an hour reading this shit, my brain actually hurts." She massaged her temples with both hands.

The phone rang and Jess leaped up to answer it. Giselle could tell she was talking to Vonnie, who was at the bar talking to some acoustical engineer about a new sound system. While Jess was on the phone, Giselle slid the book, *Prosser on Torts,* over to in front of her and opened it. She flipped the pages, skimming the boldface headings, occasionally stopping to read something Jess had highlighted in yellow or green. An italicized subheading, "Capacity to Bear Loss," caught her eye, and she read:

> Another factor to which the courts have given weight in balancing the interests before them is the relative ability of the respective parties to bear the loss which must necessarily fall upon one or the other. This is not so much a matter of their respective wealth. . . . Rather it is a matter of their capacity to absorb the loss or avoid it.

Who, she wondered, in their situation — herself, Dan, Teddy, Trina — had the better capacity to absorb the loss or avoid it? It didn't seem to apply to their situation at all. She supposed the law must be thinking of financial losses. But what about other sorts of losses? The unbearable losses?

Jess turned to her and said, "Vonnie wants to know if you want to meet for dinner downtown. Around six. She doesn't have time to come home."

Giselle looked up and said, "What?" She was still absorbed in the book. Jess repeated what she'd said. Giselle shook her head. "Tell her I'm not up for it. I just got back from lunch."

"She says she's not up for it," Jess repeated into the phone. "She just got back from lunch."

Giselle stood up and walked into the guest room just in case Vonnie wanted to argue with her. Her sister never liked to take no for an answer. She would have made a good lawyer.

Her room was even hotter than the living room. She made a mental note to buy a fan the next time she went out. It was a different, more wilting kind of heat than what she was used to in California. She stripped to her underwear and lay down on the futon. She shut her eyes and tried to imagine making love with Jess, but she couldn't. She got as far as Jess's coming into her room and lying down beside her — and then nothing. It disturbed her to think she was still so uptight that she couldn't even imagine making love to a woman. Or maybe it was because she used to baby-sit for Jess. And Jess's thin, frail rib cage reminded her of Teddy's. How she used to pull up his T-shirt and tickle his ribs while he squirmed and laughed, before he got too old for that sort of thing. A year ago, two years ago? Not that long ago, really, although already it seemed like another lifetime.

She must have fallen asleep, stunned by the heat. When she woke up, it was dusk. The sheets were soaked with sweat. A terrible, heavy lethargy pinned her to the bed. She struggled to summon the will to stand up before the depression paralyzed her. Loud music thudded down below; she heard the clatter of dinner dishes, convivial voices shouting to one another above the music. The aroma of barbecued meat wafted through the open windows. It seemed to her that she had never been more alone, not even when she left Ed — those first few shaky nights in cheap motels en route to California — or in the ugly furnished apartment in Northridge with its bare walls. Then she had Teddy to keep her going. And she had hope for a new life. Now she'd had her new life and lost it. She could feel the self-pity lengthening like shadows, stealing across her, and she forced herself to stand up. *The capacity to bear loss.* The phrase kept running through her brain. She pictured Rose Kennedy. How had she kept going? There was her faith; in interviews she always spoke of her faith. But what if Bobby had shot Jack — not on purpose, of course — say, a hunting accident? Maybe that would have shaken her faith. Not that Giselle had had any faith to begin with. Except for the usual belief that these things happen to other people, the people you see on the evening news.

Once she was up, she forced herself into the bathroom. The cold shower helped revive her. She borrowed an old madras sundress that she had found in the back of her sister's closet, a dress that Giselle had actually given to Vonnie for her birthday about a decade ago. The cat was meowing in the kitchen, a plaintive whine. Giselle found a bag of Cat Chow and dumped some in a dish. She had never much liked cats, and the cat seemed to sense it. She checked to make sure the answering machine was on, and locked the door behind her.

It was warm but pleasant walking downtown, looking at the trees and flowers. At the bar everyone greeted her by name and seemed pleased to see her. Giselle put on an apron; when she wasn't busy, Val taught her how to mix a few of the more exotic drinks: Singapore slings, fuzzy navels, golden Cadillacs. The time passed quickly. She fantasized about becoming a bartender and moving to a strange city where she didn't know anyone, maybe even out of the country, Mexico or the Bahamas, someplace by the ocean where people on vacation from their real lives drank foamy elixirs with pineapple spears and paper umbrellas, and took snapshots of each other having the time of their lives. Or Japan. She could wear a kimono and serve sake in tiny cups and wait for the culture shock, like a giant tsunami, to wash the past away. She heard a laugh and glanced over to see her sister standing next to Jess, their hips touching, their arms around each other's waist. Apparently Vonnie had moved on, even if there were still photographs of Bev all over the apartment. And Giselle was glad. Probably even Bev would be glad. But with a child it was different. What kind of parent would go off and leave a child behind? Even a dead child. Especially a dead child, who couldn't cry out in protest, *Mommy, don't leave me!*

Before she started going out with Dan, she had slept — or almost slept — with the mechanic who had replaced the fuel pump on her Honda. It was shortly after she arrived in California. He was handsome in a Tom Selleck sort of way — dark hair, dark mustache, white teeth, nice smile — and she was terribly nervous. He had come over — she had called him — after Teddy was in bed. So Teddy didn't even know he was there. But just as the man entered her, at the moment of penetration, there was this shriek, like no noise Teddy had ever made before. "Mommy, Mommy, where are you?" he shouted over and over as she pushed the man off her, leaped out of bed, and ran to Teddy's room.

"I'm right here," she said, snapping on the bedside lamp and rocking him in her arms. "I'm here. Where else would I be?" She had rubbed his back through the thin pajamas until his shudders slowed enough for him to catch his breath.

"I dreamed I was dead," he said. "I was in the dirt by myself." He started to whimper again. She held him closer, wishing that the man in the next room would just get dressed and leave. Right before they had left Nebraska, Ed's grandfather had died. Teddy hadn't gone to the funeral, but they had taken him to visit the grave and leave some flowers for Granpa Bert. Later, on the ride home, she remembered Teddy sitting in the backseat chanting, "Granpa Bert is in the dirt." She and Ed had exchanged a helpless look and shrugged.

When she got back to her bedroom, the man was already dressed; he said he'd better go. To his credit, he seemed more sad than mad. He was divorced and had a little girl who lived with her mother in Hawaii. And he had grown up in Omaha, which is how Giselle happened to strike up a personal conversation with him at the garage. He had noticed her Nebraska plates and walked over to say hello. They seemed to hit it off right away. But after that ill-fated night, he didn't call back. And when the ignition switch needed to be replaced a couple of months later, she went to a different garage.

On Thursday she was sitting out on the front lawn when Ed drove up in his white van at five o'clock sharp. One thing she had always appreciated about Ed was his punctuality. They had argued on the phone earlier, when she told him she didn't like Teddy riding around on that motorcycle. It was too dangerous. Ed blew up and said it wasn't that dangerous, they always wore their helmets, and Teddy loved it. "He's my kid, too," he'd said. "Do you think I want anything to happen to him?" Giselle had conceded, grudgingly, that she knew he had Teddy's best interests at heart, but that didn't make motorcycles any safer. Ed had muttered something under his breath that he refused to repeat when she said, "Pardon me?" It felt just like old times. But she interpreted the fact that he'd chosen to drive the van as his way of extending an olive branch.

She walked to the curb to meet them. Teddy jumped out of the passenger seat and pointed to the van. "Look, we got it painted!"

ED'S ANIMAL FARM was painted in bright red with PET BOARD-ING AND GROOMING painted in blue underneath, along with the address and phone number. The pièce de résistance was a painted cartoon of Garfield and Snoopy tucked into bed together.

"Very nice," she said.

Ed smiled and shrugged like it was no big deal, but she could tell that underneath he was as excited as Teddy. She hadn't seen him this happy since high school. "It's coming along," he said. "It's really happening."

Teddy bent over to straighten out the leg of his jeans that was caught on the cuff of his cowboy boot. He was dressed just like Ed in clothes that seemed too warm for the weather. She didn't know why he wasn't wearing the shorts and sandals she'd packed. While Teddy was bent over, Ed had a clear shot of his skinny butt. He gave him a light shove with the sole of his boot, and Teddy toppled onto the grass, spread-eagled. Teddy let out a war whoop as he scrambled to his feet and tackled Ed around the knees, hanging on like a pit bull until Ed fell down on the lawn beside him. Then Teddy threw himself on top of his father and pinned his wrists to the ground while Ed pretended to resist with all his might. They were both laughing like loons. Giselle leaned against the van and watched, her smile half real and half fake. It was good to see Teddy laughing and acting silly again. But she couldn't help thinking about Dan and Teddy, how she'd never once seen them get physi-cal like this, rolling around on the ground like two pigs in mud. She couldn't blame Dan. Or Teddy. But it made her feel bad. "Hey," she said, nudging Ed with her toe. "That's enough, you guys."

Ed sat up and held Teddy at bay as he attempted to pull him back down. "Uncle!" he called out. "Uncle!" But Teddy was so revved up, he kept coming at him until somehow Ed was back up on his feet, holding Teddy upside down by his ankles like a prize trout. Giselle had forgotten how strong he was. In high school he'd worked part-time for a piano-moving company. Next to his dad Teddy looked like a real pip-squeak. He was never going to be that big. In terms of physique, the poor kid took after her side of the family.

"I ordered a pizza," she told Teddy when Ed set him back on his feet.

"I feel dizzy!" Teddy said, stumbling around like a drunk. "I think I'm going to throw up." He wrapped his arms around his stomach and doubled up.

"Does it hurt?" She frowned and took a step toward him.

"He's fine," Ed said. "Quit faking." He leaned over and poked Teddy in the belly. Teddy giggled and straightened up.

"Well, I guess I should take off." Ed brushed the dirt and loose grass from his hands and pants. He reached through the open window of the van and pulled out Teddy's red backpack and handed it to her. "We packed his toothbrush and stuff."

"Thanks," she said. "About noon tomorrow?"

"Right." He slid his sunglasses on and gave Teddy a knock on the noggin with his knuckles. "Have a good time and mind your mother."

Teddy had stopped joking around and was looking forlorn as he watched his dad climbing into the van. Giselle wanted to walk over and put her arm around him, but she was afraid he might push her away, and she wouldn't want Ed to witness that. He was taking his sweet time starting the engine. She wished he'd just get going. He had this hangdog expression on his face, like a dog scratching at the door to be let inside. On the phone he had suggested that the three of them go out for pizza, his treat. But she'd declined the offer. She wanted to keep the boundaries straight. Things were confusing enough already.

The two of them climbed the stairs to the apartment in silence. As she opened the door, the cat whisked past to find a safe hiding place. But Teddy managed to grab the tip of her tail and reel her in.

"What's his name?" he asked, attempting to cuddle the frantic cat. "Teena," she said. "It's a her." Jess had explained to her that the cat was named after Brandon Teena, a lesbian cross-dresser attempting to pass as a man, who had been murdered in a little town not far from Lincoln. She/he had become a cause célèbre in the gay community.

"Ouch!" Teddy dropped the cat and covered his cheek. The cat took off like a missile.

"Let me see," Giselle said, pulling his hand away from his face. There was a thin bright beaded trail of blood running from just below his eye to just under his nose. He was trying not to cry. Even though she wanted to point out that it was his own fault, she said, "Let's see if Vonnie has any ointment."

He followed her inside to the bathroom. "Wow, neat bathtub," he said, sitting on the edge of the claw-foot tub. In the medicine cabinet mirror she saw his reflection checking out the shower curtain: a black-and-white orgy of naked women depicted in a vaguely classical Greek style. Naturally, her childless sister didn't seem to have any sort of first-aid supplies. Not even a Band-Aid. "She doesn't have anything," Giselle said. "Let's just wash it."

Teddy sat there stiff and sullen as she gently cleaned the scratch with the washcloth and soap. After she had patted it dry, she said, "I think it's okay. You've stopped bleeding."

"I want some ointment," he said stubbornly. "I could get lockjaw. Or cat scratch fever." He stood up and examined the scratch in the mirror. They made quite a pair. Her black eye had faded to shades of yellow and lavender. Framed in the medicine chest mirror, they looked like a poster for domestic violence.

"Dad has Neosporin," Teddy informed her.

"Okay, okay," she sighed. "Let's go to the store. Russ's is only a couple of blocks away. We can pick up a movie at the same time." Then she remembered the pizza that was on its way. She looked at her watch. "I think we better wait for the pizza. We can go afterward."

Teddy shrugged and walked around the small apartment, checking it out. His boots echoed on the wooden floors. Those narrow toes had to be bad for his feet. "Don't you wear your sneakers anymore?" she asked. They were expensive Nikes she had bought on sale at The Athlete's Foot.

"Sometimes," he said, "but I like these better." He stomped back to the living room and sat on the sofa.

"Want a Coke?" she asked.

He nodded. He had the remote in hand and was flipping through the channels. When she returned with his Coke, he was looking at the local news with the volume off. "She doesn't have cable?" he said in disbelief.

"I don't know. I guess not." She handed him the Coke. "But we're going to rent a video after supper."

"I like to watch *Bill Nye, the Science Guy*. It's on at five."

She looked at the kitchen clock. "Well, it's almost five-thirty. It would be just ending anyway." She smiled and shrugged, feeling self-conscious and tongue-tied. It felt like a first date that had gotten off on the wrong foot, doomed already. But maybe after the pizza arrived, things would lighten up. She wished that Vonnie were here. Teddy thought that Vonnie was funny and cool. He always credited Vonnie with teaching him how to whistle. But one of the bartenders was sick and Vonnie couldn't get away.

"Jeez, it's hot in here." Teddy blew at his bangs and fanned himself with a magazine. "Doesn't she have A/C?"

Giselle unplugged the box fan from the kitchen and set it up on a chair right opposite Teddy. "Here you go," she said as she turned it on, "your own private breeze."

"Shhh! I want to hear this." Teddy turned the volume on the TV up high. He was watching Alex Trebek introduce today's contestants on *Jeopardy!* Since when did he watch quiz shows? "Dad's really good at this," he volunteered. "He knows all the answers."

The doorbell rang.

"Pizza's here!" She jumped up, grabbed her wallet from her purse, and ran downstairs to let in the delivery person. The delivery person turned out to be a young guy, cute and friendly. He seemed to be flirting with her as he counted out her change. For a moment she fantasized asking him to stay and share the pizza with her, a picnic on the lawn with someone who seemed to enjoy her company. Instead, she trudged back upstairs and set the flat white box on the coffee table in front of Teddy, who didn't take his eyes off the TV screen. She grabbed a beer from the fridge and some napkins and paper plates. They ate the pizza and watched *Jeopardy!* At least he didn't have any complaints about the pizza. And his appetite seemed to be back. After the accident he had lost five pounds, and he didn't have that much to lose to begin with.

The television was on too loud, but she didn't want to ask him to turn it down. This was an annoying habit of Ed's that Teddy had obviously picked up already. She didn't know how many times she had walked over and turned down the volume when Ed was watching something. The most annoying was when he fell asleep with the TV blaring so loud that you could hear it a football field away. It had always made her regard him as a dim-witted cretin. Only ten more minutes, she told herself, and the show would be over and they could walk to the market. And talk. She wanted to catch up on what he'd been doing and thinking since he'd been gone. When Teddy was younger, they used to drive out to the beach for what he called walkie talkies. It was one of their favorite things to do, just stroll along the shore and talk about stuff. In those days, like most kids, he was full of questions. What do you call X? Why does Y do that? How come Z is like this? It was the kid's version of *Jeopardy!* every day. Back then he thought she was the one with all the answers.

She knew that it wasn't fair, but she resented Ed's ease with Teddy — the way they horsed around and teased each other, like it was no big deal, like they didn't have to worry about every word and gesture being taken the wrong way. She was afraid that Ed was stealing her son away from her. Stealing him back, to be fair. But it wasn't fair! Ed had not lost a daughter. Lost her forever. No visitation rights, no holidays, nothing. Watching Ed and Teddy wrestling on the lawn, she had suddenly understood for the first time how Dan felt. She recognized it: this is what Dan must feel. In the law of cosmic accounts, her loss was not as great as his. It took her by surprise, this petty bean counting in the face of tragedy. You would think that tragedy would be a great leveler. The democracy of disaster. After the big disasters — the Oklahoma City bombing, the Pan Am crash, the Northridge earthquake — the families of the victims always seemed so united in their shared grief whenever you saw them on the news. Yet now she knew the ugly truth. She knew that down deep, the woman who lost two children was looking at the mother who lost only the one child, and the mother who lost the one child was looking at the woman who lost only a sister, thinking, *My loss is greater than yours.* The inspirational esprit de corps was all just a media conspiracy. The silver screen's silver lining. And nobody had the guts to say it was bullshit. Even in the midst of their grief nobody wanted to look bad on national television. Smile, everybody, you're on *Candid Camera!*

During Final Jeopardy, which signaled that the show was almost over, Giselle tossed their paper plates and napkins into the pizza box and threw it in the trash. "Okay," she announced, walking back into the living room. "Time to go to the store."

"What?" Teddy was busy channel surfing.

She bent over and wrestled the remote out of his hands. "I said, Time to go to the store."

"I don't want to go."

"I thought you needed your ointment. What about cat scratch fever? Besides, we need to rent a movie."

"Can we get some ice cream?"

"I think that's an excellent idea." She held the door open for him and then locked it behind them even though Vonnie rarely bothered to lock up. Slipping the key into the pocket of her shorts, Giselle led the way downstairs and across the lawn, with Teddy clattering along behind her. At the curb she started to cross the street but Teddy balked.

"Hey," he said. "Where's the car?"

"We don't have a car. Vonnie's got it at work." Giselle pretended not to notice the scowl stealing across his face. "Come on, it's only a couple of blocks. And it's a beautiful evening." The quiet neighborhood was a beehive of benign activity. A man in Bermuda shorts mowing his lawn. Two little girls jumping rope. A kid on a flashy bike doing wheelies down the block. An old woman walking two white Scotties on bright red leashes.

"But these boots hurt my feet," he grumbled. "I didn't know we were going to have to walk. Can't I wait for you here?"

"Teddy!" She counted to ten and began again in a calmer tone of voice. "I'm going to the store and you're going with me, and that's final. Do you hear me?"

She thought she'd really blown it now, but to her surprise he fell into step beside her, and amazed her further by offering a polite observation. "The grass is so green here," he said. "It almost looks fake. Like AstroTurf."

"That's true." She nodded her head in agreement. "It rains a lot here in the summer."

"Not like California." He stooped down and petted one of the Scotties as they passed by. The old woman smiled at him, and he smiled back. Giselle put her hand on the back of his skinny neck and gave him a little squeeze, and he didn't shrug her off. She began to relax. Every transition required a little adjustment period, she reminded herself. They were just settling in to being together again.

"You know, you used to live just around the corner here," she said. "I'll show you the house when we pass it. Maybe you'll even remember it."

Teddy looked mildly interested. "How old was I?"

"Well, from the time you were a baby until you were four."

As they got closer to the boy on the flashy bike, he rode past them once and circled back around, then hopped off his bike and stood there watching them approach. "Hey," he said, "Ted?"

Teddy stared at him for a moment and then grinned as a look of recognition lit up his face. "Hi, Brent. Neat bike."

"Thanks. I live over there." He pointed to a big brick house with green trim a couple of doors down. "You live near here?"

Teddy shook his head. "I used to live in California, but now I'm staying with my dad off of Old Cheney Road. My aunt lives here." He pointed to the top floor of the house across the street.

Giselle stood there waiting to be introduced, frowning at the phrase "used to live in California." She decided to let it go. This didn't seem like the appropriate time or place to get into anything. Finally Teddy noticed her standing there and said, "This is Brent. He's on my soccer team."

Giselle nodded and smiled, pleasantly surprised when Brent stuck out his hand and gave her a gentlemanly handshake.

"You want to play?" Brent asked. "I just got this cool new computer game. Sim City. Ever played it?"

"Yeah," Teddy said, "with my uncle." He looked at Giselle. "Can I, Mom? Please?"

Shit, she thought, *this is swell, really swell. I haven't seen him in two weeks and he comes over for one measly night and now this. Talk about quality time.* She sighed and looked at her watch. "Okay. It's five-forty. You can play until seven-thirty. Then I want you to come home and we'll watch a movie together. Got that?"

"Got it!" He looked so happy as he ran off with Brent that she couldn't really hold it against him. He was a kid, after all. Kids liked to play with other kids. It was good to see him acting like a normal kid again. His aching feet didn't seem to be giving him any trouble as he chased after Brent on his bike.

She continued on to the store alone. An undulating lawn sprinkler set too close to the sidewalk doused her as she walked by. The cool water felt good against her sweaty skin. As she turned the corner onto Eighteenth Street, she wondered if she should have gone to Brent's house and introduced herself to his mother. She wondered how Brent's mother would react if she knew that her son's nice new friend had shot his little sister. *What a relief it must be to Teddy,* she thought, *to be in a new place where no one knew.* Fame might have its rewards, but anonymity was the true blessing. *Used to live in California.* Teddy's voice kept running through her head. When he'd said that, it had taken all her self-restraint not to protest, to set him straight. It had hit her like a punch in the gut. Their home was in California. It was too soon to even think about moving. It had been only two months. They were all still in shock. Even Hannah, the inept therapist, had cautioned them not to make any major decisions too soon.

The peonies were in bloom, a riot of deep pink and white bouffant blossoms. The bushes bloomed for only a couple of weeks; they were already looking a little blowsy. She thought of her own desiccated garden back home, the parched brown lawn. Their landlords, a nice young couple who had been transferred to Fort Worth and still hoped to return to California someday, would be disappointed when they saw the place. Last year Giselle had sent them a Polaroid of the newly planted garden in all its modest glory.

At the corner of Eighteenth and A Street, as she waited for some traffic to pass, a young stud in a red Camaro whistled at her. It caught her by surprise and lifted her spirits a notch. Every day she waited to hear from Dan. Something, anything. A phone call, a letter, even a forwarded bill. But she hadn't heard a word. She couldn't believe it. When her first marriage had fallen apart, there had been months of bickering, door slamming, name-calling, and sleeping on the sofa. By the time she had actually packed her car and split, they were both exhausted. There had been nothing left to say. Which seemed like the way it should be. Not like this, so quick and quiet. It didn't seem possible that a marriage could just suddenly vanish like a puff of smoke, or a house of cards in a gust of wind — now you see it, now you don't! — with so much left unsaid. It felt surreal. It felt like a dream that had turned into a nightmare and then she woke up and here she was — back in Kansas. Only it happened to be Nebraska. Except for the thin gold band on her finger, it might all have been in her mind.

The market was crowded with people buying food for supper and so air-conditioned that she could feel the goosebumps rising on her arms and legs. The video rental was in the rear of the store. As she perused the new releases, it occurred to her that she had no idea what movies Teddy had seen since he'd been staying with his dad, and she felt a fresh twinge of annoyance at his ditching her. The new releases were pretty well picked over anyway. She couldn't seem to focus. She felt out of touch and indecisive, sure that whatever she picked would be a bad choice. Finally, anxious to be done with it, she grabbed a copy of *Jurassic Park*. She figured he'd already seen it so many times that one more time wouldn't hurt. She paid for the movie and made her way back into the grocery section to the ice cream freezers. Here at least she felt on solid ground; she knew what Teddy liked. Ben & Jerry's Chocolate Chip Cookie Dough was his favorite, just as she knew that Häagen-Dazs Rum Raisin was Dan's favorite. And suddenly as she picked up the small container of Ben & Jerry's, it struck her that it was not impossible that she and Dan would never see each other again. Even though they knew all each other's little likes and dislikes, it was not inconceivable that they could just split and go their separate ways. The divorce, if it came to that, could be conducted via mail, telephone, fax. There was nothing holding them together. They didn't own a house or stocks or even a car jointly. Most of the furniture came from Dan's mother's house. Aside from their daughter, they had accumulated very little, certainly nothing worth squabbling over. They could just walk away and never lay eyes on each other again. For as long as they lived. The idea chilled her to the bone. She was shivering as she hurried to the express line, grabbed a five-dollar bill from her pocket, and paid for the ice cream.

Back outside, she walked quickly, trying to warm herself up again. Thinking about how when she and Ed split up, they knew that they would be bound together for life. They might no longer be husband and wife, but they would always be Teddy's father and mother. You could set asunder marriage, but parenthood — for better or for worse — was until death do you part. The real thing. At the time, the thought of never being free of Ed had seemed burdensome and unfair. Un-American. Didn't everyone have some inalienable right to start over? Three strikes and you're out? This was only her first strike and yet there they were, yoked together forever. But now, for the first time, she realized how grateful she was that she had not been free to leave Ed behind in a cloud of dust, how grateful she was that he was still in her life, how grateful for having the opportunity to pick up the pieces of the marriage and build something new out of them. Not that it was easy. At first it had been especially fucking miserable. Sometimes it was still a pain in the ass, but considering the alternative — well, she didn't want to consider the alternative. The alternative was unacceptable. And an unacceptable alternative was no alternative.

As she walked up the steps to the apartment, one of the guys opened the door of the downstairs apartment and said, "Hey, we got a package for you. Special delivery." He was bare-chested, tanned with a furry map of dark hair, which he scratched unselfconsciously as he handed her the flat envelope. *From Dan,* she thought, *at last,* and smiled brightly as she thanked him, her heart accelerating as she ran upstairs. Since she had been away, she kept imagining ways they could start over. They could move to Santa Barbara, say, or San Francisco. Dan was always saying how much he preferred northern California. Part of her still couldn't believe he wouldn't come around. On the landing, fumbling in her pocket for the key, she turned over the envelope and saw that the return address was Chicago. It was addressed to Vonnie. She felt all the energy drain right out of her. *Don't cry,* she told herself. *Teddy will be back any minute.* She dug deeper into her pocket and then tried the other pocket even though she knew the key was in her right-hand pocket. Which was empty except for some change. The damn key must have fallen out when she paid for the ice cream. They were locked out. *This is the last straw,* she thought, *the last fucking straw,* as she trudged back downstairs to ask the hairy-chested guy if she could use his phone.

A T SEVEN-THIRTY ON THE DOT HE TELLS BRENT
that he has to go. Brent says, "Can't you stay a little longer?
Your mom won't mind." But Teddy says no. He has been keeping an
eye on the clock because he feels a little guilty for leaving his mother
like that when he's only spending the one night. Even though he's
really had a good time with Brent. The only sort of bad thing about
his dad's place is that there's no other kids around. The nearest neighbors are too far away.

When he walks across the street, he's surprised to see his mother
sitting out on the steps with her head in her hands. She doesn't even
see him. He has to say, "Mom?" And then she looks up, and he sees
that she has been crying. Her eyes are all red. "What's the matter?"
he asks, his heart pounding. "Are you sick?" He knows that she has
made it a point not to cry in front of him. Sometimes back in California he would hear her crying in her room. He knows she's probably
thinking about his sister again. Seeing him has probably just reminded her. He wishes he were back at his dad's.

She shakes her head and says, "I'm sorry. It's nothing, really." She
fakes a smile. "It's just that we're locked out — I lost the key — and
the ice cream's all melted." She holds up the paper bag for him to see.
"Your favorite. Chocolate Chip Cookie Dough. I'm sorry, honey."

"That's okay," he says, feeling relieved. "I had an ice cream sandwich at Brent's house anyway." He says this to make her feel better, but it only seems to make things worse. She says, "Oh," and her fake smile disappears.

"The key must have fallen out of my pocket," she tells him. "I called Vonnie and she said she'd come let me in but" — she shrugs and frowns at her watch — "it's been almost forty minutes." Suddenly she looks angry. "I think that's pretty inconsiderate, don't you?"

Teddy nods. "You could call her again."

"Yeah, well, the thing is, I don't like to keep disturbing the neighbors. It's embarrassing."

"I could ask them," Teddy offers, trying to be helpful. "Or I could call my dad."

"What's he going to do?" she snaps at him. "He doesn't have a key."

"You don't have to yell," he mutters. "It's not my fault."

"I'm sorry." She lets out a deep sigh. "I just wanted us to have a nice night. And everything seems to be going wrong."

He picks up the movie lying on the ground next to the bag. Jurassic Park.

"I couldn't think what to get," she says, sounding depressed.

"That's okay. I haven't seen it in a while." He looks up at the apartment. "If there was a ladder, maybe I could crawl in the window. I bet Brent's dad has a ladder," he says, excited by the possibility of climbing the ladder like a fireman to the rescue.

"I don't think —" His mom stops talking as Vonnie drives up and toots her horn.

He runs to the curb to meet her. She gets out of the Tracker and whirls him around. "Hey, Buster!" she says. She's always called him Buster, which he sort of likes.

"Sorry it took so long," she says to his mother.

"It?" His mother glares at her.

Vonnie ignores her. She keeps joking with him as they race up the stairs. His mom follows behind, walking like an old lady. Sometimes he finds it hard to believe that his mom is Vonnie's little sister.

His mother is about to throw the ice cream in the trash when Vonnie says, "What are you doing? Don't be silly." She grabs the carton and puts it in the freezer, then announces that she's taking the rest of the night off. Suddenly everyone's mood seems to improve. Vonnie makes popcorn in the microwave, and the three of them sit on the sofa in front of the fan watching Jurassic Park, which Vonnie claims is one of her favorite movies. His mom drinks beer. Vonnie and he drink Diet Coke. After her second beer his mom starts to make up funny dialogue that cracks them up. Teddy has forgotten that his mom can be funny. One time he snorts and sputters Coke from his nose, which makes them all laugh even more. Vonnie calls time out for an intermission and comes back with the ice cream carton and three spoons. He thinks his aunt is cool about stuff like this. His mom would have insisted on serving it in bowls. Only the cat has her own bowl of ice cream, which she licks at cautiously, keeping a suspicious eye on Teddy. When he showed his aunt the big scratch on his face, expecting a little sympathy, all she said was "You ought to know better than to hold a cat that doesn't want to be held. How would you like someone to hold you against your will, Buster?" And she reached over and locked her arms around him while he struggled to break free until he finally had to give up. She was really strong for a girl. "You would've made a good wrestler," he told her. And she said, "Why, thank you. That's the nicest thing anyone's ever said to me." And he couldn't tell if she was kidding or not.

When it is time for bed, his mother says he can sleep on the futon and she'll sleep on the sofa in the living room. She carries the box fan into the spare room and sets it in the window so it will blow on him. His mother asks him if he is going to put on his pajamas, and he says no, he and his dad just sleep in their underpants. She rolls her eyes and kisses him good night on the forehead. "I missed you," she whispers. "I'll just be in the next room if you need anything." Then she turns out the light and shuts the door. He hears her walking down the hall and wonders why she doesn't just sleep in Vonnie's room, in the big bed. He thinks it has something to do with the fact that his mom isn't a lesbian like Vonnie is. He knows that Vonnie is a lesbian and *that Frito doesn't like lesbians. He always refers to Vonnie as "one of those damn dykes." His dad explained that lesbians love other women and that there was nothing wrong with that, he should just ignore Frito, who could be ignorant about some matters. His dad said hate causes a lot more trouble in this world than love does. And Teddy wanted to ask him,"Do you still love my mom?" but he figured his dad would tell him to "mind his own beeswax," which is another of his dad's expressions.*

He knows that his dad has girlfriends. Sharon, the woman who painted the lettering on the van, for example. His dad has a lot of snapshots stuck to his refrigerator, and one of them is a picture of his dad and Sharon whitewater rafting in Colorado. They have on match-ing red plaid shirts and are laughing with their arms around each other's waists. And Teddy could tell that she really likes his dad. When she came to paint the van, she brought some homemade brown-ies and a present for Teddy: a set of watercolors and a pad of paper. She smiled and laughed at everything his dad said, even when it wasn't funny. She is pretty, too. He could tell that Frito had a crush on her the way he hung around and kept complimenting her on what a great job she was doing, even when she was only using stencils.

On the round table next to his dad's bed, next to the picture of his dad's dead brother, there is a picture of the three of them in a silver frame. His mom, his dad, and Teddy sitting in between them on the porch swing holding a Popsicle. His mom and dad are both smiling. His dad's arm stretches along the back of the swing, his finger-tips resting on her shoulder. They don't look like they are going to get a divorce.

AFTER TEDDY AND VONNIE WERE ASLEEP, GISELLE sat with the phone on her lap, debating the wisdom of calling Dan. On the one hand, he was the one who pulled away, so it would seem that he was the one who needed to take the first step back. On the other hand, what was wrong with her meeting him more than halfway if that's what it took? After all, this wasn't some run-of-the-mill lovers' quarrel. They were fighting for their lives.

It was still only nine o'clock in California. She dialed the number. When his mother answered, Giselle hung up like some teenage girl afraid to seem too forward. She stared at the phone in its cradle and then at her hand, which seemed to have acted on its own accord, some involuntary nerve impulse. She couldn't believe she had done something so juvenile. It seemed she was regressing day by day. And the worst part was that she was sure Luisa knew it was her. She was ashamed of herself. You would think, at the very least, tragedy would bestow dignity and maturity. *Mourning Becomes Electra*. And here she was, trapped in *Gidget Goes to Nebraska*.

She got up and sat down at the kitchen table, where Jess had left her yellow legal pad and pen lying out. Everything was so complex, maybe it would be better to take the time to compose her thoughts. She had always expressed herself more clearly on paper anyway.

> Dear Dan,
> This afternoon I had this insight into what you must be feeling. How it must seem to you that I still have a child, so I can't know how you feel to have lost your only child. Well, it's true that I'm still a mother, but in some ways it's worse because I . . .

No, she scratched that out. Wrong tack. She shouldn't get into this comparative misery index. She started over.

> Dear Dan,
> This is so hard. I miss you all the time. Sometimes I think we just didn't have enough time before this hit us. Maybe if we had been married ten or fifteen years already, we'd have accrued enough good years to better withstand such a shattering blow as losing our child. But Trina was born a month before our first anniversary. We barely had any history before Trina. She was our history. So it's natural we wouldn't know how to proceed from here.

She froze, pen in midair, and sighed. *Accrued. Proceed from here.* It sounded like some sort of legal brief. Maybe it was the yellow-lined paper. She imagined Dan scribbling professorial comments in the margins in green ink, red ink being too authoritarian. Maybe — she sighed and set the pen down — it would be best to wait, to be patient and wait for him to make the first gesture in his own time. He knew where to find her. It wasn't as if he could just forget about her. They were still married, after all. She was still his wife. Their clothes were still hanging side by side in the closet.

BY THE TIME HE WAKES UP THE NEXT MORNING, *his mother has been to the store already for Bisquick and maple syrup. The batter is ready to go, sitting in a blue bowl. He and Vonnie have a contest to see who can eat the most pancakes, and she wins. She eats five to his three. Then she winks and lets out a huge belch just like a man. His mother says, "That's disgusting!" but she laughs. Then the phone rings. Vonnie answers it and hands it over to his mother, mouthing something to her that he can't make out. But he sees his mother's face tighten up like a pinch. He is trying to eavesdrop when Vonnie drags him into the other room by the sleeve of his T-shirt. She sets him down in front of the TV, snaps it on, and hands him the remote. Then she says she has to take a shower. As soon as he hears the water turn on in the bathroom, he mutes the volume. After a couple of minutes he can tell that his mother is talking to his stepfather. Some problem with the house. His mother is mostly listening, saying "uhmmhumm" and "oh" a lot. Her voice sounds small and shaky, like a little girl's. Once she says, "I see," and then, "It's up to you, I guess." Then, "I don't know what to say." And finally, "Okay, then, talk to you tomorrow night." He unmutes the volume as she hangs up.*

He pretends to be watching something — he doesn't even know what — when she walks into the living room. She doesn't say any-thing at first, so he mutes the volume again and says, "Who was that?"

She looks as if she didn't hear him, but then she says, "That was Dan." She looks down at her hands in her lap. "He says someone broke into the house and stole some stuff. They bashed in the back door." She shakes her head and sighs. "The police don't have any clues."

"Wow," Teddy says. "What did they steal?"

"I don't know. The TV and VCR, the stereo —"

"My computer?"

She nods.

"Oh, man," he says, "that really sucks."

She nods and pats his thigh, not really paying any attention to him. "Dan thinks we should move out. He wants to give the landlords notice and put our things in storage." He can hear her voice crack like she's going to cry, but she clears her throat and continues in a stronger voice. "He's going to call back tomorrow night. So we don't have to decide right away." She stands up. "I'm going to wash the breakfast dishes."

Teddy flips through the channels — without cable there aren't many choices — and he can't find anything that looks good. He is pretty shocked about the burglary, mad about losing his computer that his uncle gave him, but if it means they don't have to go back there to live, it's worth it. He never wants to go back. He doesn't know why his mom would want to go back there either.

He shuts off the TV and looks out the window at the street, to see if maybe Brent's out there riding his bike. He doesn't see him, but he can see Brent's house and there's a car in the driveway, so he figures they're probably home. Brent has a baby sister named Melody. Only nine months old, too young to walk yet. Last night she was crawling around in her pink rubber pants. At one point Brent's mother put her down on the carpet in Brent's room and told them to watch her while she helped Brent's father for a minute in the backyard. When they weren't paying attention, the baby picked up a floppy disk and put it

in her mouth the way babies do. Brent grabbed it from her and yelled,
"No! Bad girl!" The expression on her face broke Teddy's heart.
"She's not a dog," Teddy said. "You should be nice to her." Brent
looked at him as if he were a weirdo. When Brent went out of the
room to get them some ice cream sandwiches, Teddy picked up the
baby and cuddled her. He remembered that smell of powder and wet
diaper. He kissed the soft, wrinkly folds at the back of her neck. Then
he heard Brent's footsteps thundering up the stairs, and he set her
down so fast that she was bawling by the time Brent burst into the
room. "What did you do to her?" he asked suspiciously. Teddy
shrugged. "Nothing," he said, "I didn't do anything." He was relieved
when Brent's mother heard the crying, swooped up the baby, and took
her away.

In the bathroom he can hear Vonnie singing. She's a good singer. At
first he thought it was the radio, but then she dropped something,
cursed mid-sentence, and started the song over again. He walks into
the kitchen and says, "Is it okay if I go over to Brent's for a little
while?"

His mother nods and looks at her watch, just barely glancing at
him. "Okay. Be back by eleven-thirty. Just in case your dad's a little
early."

"Okay." He can see she's upset, but he doesn't know what to say.
"Thanks for the pancakes. They were really good," he says.

"You're welcome, honey."

He is walking out the door when his mother calls out his name and
says, "Maybe I'll just come get you. I think I should introduce myself
to Brent's mother."

Teddy freezes, trying to think what to say. He doesn't want her to
go over there.

"What's their last name?"

"Ronalds," he says.

If he says that Mrs. Ronalds isn't home, his mother won't let him
go over there. But he definitely doesn't want his mother to go over
there and see the baby sister. He's afraid she'll start crying. She might

even tell them about Trina, but he doubts it. He knows she feels just as guilty as he does — she has told him so more than once — although he doesn't really see why.

"Okay" — he nods — "cool." He figures he'll just come home early, before his mom has a chance to go over there.

"See you later," he shouts as the door slams shut behind him. He races down the stairs, relieved to be out of there and eager to tell Brent all about the robbery. He seriously doubts that Brent has ever been robbed, since there isn't any crime in Nebraska.

THEY WERE SHOPPING FOR TEDDY'S BIRTHDAY presents. It was the first time she could remember being alone with Ed in years, since before Teddy was born, although there must have been other times. When Ed called to suggest that they go shopping together, she had hesitated. She knew that Teddy harbored this secret fantasy that his parents would get back together. Didn't most kids? There were countless movie and sitcom plots that revolved around this very issue. She had grown up on the cusp, between the sweet, comic movies like *The Parent Trap* (in which Hayley Mills plays her own twin sister) where the kids plot and scheme to get the parents back together and — presto! — they are just one big happy family again, and the more contemporary movies in which the divorced parent sits down with the hopeful child and has a serious heart-to-heart, giving him or her the straight dope about how sometimes things just don't work out between adults — this doesn't mean we don't love you, because we do — but Mommy/Daddy and I are never going to live together again, pumpkin, capeesh?

However, it just made sense to pick out his presents together, particularly since she didn't have a car, and now that Teddy was getting older — his tenth birthday — she found herself more at a loss picking out boy toys. Despite the women's movement and all this talk about gender bending, the aisles at Toys "Я" Us were still as clearly divided as public lavatories: girls on this side, boys on that side. The girls' stuff was still predominantly pink. About the only difference that Giselle could see was Veterinarian Barbie. In her day, Barbie had been a nurse.

"How about this?" she said, holding up Veterinarian Barbie. "It seems apropos, given the kennel and all."

Ed laughed. "Sure," he said, "why not?"

Giselle put it back on the shelf. She avoided looking at the little girls toys, ages three and younger, as she walked around to see what Ed was holding. Some tall neon-colored poles made of Styrofoam. "Fun Noodles," he said. "For jousting." He bopped her on the shoulder with the shocking-pink pole. "I think he'd get a kick out of these. What do you think?"

"Okay," Giselle nodded. "I think I'll go look at the books and videos. I'll leave the action stuff to your discretion."

They had already picked out his big present: a bicycle similar to the one Teddy had back home. A miniature Harley-Davidson. Since she didn't know when or if they would be going back to California, she hadn't objected. She had gone along with Dan about giving notice and putting their stuff in storage. Beyond that, she didn't know. One step at a time. They had both been too chicken-hearted to press the issue, anxious to avoid a big showdown.

She threw a couple of books into the shopping cart. Abridged and illustrated classics. *Robinson Crusoe* and *Call of the Wild*. She knew that Dan would object if he were there, but he wasn't there, was he? He had remarked once that you might as well give the kid Cliffs Notes.

Earlier, at lunch in the Garden Cafe, conveniently located in the same strip mall as Toys "Я" Us, Giselle had asked Ed how Teddy seemed to him. "Do you think he's all right?" she asked anxiously, half afraid to hear his answer. Because if Teddy was not all right, whose fault was it?

She panicked when he didn't answer right away. She supposed

she had expected him to dismiss her fears, to shoot right back with some pat, hale-and-hardy response: "Relax, he's fine" or "Give him a few more months, and he'll be as good as new." The verbal equivalent of a slap on the back. And while she would have been relieved on the surface, down deep she would have been thinking what a simpleton he was, how unattuned to life's complexities.

"I don't know." He worried the little turquoise post in his ear, turning it back and forth as if he were winding a watch. "He seems to be doing okay, but it's hard to know, you know, about down deep. 'Cause he's a good kid, and I know he wants us to feel okay."

Giselle nodded and mumbled, "Yeah." The waiter set down the bill. Ed grabbed it and waved away her offer to pay her share.

"I read something about how they hadn't done any follow-up research about kids in Teddy's position, but that they are almost certainly at increased risk for acute and chronic emotional and be-havioral disturbance," she said, quoting from the book she had seen lying on Dan's desk.

"Yeah, well, you don't have to be a rocket scientist to figure that one out." Ed shook his head. "You think I should make an appointment for him with that psychologist? I've been sort of putting it off, I guess."

"I think it would be a good idea," she said. "Couldn't hurt." Not that their therapist back home had worked any wonders.

Ed nodded and reached for his wallet. "It's a hell of a thing. He's had a couple of bad nightmares. Wakes up shouting and crying. Of course, he had some of those even when he was real little, so — who knows? — maybe it's not even related. But that's the thing, something like this changes everything. You keep looking for signs he's screwed up. Like I noticed he seems sort of obsessed with George, my brother, the one who died?"

Giselle nodded but didn't interrupt. She couldn't remember ever hearing Ed go on like this, at length. It might have been his personal best in contiguous sentences uttered.

"He asks a lot of questions about him. You think that's normal behavior for a ten-year-old?"

"I don't know," she said. "It could be. Then again, maybe it's symptomatic." It dawned on her suddenly that he hadn't lit up a cigarette. "You quit smoking?"

"Yeah."

"Me, too. When my daughter was born." She had almost censored that last part and then thought, *Why?* She couldn't very well spend the rest of her life editing out such a big part of it.

He reached across the table and laid his large suntanned hand on top of her pale fidgeting fingers. "I know you're doing the best you can," he said. "And Teddy knows it, too. I wouldn't want to be in your shoes."

Her eyes filled up and she snatched away her hand to grab her paper napkin and blow her nose. *What happened to all the anger?* she wondered. She remembered him as edgy and moody. Pounding his fists into doorframes and dashboards. "You've changed," she said hesitantly, afraid he might take offense. "You used to be so angry."

He popped a mint from the change tray into his mouth and offered her the other one. "It's the first time in my life I'm doing what I want to do." He shrugged and smiled. "It feels pretty damn good."

"Let's look at toys," she said, scraping back her chair and standing up, colliding with a waitress. Ed reached out to steady her and kept his hand at the small of her back, guiding her out of the crowded restaurant, into the sudden blast of sunlight. She was fumbling in her purse for her dark glasses. Ed was whistling something cheerful sounding. She felt a twinge of resentment and envy. Her life was falling apart and his was just coming together. When she'd left for California, the Golden State, Ed was the last person on earth she could ever have predicted envying. The odds of dying in an earthquake would have seemed much greater. And she almost had. She had ended up moving right to the epicenter. Six point six on the Richter scale.

As they walked over to the toy store, she thought about her last conversation with Dan. After they had agreed to give up the house, he told her that he was going to some writer's conference in Vermont next month. He said he'd been dabbling with poetry, and there was some famous poet at this place in Vermont whom he was hoping to study with. Maybe she could fly out and join him for a weekend, he suggested a bit tentatively. She didn't know whether to attribute his hesitation to insecurity or indecision, whether he was afraid she'd shoot him down or afraid she'd take him up on the offer. Giselle wanted to ask whether this poetry business meant he had abandoned the ill-conceived book about the accident. His desk drawers were full of abandoned articles in various stages of incompletion. Two years ago he had sweated through the tenure process, squeaking by with a split vote, and since then hadn't finished a single article, let alone his book on the confessional novel. So it wouldn't be inconceivable for him to abandon this new book, even without her opposition to it.

Somehow from a distance of fifteen hundred miles, her anger had stretched itself a little thin. It was hard to keep the fire of righteous indignation burning brightly, especially when she missed him so much. She kept thinking of all the things they would never do again if the marriage was really over. No more reading in bed. No more anything.

"So, what do you say?" he said, nudging her.

"I'll think about it. It would be nice to get away from this humidity for a couple of days."

"Okay then." He cleared his throat a couple of times. "I'll check into the dates, what dates would work for me, and I'll call you tomorrow or the next day." Then he switched the subject to the damage deposit. He couldn't remember exactly how much it had been, did she?

"Three hundred dollars," she said, not really listening.

She had never been to Vermont. It sounded so cool and green. And she remembered seeing a list of all the states ranked by their relative safety. In the newspaper or *Time* magazine. Vermont was number one.

On the ride home from the toy store, the talk was mostly about the kennel. They were opening at a good time, people were taking off on summer vacations, Ed told her. They already had the dog kennels more than half booked and had a pretty fair number of cats, too. A lot of people tended to leave their cats at home and just hire someone to come by and feed them, he explained, since cats were such homebodies. He had also hired a pet groomer who was teaching him the tricks of the trade. "Groomed my first French poodle yesterday," he said, smiling like a proud first-grader. "Simone. A former show dog, no less."

"I could use a trim," she said, and they both laughed. She had always liked his deep, goofy laugh. Her feet were propped up on the dashboard, the cool air from the vent blowing up her skirt. The radio was playing a golden oldie that sounded familiar, though she couldn't have named it. For a moment, they could have been back in high school, cruising around in his father's new pickup. Then a commercial came on, and Ed turned the volume down.

"So Teddy tells me you moved your stuff into storage out there," he said. He waited for her to say something.

She knew what he wanted to know. Was she going back? Was the marriage over? Her good mood went up in smoke. She glared at him, then forced a smile. "I might be going to Vermont for the weekend," she told him.

He looked surprised. "This weekend?" She knew she didn't have to say who she'd be visiting in Vermont.

She shook her head. "Soon. I don't know when exactly."

Ed shrugged and turned the volume back up. She looked out the window and bit her lip to keep from crying. Somehow, the instant the words were out of her mouth, she knew it wasn't true. She wasn't going anywhere. Dan hadn't called her back. She hadn't heard a word from him in three days.

A couple of nights later she was working at the bar, as usual, washing glasses and emptying ashtrays, when Vonnie grabbed her by the elbow and led her over to the small TV mounted at the far end of the counter. Vonnie had protested against having a TV in the bar, but Val, a football fan, insisted that you couldn't have a bar in Lincoln with no television. Most of the other bars had huge screens and all sorts of Big Red promos. Giselle looked at the screen. Some young couple was sitting on a sofa in a tacky but expensive-looking living room, talking to a blond interviewer, a Diane Sawyer clone. Giselle opened her mouth to ask what the big deal was when Vonnie said, "Shhh. Just wait." They were standing in the smoking section; Giselle waved away a cloud of smoke as it drifted into her face, then let out a gasp as the camera panned to Dan sitting there looking casually professorial in his tweed jacket and black T-shirt, his longish hair falling into his face as he leaned forward toward the interviewer, hands clasped earnestly in front of him.

"In our case," he said, "it was a member of our own family, my nine-year-old stepson. He was next door, at a neighbor's house. The mother was at home in the rec room, exercising. My wife was in our backyard, adjacent to the neighbor's, watching our twenty-three-month-old daughter, Trina, playing in a wading pool. The neighbor boy took out a .38-caliber Colt from its hiding place" — here Dan made quotation marks with his fingers around the word *hiding* — "and handed the gun to my stepson. Somehow the gun went off, and our daughter was pronounced dead in the ER an hour later." His voice choked up, he hung his head and took a deep breath. As the woman and the man sitting on either side of him patted him on each shoulder simultaneously, it dawned on Giselle that this was one of those support groups. And sure enough, the handsome, prematurely gray man to Dan's left spoke up and said, "We knew there had to be other parents who had been through this, or at least through similar situations, and we wanted to know how they were coping. Carol and I felt" — here he paused and covered his wife's hand with his — "that it always helps to know you are not alone. So we opened up a web site on the Internet, looking for other parents whose lives had been shattered as the result of guns in the hands of children. In the first month alone, we made contact with fifty-two people, mostly parents. One for every day of the week."

"Week of the year," Dan corrected him.

The web site address flashed onto the bottom of the screen:

www.kidsnguns.com

"Kids 'n' guns!" Vonnie screamed out, like a contestant on *Wheel of Fortune,* and snorted derisively.

Giselle felt sick. She had broken out into a cold, clammy sweat and felt her intestines knotting up, roiling inside her. She wanted to turn off the TV and run to the bathroom, but she was afraid of missing any of it. Of not knowing. Of not knowing what everyone else would know. After all, this was national TV. And those who hadn't actually seen it would hear about it.

The interviewer turned back to Dan. "And I understand you're writing a book about your family's experience."

"Fucking asshole," Vonnie hissed and flipped him the bird, "thinks he's Fred Goldman. Or what's-his-name, Polly Klass's father."

Val gave him a Bronx cheer.

"Shut up!" Giselle glared at them.

A large-breasted woman in a too-small Kansas City Royals T-shirt stared at them, trying to figure out what the story was.

Dan nodded and cleared his throat — a classroom trick he used to get everyone's attention. "Yes, I am. It's called *Johnny's Got Your Gun.* It's not an easy decision to write openly about such a painful and personal experience, but if it will help just one other family avoid such a loss, then the book will have been a success."

"Yes, and where is your family, your wife, tonight, asshole?" Vonnie interrupted, perfectly mimicking the interviewer's tone of voice. "And your beloved stepson?"

The interviewer moved on to another couple for some last words. The couple was holding a picture of their little boy, a grinning freckle-faced redhead who looked to be about four or five years old. The camera zoomed in for a close-up of the boy's face. Then a row of children's photographs flashed on the screen, including Trina in her red velvet dress. And below each child's photograph was a caption with the child's name and dates, like a row of tombstones. Vonnie groaned and snapped the mute button just as the network cut to a commercial. For Huggies disposable diapers.

"Jesus, diapers," Vonnie shook her head. "They're fucking shameless."

Giselle was shaking. She reached over and swiped two cigarettes from a pack lying on the bar, along with someone's Bic lighter. She walked outside and lit up. Standing in the dark, she smoked one, then the other. The smoke went to her head. She felt dizzy and nauseous. Vonnie came outside. "Are you all right? Do you want a drink or anything?"

Giselle shook her head.

"I swear, if I had a gun, I'd kill that pompous, self-centered bastard. I never did see what you saw in him." Vonnie sat down on a wooden crate. "How do you feel about him now?" When Giselle didn't say anything, Vonnie glared at her. "You can't still love him."

On the sidewalk across the street, in front of another bar, a young couple was arguing about whether he was too drunk to drive home. She kept trying to snatch the keys from his hand. He held them over her head, teasing her with them, as if she were a dog begging for a bone. But then he dropped them, and she scooped them up and he fell over reaching for them. Too late. She dangled the keys in front of his face. "Bitch!" he shouted, but then he started to laugh and she laughed with him.

"I think I'll just walk back," Giselle said, untying the green apron and handing it to her sister.

"Are you sure?" Vonnie asked. "I can give you a ride." She leaped up, eager to be of service.

But Giselle was already gone. *How do you feel about him now?* Vonnie's question kept echoing in her mind as she half walked, half ran, from the brightly lit downtown area into the dark, quiet residential streets of the Near South, working her way, block by block, up the alphabet.

The message light was blinking on the phone. The first message was from her parents. *My God, did you see it? He was on that show. Dan. Talking about . . . well, you know. Did you know about this? Call us. Don't worry about waking us up.* The second was from some friend of Vonnie's in Madison, saying she was coming to town the weekend of the Fourth. The third message was from Lois. She had seen it, too.

Giselle jotted down the message for Vonnie and erased the other two. She didn't want to call them back. She sat on the sofa, holding the phone in her lap and trying to think what she wanted to say to Dan. The short version if she got a machine, and the long version if he actually answered. She felt like a flat tire, deflated and immobilized. It was too much. Too much to think about. Too much to feel. She wanted a shot of Novocain in her brain.

She wanted to blame Dan — she needed to blame someone — and he seemed, by process of elimination, the only choice. Teddy was a child at risk; he needed all the support she could muster. She was doing what she had to do as Teddy's mother. And although she wanted to be morally indignant, energized by righteous wrath, she knew that Dan was doing what he had to do as Trina's father. Early on he had seen how things would go. In a latter-day sort of *Sophie's Choice,* she would choose her son over her husband. One of those choices that was really no choice at all. And he would choose his daughter's memory over his stepson and his stepson's mother. They were on different sides. Like two soldiers in opposing armies. It was, in a sense, nothing personal. There were forces at work, forces beyond anyone's control — laws of nature. She understood this, but she would blame him anyway because she was Teddy's mother. She had known almost from the beginning that it would come to this. From that very first night when he had said to Teddy, "You're lucky you're not my son," and she had seen the expression on her husband's face as he looked at her son, she had known in her gut that was it. If she had had the courage of her convictions, she would have taken Teddy and left right then and there. But she hadn't. She couldn't. She wasn't strong enough — any more than Dan was strong enough to forgive Teddy for what he'd done.

She dialed Dan's number — actually, Harvey's number. Harvey and Lynn were in Europe for a month, and Dan was house-sitting, so at least she didn't have to worry about getting Luisa. The machine picked up, Harvey's voice telling her to leave a message. Some sort of high-brow jazz played in the background. She knew that Harvey had never really approved of her. The sound of his self-important, self-satisfied voice suddenly struck her like a lit match — *phoompf!* — and the fumes ignited. "You goddamned coward!" she shouted. "You could have at least warned us. This pseudo-crusade of yours makes me sick. Hope you sell a lot of books. You're going to need it for the divorce settlement." She slammed down the phone, shaking, waiting to see what would happen. She thought she might burst into tears. But she felt as cold as ice. Dry ice. Her heart was a steaming, freezing block of ice. If she touched it for an instant, it would rip the skin off her fingertips when she tried to pull her hand away.

It's over, she thought, *it's really over.* She knew the pain wasn't far away, but for the moment she felt almost peaceful. Calm and full of resolve. She would find an apartment. She would find a job. She would get one of those quick-and-easy no-fault divorces. Look on the bright side — it would be a piece of cake — no custody issues to complicate things. And wasn't California the state that had invented no-fault divorce? Or maybe that was car insurance. Whatever. The underlying principle was the same. She got up and fished the newspaper out of the trash can in the kitchen. Vonnie had emptied an ashtray on top of it. Giselle shook the ashes off the classified ads and then plucked two of the longest butts from the trash. There weren't any matches in sight, so she bent down and lit the butt off the stove burner. *It's really over,* she thought as she took the first

drag. The smoke burned her lungs. She felt light-headed. She inhaled deeply and held in the smoke, trying not to cough. She
wanted it to burn. She wanted to chain-smoke an entire carton.

The next afternoon when she returned from apartment hunting,
there was a letter from Dan waiting for her in the mailbox. Post-
marked from New York. Jess was in the kitchen with her law books
as usual. It was hotter than hell. The plant mister was sitting on
the table; every so often Jess would stop and spritz herself, then go
on highlighting her casebook.

"Find anything?" she asked.

"A couple of places weren't too bad." Giselle kept on walking,
into the bathroom, as if answering an urgent call of nature, and
locked the door behind herself. Just the sight of Dan's handwriting, so familiar from all those compositions she'd written what
seemed like a century ago, made her break out into a cold sweat.
She ripped open the envelope and didn't know if she was relieved
or disappointed to see that it was a short note.

> Dear Giselle,
>
> I'm on my way to Vermont, stopped off in New York for a cou-
> ple of days. I wanted to give you the address where I'll be and a
> phone number. I still don't know about the dates. I thought maybe
> I should get there and check it out first.
>
> I hope Teddy is doing better. A day at a time is what they say,
> right? Don't think I don't miss you, because I do. Every day I'm
> alone I wonder what the hell I'm doing.
>
> Every day I blame myself for not being a bigger person than I
> apparently am.
>
> Love, D.

Enclosed was a check for a thousand dollars and a key to the
rented storage unit where he had stashed their belongings.

She sat there staring at the note. It pissed her off that there was
no mention of his television appearance. Was he crazy? Did he

think they didn't have TV in Nebraska? Did he think she wouldn't hear about it? Or did he just think there was nothing to say? Nothing he could say. And then it dawned on her that he was no longer staying at Harvey's, which meant that Harvey, that pompous ass, would come home and play back her message. She could just hear his ironic tone as he related the message to Dan verbatim. She wanted to tear up the check into tiny pieces and flush it down the toilet, but she couldn't. And the humiliation of being financially dependent upon him further enraged her. She stormed out to the living room and retrieved the morning newspaper from the trash.

"What are you doing?" Jess said, sucking on one of Teddy's Popsicles. She looked as if she were giving it a blow job.

Giselle ignored her. "Can I borrow this?" She pointed to one of Jess's highlighters.

"Be my guest."

Giselle took the paper back to the living room and started skimming through the want ads. By the end of the first column, her eyes filled up; the fine print blurred. A tear torpedoed an ad for a part-time cashier at Hobby Lobby. She wrote the phone number down. *Want ads.* The term suddenly struck her as terribly poignant, and sad. The terse, businesslike ads seemed so far removed from everything she had ever really wanted in this life.

By the end of the week she had rented an apartment in a rickety triplex on F Street. "F Street," she had joked to her friend Laura when Giselle called to tell her she was staying in Lincoln. "It seems appropriate. Like I flunked out big-time."

"Don't say that," Laura had chided her. "There's no point blaming yourself."

Easy for you to say, Giselle had thought to herself. How could Laura — how could anyone — know what it felt like to have a child die on your watch? A dead child was worse than no child. "'Tis better to have loved and lost" did not apply to children.

When she told Ed about the apartment, he sounded pleased. He offered to help her move even though she didn't have anything to move.

"I made reservations to fly back to L.A. the week after Teddy's birthday," she said. "To sort out our stuff and drive the Honda back. Just a quick trip. Teddy can stay with you."

"Jesus," he said, "how many miles does that car have on it?"

"I don't know. A hundred and ten thousand, something like that." She was standing in the kitchen, chopping onions for tuna salad, and tears were streaming down her face as she spoke. She sniffed a couple of times, and Ed asked, "Are you crying?"

"Chopping onions."

"Oh." He was silent for a couple of seconds. She could hear voices in the background and what sounded like a jackhammer. They were still rushing to get things ready for the Fourth, which was only a couple of days away. "We could go with you. Teddy and me," he said. "I'm worried about that old car making it. And you know, I'm not a bad mechanic. Besides, I've never seen California. I probably ought to go out there so I can have a more informed prejudice."

She laughed. She knew that Ed had no desire to see California. He was just worried about her. She sniffed again, and this time she *was* crying. "Thanks, but I don't think so. There are some things you've just got to do alone." She picked up the dish towel and wiped her eyes. She was glad he couldn't see her. "Besides, it wouldn't be good for Teddy."

"Yeah."

She knew what he was thinking. In the old days she would have thought it was none of his business, but she said, "Dan's not going to be there. He's in Vermont or New Hampshire or someplace, trying to be the next Anne Morrow Lindbergh."

"Royalties from the Sea," Ed snorted.

She was about to rebuke him, to say that Dan wasn't doing it for the money, but she let it go. She didn't know at what point she and Ed had stopped being adversaries and started playing on the same side, but somehow it had happened. Maybe it wasn't a winning team, but at least it was a team. She was surprised Ed knew who Anne Morrow Lindbergh was. He seemed full of surprises lately. She had begun to wonder if she had ever really known him.

"I think I might have a job," she said. "They're supposed to call me by Friday and let me know."

"Really? Doing what?" She heard Teddy calling him in the background, and Ed covered the mouthpiece and hollered back, "Just a minute!"

"Taking classified ads for the *Journal-Star*," she said. "Part-time. And Vonnie is going to pay me to bartend on the weekends."

"Hey, that's great!" Then, as if anticipating some sarcastic comeback, he added, "I mean, you know, for now."

"Yeah, I guess." She washed her hands, raising her voice over the running faucet. "And I've got an appointment to talk to some adviser at the university about finishing my degree."

"No shit. Sounds like you got it going on, girl." She could hear Teddy whining at him to hurry up. "Keep your shirt on, bud. Come say hello to your mom," Ed told him. He handed the phone over to Teddy, who said, "Hi, Mom. See you tomorrow." And hung up. She stood there staring at the dead phone in her hand and then shook her head, smiling to herself. "Didn't anyone ever teach that kid any manners?" she muttered to herself. But she didn't take it personally. She knew he was just busy being a kid again.

WHEN SHE SHOWS IT TO HIM, TEDDY ACTS really enthusiastic about his mom's new apartment even though it is just five empty rooms with dirty white walls crying out for fresh paint. You can see the nail holes and tape marks where all the previous tenants had hung their posters. And it smells like the inside of his old tin lunchbox when he forgot to empty it out.

"It's really big," he says, "and it has a lot of windows." He knows his mother likes light. She thought a lot of the houses they looked at in California were depressing because there weren't enough windows.

"Well, it's not really that big," his mother says, frowning faintly as she surveys the place. "It just looks big without any furniture." She walks down the hall and looks into the two bedrooms, which are about equal size. "Which room would you like?" she asks him.

He doesn't care. He doesn't care if he sleeps in a closet, as long as he doesn't have to go back to California. "Either one," he says, "they're both nice." She looks a little disappointed, so he points to the one next to the bathroom that has one less window than the other bedroom. "Maybe this one. So I can be close to the bathroom." He thinks she'll like the extra window. Both rooms are painted a dingy beige, the color of old Band-Aids.

"I'll help you paint," he volunteers. He remembers the two of them *painting what would be the baby's room, listening to Spanish tapes and joking around. He can tell from the look on her face that she is thinking the same thing. "Dad has a whole lot of extra paint," he says to change the subject. "I'm sure he'd let you borrow it."*

"You can't borrow paint, you dummy." She smiles and tousles his hair, which is growing out fast. He can get it all into a rubber band now, but it still looks pretty stupid. The other day when he tried it out, Frito walked by and said, "You get your tail caught in a door?" Sometimes, like his dad said, Frito could be a real pain in the ass. He isn't really sure why his dad puts up with him. They argue all the time about everything. Like when Frito overheard his dad offering to help his mom move in to her new place, he made a big deal out of it. When his dad got off the phone, Frito was standing there looking all glum. "What's wrong with you?" his dad asked him. And Frito just shook his head and looked even glummer. He was like that — you had to pull it out of him. Finally, when his dad started to walk away, Frito said, "You're too busy here to be helping her move. We've got a ton of shit to do before the Fourth."

"It'll only take a couple of hours, if that," his dad said. "She hardly has any stuff. Just relax, for Pete's sake."

"I just hope you're not thinking about starting anything up with her again," Frito muttered. "'Cause she's bad news. It's bad enough being a fool for love once, but twice means you're a goddamned moron who deserves what he gets."

His dad looked mad, like he wanted to punch Frito out, but he just shook his head and said, "It's all in your head. You've been watching too many soap operas." He picked up the hammer and headed downstairs. "I'm just giving my son's mother a hand."

"Yeah, right," Frito mumbled as he followed him down the stairs.

"Look" — his dad wheeled around and pushed his index finger into Frito's big chest — "it's better for me if she stays here. That way I can see my son whenever I want to, and that means a lot to me. So I'll do whatever I can to make it easy for her to be here, understand?"

Frito shrugged. He saw Teddy spying on them from the landing. "You're the boss," he said, and kept on walking out to his truck and took off somewhere. But he was back the next morning, same as always.

"I can stay here with you," Teddy offers, worried that his mom will feel too lonely by herself in an empty apartment.

"That's sweet of you, Teddy. I appreciate it." She looks as if she's about to cry, and he thinks maybe he said the wrong thing. "But there's nowhere for you to sleep yet. I need to get some beds."

"I can use a sleeping bag."

"Next week," she says. "When the place is all fixed up. I want us to start off on the right foot here."

"Okay." He is just as glad, since things are pretty exciting right now at his dad's place — they're counting down to the big day — and he doesn't want to miss any of it. Although he would have if his mom needed him. He knows the only reason that she is here, in Nebraska, in this empty new apartment, is because of him. He knows she is trying to make the best of it for his sake. He knows there is really nothing he can ever do to make it up to her.

THE TENANTS MOVED OUT OF HER NEW APART-ment on the last day of June. They were two college girls, blond and overweight with sad-looking perms, going home for the summer. They were from the same small town in the western part of the state, Broken Bow, and could have passed for sisters. Although they were friendly and generous, leaving Giselle two old wooden dressers and a battered coffee table free of charge, as well as a six-pack of Bud, the place was filthy. The linoleum floors looked as if they had never been washed. Something dark and sticky had spilled all over the refrigerator shelves. Giselle spotted a can of 100 percent pure Vermont maple syrup in the trash can sitting by the front door and thought of Dan scribbling away in some pristine knotty-pine cabin in the woods, where the air smelled like room freshener all the time. The two window air-conditioners in the apartment banged and chugged like old airplane engines in a valiant but doomed attempt to defeat the heat.

She spent the first day after the girls moved out cleaning. And the second and third days painting the dingy beige walls white. Vonnie and Jess brought over pizza and a boom box and spent an afternoon helping her. As soon as they left, as if he'd been parked around the corner waiting for them to leave, Ed stopped by with some housewarming gifts: a ficus tree, some potted yellow mums, and two beautiful old wing chairs from the farm that he said were just going to waste since the guys thought they were too uncomfortable to sit in.

He said he had dropped off Teddy at his appointment with the new shrink just a couple of blocks away and had fifty minutes to kill until he picked him up again. They talked about the new psychologist and how Teddy seemed to have warmed right up to him. It was "Dr. Bauer says this" and "Dr. Bauer says that." Giselle offered Ed one of the beers the girls had left behind, and they sat in the two wing chairs in the otherwise empty living room, discussing Teddy's choices for school in the fall. Giselle was conscious of her sweaty clothes and limp hair, both liberally spattered with paint. Ed looked as though he just stepped out of the shower, in a loose Hawaiian shirt and baggy white pants. For once, he'd even traded his cowboy boots for rubber thongs. She stared at his long pale toes, thinking that she couldn't remember ever having seen them before, although she must have. You couldn't be married to someone for five years and never see his toes, could you? She thought of *M. Butterfly,* the film version. She and Dan had rented it one night. Jeremy Irons, a diplomat, falls in love with a Chinese opera star and loves her for years and years, supposedly never knowing, until the end, that she was a man. Dan said he didn't believe such a thing was possible, but she wasn't so sure, then or now. Lately she had been thinking a lot about why Dan had married her, and she had come to the conclusion that it was all timing. Like a game of musical chairs. She was the one left standing when his father died.

Before he left, Ed asked if he could use the bathroom.

"First door on the right," she said. "But I warn you, it's a disaster area."

While he was in the bathroom, she peeled some masking tape from around the window trim. Vonnie had done a great job with the trim. She was neat and precise, unlike Giselle, who tended to slop and dribble paint all over. The toilet flushed, and Ed walked back into the living room.

"It's looking good," he said. "There's lots of light."

He looked at his watch but didn't go. He seemed as if he had something on his mind. She peeled another long snake of masking tape off the doorframe.

"I was wondering," he said finally, "if you had a picture of your daughter I could see. I've never seen her. I don't even know what she looks like."

Giselle's hand froze in midair. She looked at him as if he were crazy. Everyone else, including herself, avoided bringing it up. Or alluding to it in any way. She felt a flash of anger. She stalked over to her purse sitting on the kitchen counter and took out her wallet. He looked nervous but stubborn, as if he were prepared to stand his ground. She walked back over and shoved the open wallet into his hands.

"May I?" He looked at her, and she shrugged as he slipped a 2 x 3 photo of Trina in the red dress out from its cloudy plastic envelope. He stared at it for a good long minute without saying anything. Not so much as "She's pretty" or "What a beautiful child." She reached out and snatched it back. He looked up at her, startled, and she could see the tears in his eyes. Then, as if to change the subject, lighten things up, he pointed to a messy stack of books and magazines lying on the kitchen counter. "What's all this?" He picked up a book entitled *Money Matters*. Half a dozen bookmarks fluttered between the pages. "You studying for an exam?"

"It's my women's investment study group," she said, taking the book from him, "if you must know." She expected him to make some sexist joke, but he looked interested, as if he were waiting for her to tell him more. "We meet once a month. We each do research on particular mutual funds or Treasury certificates or whatever and report on them. Then we decide what to invest in."

"Really? That's great." He walked out onto the front porch.

"I've been thinking I should learn about this stuff. Maybe you could teach me."

"I don't know that much." She shrugged. "But sure. I mean, we've got to think about Teddy's college fund and all."

"Please," he groaned. "I'm not ready for junior high."

She smiled and patted him on the shoulder. "Poor dad."

"See you on the Fourth," he said as he started across the lawn to his van. "Shit. I almost forgot." He smacked his forehead with the heel of his hand, a gesture she remembered from high school. "You don't need to worry about the cake. Aunt Lou volunteered to bake one." She nodded and tried to look enthusiastic. She wasn't much in the mood for crowds, but seeing as how it was Teddy's birthday, she didn't have much choice. After Ed left, she went back inside and slipped the photo back into its plastic sleeve. The anger was gone. She appreciated the gesture. She knew that it couldn't have been easy for him to ask.

The first night she spent in her apartment, it rained all night. A violent crash of rolling thunder and then the downpour, clattering against the metal air-conditioner like a stampede of horses. She gave up trying to sleep and painted the bathroom until dawn. The fresh paint seemed to brighten her mood, as if she'd applied a coat to the walls of her mind. There was something about new paint, pristine walls, that just made you feel good. All the old nail holes and cracks covered up like so many old mistakes erased and forgiven. The apartment, she had to admit, was looking good. Better than she had imagined. Their house in California was just a cracker box, really, with wall-to-wall carpeting and low ceilings, like a glorified mobile home. It would be nice to have hardwood floors and crown moldings, not to mention a fireplace. Maybe she would volunteer to have the women's study group meet at her place next month. A sort of housewarming.

The birds chattered and the sun shone. She felt tired but not so bad, considering she'd been up all night. She was glad to see that

Ed and Teddy were going to have a nice day. Ed had been fretting about the weather for days, worrying about rain, mumbling about omens. She had to admit the sun seemed like a good omen. She looked at her watch and yawned. As she poured herself some iced coffee, she looked at the huge gaily wrapped package sitting on the floor next to one of the wing chairs. A birthday gift from Dan for Teddy. When it arrived yesterday, via UPS, she had been so curious to know what he'd sent — what he felt was appropriate under the circumstances — that she had unwrapped the gift and then rewrapped it. It was a new computer like the one that had been stolen. *Guilt money,* she'd thought. But maybe she was being unfair. All her thoughts about Dan seesawed back and forth like this. One minute she was so furious with him, she knew she'd kill him if she ever laid eyes on him again. Then the next minute she missed him so much that it took her breath away, literally, and she'd have to steady herself against the nearest solid object. She had been so in love with him — that weak-kneed, swooning, melting sort of love that every young girl fantasizes about. But she wasn't a girl anymore. She was a mother. *You're a mother,* she kept reminding herself. *Think of your son.* She was like the captain of a sinking ship, bound by duty and honor to save herself last. She was glad her phone wasn't hooked up yet. It made it easier not to break down and call him in a weak moment. At times she gave in to the temptation of thinking there was still hope. It went against the grain — it was un-American to believe that you couldn't have what you wanted if you worked for it. Maybe they just hadn't worked hard enough. She hadn't been patient enough. She hadn't been willing to compromise enough. But in her more clear-eyed moments, she always came back to the expression on Dan's face when he looked at Teddy. There was nothing she could do about that. She slid the box to the back of the coat closet.

It looked like a county fair. Cars lined the gravel road leading up to the newly painted farmhouse festooned with red, white, and blue balloons. A giant white rabbit was handing out free dog and cat treats to people who had brought along their animals. Kids were lined up for free pony rides. Mac was manning the barbecue grill, and Frito was in charge of the beer kegs. Ed's brother, Brice, was handing out free ED'S ANIMAL FARM seed caps. Teddy was all revved up, higher than a kite, riding his birthday bike around in manic circles until he smashed into the fireworks table and his dad told him to knock it off. Everyone seemed to be having themselves a fine Fourth of July.

It had been so long since Giselle had been in a social situation, aside from Vonnie's bar, that she felt a knot in her stomach like a small grenade of panic ready to explode at any slight misstep. She practiced deep breathing, sipping her wine in slow, deliberate doses, as she strolled around the property, trying to look like a potential customer checking out the accommodations for her beloved Rover or Snowflake. Her pulse was just starting to slow to normal when she recognized Gail Svoboda standing by the barbe-cue grill talking to Mac, who was flipping hamburgers with a showman's flourish. A year ahead of Giselle in school, Gail had been her role model. Giselle had followed in her footsteps as edi-tor of the yearbook when Gail graduated and went off to North-western. The last Giselle had heard, Gail was married, working for a big ad agency, and living in Chicago. Maybe she had moved back, too. Or maybe, more than likely, she was just visiting her family. They owned a big funeral home — white with pillars — like something out of *Gone With the Wind*. Giselle was working up her nerve to go over and say hello when a dogfight suddenly broke out. Mac had accidentally flipped a burger onto the ground. A German shepherd and a boxer were going at it in a cloud of dust. The owners were screaming at each other while the other dogs raised a deafening ruckus. Everyone seemed paralyzed ex-cept Ed, who charged over and blasted the dogs apart with the garden hose. The crowd calmed down again except for the boxer's owner, who left in a huff. Giselle walked over to Ed and said, "Nice work."

"Thank you, ma'am." He tipped his ED'S ANIMAL FARM seed cap. "You think it's time for Teddy's cake yet?"

She squinted into the sun that was just beginning to sink, sending out its own natural fireworks, shimmery gold against the flat blue sky. "Let's wait a bit." They looked over at Teddy, who was presiding over a little petting zoo he'd talked his dad into rigging up. Half a dozen smaller kids were crowded round him as he passed around a brown bunny. Giselle could hear him saying, "Be gentle. Don't scare him." There was also a goat, a litter of kittens, two hamsters, a box turtle, and a snake.

"Seems like you're off to a great start here," she said.

Ed shrugged modestly. "I had a lot of help."

A pretty blond woman in cutoffs and a white halter walked up to Ed and handed him a beer. "You look thirsty." She glanced over at Teddy, who was hamming it up for the little kids with the big old black snake wrapped around his neck. A little girl squealed and ran away as he waved the snake in her direction. "You must be Teddy's mother," she said to Giselle.

Giselle nodded coolly. She recognized the woman from a photograph stuck to Ed's refrigerator. The two of them standing by some river with their arms around each other's waist in matching plaid shirts.

"This is Sharon," Ed said. "She's an artist. She painted all the signs. Did a hell of a job, too."

His use of the term *artist* irked Giselle, and she was surprised by the completely unwarranted hostility she felt toward the woman, who seemed, she had to admit, perfectly pleasant.

"Teddy's such a sweet boy," the woman said.

"He has his moments," Giselle said.

Ed shuffled his feet nervously and cleared his throat. "I better see how the food supply's holding out." He walked off and left them standing there.

To compensate for the childish bitchiness she was feeling inside, Giselle smiled and said, "The signs are great. Where'd you learn how to paint like that?"

"I majored in art in college." Sharon made a self-deprecatory face. "Then I had a baby and my husband left me, and I figured I better figure out a way to make some money." The woman took a sip of beer. "I mean, it's not like I dreamed of being a sign painter."

Giselle nodded, liking the woman despite herself. Maybe they could even become friends. God knows she could use a friend. "Do you have a boy or a girl?"

"Girl." Sharon looked around as if she were going to point her out but then said, "She's with her father for the month. In Boulder. He went to some Robert Bly lecture and converted to fatherhood. A bit belatedly but still . . ." She shrugged. "Chloe's crazy about him. She's five and a half. Honestly, sometimes I don't know if it's healthy. It's like she's going on a date. She changes her clothes five times before he picks her up. We had a big fight this last time 'cause I wouldn't let her wear her tutu on the airplane."

Giselle laughed.

"You're lucky to have a boy," Sharon said.

Giselle could see the precise instant it hit her. The woman clapped her hand to her mouth and said, "Oh, my God, I'm so sorry. Ed told me and —" She shook her head. "I feel just awful."

"Please." Giselle reached out and touched her hand. "It's okay. Really." She actually felt a rush of sympathy for her. It was the sort of clumsy thing she might have done and then lain awake half the night, kicking herself. But she could see that Sharon was too mortified and flustered to recover anytime soon. To let her off the hook, Giselle said, "I think maybe it's time for the birthday cake."

On her way into the house she passed by Ed, who was busy giving some people a tour of the new facilities, explaining about the outdoor run and the indoor run. Giselle signaled to him that she was going to bring out the cake. She made little cutting motions with a pretend knife and then blew out the candles. Ed looked puzzled at first and made a charades gesture back: *Sounds like?* She pretended to blow out the candles again. He nodded and gave her a thumbs-up sign.

Along with the ten-foot Milk-Bone, Aunt Lou had baked

Teddy's cake. It was a large sheet cake, chocolate with white icing, that said, HAPPY FIRST DECADE, TEDDY, decorated with miniature soccer balls around the edges. Aunt Lou's husband, Edgar, had delivered the cake earlier in the afternoon. Ever since she had her left foot amputated as a result of diabetes a couple of years back, Aunt Lou rarely set foot out of the house anymore. Those were Edgar's exact words. "Set foot." Teddy had giggled when he heard them and hopped around on one foot the minute Edgar took off. As Giselle lit the ten candles, she wondered just how happy Teddy's first decade had been. She could only hope the next one would be better. She mumbled a little prayer under her breath — one of those little "Please, God" bargains, even though she had never been much of a believer, then or now — and carried the cake out the door onto the front porch. She walked gingerly, afraid that the breeze would blow out the candles before Teddy had a chance to make his wish. Ed saw her and hurried over, walking beside her, attempting to block the wind.

"Hey, Ted-head!" he hollered. "How 'bout trading that snake for some cake?"

Teddy unwound the snake that was curled around his arm and dumped it back into its cage. "Come on," he told the little kids. "Come have some birthday cake."

Giselle handed Ed the cake knife. "You cut the cake, and I'll serve. But first I want to take some pictures." She pulled a disposable camera out of the pocket of her baggy sundress and pointed the camera at Teddy as he took a deep breath and held it in for as long as he could and then exhaled. She snapped the picture. The candles wavered and went out. Everyone cheered. She looked around for Ed, to share this classic parents' moment, but didn't see him anywhere. Gail waved to her and walked over. She looked even better than she had in high school, thinner and sleeker. Gail asked her if she'd heard about Mrs. Van Dorn's mastectomy and when Giselle said she had, they began to swap stories about their former yearbook adviser. It turned out that she had also given Gail a copy of Margaret Bourke-White's biography as a graduation gift.

Giselle was laughing when she heard Ed yelling. She turned around and saw him standing in front of two men over by the driveway, on the fringe of the crowd. One man had a fancy camera with a camera strap slung over his shoulder.

"You get the fuck out of here, or I'll throw you out," Ed was shouting at them. "You've got a lot of nerve, you scumbags."

Giselle's blood froze. She knew who they were. Reporters. Here for the perfect photo op: a local-interest story about the boy who shot his sister. She had held her breath for a day or two after the TV show, expecting the media to appear on her doorstep, but nothing happened. When Lois had called, all concerned, having seen Dan on television, Giselle had told her that everything seemed to be all right. Apparently, no one in Lincoln was the wiser. Since Teddy had his father's last name, Bedford, no one seemed to associate Dan Trias with Teddy Bedford. But now, obviously, some eager beaver would-be Woodward and Bernstein duo had caught wind of the story. She saw Teddy looking over at his dad. He had been so happy all day. This would ruin it for him for sure. Beowulf was barking at the men, excited by Ed's angry tone and gestures. A few people were beginning to get curious.

"Hey, Teddy!" She hurried over and grabbed his arm and spun him back to the table. "We've got to cut up this cake. There's hungry people waiting." She set down the camera and picked up the big knife and started carving the cake into squares. "You scoop the ice cream." She handed Teddy the ice cream scoop before he could protest. "Hurry, before it melts."

Out of the corner of her eye she saw the two men trotting, half running, down the gravel drive. Ed was brandishing a spade. He looked like one of those crazed Freemen in Montana, holding the FBI at bay. She started to breathe again as the two men got into a green Jeep and drove off.

"Who were those guys?" Teddy asked.

"Inspectors," she improvised. "Building inspectors for the new kennel."

"Oh." Teddy licked some frosting off his fingers. The explanation seemed to satisfy him. Two of the littler kids were bashing each other with the Fun Noodles. Teddy ran over to join in. He pretended to let the little kids beat up on him, falling to the ground and begging for mercy.

Ed threw the spade into some bushes by the side of the barn and started back toward the party. You could tell a mile away that something was wrong. One look at his face, and everybody would be wanting to know who those guys were and what the story was. She hurried over and linked her arm through his and walked him around behind the barn. He was breathing heavily and shaking his head. "You know who those bastards were?" he asked.

"I think so." She led him up a gently sloping hill to a patch of shade underneath two old oak trees. "You were pretty impressive," she said. "Just like Alec Baldwin punching out the paparazzi." She was trying to lighten things up. She didn't want him to go back to the party looking like he could kill someone with his bare hands.

"Who's Alex Baldwin?" He pulled a red bandanna out of his back pocket and swiped at his neck and face. She remembered how he used to sweat a lot, but his sweat never seemed to smell sharp and unpleasant like other men's.

"A movie star. He was bringing his new baby home from the hospital and this photographer got too close, and he decked him."

"Oh yeah." Ed worried the little post in his ear. "Didn't he go to jail or something?" He sat down next to her on an old tree stump.

"I don't remember. Maybe he paid a fine. I forget." She reached over and took his hand. "Have I told you lately that I'm glad you're Teddy's father?"

He nodded but didn't say anything to that.

On the phone when she had told Laura that she was planning to rent an apartment and stay in Lincoln, Laura had protested. "But why? Why go backward? I think you're making a big mistake."

And Giselle had said, "You don't understand. Ed's the only person on this earth who cares about Teddy as much as I do. I owe it to Teddy to be here."

"Well," Laura had sighed, obviously unconvinced. "I guess that's why I don't have children."

After she hung up, Giselle had brooded over what Laura said about going backward. She had thought the same thing herself at first, but in the past few days, since painting the new apartment and getting the job at the *Journal-Star,* unglamorous as it was, she had started to think about the move in more positive terms. Maybe she wasn't going backward so much as returning to the point where her life seemed to have veered off track. Where she seemed to have lost her momentum, like a kid who'd fallen off her bike and had the wind knocked out of her. And then, later, when she finally picked herself up and got back on, she was wobbling like crazy, like someone who had lost her confidence, and before she was really up and running, she'd met Dan. Which might have worked out just fine, under other circumstances — who knows? — but this time she was determined to steer her own course. To go the distance. To pick up where she had left off a decade ago.

She had actually pilfered a picture of herself in high school, her yearbook portrait, from a collage on Vonnie's refrigerator and tucked it into the frame of her medicine chest mirror at the new apartment, where she would see it first thing every morning. To remind herself of the girl she used to be. The future Lois Lane. If Ed could get this kennel up and running, surely she could get a lousy B.A. And go on from there. The adviser at the university had seemed enthusiastic and encouraging. She said she had been a returning student herself, a mother of four. *But all your children are alive,* Giselle had wanted to say, sinking for a moment into self-pity, as she struggled to get a grip on herself and ask another question about the English major, which, the adviser assured her, law schools would look upon favorably. If you can read and write well, she said, you'll have a real advantage over most of these kids, as if to assure Giselle that she hadn't really lost all those years after all:

she wasn't just older; she was wiser and better prepared. It was a hard sell and Giselle was a tough customer, but she appreciated the effort.

They could hear the music carried on the wind from down below. Mac's band was playing old rock 'n' roll songs, the same songs he used to play in high school, only a little more out of practice. Still, the folks all seemed to be having a good time. She looked over at Dinky's grave, marked with a wooden cross and a pile of stones, and she remembered the afternoon she had sat here drinking coffee from a thermos while Ed dug the grave. It took a long, long time. It was a warm spring day, but the ground was still half frozen from a late snow. And Dinky was a big dog — part Great Dane. She had her sociology textbook with her, studying for the final exam. But mostly she had watched Ed digging. He had removed his red flannel shirt, which was waving like a flag from one of the branches. She had sat there admiring the way his muscles worked under the white T-shirt and how silently and swiftly he dug the hole, deeper and deeper, without stopping to complain about how hard the ground was or how long it was taking. She knew how much the dog meant to him. He'd had Dinky since he was five years old. The dog was fifteen — 105 in dog years — half blind and crippled from arthritis, but he still followed Ed everywhere. She remembered saying to Ed, "From now on, I guess I'll have to be your best friend." She had actually said that to him. And he had hugged her to him, crushing her, as if he actually believed her.

The fireworks from down below sounded like scattered gunfire. It wasn't even quite dusk yet. Someone was jumping the gun.

"You should get back to your party," she said.

He stood up and held out his hand to her. His hand felt like an old worn baseball mitt, large and leathery. They walked back down the hill to the party. Teddy ran up to greet them, waving a lit sparkler in his hand. She was afraid of firecrackers. One of the kids in their neighborhood, Denny Mahoney, got his thumbs blown off by a cherry bomb one Fourth of July. The plastic surgeons had fashioned something called thoes, sewing his big toes onto his hands. It had seemed like a miracle at the time.

"Where were you guys?" Teddy asked them.

"Just up there." Ed pointed to the fields behind the barn.

"Doing what?" Teddy said.

"Talking." Ed shrugged.

"Talking about what?" Teddy asked suspiciously.

"Stuff," Ed said.

"Good stuff," she added, seeing the anxious look on Teddy's face.

He smiled as his sparkler fizzled out and then he ran to get a new one.

"I don't know how you do it," Laura had blurted out during that same phone conversation, just as they were about to hang up. "Don't you ever blame him?" She didn't have to say his name. Giselle knew who she meant.

"All the time," Giselle had said. "Every day."

"Really?" Laura had sounded surprised, or maybe just surprised that Giselle had admitted it. "But Teddy doesn't know?"

"He knows," she said.

"And how does that make him feel?"

"How do you think?

"I don't know," Laura said.

"I don't know either," Giselle had said. "I can't even imagine."

Giselle looked over at her son. He was waving a sparkler in each hand, drawing circles in the air, bathed in a shower of white sparks.

She remembered last Fourth of July. They had driven to the beach. Trina, just barely a year old, squatted in the sand, digging a hole with her new shovel and bucket. Teddy, the big brother, squatted beside her, giving her pointers. And Dan stood in the surf up to his waist smiling and waving at them. She had shot a whole roll of film that day with a brand-new Minolta Dan had given her for her birthday. Then Dan motioned for her to come in. "Water's great!" he'd shouted. And she had carried Trina to the water's edge, with Teddy galloping along in front. She handed the baby over to Dan, who held her on her stomach while she paddled her arms and legs gamely in the waves. "A real little Esther Williams," Dan bragged to an older woman in a white sailor hat who was smiling indulgently in their direction. And Teddy, feeling ignored, had shouted, "I can do the backstroke. Watch me!"

The water was chilly, as always in California, and after a few minutes Giselle had waded back to shore alone. When she picked up the bright beach towel to dry herself off, she realized that the camera was gone. At first she couldn't believe it. She picked up the beach blanket and shook it out. Then she dumped the contents of the straw beach bag onto the blanket and sifted through it twice. But the camera was definitely gone. Nothing else, just the camera. At the time she was more upset about the camera than the film. The roll of pictures that would never be developed. At the time she didn't even realize what had been stolen from her.

"Mom, Dad, look!" Teddy shouted at them. "Smile!" He had picked up her disposable camera from the table where she'd set it down and was aiming at them through the viewfinder. Even from this distance she could see that his fingers were sticky with chocolate frosting and she wanted to tell him to wash his hands first, but she didn't. She felt Ed's arm encircling her waist. She smiled obediently.

The day they brought Teddy home from the hospital, they had sat on the front porch and taken turns taking pictures of each other holding him. After maybe a dozen pictures Ed said, "We don't have any of the three of us, you know, together." And he had run next door to ask old Mrs. Knapp if she'd mind helping them out. The widow Knapp, as Giselle had dubbed her, was crazy about Ed. She was always calling him over for some fresh-baked pie or bread pudding. But Mrs. Knapp's middle-aged daughter answered the door and told him that her mother was dead. She had died of a heart attack the night before, in the same hospital where Teddy had been born. Despite Ed's protestations, the daughter had insisted upon coming over and taking the pictures herself. Later, after the woman left, Ed said he didn't want to get the pictures developed. He felt as if it would be bad luck. And Giselle had said, "Don't be ridiculous." In those days they argued constantly, about everything.

A couple of days later Giselle had dropped off the roll of film at the drugstore to be developed, and then forgot all about it in the ensuing chaos and exhaustion of new motherhood, until the drugstore called and reminded her a month or so later. The next morning she picked up the photos in their yellow envelope, distracted by Teddy's crying in the store, and didn't look at them until she got home and Teddy was in his crib napping. Then she collapsed on the sofa and opened the envelope, eager to see the first photographs of her beautiful new son.

But instead of a wrinkly pink infant in a blue receiving blanket, there was a tall, gangly high school boy in a mortarboard and graduation robe, grinning and waving his diploma like a blank check. Confused, she sat frozen for a moment, as if staring at some time-lapse photograph of Teddy already grown up. A sharp pang of loss shot through her, and she shuffled rapidly through the other snapshots, looking for pictures of her baby, only to find more of the graduation boy. The boy and his parents, hugging. She could almost hear the teary-eyed mother saying, "It seems like just yesterday . . ." The boy and his siblings, friends, girlfriend. The roll ended with some shots of the crowd, the stage, and what appeared to be a brand-new car — a shiny red convertible, the graduation gift, no doubt. Suddenly Giselle was sure the kid was a spoiled brat. A cocky, callow future frat boy. It was an eerie, unsettling experience. She shoved the pictures back into the envelope and checked the name on the outside label: Bettendorf, J. The frazzled clerk had grabbed the wrong envelope. A stupid, understandable mistake. Tomorrow, bright and early, she told herself, she would exchange the pictures. She had heard a whimper then and leaped up — feeling suddenly young and energetic — to check on her son, relieved that the future still lay ahead of them, that it wasn't too late. Everything was still possible.

Teddy snapped the picture and handed the sticky camera back to Giselle. It smelled like chocolate.

"Okay, my turn," Ed announced. "I'll take one of you and your mom." He motioned Teddy over to where Giselle was standing in front of some rosebushes.

"I don't feel so hot," Teddy said as he stood beside her. "My stomach hurts." He didn't protest when she brushed his sweaty hair out of his face and felt his flushed forehead.

"Ready?" Ed said. "One, two, three." He clicked the shutter just as Teddy bent over and vomited on the grass.

"Great picture," Ed joked. "Real nice."

"Too much cake and excitement," Giselle said to Ed. She was massaging Teddy's bony shoulders, sharp as coat hangers, while he retched again, spattering her sandals. But she didn't move away. She just kept rubbing little circles on his back and whispering soothing words: "It's all right, you're fine now, you're gonna be all right." Ed ran into the house and returned with a glass of 7-Up.

"I'm okay," Teddy said, taking a sip and spitting it out.

"Get out of there!" Ed yelled at the dog that was sniffing around the mess on the grass. He picked up the hose coiled by the side of the house and sprayed the area clean. Giselle danced a little jig as he skittered the cold spray over her bare toes.

"Wow" — Teddy perked up — "you think we'll actually be able to see the barf in the picture?"

Giselle rolled her eyes and Ed laughed.

It was dusk. The guests were starting to leave. "So long, Ed!" a large man with red suspenders called out. "Hell of a shindig!" Ed walked over to shake the man's hand and say good-bye. Out of the corner of her eye she saw Sharon sidle up to them, all smiles, carrying a huge wooden bowl that had contained potato salad. Good potato salad, almost identical to Giselle's mother's recipe.

"I want to go with you," Teddy said to her. "Can I?"

Giselle was surprised. "You mean, spend the night?" She reached out and pushed his sweaty hair out of his eyes. His damp skin still looked faintly green.

He nodded.

"Sure," she said. "But you better bring a sleeping bag."

"Okay." Teddy ran inside the house.

When Ed walked back over, she cleared her throat and said, "Teddy wants to go back to my place for the night." She tried to sound casual — like no big deal — but her throat squeezed shut. She stared down at her muddy toes, blinking back the tears. "He's getting his sleeping bag. Do you mind?"

Ed put his arm around her shoulder and gave her a hug. "There's nothing like Mom when you're feeling sick."

Teddy ran out dragging an old faded blue sleeping bag in the dirt behind him. She thought of the matching orange sleeping bags Dan had bought them for the soccer team's camping weekend. Just last fall. She wondered if Dan had taken his to Vermont or if it was in the storage locker.

"Jesus Christ, Teddy. Pay attention." Ed grabbed the sleeping bag, rolled it up, and handed it back to him. "Come on. I'll walk you guys to your car."

The sunset was fading out, the final flickering fireworks, as they walked down the gravel drive to the magenta Tracker. Giselle had parked it off by itself where it would be safe from careless people banging into it. She was looking forward to having her own car back, even if it was just an old piece of shit — although she was dreading going back to California to get it. *One day at a time,* she told herself as they climbed into the jeep.

"This thing looks like a goddamned toy," Ed said, slamming the passenger door shut. "I'll take my chances on the Harley any day."

"Me, too," Teddy said.

"We'll give you a call tomorrow," she told Ed. Her new phone still wasn't hooked up. The phone company had screwed up. Tomorrow, they'd said, for sure.

As she started the engine, Ed gave her a quick kiss on the cheek. "Sounds like crap," he said. "Tell your sister she needs new plugs."

"You tell her yourself," she said, shifting the car into gear.

As they jounced along the unpaved drive, she cursed softly and winced at the loose gravel dinging the doors. She would take the car to the car wash, she thought, before she returned it to Vonnie, who had really been very generous. At the bottom of the hill, she glanced in the rearview mirror. Ed was still standing there, waving at them as they turned onto the main road. Teddy yawned and slumped in his seat.

"Big day," she said.

He nodded and yawned again.

"You know, I'm really glad you decided to come with me." She smiled at him. He smiled back sleepily. His eyelids seemed to descend in slow motion. He was holding his belly like a little Buddha. "How's your tummy?" she asked.

"Okay," Teddy said. "It doesn't hurt anymore."

By the time they pulled up in front of the apartment house, he was sound asleep, dead to the world. She didn't know what to do. It had been a long time since she had attempted to lift him up; she didn't know if she was strong enough. She ran up the steps and unlocked the door to the apartment. She had left all the windows open, and the smell of fresh paint had already begun to fade. It was a pleasant smell, like the smell of just-sharpened pencils or newly cut firewood. She went back out to the car. Teddy moaned a little as she unbuckled his seat belt and slid her arms under him, but he didn't wake up. She bent her knees and then slowly straightened her back, staggering a bit until she found her balance, her center of gravity. She was surprised by how easy it was. She felt as if she could carry him around the block if she had to, although she was certain she couldn't budge a seventy-five-pound dumbbell if her life depended on it. *It must be something to do with the distribution of weight,* she thought, *some law of physics. Or metaphysics.* She remembered that phrase from the law book: the capacity to bear loss.

Inside, she set him down in one of the wing chairs next to the fireplace. Teddy frowned and mumbled something she couldn't make out. "Shhh," she whispered, "it's all right. I'm going to make up your bed now."

As she arranged his sleeping bag in the corner of his new bedroom, she began making a mental list of what she needed from the grocery store in the morning. Cereal, milk, peanut butter, bread, Oreos, noodles, apples. The list was endless. It seemed to her that they needed everything. She went into the bathroom and, as she brushed her teeth, thought: Q-tips, bubble bath, Band-Aids, ointment. She thought about looking for a scrap of paper to write the list down on. She knew she should, but somehow she didn't feel like it. It almost didn't matter what she wrote down. Since there was nothing they didn't need, anything would do. She couldn't very well go wrong. In its way, it was a comforting thought.

Even though it was still early, not long past dark, she was tired. It had been a big day and she hadn't slept last night. She dragged the borrowed futon from her room into Teddy's bedroom. She just wanted to be next to him. Teddy was snoring softly. His nose sounded stuffy. Children's Tylenol, orange juice, tissues. Tonight, she had a feeling, she was going to sleep like a baby. On the street outside someone set off a burst of fireworks that lit up the window. A series of loud pops, like gunshots, followed by a long, shrill whistle. Teddy snored on, oblivious to the commotion. She thought of *Koko's Kitten,* Trina's favorite book. Koko's full name was Hanabi-Ko, which means Fireworks Child in Japanese, and then shoved that, all of it, out of her mind. She forced herself to focus on her list. Napkins, popcorn, salt and pepper. The items formed a singsong lullaby in her mind — sugar, flour, rice — and she drifted off to sleep, still adding to the list, as if she were counting sheep.

EPILOGUE

HIS MOTHER IS LYING IN A CHAISE LONGUE BY *the swimming pool, reading some courtroom thriller she picked up at the airport. Teddy had thought about making her reservations at an elegant B and B on Gilbert Street, just around the corner from the house he shares with three friends, including Cathleen, his now ex-girlfriend, but his mother said she would like a pool. And now he's glad she's not staying there, because that's where Cathleen's parents are staying. He still can't believe that Cathleen picked the weekend before graduation to break up with him. He still can't believe it, period. All weekend he has been dragging himself through the festivities, this great rite of passage, weighed down by this heaviness in his chest; he feels as if he's sitting in the dentist's chair with one of those lead X-ray aprons pressing against his heart. But instead of shielding him from harmful rays, it is trapping all the bad stuff inside.*

His mother catches sight of him and waves her sunglasses in his direction, smiling brightly. In her black one-piece suit from this distance, she looks like a college girl. He sits down in a chair under a red-and-white umbrella, feeling constrained and conspicuous in his good khaki slacks and white shirt. He bends over and gives her a peck on the cheek. "I thought we were supposed to meet Dad and Sean at six," he says, glancing pointedly at his watch; it's already ten of six.

"I guess I lost track of the time. It's so great to just relax." She sighs and sits up, tossing her personal effects into a beach bag. "I'll be ready in ten minutes. Meet you in the lobby or up here?"

"The lobby, I guess," he says, watching some beautiful blonde sitting in the shallow end of the pool talking earnestly with her handsome gray-haired father. The town is overrun with graduating seniors and their parents.

His mother reaches out and touches his shoulder. "How are you doing?"

"Fine." He shrugs. "A little tired. I was up till three."

Even though he had been determined to hide the fact that anything was wrong, his mother had picked up on his emotional state at the airport, before her suitcase even appeared on the luggage carousel. This weekend would be the first time they were all together in five years, since the summer before he left for college and his mother moved to Phoenix. Teddy wanted it to be pleasant. When she asked him what was wrong, he said, "Nothing. I'm just tired from finals." But he knew she didn't believe him. And by the time they left the airport parking lot, he had confessed that Cathleen had dumped him; she wasn't moving to Ann Arbor with him as they had planned. He was going to have to go alone. His mother had looked at him with that sad, worried look he hated. He knew she still thought of him as a child at risk, a statistical long shot.

His dad and his stepbrother were staying at the Hawkeye Inn in Coralville. His dad thought the Holiday Inn, the only hotel in Iowa City proper, was too pricey. "Let your mother, the hotshot lawyer, stay there," he'd joked on the phone. Sharon, his father's wife, had stayed in Lincoln with Chloe, her nubile daughter from a previous marriage, who had a big crush on Teddy. His mother's new beau, as she called him, had also discreetly chosen to remain at home. Hal was considerably older than Teddy's mother — though his exact age was a well-kept secret — and not much to look at. He was balding and soft around the edges but incredibly energetic and magnetic somehow — a prominent retired trial attorney who could mesmerize a jury, allegedly hold them in the palm of his hand. Teddy had to admit, when *he visited them last Christmas, that his mother had never seemed so present and casually affectionate. And girlish, almost giggly.*

The Holiday Inn pool is on an upper deck that looks out over the walking mall. Down below, Teddy sees his father and Sean walking toward the hotel, holding hands. As they near the fountain, Sean nearly trips on his shoelace on the uneven cobblestones. Teddy feels his throat knot up as he watches his dad kneeling down to tie Sean's sneaker laces. He knows that his father saved him. His mother did her best — and Teddy doesn't think that anyone could have done better under the circumstances — but he doesn't think he could have made it without his dad. With his mother, there was always that shadow of tension, that hairline crack in her smile, the faint limp in her laugh. Everyone else seemed to think his mother's recovery bordered on the miraculous. When it came to bucking up and shouldering onward, his mother was Exhibit A. He knows how much she loves him, but he also knows what an act of will that love was, how she worked at it, like an alcoholic: God grant me the serenity to love my son one day at a time. Don't let me blame him for what happened, not even in a moment of weakness. She made him aware of the fact that the heart is a muscle. He used to imagine he could see her heart working inside her chest, pumping and flexing. For his mother, loving — at least loving him — required strenuous daily exercise. Whereas his dad just loved him. Like it was no big deal, as if he didn't have to think twice about it.

Teddy stands up and hollers over the railing, "Hey, Dad! Sean!"

His father looks up and waves while Sean keeps scanning the sky, as if he thought a pilot in a passing airplane had shouted his name, until their father picks him up and points at Teddy on the balcony. Then Sean's face breaks into a big grin, and he waves like mad. It breaks Teddy's heart. Even though he is hardly ever home, Sean is crazy about him. He follows him around like a devoted puppy nipping at Teddy's heels.

When Sean was born, Teddy was relieved that it was a boy. He thought it would be easier for his mother to take. And for him. He still dreamed about his baby sister all the time, even after a decade of therapy. Cathleen had said it was what made him special, different from the other guys, the reason she had fallen in love with him. Despite the fact he hadn't told her about Trina until they had already been living together for a month. And only then because he'd had a nightmare in which he'd called out her name in his sleep, and Cathleen had woken him up, demanding to know who Trina was, with such a sick, wounded expression in her eyes that he had to tell her. Then when she poured all this love and sympathy on him, he felt guilty and pushed her away. He didn't feel right being somehow rewarded for having done something so terrible. He deserved less love, not more. It was all backward.

It was the same with his admission to medical school. On the application they asked you to write a personal essay on why you want to be a doctor. He had started out writing the standard bullshit — how he had changed his major from philosophy to pre-med because he realized he wanted to make a concrete contribution to society, blah blah blah. But suddenly he found himself writing about his baby sister: How many lives will I have to save to equal my little sister's? A hundred? A thousand? Ten thousand? At a young age, I learned the hard way what every doctor needs to know. That every life is unique and irreplaceable. *The admissions officers fell for it big-time, not that it wasn't true, but somehow he came away feeling like a con man. He thought about sending the essay to his mother, but he keeps putting it off.*

Since Cathleen announced she isn't moving to Ann Arbor with him, he has been plagued with second thoughts. Wild fantasies of bumming around India and South America, or buying an old Harley like the one his dad used to have and just taking off with no particular destination in mind. He envies his housemate Keith, who is going to film school in the fall, some new high-tech program near L.A. He wants to be a special effects wizard. Teddy has already put him in touch with Uncle Todd, who, as Teddy gets older, strikes him more and more like some perpetual kid with his computer models, blowing up cities, creating new galaxies. Except for the fact that the big stu-

dios are in California — a place he never wants to see again — it sounds like an appealing way to earn a living. But Teddy feels he has forfeited his right to a frivolous career. Most of the time he still thinks he genuinely wants to be a doctor for all the right reasons; other times he worries that it was just the most obvious solution to the problem of his life.

When Cathleen broke up with him, just last week, she had said she loved him but was giving up on him. She said it was too much work to love him, to love someone who thought he didn't deserve to be loved. And Teddy had thought of his mother. Somehow she had managed to love him all these years. Even though he didn't always enjoy being around her, he loved his mother more than anyone. He worried sometimes that he would never be as close to anyone as he was to his mother. They were like the last two living veterans of some terrible, senseless war.

Teddy takes the elevator down and enters the lobby just as his father is kissing his mother hello, telling her she looks great, which she does. She is wearing a killer black dress and heels. His father, by comparison, looks like he just stepped off a tractor, but he's still a big, good-looking man with a thick head of shaggy hair. Somewhere along the way — Teddy doesn't remember exactly when — the turquoise earring disappeared.

"And this must be Sean." His mother is squatting on her heels looking into Sean's benign but puzzled face with tears in her eyes. "You were just a baby the last time I saw you. This big." She holds her hands a foot apart.

Sean looks up at his dad, who gives him a reassuring squeeze on the back of the neck, just the way he used to do to Teddy. Then Sean catches sight of a water fountain and veers off, shouting, "Water! Water!" like someone who has been lost in the desert for a week. Everyone laughs as Ed excuses himself and walks over and lifts Sean up so that his mouth can reach the faucet. His mother pulls a tissue from her purse and dabs at her eyes with a faintly self-conscious smile. As they walk outside, Teddy glimpses their reflection in the *mirror. Like a family portrait. Another one of those odd, complicated, patchwork families.*

At the restaurant, a casual but upscale pasta place called The Kitchen, there is none of the awkwardness that Teddy had worried there might be. The place is bustling, there is plenty to talk about (even though his dad is not a big talker), and a perpetual-motion, revved-up five-year-old is an entertaining distraction. At first Teddy thought that his father had decided to bring Sean along for the trip because little kids were always a good buffer, but now he thinks it was because his dad just couldn't stand to be away from him for that long. Teddy can't decide how he feels about seeing his dad so gaga over this kid. Then he remembers something his dad told him on the phone: "You know, when you were Sean's age, you were off in California. It used to kill me not seeing you. I feel like I'm making up for what I missed out on." And Teddy had felt both touched and miffed, as if any five-year-old would do. He knew that this was something his mother would never feel.

When Sean announces that he wants to switch places in the booth and sit next to Teddy, instead of his father, Ed makes a big show of being jealous. He pounds his heart and says, "I'm wounded to the quick." Sean manages to knock over a glass of white wine as he wriggles underneath the booth. Some of the wine splashes on Giselle, who says it's no big deal and smiles indulgently as she dabs the napkin at her dress. Teddy thinks how when he was Sean's age, she'd have whacked him with the folded napkin for behaving like this. At least before the accident. After the accident she was more polite; she hardly ever yelled at him, even when he wished she would.

"Hey, settle down." Ed finally wags his finger across the table at Sean. "What's your problem? You got ants in your pants?"

Teddy remembers his dad saying the same thing to him when he was a kid. Sean giggles and wiggles his butt.

After they order their food — plain spaghetti with butter for Sean — they attempt to have an adult conversation, which isn't easy *with Sean interrupting every few seconds. But maybe it's just as well. Things can't get too heavy. Not that they probably would. Although they don't have much contact anymore, his parents have remained friendly. He waves to the waitress and pantomimes needing another glass of wine.*

His mother is talking about Phoenix, how bad the traffic is getting to be. She had moved there to edit a magazine called Southwest Lawyer *that some friend of her old friend Laura was starting up. The job offer had come at the right time. She was tired of private practice, tired of winter, and Teddy was about to go off to college. He has always suspected that his father's new baby might have also had something to do with it. Maybe his mother wanted to have her own new beginning.*

The waitress, a pretty Asian girl with short angular hair and lots of earrings, brings their food. The conversation ceases while she shuffles the plates around, trying to match the right order to the right person. Teddy thinks she must be new and flashes her an encouraging smile. The place is really crowded, and she looks about ready to run screaming into the night. Teddy knows how she feels. Although he loves his parents, the whole scene is just a little too weird. He excuses himself to go to the men's room.

When he gets back to the table, the waitress is clearing away the dishes. Sean has eaten maybe three noodles, and Giselle hasn't done much better. The waitress asks her if she'd like it wrapped up to go. His mother says yes, then turns to him and says, "You can eat it for lunch tomorrow." As if she's worried he's wasting away from malnutrition, even though she was never that sort of mom. Her worries always seemed darker and more mysterious. Sean suddenly conks out as they are waiting for their desserts to arrive, like the Energizer Bunny whose battery suddenly ran out of juice. He slumps against his dad, with his head wobbling, his eyelids fluttering as he struggles to keep them open just a second longer. Teddy's eyes meet his mother's and bounce away; he knows they are both thinking of his sister. Ed reaches over and smoothes Sean's hair out of his eyes.

"This guy's had it," he says. "I'm going to take him back to the

motel." He reaches for his wallet, but Giselle motions for him to put it away. He hesitates and then shrugs and says thanks. One thing about his parents he always liked, Teddy thinks, was how they never argued about money. Unlike Cathleen's parents. The one weekend he spent at their house in Des Moines was like switching channels between Moneyline and Crossfire.

His father turns to him and says, "You eat my dessert." He pats his belly, which is still impressively flat. Then he gently hoists Sean, like a big sack of potatoes, onto his shoulder. "Dead to the world." He claps Teddy on the shoulder. "How about breakfast before we get on the road?"

"Sure." Teddy nods. "How 'bout I pick you guys up around ten?" His mother's plane leaves at 8 A.M. She has already insisted upon taking a limo so as not to inconvenience anyone.

"How 'bout nine?"

Teddy heaves a sigh. "Nine-thirty?"

"It's a deal."

After they leave, his mother stifles a little yawn. She looks tired and older than she did this afternoon. "We could get the dessert to go," he says.

"I'm okay. It's just such a beautiful night out." She looks out the window. "I'd like to get some fresh air."

"We could go back to my place and sit on the porch swing," he suggests almost shyly, as if he's asking her out on a date.

"That sounds perfect." Her face lights up. "The one thing I always loved about the Midwest was the porch swings."

They ask the waitress to wrap up the desserts — an apple tart and some sort of fudge pie that his father ordered. His mother extracts a slim wallet from a svelte little bag and sets her credit card on top of the bill. The waitress whisks the card away. While they are waiting for her to return with the slip, his mother says, "Your father seems to be doing well."

Teddy nods noncommittally. He has never much liked talking about one of them with the other one, even though they only say nice *things about each other. And besides, now that they are alone, he's getting nervous. There's something he's been wanting to tell her but not in the presence of his father. It is something about his stepfather. Talk about an incredible blast from the past.*

The drive to his house is short, six blocks, and he doesn't say anything about it. He waits until they are settled on the dark porch with some citronella candles burning and a jug of cheap wine on the railing next to the porch swing. His roommates are at a concert at Hancher Auditorium and won't be back for at least a couple of hours. He feels anxious and keeps changing positions as if he, too, has ants in his pants, but his mother doesn't notice. Or more likely, pretends not to notice, as she asks him questions about the courses he will take during his first year of medical school. And tells him a couple of amusing anecdotes about her first year of law school.

Finally he clears his throat and says, "There's something I want to tell you." He feels her body snap to attention beside him. Her hand crawls up to her throat. She holds her throat as if, if she doesn't like what he's saying, she can silence him by squeezing her own larynx shut. "It's about Dan. He called me. I talked to him on the phone. Maybe a month ago."

"He called you?" she asks after a brief pause. "Just out of the blue?"

"Well, no, not exactly out of the blue." He pauses for a slug of wine. He knows that his mother and stepfather, ex-stepfather, haven't spoken in a decade. He can feel the shock waves radiating from his mother's brain. "What happened is, I came across this book of poems of his at Murphy-Brookfield, you know, that used-book store we went to yesterday?" She nods. "I recognized the name, of course, but thought maybe it was just a coincidence or something. Then I opened the book and saw his picture on the back flap. It was kind of a jolt, to say the least."

"What was it called? I mean the title."

Oh, God, he thinks. He should have known she'd ask, and he can't bring himself to say it. "I've got it in my room," he says. "I'll go get it." *He's relieved for an excuse to get away for a moment. He can feel the adrenaline pumping as he takes the stairs two at a time. The book is lying next to his bed on the floor.*

When he walks back outside, his mother isn't there. He thinks for an instant that maybe she just took off. It isn't as if they had these cozy little conversations about the past every day. But then he hears the toilet flush inside and hears her high heels tapping on the wooden floor as she makes her way back to the porch. He thinks she looks a little pale as she takes the book from him and examines it. First the dust jacket, the inside flap that describes the poems, then the back flap with the photo and bio.

Daniel Trias teaches literature and creative writing at Ohio College in Athens, Ohio. His poems have appeared in Antioch Review, Ploughshares, Kenyon Review, *and* Virginia Quarterly. *He is the author of* Constructing the Self: The Confessional Novel, *published by the University of Connecticut Press. This is his first book of poetry.*

"Ohio!" She smiles, amused at the irony of his being in the Midwest. "I wonder how long he's been there. He used to brag he never owned a winter coat."

The bio mentions nothing about his personal life, and Teddy knows what she's wondering. He saves her the indignity of having to ask. "He's not married. Never remarried."

His mother nods her head vaguely. She is hunched beside one of the citronella candles, leafing through the poems in the book, pausing now and then to read a phrase. He suddenly realizes that he has left out an important link in the story. "So after I read the book, I wrote him a letter, a note really, care of the college. And he called me the next week. And we talked for a while. He asked me about myself and about you, what you were doing, and I sort of filled him in on the last ten years." His mother is just looking at him now, waiting for more, looking as if he hit her with a stun gun. "He said he was really happy to hear from me."

She shuts the book and starts to cry. When Teddy takes an awkward step toward her, she waves him away. "It's just so ironic. The thing that drove us apart was this book he was going to write about the accident. I couldn't stand it. I thought it was a terrible, selfish thing to do." She fishes a tissue out of her purse and blows her nose. "I guess he never actually wrote it."

Teddy shrugs. "I don't know. He didn't mention it."

"Did you read the poems?" she asks, handing the book back to him.

"Yeah. You know I'm not that into poetry, but they seemed pretty good. I mean, it won a prize and everything. But it was kind of hard to be objective, under the circumstances. You want to borrow it?" He holds the book out to her. She hesitates and then shakes her head. He doesn't blame her. The book is called Raising the Dead: Confessions of a Childless Father.

"Maybe someday," she says. She reaches up and touches the side of his face. "I'm glad you spoke with him."

"He said he's giving a reading in Ann Arbor in the fall. He suggested maybe we could get together for dinner." Teddy watches his mother closely to see how she really feels about this prospect. Her face is in the shadows, but he can sense rather than see her smile.

"That's good," she says. "Good for him."

Teddy doesn't know if she means it is good of his stepfather to see him or if it is good for his stepfather to see him. Either way, he's just relieved to have got it off his chest.

The phone rings and Teddy excuses himself to go answer it even though he's sure it is for one of his housemates. It seems a good idea to give his mother a couple of minutes alone. It's Keith's girlfriend calling from California. Even though it's not that late, Teddy feels annoyed. She frequently forgets about the two-hour time difference and has woken him up on more than one occasion, then laughed about it as if she thought such dim-wittedness was cute. He scrawls a message on the blackboard — Keith, Call Christy *— and then stops in the downstairs bathroom to take a piss. As he washes his hands, he stares moodily at his reflection in the mirror and imagines that Cath-*

leen is outside on the porch, talking to his mother. He imagines the two of them teasing him until he blushes and begs for mercy. But when he goes back outside, he is surprised to find his mother lying on the porch swing, her head propped up by a nest of dirty throw pillows, sound asleep. Or passed out. He picks up the wine bottle and sees that it is almost empty. That plus all the wine at the restaurant. The rusty chain squeaks as the swing sways back and forth under his mother's weight. He stands there with his hands in his pockets trying to decide whether to wake her up. He knows she would be more comfortable in her hotel room with its queen-size bed, but it seems a shame to wake her when she's sleeping so peacefully. He goes inside, runs upstairs, grabs the comforter off his futon, runs back downstairs, and drapes the quilt over his mother. The night is warm, but he wants to keep the mosquitoes away. Then he sits down on the front steps, like a guard dog, and waits.

WHEN GISELLE WAKES UP IT IS DARK AND RAINing softly. A cat mews plaintively, asking to be let in or out. The porch swing lurches as she sits up and stretches the kinks out of her stiff bones, particularly her neck, which feels as if some deranged chiropractor has wrenched it out of alignment. Teddy has fallen asleep in a decayed armchair in the corner of the porch. All the furniture looks as if it was salvaged from the curb. It makes her nostalgic for the college days she never really had.

The sky is just starting to brighten, and the air is fresh, cool. Despite the kinks, she feels surprisingly rested. Then, with a jolt, she remembers her early-morning flight. She tiptoes over to the edge of the porch, where there's more light, and peers at her watch. She can still make it. The limo is scheduled to pick her up at the hotel in an hour. Teddy appears to be sleeping so soundly, she hates to wake him. She knows what an effort he's been making all weekend to hide his heartache. His arms are crossed over his chest as if he were attempting to protect himself in his sleep. She has always thought of him as something fragile, just barely mended, someone for whom rest does not come easily. Besides, she feels like walking, and it is only five or six blocks back to the Holiday Inn. The whole town is small enough to be a movie set.

She looks around for something to write a note on. Normally she carries a large shoulder bag with all kinds of supplies, but last night she used this silly little bag just big enough for some money, a comb, a lipstick, tissue, and a pen — but no notepad. She sees the book of poems sitting on the floor next to the steps with a piece of paper sticking out. Thinking maybe it's scrap paper, she picks up the book and slips the paper out. It is folded in half. With something typed on it. She opens it up and skims the first couple of sentences and stops breathing. It is Teddy's essay for his medical school application. It begins:

> I know what it feels like to take a life. When I was nine years old I was playing with a gun and I accidentally shot my two-year-old sister, Trina. My whole life, my family's whole life, has been one long painful process of recovery, and we're not fully healed yet. Now I want to learn what it feels like to save a life. I realize that there's no way to undo what I've done. How many lives would equal my sister's life? One hundred? One thousand? Ten thousand? At a young age I learned the hard way what every doctor needs to know: that every life is unique and irreplaceable. Part of me died with my sister. It has been difficult living with myself even though my mother and father have given me more than any kid has a right to ask for. If given the chance, I will work as hard as humanly possible to be the best possible doctor I can be. For me it's not just a profession but a salvation. In my case, I think of that old billboard or bumper sticker that says THE LIFE YOU SAVE MAY BE YOUR OWN.

The letters blur on the page as she reads the last couple of lines of the first paragraph and then tucks it back into the book of poems. She looks over at him slumped in his chair, his head dangling at an awkward angle, and has a sudden clear image of him as a toddler in his car seat. What a sweet, tender boy he was. During the past decade she has rarely flashed on Teddy as a small boy, as if Trina's memory has somehow usurped those early years. Since Trina was stuck in the role of eternal toddler, like a permanent kitten or puppy, Teddy had — in her mind — somehow forfeited his claim to babyhood. It was as if Giselle's memory were a photo album with limited space, so she had made a judgment call to toss out all of Teddy's cuddly, innocent baby photos. And anyway, he wasn't innocent. At least not completely. Under the doctrine of strict liability, if you did it, it's your fault.

When she first started law school, she was obsessed with theories of causation. All the various legal tests for assigning blame. The last human wrongdoer test. The "but for" rule. But for X, Y would never have happened. They all sounded reasonable enough until you started applying the theory to messy real-life cases. Her favorite was a Mississippi case in which a custodian was cleaning a vending machine with an oil-soaked rag. The oil fumes permeated the fur of a rat hiding under the machine who then ran over to some docks that subsequently burst into flames, resulting in thousands of dollars in damages. It was obvious that but for the rat, the fire would never have occurred. But since you couldn't sue a rat, the last human wrongdoer was the custodian. So the real issue was whether it was foreseeable that the oily rag would turn the hidden rat into a Molotov cocktail. Under the highly extraordinary consequences test, also known as the hindsight test, the custodian could not be held liable for such consequences that a reasonable person could not foresee.

Giselle would, of course, lie awake at night applying the various theories to her own life. But for Bill Beemer's buying the gun. But for Eric's finding the gun. But for Lois's being in the rec room. But for Giselle's not taking the kids to the beach that day instead of putting Trina in the wading pool. But for moving to California. And so on. The test was stupid. It reminded Giselle of one of her mother's favorite homilies: But for the grace of God . . . And it was really just your basic "if only" all dressed up in legalese with nowhere to go. And as to whether it was foreseeable that Eric would find the gun and that Teddy would fire it, who knows? After all these years she still remembers, word for word, her favorite sentence from Prosser: "To one gifted with omniscience as to all existing circumstances, no result could appear remarkable, or indeed anything but inevitable, as a matter of hindsight."

The law was useless. It was nobody's fault; it was everybody's fault. She started reading books about Buddhism instead. The books told you to put aside logic. They gave you koans, Zen brain-twisters, that forced your rational mind to short-circuit. Does a dog have Buddha-nature? What is the sound of one hand clapping? Who is this I you call yourself? How can something be nobody's fault? And gradually she began to understand that even if she could understand, it wouldn't make any difference. She tucked a quote by Takuan into the mirror over her bureau: "One may explain water, but the mouth will not become wet. One may expound fully upon the nature of fire, but the mouth will not become hot."

She flips the back cover of the book open and stares at the photograph of Dan, barely larger than a postage stamp. *He looks the same,* she thinks, and imagines that the young women in his poetry classes must hang on his every word. The sensitive, wounded poet. Somehow she is not surprised that he has never remarried. She is, in fact, surprised that she feels no bitterness at the thought of Dan seeing Teddy again after all these years. The two of them eating pizza at some college hangout. She can't imagine the conversation, but she hopes it goes well, for both their sakes.

Her high heels are sitting under the swing. She takes off her panty hose and tosses them into a pile of dead leaves beside the porch. Teddy still shows no signs of stirring. She decides she will call him from the airport to say good-bye. At the last minute she slips his essay out of the book and into her purse. She wants to keep it. As proof that despite the odds, he has turned out all right after all. A son any mother would be proud of. Giselle picks up her shoes and walks barefoot across the wet grass. It is quiet, pristine, just before the morning rush. A pretty girl with a perky ponytail jogs by with her German shepherd keeping pace right beside her. She smiles at Giselle, who smiles back.

It is an extraordinarily beautiful morning. After four years in the desert, she feels almost drunk on the dew and lush greenery. Trees, grass, shrubs. She feels as if she's been transported to the Emerald City. For the first time she feels a nostalgia for the Midwest with its sober shade trees and tall, square houses, the archetypal houses of children's drawings with a scribble of crayon smoke curling from the chimney. At the same time she pictures, with pleasure, her rambling adobe ranch house with its cacti garden and postage-stamp pool in the backyard. She pictures Hal, who is an early riser, sitting in the sunny breakfast nook, reading his morning paper, waiting impatiently until it is time to leave for the airport to pick her up. It is not the romantic sort of love she felt for Dan, or the familial sort of love she felt (feels still) for Ed, but some other sort of thing that she doesn't think she could have come to any earlier in her life. Even though sometimes she wishes their wrinkles and loose skin could be airbrushed away, she knows that they are a necessary part of it. Hal has two grown daughters and an expensive ex-wife. Sometimes, lying in bed, they like to fantasize about what they would have done if they had met each other in their twenties or thirties. But then usually one of them says, "And we'd probably have gone our separate ways by now," and the other nods in agreement, grateful to have what they have. As Hal said one morning not long ago, "This is as close to enough as it gets." Not that a day goes by that she doesn't think of her daughter. And now that she knows Dan isn't even in California, the thought of Trina buried out there all alone is enough to make her cry.

But it seems to her that something is different. She feels different. She can't put her finger on it. And then it hits her: she is breathing more easily than she has in years. It feels as if some obstruction in her chest has, overnight, dislodged itself or dissolved, as if, for the past decade, her heartbeat has been stuck in phase one and has finally moved onto phase two, something she still remembers from Biology 101: Each heartbeat has two main phases. The phase when the heart muscle is fully contracted, squeezing out blood, is called systole. The phase when the heart relaxes and refills with blood is called diastole. She also remembers a children's encyclopedia of Teddy's that showed a scary-looking picture of the heart with a caption that said, "The adult heart is the size of a clenched fist." Which was precisely what hers felt like. Sometimes she would wake up in the night and hear it punching her ribs, beating her up from the inside. But now, suddenly, or maybe not suddenly, it feels as if the fist has opened its fingers and let go of whatever it has been holding on to, clutching so tightly, for all these years.

The sun is higher and brighter now, and she can see the white hotel at the end of the walking mall. A couple of stray dogs are chasing each other around the fountain. A young man with copper-colored dreadlocks and a Rasta cap is playing the flute; an open case lined with gold velvet shimmers in the bright sunlight. Giselle digs a five-dollar bill out of her skinny purse — something a teenage girl would carry — and drops it into the case. He nods his head and launches into a silvery, birdlike trill of gratitude.

Then she remembers something else, something she hasn't dared to think of in a long, long time. A bedtime ritual. It went like this: Trina would be lying in the crib and Giselle would say, "Anybody want a nighty-night kiss?" Trina would wriggle her arm out from under the pink quilt and hold up her cupped palm for Giselle to kiss. Like a little pink flower. Giselle would bend over the crib, inhaling her sweet baby scent, making a *bzzzz-bzzz* sound like a bumblebee, and land a kiss in the center of her pudgy hand. The instant that Giselle's lips brushed her skin, Trina's fingers would curl shut, into a small, tight fist. And she would fall asleep, still holding on to the kiss.

It was enough to break your heart. Even then.

ACKNOWLEDGMENTS

I would like to thank Sarah Burnes, my editor, for her encouragement and advice; Kim Witherspoon, my agent, for her invaluable guidance; and the English Department at the University of Nebraska for helping me find the time to be a writer as well as a teacher.